AODHÁN

*Book 1 of the **DEOS IRÆ** series.*

By Adrian Buckle

© Adrian Buckle 2024

Chapter 1

A sinister snap echoed through the moonless night as the old tree's body splintered and cracked.

In the quiet town of Rashford, more precisely on the outskirts by Helen Road, where time seemed to stand still and the air was always heavy with the scent of honeysuckle and moss, a timeworn, gnarled oak tree stood as a silent sentinel. Stories whispered by the wind spoke of its ageless power and the spirits it harboured. As dusk fell on this seemingly ordinary day, a sudden tempest erupted, shattering the tranquillity with its deafening roars. The wind howled like a tortured beast, ripping through the town with an uncharacteristic ferocity. Amidst this chaos, the eerie snap echoed through the air - a sound that seemed to come from deep within the oak itself. As if in response, a spectral figure emerged from its bowels - a boy who looked no older than sixteen, his skin as pale as moonlight and eyes alight with a terrifying power.

His arrival marked an unexpected shift in the town's dynamics; his very presence radiating an energy that hinted at both danger and intrigue. The peaceful monotony of Rashford Town was shattered, replaced by an atmosphere thick with suspense and anticipation. Even as the tempest

threatened to consume him, he stumbled forward - a harbinger of events yet to unfold.

Each faltering step sent tremors through his fragile form, the sensations overwhelming and alien. The wind shrieked like a ghastly symphony of wretched souls, carrying with it the whispers of a language he could not comprehend - a vile tongue that spoke of ancient evils and unfathomable atrocities.

"Aaargh!" The boy's voice was barely audible, lost in the pandemonium of the storm. He reached out in desperation, attempting to seize the rain that thrashed his flesh. But instead of water, his fingers encountered something gelid and corporeal - a substance that should not exist in this realm.

As he cautiously ventured further from the ageless tree that gave him birth, a creeping terror began to permeate his very marrow. The darkness seemed to contort and pulsate as if ravenous for his soul. His heart pounded relentlessly, his breath coming in short, panicked gasps.

A jagged streak of lightning tore across the sky, momentarily illuminating grotesque figures lurking at the road's fringe—monstrosities stitched from the fabric of nightmares and steeped in raw evil. The crackle of thunder echoed, deep and menacing, as if nature itself recoiled from these lurid spectres, once more scaring the life out of

him. The air was thick with an acrid tang that clung to his throat, while an unsettling chill crept over his skin like cold velvet.

He stood rooted in place, every fibre in him demanding he ran, but something about those shadowy forms tugged at his sheer curiosity—a whisper of innocence wrestling with primal fear. His mind reeled as if he'd tasted bitter despair—an unfamiliar flavour that left him trembling inside.

But where would he go? This world was alien and horrifying, and he was nothing but a forsaken spirit ensnared in a decaying vessel.

"Aaargh!" he cried out again, his voice quavering with fear.

Only the howling wind responded, bearing with it the stink of putrefaction and despair. The boy embraced himself tightly, his slight frame quivering uncontrollably in the cold. He took another tentative step forward, ignorant of the malignant presence that lurked within the shadows.

The boy's thoughts raced, desperately searching for some kind of refuge amidst the chaos and destruction surrounding him. Blank thoughts flooded his mind, taunting him with the realisation that he was all alone now, beyond safety's grasp.

He longed for sanctuary, but in this strange and dangerous world, he had no idea where to find it.

Battling through the remorseless tempest, the oppressive darkness engulfed him, draining every iota of hope from his trembling frame. Each gale of wind carried a sinister voice, deriding and tormenting with malevolent promises of unspeakable torment. The boy's tormented cries were smothered by the deafening din of thunder and rain, yet still he called out for deliverance, only to be met with a disquieting silence. As the storm raged on, a vile premonition took root - something depraved and insatiable slithered just beyond his grasp, eager to rend him asunder without an ounce of mercy.

The windshield wipers thrashed against the torrential onslaught, their frenzied thump-thump echoing Meredith Caldwell's frantic thoughts. She gripped the steering wheel with a vice-like grip, her knuckles turning pale as she navigated the perilous twists and turns of the slick road.

"Brian!" she whispered, her voice barely audible over the raging storm. Rain continued pouring from the sky, pattering against the windshield as she drove her car. She looked at the folded flag on the dashboard, tears streaming down her face as she remembered the phone call that shattered her

world. Her son's medals hung from the front view mirror, glinting in the dim light of the of the night.

Her heart was heavy with the weight of grief, just as it had been on this very night when she had received the devastating news of his death in the army. The memories of their love flooded her mind, mixed with the agony and anger at his sacrifice. She couldn't decide if she wanted to hold onto those memories or push them away, as they only brought her more pain.

Her mind flooded with memories of her son, each one hitting her with the force of a crashing wave. His laughter, his smile, the way his eyes crinkled when he was truly happy. And then, the crushing weight of his absence, a void that threatened to consume her whole.

Tears threatened to spill anew from Meredith's eyes as she spoke. "I wish I had never let you go," she whispered, regret gnawing at her heart. "But deep down, I know that you needed to leave, even if it tore me apart."

A sudden movement caught her eye. In an instant, her headlights illuminated a small, ghostly figure standing in the middle of the road. Her heart leapt into her throat.

"Oh God!" she screamed, slamming on the brakes.

The car jolted violently, tires screeching against the slick pavement. Meredith's world spun wildly, a dizzying blur of rain and darkness. She felt the sickening impact, heard the sickening crunch of metal.

When the car finally skidded to a stop, Meredith sat frozen in shock, gasping for air. The windshield wipers continued their relentless beat, clearing away sheets of rain to reveal... nothing.

"No, no, no," she whimpered, fumbling with her seatbelt. "Please, not again."

Her hands shook as she reached for the door handle, her mind reeling. Had she imagined it? Was the grief finally driving her mad? Or was there truly a child out there, broken and bleeding on the unforgiving road?

"Hold on," Meredith called out, her voice cracking. "I'm coming. Just... just hold on."

Meredith wrenched the car door open, the storm's fury assaulting her senses. Rain lashed her face as she stumbled onto the road, her feet slipping on the slick surface. Her heart pounded a frantic rhythm against her ribs, each beat a desperate prayer.

"Where are you?" she cried, squinting through the downpour. "Please, answer me!"

Lightning split the sky, illuminating the scene in stark relief. And there, just beyond her headlights, a small figure lay crumpled on the asphalt. Meredith's breath caught in her throat as she rushed forward, her soaked clothes clinging to her trembling frame.

"Oh, sweetheart," she whispered, dropping to her knees beside the child. "I'm so sorry. I'm—"

The words died on her lips as the boy's body suddenly jerked to life, his head lurching up to meet Meredith's gaze. She gasped in shock, unable to look away from the piercing eyes that seem to hold the entire universe within them. A strange, otherworldly glow surrounded the boy's flawless skin, defying all logic and reason.

"You...you're not hurt," Meredith stammered, her voice trembling with disbelief and wonder. She tentatively reached out a hand, expecting it to pass through the boy's ethereal form like a mirage. "How is this possible?" But as she looked at her car, she saw a deep dent in the bumper where they had collided. The evidence was undeniable - there was physical contact. Meredith could feel her mind reeling as she tried to make sense of this supernatural encounter.

The youth tilted his head, regarding her with an expression of innocent bewildered curiosity. She could see his hesitation. Raindrops clung to his

impossibly long lashes, and for a moment, Meredith was struck by a memory of her own son, eyes wide with wonder as he explored the world.

"What's your name, sweetheart?" she asked gently, even as a part of her screamed that this was wrong, that no human child could survive such an impact unscathed.

The boy's lips parted, but no sound emerged. He looked around, confusion etched across his delicate features, as if seeing the world for the first time.

Meredith's maternal instincts surged, warring with the growing unease in the pit of her stomach. "We need to get you out of this rain," she said, her voice wavering. "I... I should take you to a hospital, make sure you're really okay."

Meredith's heart ached as she struggled with the decision. She knew she should hand over the youth to the authorities, but the mere thought of it sent shivers down her spine. How could she subject this innocent being to the scrutiny and uncertainty of strangers? Yet, if she didn't turn him in, what would happen to the child in the long run? Meredith was torn between a sense of duty and a deep-rooted fear.

"Brian," she whispered, her late son's name a prayer on her lips. "What would you want me to do?"

The boy reached out, his small hand grasping hers with surprising strength. In that touch, Meredith felt a surge of warmth, of purpose, that she hadn't experienced since losing her son. It was reckless, perhaps even dangerous, but in that moment, she made her decision.

"Come on, little one," Meredith said, her voice steadier now. "Let's get you somewhere safe."

As she helped the youth to his feet, a nagging voice in the back of her mind whispered warnings of the unknown. But Meredith silenced it, focusing instead on the familiar ache of protectiveness swelling in her chest. Whatever mysteries this boy held, whatever dangers might follow, she would face them. She had failed to save her son once; she would not fail this boy.

Meredith steadied him, her weathered hands gentle against his rain-slicked skin. As she guided him towards the car, a sudden chill crawled up her spine. Her gaze darted to the side, drawn by an unseen force.

Perched menacingly on a gnarled branch sat a raven, its inky feathers glistening with the blood of the storm. Each droplet seemed to refract some

unfathomable darkness. But it was the bird's eyes that froze Meredith's very soul—twin orbs of liquid night, gleaming with an intelligence that sent violent tremors through her very being.

"It's okay," Meredith murmured, more to herself than the youth. "It's just a bird. Nothing to be afraid of."

But the words rang hollow, even as she spoke them. There was nothing "just" about that raven. Its presence felt like a portent, a harbinger of something vast and terrible looming on the horizon.

Shaking off the dread, Meredith turned her attention back to the boy. His wide eyes darted between her and the raven; confusion etched across his delicate features.

"Can you understand me, sweetheart?" she asked, her voice soft and soothing despite the storm's howl. "What's your name?"

The youth's brow furrowed, his lips moving silently as if tasting unfamiliar words. When he spoke, it was in a language Meredith had never heard – lilting and ethereal, like wind through ageless trees.

"I'm sorry, I don't... I don't understand," Meredith said, frustration and concern warring within her.

How could she help him if they couldn't even communicate?

Her nervous fingers fumbled through her pockets, searching for something to offer as a peace offering. She finally grasped the crinkling edge of a solitary candy bar, its wrapper smooth and shiny from being tucked away for so long. She considered it briefly, then extended it towards the boy, who regarded her with sceptical eyes, his brow knit in uncertainty. "Go on, it's yours," she encouraged softly, peeling back the wrapper's metallic sheen to reveal the deep brown chocolate beneath and gently placing it into his open hand. The scent of cocoa and sugar filled the air and her mouth watered at the thought of taking a bite.

The boy hesitated for a second, bringing it closer to inspect with his nose flaring ever so slightly to catch its rich aroma mingled with the sweet scent of cocoa and sugar. Finally convinced, he nibbled tentatively at first before yielding to hunger. His teeth tore into it eagerly as though each bite was an event savoured after long days without food.

Around them, fallen leaves rustled like whispered secrets across the ground, adding sonic texture to this quiet exchange. The air carried with it a musty autumnal smell that blended with the lingering chocolate fragrance now fully under assault by

enthusiastic chews – chewy and creamy in each gratifying mouthful.

"My name is Meredith," she signed. "Meredith!"

The boy's eyes widened with recognition. "Aodhán!" he smiled.

"Aodhán," Meredith breathed, the name feeling both alien and achingly familiar on her tongue. "Your name is Aodhán."

As their eyes met, Meredith felt a connection spark between them, transcending language and logic. In that moment, she knew with bone-deep certainty that her life would never be the same. She felt a growing unease settle within her. His mysterious words spoken in a language unheard before hinted at secrets untold and mysteries yet unfolded. The exchange of the candy bar carried an air of significance beyond mere sustenance, as if it was a catalyst for something greater, something unseen but palpably looming on the horizon.

And as their shared moment unfolded amidst the rustling leaves and fading light, a connection formed between Meredith and Aodhán that transcended mere understanding. It was as if fate itself had woven their paths together in that ephemeral instant, binding them inextricably to a

future fraught with uncertainty and unforeseen dangers.

Unbeknownst to them, as they stood locked in this silent exchange, the raven took flight into the swirling abyss of the night, its departure marking only the beginning of an enigmatic journey filled with shadows and revelations yet to come.

Meredith gently guided Aodhán towards her car, her hand trembling slightly as she opened the passenger door. The boy's otherworldly grace was a stark contrast to his bewildered expression, his eyes darting about like a frightened fawn.

"It's alright," Meredith murmured, more to herself than to Aodhán. "You're safe now."

As she settled into the driver's seat, her mind raced with a torrent of questions. Who was this boy? Where had he come from? And why did she feel such an inexplicable, visceral need to protect him?

The engine sputtered to life, headlights cutting through the deluge as Meredith eased onto the road. Aodhán pressed his palms against the window, mesmerized by the rivulets of rain cascading down the glass.

"I don't suppose you can tell me where you're from?" Meredith asked, knowing full well she wouldn't get an answer she could understand.

Aodhán turned to her, his eyes reflecting an impossible depth of starlight.

"I'm sorry," she said, shaking her head. "I wish you could understand me."

As they entered Rashford proper, the familiar streets took on an eerie quality. Shadows seemed to lengthen, writhing in the corners of Meredith's vision. The rain-slicked cobblestones glistened like the scales of some great, slumbering beast.

"Welcome to Rashford," Meredith said, her voice barely above a whisper. "Though I'm starting to wonder if I even know this place anymore."

Aodhán's gaze was fixed on the town beyond the windshield, his expression a mixture of wonder and something darker – recognition, perhaps? But how could that be possible?

The car crept past shuttered storefronts and dimly lit houses. In the oppressive silence, Meredith could almost hear the secrets seeping from between the bricks of every building they passed.

Panic gripped her like a vice once again as she tightened her grip on the steering wheel, knuckles turning white. "What am I doing?" she screamed internally, heart racing. "I should be getting him help, taking him to hospital or calling the police. This is completely wrong." Her mind swirled with

conflicting thoughts, torn between fear and responsibility as she sped down the empty road.

Yet something deep within her rebelled against that notion. The mere thought of handing Aodhán over to strangers filled her with a dread she couldn't explain.

As they passed the old church, its spire barely visible through the downpour, Aodhán suddenly stiffened. He pressed himself back against the seat, a low keening sound escaping his lips.

"What is it?" Meredith asked, alarmed. "What's wrong?"

But Aodhán only shook his head, his eyes squeezed shut as if to block out some terrible vision. And in that moment, Meredith felt it too – a weight pressing down on her chest, a sense of ancient malevolence stirring in the shadows of her beloved town.

"It's okay," she said, though her voice quavered. "We're almost home. You'll be safe there. I promise."

Then, Meredith made a sudden decision to veer off the main road. The turn to her farm loomed ahead, a dark mouth in the rain-slicked night.

"I can't take you to the hospital," she said softly, glancing at Aodhán. His eyes met hers, filled with

an innocence that pierced her heart. "There's something... different about you. They wouldn't understand."

The boy tilted his head, a question in his gaze.

Meredith swallowed hard, memories of her lost son flooding her mind. "I... I lost someone too."

As they bumped along the rutted drive to her farmhouse, a dark shape swooped low over the car. Meredith gasped, swerving slightly.

"Did you see that?" she asked, her voice trembling.

Aodhán nodded, his face pressed against the glass. Outside, a massive raven alighted upon a fence post, its eyes gleaming with malevolent intent.

"It stalks us," Meredith whispered, a chill snaking up her spine as though Death itself caressed her. The bird's presence was an ill omen – a harbinger of unspeakable horror awakening within Rashford.

She could feel it now – the wicked energy seeping from the very core of the earth itself, reaching out for them with ravenous tendrils like a vile spider weaving its web.

Meredith's hands shook as she parked the car, her resolve wavering.

As she stood in front of the looming farmhouse, her mind raced with doubts and fears. Was this the right decision? What consequences would this bring to her quiet home?

What have I done? She thought, afraid of what the answer might be.

But as Aodhán turned those trusting eyes to her once more, Meredith knew she couldn't abandon him. Whatever storms were gathering on the horizon, they would face them together.

The key groaned in the lock as Meredith pushed open the weathered farmhouse door. A gust of wind chased them inside, slamming it shut behind them with a resounding thud. Aodhán flinched, his eyes wide as saucers in the dim entryway.

"It's alright," Meredith soothed, her voice barely above the storm's fury. She fumbled for the light switch, flooding the room with a warm, golden glow. "We're safe now."

But even as the words left her lips, doubt gnawed at her. The raven's watchful gaze lingered in her mind, a portent of darkness she couldn't shake.

Aodhán stood motionless, drinking in his surroundings. His fingers traced the peeling wallpaper, marvelling at its faded floral patterns.

He murmured something, the word clumsy on his tongue, but verging on awe.

Meredith's heart clenched. "You've never seen anything like this before, have you?"

He shook his head, those otherworldly eyes brimming with wonder.

"Come," she said, gently guiding him towards the kitchen. "Let's get you dry and warm."

Meredith bustled about, gathering towels and setting the kettle to boil.

Thunder shook the windows, and Aodhán trembled. Meredith instinctively moved closer, her maternal instincts overriding her fear.

"What happened to you?" she whispered, more to herself than to him. "Where did you come from?"

As if in answer, a gust of wind howled through the chimney, carrying with it the acrid scent of something burning. Meredith's nose wrinkled. "That's odd. I haven't lit a fire in months."

She crossed to the fireplace, peering up into the darkness. For a moment, she could have sworn she saw something moving, writhing in the shadows. A chill ran down her spine.

"Meredith?" Aodhán's voice was tentative. When she turned, he was holding out a steaming mug of

tea, his expression a mix of concern and confusion.

"Thank you, dear," she said, forcing a smile. "How did you...?"

But the words died on her lips as she noticed the kettle, still cold on the stove. The tea in her hands was scalding hot, steam rising in delicate curls.

The raven's screech echoed through the night, a chilling omen ignored as the shadows thickened, ready to pounce at any moment.

Chapter 2

Apollo's fingers trembled as he clutched the cold vial, its chipped edges mocking his fading radiance. The shadows danced wildly in the flickering candlelight, their shapes both ominous and eldritch. "What dark revelation does this latest prophetic vision foretell?" he pondered. "Will I unravel the cryptic words in time to save myself, or have the Fates finally forsaken Zeus' once-favoured son?" Slowly taking a deep breath, he downed the Blood of the Vine liquid in the vial.

And lost consciousness.

When Apollo came back to himself, he found himself in the arms of the archangel Micha-El. Micha-El's face twisted in a mix of concern and dread as he looked down at Apollo, this once powerful god now weakened and drained. "What did you see?" he whispered urgently.

Apollo's trembling hand concealed the small vial, his eyes dark and empty as he gazed at its contents. A thin stream of blood dripped from his nose, a sharp reminder of his frailty. Against Micha-El's advice, he had consumed the vine's blood and now a violent, all-consuming vision tore through his mind, tormenting him with its brutal clarity.

"I'm tired," he finally admitted, his voice strained and weary.

Micha-El's voice shook with a mix of rage and fear, his teeth clenched in frustration. The burden of his divine powers weighed heavily on him, a constant reminder of the curse that ran through Apollo's blood. As he searched the looming shadows around them, a gnawing worry consumed him, knowing that his beloved was tainted by the cursed lineage of the Greek gods who so obstinately refused to embrace their divinity. A part of him yearned to protect and understand Apollo. He was desperate to understand what it was like to become human flesh and blood like him, to experience the raw intensity of human emotions together as equals, while another part resisted the thought of giving up his godly qualities.

Apollo limped away, his head spinning with dizziness and pain. His heart raced as he tried to escape the wrath of Micha-El's snarling voice.

But as he stopped in his tracks, Apollo's thoughts became muddled and clouded. He could feel the weight of defeat looming over him, pushing him down towards the ground.

"Where do you think you're going?" Micha-El growled, his words like shards of ice cutting through Apollo's already fragile state.

With a heavy sigh, Apollo closed his eyes and let out a shaky breath. "Home," he whispered, the word laced with both sadness and resignation. His mind drifted to memories of warmth and safety, a place where he longed to find solace and comfort once again.

Despite his longing, Micha-El could sense the distance and resistance in Apollo's embrace. He craved to hold him tighter and prove their love, but Apollo pushed him away with a ragged sigh.

"I can't do this right now," Apollo pleaded. "Please, just let me go."

Feeling torn between wanting to comfort his lover and needing answers, Micha-El asked again, "Can you at least tell me what happened?"

Apollo's tear-filled eyes gazed into Micha-El's with a mixture of pain and fear. Unable to sustain the intense gaze, he looked away, his face streaked by blood and tears, leaving Micha-El torn between wanting to protect him and desperate for the truth.

As he neared the ancient mansion where he and his family of remaining Greek gods resided, the scent of rain-soaked earth and fresh pine filled his nostrils. The air was thick with a heady mixture of nature's fragrances, a gentle reminder of the world beyond –the dimension of the gods; a world that

he had once revelled in but now rejected to live among mortals. He couldn't help but feel a twinge of sadness at how far he had fallen from his potential glory. He was the only god to retain his powers but had no access to his divine self. That was his curse. He was a god without being a god.

As he entered the grand entranceway, adorned with marble columns and intricate friezes, he couldn't help but feel a pang of nostalgia for the days when he ruled from the heavens. But now, this luxurious mansion served as their refuge and sanctuary, a small haven in a world that no longer welcomed them.

With his heavy, weary steps echoing through the grand hall, Apollo's eyes were immediately drawn to Athena. She stood like a marble statue, her lithe figure outlined by the dark clouds outside the window. Her once-perfectly styled hair fell in loose waves around her face, a visual representation of their shared downfall.

"Athena," Apollo's voice rang out, a mix of urgency and fading power. "Sister, I've seen him. The Eldar— he's coming." His words hung in the air like a thick fog, as if foretelling the impending storm that was about to break upon them.

Athena turned, her grey eyes sharp as steel. "Another vision, Apollo? And what good have your prophecies done us lately?"

Apollo flinched at the barb but pressed on. "This is different. I saw him clearly this time. He's the key, Athena. The key to everything."

"And what of the Semites? What of your beloved Micha-El?" Athena's voice dripped with bitterness. "Will your precious Eldar protect us from Yahweh's watchful eye?"

Apollo's mind raced, memories of celestial war and divine betrayal threatening to overwhelm him. "I... I don't know. But we can't just sit here and do nothing. We're dying, Athena. Slowly, painfully... fading into obscurity."

Athena's laugh was hollow, devoid of mirth. "Obscurity? We're already there, brother. Look at us – cowering in this ancient mansion, shadows of our former selves."

"But wait," she continued to press. "You're not facing that fate because, unlike us, you retained your powers."

Apollo frowned. Athena had always blamed him for the downfall of the Olympians. She always blamed his recklessness and his impulsivity . . . and, in a way, he admitted she was right.

His hands shook as he clutched the worn vial, the same vial threatening to shatter under his grasp. The weight of prophecy and destiny hung heavily over him, a constant reminder of his power and

limitations. He was torn between wanting to use his abilities for good and fearing the consequences of acting on them. It was a never-ending battle within himself, one that left him feeling helpless and trapped.

"We can't give up," Apollo insisted, his voice dropping to a whisper. "Not now. Not when he's so close."

With each step towards his sister, Apollo's heart raced faster, anticipation rising in his chest. He approached Athena, her presence commanding and powerful as always. He couldn't help but catch a whiff of the faint scent of olives that still clung to her - a cruel reminder of their lost Olympus. The room was dimly lit, with only the occasional flash of lightning illuminating it in stark relief. In those brief moments, Apollo could almost see the golden aura that once surrounded her, now nothing more than a fading memory. Time had washed away her godly powers, leaving her a mere immortal human, trapped in an endless cycle of longing for the past and it was partly his fault.

"What did you see?" Athena asked, her tone softening slightly.

Apollo closed his eyes, recalling the vision. "A boy... no, a man. Walking through fire, yet

untouched. The Darkness cowered before him, Athena. And behind him... I saw us. Restored."

He opened his eyes, searching Athena's face for a glimmer of hope, of belief. Instead, he found only weary scepticism.

"And how many times have your visions led us astray?" she asked, her voice tinged with a mixture of pity and frustration. "How many times have we chased shadows, only to find ourselves further entangled in this mortal coil?"

Apollo's jaw clenched. "This is different. I swear it on the Styx."

Athena's eyebrow arched. "Bold words, for one so far from the river's banks."

The silence in the mansion was suffocating, only interrupted by the thunder rumbling outside. Apollo's thoughts were racing, desperately searching for the right words to rekindle the hope that had been lost between them. But he couldn't deny the doubts and fears creeping in, threatening to drown out any glimmer of optimism.

"We have to try," he finally said, his voice barely above a whisper. "What other choice do we have?"

Athena's eyes blazed with a sudden, searing rage. "Choice?" she hissed, her words laced with the venom of a thousand snakes. "We surrendered

our right to choose when we lost our divinity, Apollo. We are nothing more than mere humans now, clinging to the fading memory of our once-great powers."

"You're . . . We're still immortal," Apollo tried but his words were only met with scorn.

Athena turned away from him, her back rigid with fury. The rain outside pounded against the windows, mirroring the tempest of emotions raging within the grand hall.

"Your visions are nothing but hollow echoes of a past that can never be resurrected," Athena spat, her voice dripping with bitterness and disdain. "This Eldar, the Darkness, our salvation... they are nothing but delusions spawned from our desperation."

As Apollo listened to her words, his heart felt like it was being squeezed in a vice. He wanted to protest and defend himself, but with each passing moment, his doubts only grew stronger. He couldn't deny the truth behind her accusations, and he found himself at a loss for words.

"Is that all you saw?" Athena's piercing question made Apollo's heart race. He knew he couldn't tell her the whole truth, so he held back and just shook his head. The image from the vial containing the blood of the vine still burned in his

mind, but he couldn't bring himself to reveal it to his sister. How could he explain what he had seen?

From the shadowed corner of the grand hall came a soft rustle of fabric, like the whisper of satin against stone. Aphrodite, former goddess of love and beauty, rose from her seat at the head of the table. Her ethereal form stood out against the sombre atmosphere that seemed to permeate the mansion. The once sparkling light in her eyes had dimmed, replaced by a haunting melancholy that deepened with each passing day.

"Perhaps," Aphrodite murmured, her voice a melodic whisper that echoed through the hall, "we should not be so quick to dismiss hope, however faint it may be."

Apollo turned to her. A flicker of gratitude warmed his chest at her words. But before he could speak, Aphrodite glided past him, her movements as graceful as ever despite the heavy weight of her curse. Her long, flowing gown trailed behind her like a river of moonlight, adding to her otherworldly beauty as she moved through the shadows.

"Where are you going?" Athena demanded, her tone softening slightly in the face of Aphrodite's ethereal presence.

Aphrodite paused at the threshold, her hand resting on the ornate doorframe. "To seek solace in the only way left to me," she replied, a hint of self-loathing colouring her words. "In the arms of those whose lives I'll inevitably destroy."

With that, she vanished into the dimly lit corridor, leaving Apollo and Athena alone with the echoes of their shattered dreams and the relentless drumming of the rain.

The rain pounded against the windows, but Hermes sat comfortably in his cozy apartment, swiping through profiles on Tinder with a yearning grin on his face. He knew he shouldn't be using mortal dating apps, but as a fallen god, he couldn't resist the temptation for some excitement and possibly a romantic encounter.

Apollo and Athena's serious discussions about their lost powers and shattered dreams seemed like a real-life drama show Hermes would binge-watch while snacking on ambrosia. He imagined tuning in weekly to hear Athena's sharp retorts and Apollo's heart-wrenching dilemmas, thinking, "Move over, soap operas – the gods are stealing the spotlight now! And who knew that divine interventions could be so relatable? I mean, forget about reality TV, Olympus drama is where it's at! I bet even Zeus would be taking notes on how to

handle family disputes from Athena's epic comebacks!"

And as Aphrodite would float elegantly away to seek solace in the arms of unsuspecting mortals, Hermes would wonder if she'd be sharing relationship advice along with her divine curse. "Ah, the things we do for love... or should I say, for a good story?" he chuckled mischievously to himself.

In the midst of all this divine drama and mortal intrigue, Hermes found himself grateful for the simple pleasures of swiping through Tinder profiles. After all, even a fallen god needs a little laughter and romance in his immortal life.

A notification beeped and he eagerly clicked on it, hoping to finally find someone who could satisfy his insatiable desire for sex and attention. But as he looked at the profile, his excitement quickly faded. He just wasn't interested in another shallow conversation with an average mortal.

Just as he was about to close the laptop in frustration, another notification popped up. His curiosity piqued when he saw the username "Truly Scrumptious." Intrigued, he clicked on her profile and was met with a stunning image of a girl with golden hair and dark eyes.

Without hesitation, he typed out a message, hoping to charm her with a story from his past. As he typed, memories flooded back of his days as a mischievous infant, causing trouble and outsmarting even Apollo.

As he waited for Truly's response, a sense of longing crept over him. He couldn't help but wonder what thrilling secrets lay beneath the surface of these mortal humans. His eyes darted around the room, taking in every detail with a predator's precision.

Lost in thought, his fingers traced over the tattoo of a winged staff on his forearm - a symbol of his former divinity. And then suddenly, he asked Truly if she would be willing to indulge in forbidden experiences with a fallen god. The words dripped from his lips like honeyed venom, revealing a desperate craving for something more than just mundane human interaction.

"Meet me at Elm Mansion," beeped the reply from Truly Scrumptious.

As he closed the laptop and laid back on his bed, images of tantalizing experiences filled his mind - ones that only a god like him could imagine and crave. With one last devilish smirk, he surrendered to an intoxicating moment of rapture by pleasuring himself, the only thing that made his skin hum with life in this mundane, mortal world.

With hesitant steps, Aphrodite braved the dark and rainy night, feeling the scattered raindrops as a constant reminder of her curse. Apollo's misguided attempt to cure her only added to her inner turmoil. A part of her yearned for her divinity to be restored, but another part feared the consequences and wondered if she even deserved it. As she trudged along, tears mixing with the rain, she couldn't help but question the complexities of love and family ties.

The worn cobblestone streets of Rashford glimmered beneath her feet, shimmering with the warm glow of streetlamps like a constellation of shattered stars. The sound of her footsteps echoed off the ancient buildings, their rough stone walls steeped in history and secrets. She couldn't help but feel small amidst the towering structures, each one telling its own story from centuries past. As she walked, her eyes caught every detail - the intricate carvings on doorways, the flickering lights behind windows, the lingering scent of freshly baked bread wafting from a nearby bakery. It was a city alive with magic and mystery, and she couldn't wait to explore every hidden corner and unravel its mysteries.

As she walked, her thoughts swirled like a tempest. "What have I become?" she wondered,

her inner voice a mixture of longing and despair. "Once worshipped as a goddess of life, now a goddess of death. Once a bringer of love, now a harbinger of destruction."

The scent of rain-soaked earth and pine filled her nostrils, a reminder of the mortal world she now inhabited. She paused, closing her eyes and tilting her face towards the sky, letting the rain mingle with the tears she could no longer hold back.

"Is this to be my eternity?" she whispered to the uncaring heavens, as she headed for the lakeside, her favourite hunting ground. "To seek fleeting moments of pleasure, knowing it will not last?"

A group of young mortal boys stumbled out of a nearby tavern, their laughter cutting through the night. Aphrodite's gaze was drawn to them, her curse stirring within her like a hungry beast.

"No," she murmured, clenching her fists.

Yet even as she spoke, her feet carried her towards the revellers, her curse compelling her forward. The air around her seemed to shimmer, her otherworldly beauty calling to the mortals like a siren's song.

"Hey there, beautiful," one of the young men called out, his eyes glazing over with desire. "Care to join us?"

Aphrodite felt her lips curve into a seductive smile, even as her heart ached. "Why not?" she heard herself say, her voice a melody of promised pleasures and hidden sorrows.

As she allowed herself to be drawn into their circle, Aphrodite caught a glimpse of her reflection in a rain-slicked window. For a moment, she saw not the captivating goddess she appeared to be, but a hollow-eyed spectre, trailing destruction in her wake.

Meanwhile, across town, Hermes scurried out of the mansion and made his way to his favourite tavern. Once there, he pushed open the creaking door of the Key Hole, a dimly lit tavern on the outskirts of Rashford. The scent of stale beer and desperation assaulted his nostrils, a far cry from the ambrosia of Olympus. Yet he grinned, relishing the challenge that lay before him.

"Well, well," he mused inwardly, scanning the room with keen eyes. "What secrets do you hold, my mortal friends?"

He sauntered up to the bar, his movements fluid and purposeful. The bartender, a grizzled man with eyes that had seen too much, raised an eyebrow at his approach.

"What'll it be, boy?" the man grunted, his voice rough as sandpaper.

Hermes leaned in, his smile disarming. "Information, my good man," he replied smoothly. "And perhaps a whiskey to loosen the tongue."

The bartender snorted but poured the drink. Hermes raised the glass in a mock toast before taking a sip, suppressing a grimace at the harsh burn.

"So," Hermes began, his tone casual yet probing, "what's the word on the street these days? Any interesting tales to share?"

A patron nearby, his face weather-beaten and lined with years, chuckled darkly. "Careful what you ask for, boy," he warned. "This town's got more secrets than a graveyard's got bones."

Hermes felt a thrill of excitement course through him. "Is that so?" he pressed, his eyes glinting with mischief. "Care to elaborate?"

As the old man began to speak, Hermes listened intently, his mind racing. He might have lost his divine powers, but his wit remained sharp as ever. And in this town of secrets and shadows, knowledge was power.

"Tell me more," he urged, his voice a blend of charm and curiosity. "I have a feeling this is going to be a very interesting night."

The old man leaned in, his breath reeking of cheap whiskey and stale cigarettes. "They say strange things happen down by the lake," he whispered, his rheumy eyes darting nervously. "Folk go missin', ya see. And those that come back... well, they ain't quite right."

Hermes felt a chill crawl up his spine, his curiosity piqued and mingled with a sense of foreboding. "Not quite right how?" he pressed, his voice low and urgent.

"Empty, like. Shells of their former selves," the man muttered, knocking back the rest of his drink. "And the sounds... dear God, the sounds..."

The bartender slammed a glass down, startling them both. "That's enough of that talk," he growled. "You'll scare away the customers."

Hermes' mind raced, weighing his options. The lake . . . was it his sister's actions or was it connected to the strange energies he'd been sensing? Without his divine powers, he felt vulnerable, but the allure of uncovering the truth was too strong to resist.

"Well, gentlemen," Hermes announced, rising from his stool with practiced nonchalance, "I believe I'll take a moonlit stroll. Clear my head."

As he stepped out into the damp night air, Hermes couldn't shake the feeling that he was walking into something far darker than he'd anticipated. But his quick wit had always been his greatest weapon, and he'd be damned if he'd let a little mortal danger stop him now.

Back at the Mansion, Apollo paced the grand hall, his rusty hair catching the dim lamplight. His frustration radiated off him in palpable waves, filling the cavernous room with an oppressive tension.

"Damn it all," he muttered, his voice tinged with bitterness. "How am I to find the Eldar without knowing where to start?"

He paused by a towering window, staring out at the rain-soaked landscape. The weight of his duty pressed down on him like a physical force, threatening to crush him beneath its immensity. What if the Semites found him first . . . Gabri-El was just as good a seer as he was . . . What if *she* . . ?

"No," Apollo said aloud, his voice ringing with newfound determination. "I won't let them have him. I can't."

He turned from the window, his eyes blazing with an inner fire that seemed to push back the encroaching shadows. His powers may have waned, but his resolve burned brighter than ever.

"Time to act," Apollo declared to the empty hall. "Before it's too late."

As he strode purposefully towards the mansion's entrance, Apollo couldn't shake the feeling that events were spiralling rapidly out of control. But he'd be damned if he didn't go down fighting. His tongue flicked out to wet his dry lips. He could feel the weight of the decision heavy on his shoulders, knowing he would have to betray Micha-El's trust and go behind his back. The archangel's wrath was not something to be taken lightly. But the haunting vision burned in his mind, driving him towards this inevitable course of action, heedless of the grave consequences that awaited him.

The surface of Loch Rashford glistened under the pale, silvery light of the full moon, its inky depths shrouding untold secrets and mysteries. On its rocky shore, a blazing bonfire roared and crackled, casting long shadows that danced across the

faces of five young men sprawled around it. The cool breeze carried with it the smell of smoke and damp sand and gravel, while the distant call of an owl echoed through the stillness of the night. The rhythmic lapping of water against the shore added to the peaceful yet eerie atmosphere of the secluded lake. It was a place where stories were born and folk tales were made, and these five friends relished in their shared moment by its side.

Jamie Quinn, the golden boy of Rashford Town, his dark brown hair ruffled and catching the flickering light of the fire, raised a bottle of cheap whiskey in the air. The amber liquid inside the bottle glinted with an enticing shine as Jamie's calloused fingers gripped it tightly. The smell of smoke and wood filled the air around him, adding to the ruggedness of his appearance. Despite the roughness of his surroundings, he stood tall and confident, a wild spirit captured in one fleeting moment.

"To us," he proclaimed, his voice carrying a hint of slurred exuberance, "and to nights we'll probably regret but never forget!"

The others cheered, their laughter echoing across the still water. Goddard Greening's eyes lingered on Jamie's profile, his heart aching with unspoken longing.

"While we're on the topic of regrets," sneered Windsor Taser, his upper lip curling with contempt, "do you see how Goddard's pants are bulging? Are you interested in one of us, Greening?"

Jamie's smile faltered, oblivious to the fact that he was the subject of Goddard's attention. "Come on, Wind, ease up. It's not—"

"So," Jamie murmured, transfixed, turning to Aphrodite. The goddess had led the boys to a secluded part of the lakeside where she always took her prey to devour. They had lit a small bonfire to stay warm and bought cheap whiskey to celebrate their meeting. "Where did you come from, beautiful?"

Aphrodite's lips curved into a melancholic smile. "From dreams and nightmares, sweet boy," she purred, her voice a melody that sent shivers down their spines. "Won't you come dance with me?"

The boy looked at the empty space and shrugged. "There's no music," he said. Without hesitating, Aphrodite glided closer and began to sing a soulful tune that filled the boy's ears. Her voice was like a lullaby, soothing and enchanting. The boy couldn't help but smile as she danced and sang, creating her own music in the silence of the lakeside.

The boys looked transfixed, as if hypnotised by the sound of Aphrodite's song.

As if pulled by invisible strings, Jamie rose, ignoring his friends' uneasy murmurs. Goddard reached for him, a warning dying on his lips.

"Jamie, wait—" But his words were lost as Aphrodite enveloped Jamie in her deadly embrace, the curse that bound her pulsing with dark anticipation.

As Aphrodite pressed herself against Jamie's trembling body, her soft breasts meeting his chest and her legs entwining with his own. She brought her mouth to his ear and whispered seductively before capturing his lips with hers passionately. They kissed deeply and hungrily for several intense moments before she broke away, their breaths heavy and hot.

His breath stuttered in his chest, a low, primal groan rumbling from his throat as every sinew in his body tensed up and surrendered under her skilled hands.

Jamie's eyes locked onto Aphrodite's as she began to undress him, removing each article of clothing one by one, her fingers teasing and lingering on his bare skin. His body quivered under her touch, anticipation and desire making his heart race and his breath uneven.

Aphrodite then guided Jamie's hands to her own garments, encouraging him to undress her as well. As each layer of clothing fell away, the goddess revealed more of her divine form, glowing in the moonlight. When they finally stood bare before each other, Jamie could barely breathe at the sight of her perfection.

The goddess gracefully lowered herself onto the soft ground, guiding Jamie down with her. She spread her legs invitingly, exposing herself to him completely. As Jamie knelt between Aphrodite's thighs, their eyes locked once again; a silent communication acknowledging the depth of their intimate connection.

Jamie moved forward cautiously, entering Aphrodite slowly and deliberately as she had shown him. Her moans grew louder as he began to move, matching the rhythm of his thrusts with her own sensual movements. They moved together in perfect harmony, their bodies intertwining as if they were made for one another.

The sensation of their passionate union was overwhelming; any control that Jamie thought he possessed was long gone. He arched his back and buried himself deep inside Aphrodite, feeling the sweet release wash over him.

Their breathing slowed as they clung to each other in the aftermath of their passionate encounter.

Aphrodite's deadly embrace lingered just beneath the surface of their bliss; a chilling reminder that this forbidden love would eventually lead to destruction.

Jamie Quinn released a primal, intoxicating howl as waves of pleasure overpowered him. As his body shook with the intensity of his climax, he was a spectacle of raw masculinity. The muscles of his chiselled torso flexed under the bare skin, slick with sweat and flushed from desire. His deep-set eyes, normally sharp and calculating, were now clouded with unadulterated lust.

Physically, his lover was undeniably magnetic - a siren whose sensual curves were irresistible to his touch. Her supple skin beneath his rough fingers ignited a burning desire that threatened to consume him whole. The fiery-red hair that cascaded over her bare shoulders made a stark contrast against her porcelain skin, making her all the more enticing.

Her smoky eyes held a dangerous allure; they were windows into an untamed soul that beckoned Jamie like a moth to a flame. Every inch of her curvaceous form screamed sensuality, from the delicate arch of her neck to the provocative sway of her hips.

Their physical chemistry was undeniable - it was like watching lightning crackle in a stormy night

sky. Each look shared was loaded with sexual tension; each touch was like the spark that could set them both ablaze. Their bodies were drawn together by an irresistible force, aching for the intimate contact that promised sweet release.

Erotic words whispered between them carried an added layer of tantalizing seduction. His husky voice against her ear sent shivers down her spine - it was as though he spoke directly to her innermost fantasies.

"Missus," he'd growl in pure delight, tracing his fingertips along every seductive curve of her body, "you're driving me fucking crazy." And in return she'd murmur sweet nothings into his ear, her hot breath tickling his neck and causing every nerve ending to ignite.

This dance they played - part seduction, part conquest - was an artful performance that left them both consumed by the tantalizing promise of pleasure. The intensity was palpable, an undercurrent of desire that added a tangible electricity to their every interaction.

Then, Jamie began to sparkle. The others watched in horrified fascination as Jamie's skin began to sparkle and then wither, his flesh crumbling like ancient parchment.

"No!" Goddard cried out, lurching forward. But an invisible force held him back, his limbs leaden and unresponsive.

Aphrodite's mournful keen pierced the night as Jamie disintegrated, his essence dissolving into a fine, glittering dust that scattered on the breeze. She cradled the emptiness where he had been, her beauty now terrible to behold.

She glanced at the other boys. The world tilted and blurred around Goddard and his friends as consciousness slipped away. Their last thought before darkness claimed them was of Jamie's smile, now lost forever.

■■■■■■■■■■■■■■■■■■■■■■■■■■■■■■■■■■■■■

Chapter 3

Goddard jolted awake, his heart pounding violently within his breast, as the oppressive silence of the dawn was shattered by a scream that tore through the air—a cry that could only have been born from the very depths of mortal terror. Blinking against the cold, pale light, he struggled to piece together the ominous puzzle of his surroundings—the gloomy lakeshore, the sinister shadows, and an unshakable dread that something beyond his comprehension had gone terribly awry. What malevolent force could be lurking within this desolate place? And why did memory fail to illuminate the path that had led him here? An icy chill gripped Goddard's heart as the grisly tableau emerged from the receding penumbra.

"Jamie?" he rasped, pushing himself up on quivering arms. His stomach convulsed with revulsion as fragmented memories assailed him—Jamie's laughter contorted into a ghastly scream, a spectral siren of ethereal beauty, and ash swirling with malicious intent upon the wind.

"Dear God," Goddard choked out, bile seething in his throat. "Dear God in heaven above, what has happened?"

He staggered to his feet with trembling limbs, blind panic clawing at his very soul as he surveyed

the scene. His companions lay strewn about like broken dolls, their lifeblood pooling in crimson lakes beneath them; but of Jamie—Jamie there was no trace.

"This cannot be," Goddard murmured, running bloodied hands through tangled locks. "This cannot be reality."

Yet deep within his marrow—a primal voice whispered that it was indeed so. The abomination of it seeped into every fibre of his being and sent him careening towards madness. With one last anguished glance at the carnage surrounding him, Goddard turned and fled into the darkness—desperate to escape the nightmare that threatened to smother him like a shroud.

Apollo stood at the entrance of the mansion, his face dulled by the shadows that cloaked him. The weight of prophecy and duty pressed upon his shoulders, a familiar burden made heavier by the vision he had beheld. He gazed out into the rain-soaked morning, his eyes flickering with determination.

The idea of the Semitic angels discovering the Eldar before anyone else filled Apollo with fear. He could still feel the lingering effects of his father Zeus banishing him to Tartarus, thanks to those

servants of Yahweh. Apollo's hands balled into fists as he suppressed the painful memories.

"You can't keep this up forever, Apollo," Athena's sharp voice cut through his reverie. She stood in the doorway, her grey eyes cold and unforgiving. "Your visions have led us astray before."

With a fierce determination, Apollo whirled around to meet Athena's gaze. His jaw clenched with resolve as he spoke in a low, urgent voice. "This is not like any other vision, Athena. I have seen it with crystal clarity. The Eldar holds the answer to everything - our salvation or our downfall."

"And what if you're wrong?" she challenged, stepping closer. "What if this wild chase only brings Yahweh's wrath down upon us all again?"

For a moment, doubt flickered in Apollo's eyes. But then he squared his shoulders, meeting Athena's gaze unflinchingly. "Then I'll face that wrath alone. But I cannot – will not – stand idly by while this formidable being walks our land alone."

Without waiting for a response, Apollo boldly stepped out into the morning pouring rain. The icy droplets pelted against his mortal clothing, chilling him to the bone and reminding him of his current human form. Yet, with each determined step away from the mansion, he felt a sense of

rebellion against the harsh fate that had befallen him and his family. Every raindrop that fell on his skin served as a reminder of the weight of mortality and the power of resilience in the face of adversity.

"I was the god of prophecy once," he thought, a wry smile tugging at his lips. "Now I'm little more than a man, chasing visions in the dark."

The streets of Rashford Town stretched before him, glistening in the rain. Apollo's steps were swift and determined, his keen eyes scanning every alley and corner for any trace of the otherworldly boy who appeared in his visions. The weight of his quest bore down on him, a constant reminder of the danger he faced if discovered by Yahweh's agents. Each moment felt like a delicate balance between fulfilling his mission and risking everything he held dear.

As he passed a dimly lit alley, a flicker of movement caught his eye. Apollo paused, his heart racing. "Who goes there?" he called softly, hope and trepidation warring in his voice.

But the only answer was the steady drumming of rain and the distant rumble of thunder. Apollo sighed, running a hand through his wet hair. With renewed determination, Apollo pressed on into the storm-wracked night, his quest a beacon of hope against the encroaching shadows. Each step

carried him further from safety, deeper into uncertainty, yet his purpose remained clear – to find the Eldar, to harness his power, and perhaps, in doing so, to reclaim a fragment of the divinity his family had lost.

Goddard's legs moved of their own accord, carrying him away from the scene. His mind reeled, unable to process the horror he'd witnessed. Why was he the only one to remember it, albeit vaguely? Why had he and his companions forgotten every detail of that woman? The questions taunted him. He tried to remember what happened the night before, but the details just would not come back.

"I have to tell someone," he gasped between ragged breaths. "Dad . . . he'll know what to do."

Goddard's legs moved with possessed urgency, propelling him away from the unspeakable atrocity he'd observed. His mind reeled like a fevered nightmare, incapable of comprehending such depravity.

"I must confide in someone," he gasped between agonized breaths. "Father, he'll believe me . . . he shall know what recourse we must take."

But even as he fled in terror, part of Goddard knew that their world had been forever altered. An

unseen veil between dimensions had been torn asunder, and the malevolence seeping through threatened to engulf them all in its unfathomable depths.

Apollo shuffled to his home, his skin looking dull due to the heavy darkness around him. Rain pelted the weathered stone, each drop a mocking reminder of his diminished divinity. He clenched his fists, jaw tight with determination.

Amidst the peltering rain, Apollo's voice was barely audible as he whispered, "I cannot fail. Not like I failed . . ."

The memory of his son's merciless and cold assassination at the archangel Azaz-El's hands flashed through his mind, igniting a fire in his piercing blue eyes. He shook his head, banishing the thought.

"I can't fail," he repeated to the empty air. "I won't let the Semites claim another god."

Lightning split the sky, illuminating Apollo's face. For a moment, he looked every inch the god he once was, radiating purpose and power.

The rain intensified, pounding against the earth with a relentless fury. Apollo pushed forward, his determination unyielding despite the weather. In

the distance, Rashford Town's lights flickered like distant stars on their deathbeds, their faint glow offering no solace in the midst of the storm. The harsh wind whipped at Apollo's clothes and stung his skin, but he kept moving towards his goal, undeterred by the treacherous conditions. The only sound was the roaring rain and thunder, drowning out any other noises in the night. But Apollo pressed on, a lone figure against the darkness and chaos of the storm.

"Whatever it takes," Apollo vowed, his eyes fixed on the horizon. "Whatever the cost. I'll find the Eldar, even if I have to do it on my own. And may the Fates have mercy on any who stand in my way." With that final thought, Apollo disappeared into the darkness.

For a moment, Aphrodite allowed herself to pretend she was still the goddess she once was. But as heads turned, eyes widening with desire, she felt the weight of her curse more keenly than ever.

Aphrodite's heart hung heavy as she trudged down the winding cobbled streets, each step feeling like a weight upon her soul. She made her way to her brother's favourite bar, the familiar sounds of laughter and clinking glasses echoing through the night air. The dimly lit sign above the entrance

flickered with a neon pink light, casting an eerie glow on the surrounding buildings. As she pushed open the door, the warm scent of wood and alcohol greeted her, along with the boisterous chatter of patrons. She took a deep breath, steeling herself for what was to come. She spotted him immediately, his mischievous eyes catching her gaze before he turned back to the group of locals he was chatting with. As she approached, she watched as he leaned in, his voice low and filled with playful secrets.

Hermes' electric charm radiated from him like a palpable force, drawing the attention of all in the small town. His keen ears pricked at the hushed whispers that followed his question, and he could feel the weight of their secrets hanging in the air.

A woman with weary eyes and nicotine-stained fingers leaned in, her voice barely audible over the clink of glasses. "That lake," she murmured, her gaze darting nervously. "There's something... not right about it lately."

Hermes felt a chill run down his spine, a sensation he hadn't experienced since his descent from godhood. He couldn't resist the temptation to delve deeper into this mystery, despite knowing he should focus on more pressing matters, like Truly Scrumptious.

But as the woman's companion growled about people going missing and returning with twisted minds, Hermes felt a thrill course through him. The allure of danger and intrigue called to his very essence, and he knew he had to investigate further.

Suddenly, Hermes saw Aphrodite appear at the door, glaring at him with fury in her eyes. She signalled for him to come near her and warned him against entertaining the mortals. But Hermes couldn't resist one last quip before slipping away with his sister into the rain-soaked night.

Chapter 4

In the dead of night, where shadows preyed upon the weak, the cacophony of colossal wings beating against the blackened sky stirred the slick cobblestones of Rashford Town. The very atmosphere quivered under their harsh embrace. Gabri-El's piercing gaze raked over the town, a place where shadows now whispered wicked secrets and ancient sins refused to sleep. His eyes fixed upon a figure that glowed with an unholy radiance amidst the darkness.

"Who dares defy an Archangel's decree?" His voice rumbled through the air like thunder, laced with menace and foreboding. But the eerie figure did not flinch, nor did it beg for mercy as so many before had done.

The strange power pulsed, drawing Gabri-El north of Rashford. As he descended, a small farm came into view, surrounded by rolling fields and a fence made of wooden posts and barbed wire. The air was charged with the power's energy, making his skin tingle. He landed in front of the window of a room of a teenage boy, no more than sixteen human years of age, who radiated an invisible aura that only a seer like Gabri-El could sense. The Eldar! "So, he's still a child," Gabri-El mused.

Laughter suddenly echoed in the fields; soft and mirthful yet tainted with malevolence. "Dear

Gabri-El, is this how you greet an eons-old friend? So cold, so bitter—how tragic."

"Who..." Gabri-El whispered, his voice a morbid symphony of awe and trepidation.

A disturbance—a vile abomination or perhaps some accursed event—shattered what little peace remained within this town. Gabri-El observed in horror as trees swayed unnaturally in response, their wicked branches caressing an unseen entity like supplicants paying homage to their cruel master. The night itself seemed to tremor around it, reality contorted by its nefarious presence.

"Loki!"

Gabri-El's wings twitched with urgency – a visceral reaction to the magnetic trickery that now pervaded the area through the old Norse trickster. He now regretted having freed him from his prison and the serpent's grasp, even though Loki had been useful in annihilating the Norse gods. Gabri-El's thoughts raced with the dreadful implications, the blood in his veins turning cold. "Yahweh must know."

With a powerful thrust of his wings, Gabri-El ascended, the air splitting around him as he rocketed towards the celestial realm. The wind howled in his ears, carrying whispers of ancient prophecies and forgotten warnings.

"Father," Gabri-El called out, his voice echoing across dimensions, "a new player, an Eldar, has entered the game. One whose power may rival Your own."

As he soared higher, leaving the mortal world behind, Gabri-El's determination solidified. The weight of his duty pressed upon him, a mantle both glorious and terrifying.

"The boy's innocence is a double-edged sword," Gabri-El mused, his thoughts tumultuous. "In the wrong hands, he could bring about our downfall. In the right ones..."

The archangel shook his head, banishing the temptation. "No. It's not for me to decide. Yahweh will know what must be done."

With one final, powerful beat of his wings, Gabri-El breached the veil between worlds, leaving behind a town on the precipice of chaos, and a boy whose very existence threatened the cosmic balance.

The Heavenly Realm shimmered into existence around Gabri-El, its ethereal beauty a stark contrast to the mortal world he'd left behind. Rivers of liquid light flowed beneath his feet, and the air thrummed with celestial harmonies. Yet, even in this bastion of divine serenity, Gabri-El felt a creeping unease.

Yahweh's presence filled the space, vast and incomprehensible. "Speak, my messenger," the voice thundered, shaking Gabri-El to his core.

"Father," Gabri-El began, his voice quavering, "a being of immense power has arrived in Rashford. An Eldar, I believe. His aura... it disrupts the very fabric of reality."

A heavy silence fell, punctuated only by the distant chorus of seraphim. Gabri-El's wings twitched nervously.

"This is troubling news indeed," Yahweh's voice rumbled. "The Eldar were never meant to interfere in our affairs. Their power is... unpredictable."

Gabri-El nodded, relief flooding through him. "Loki knows too."

"Then we must act swiftly," Yahweh declared. "Micha-El will go. His strength and loyalty make him best suited for this task. . . We must collect this being and hold him under our clutches."

As if summoned by the mere mention of his name, Micha-El materialized beside Gabri-El. His golden hair cascaded over his shoulders, and his eyes blazed with divine purpose.

"I am ready, Father," Micha-El said, his voice resonating with quiet authority. "What is my mission?"

Gabri-El watched as Yahweh's essence coalesced into a vaguely humanoid form, its radiance almost blinding. "Go to Rashford, my warrior. Find and observe the Eldar. If he poses a threat to the balance we've fought so hard to maintain, you must bring him to me. If he resists, you know what must be done."

"He is still a child, Father," Gabri-El interjected but a sharp look from Yahweh made him regret his outburst.

Micha-El's jaw clenched, his eyes narrowing with an unnerving mix of regret and anticipation. "I understand, Father," he said through gritted teeth. "Consider it done." His voice dripped with icy determination as he stared dead-eyed at his superior, ready to fulfill whatever dark task lay ahead.

Without another word, Micha-El spread his wings, each feather gleaming like burnished gold. He cast one last glance at Gabri-El, a silent exchange passing between them.

"The farmhouse north of town," Gabri-El confided.

With a nod, Micha-El descended towards the earthly realm.

As he plummeted through the celestial spheres, his mind raced. "An Eldar child," he mused, the wind whipping past him. "Such power! What

chaos might he unleash? Is this what Apollo was hiding?"

A surge of fury assailed him as he realized that his lover had withheld such an earth-shattering revelation from him. How could he do this, hide something of such import? But he suppressed the thoughts, knowing well that confrontation with Apollo would come in due course.

The thought of confronting an Eldar, even if a child, stirred something deep within Micha-El—a mixture of duty and an emotion he dared not name. As he neared the earthly plane, his resolve hardened.

"I must protect the balance," he told himself, even as a small voice whispered of other loyalties, other loves. "No matter the cost."

Meredith's farmhouse came into view, a tranquil oasis in a sea of impending chaos. Micha-El's wings flared, slowing his descent. As his feet touched the ground, he steeled himself for what lay ahead, unaware of the dark forces already gathering to oppose him.

No sooner had Micha-El's feet caressed the damp earth, the atmosphere surrounding Meredith's farmhouse shifted in a most vile manner. The clear sky darkened with unnatural speed; even the blackest curtain could not eclipse its former

splendour so utterly. A revolting odour—as if one were inhaling liquid metal—assailed his senses, overpowering any natural scents that might otherwise have lingered in the air. Micha-El's eyes widened with unadulterated horror as crimson droplets cascaded from above, painting everything they touched with a sanguine hue reminiscent of fresh slaughter.

"Blood," he whispered, his composure crumbling like ancient stone. "Loki . . . or . . . the Eldar himself!"

Like the sinister knell of a death bell, the rain of blood intensified, staining his once-pristine wings and saturating the ground below with a hue befitting the most gruesome of crime scenes. Micha-El's mind reeled, torn between steadfast duty and a primal revulsion.

"Is this your loathsome handiwork, Deceiver?" he called out, his voice quavering despite desperate attempts to retain stoic composure. "You cannot dissuade me from my grim objective."

As if in retort, the soil before him churned and split asunder. Skeletal hands, dripping with gore and putrid decay, erupted forth to ensnare his ankles. Micha-El recoiled in horror, his wings flaring in abject terror.

"By all that is unholy," he gasped, struggling to maintain equilibrium. "What abomination have you wrought?"

The bony appendages multiplied like a plague, a grotesque forest of undead arms sprouting from the sanguine earth. Micha-El's heart raced as memories of celestial warfare assailed his thoughts. He had faced gods before—but this... this was a monstrosity born of pure malevolence.

"I must find the cursed Eldar," he muttered through gritted teeth as he endeavoured to forge ahead. "Yahweh's will shall be done."

But with each step, even more ravenous arms emerged, clawing at his robes, his wings, his very soul. Micha-El felt the icy tendrils of fear entwine about his spine—a sensation long forgotten since time immemorial.

"Eldar!" he roared, despair and dread intermingling within him. "Show yourself, craven! Face me directly if you possess an ounce of courage!"

Only the sickening patter of bloody rainfall and the nauseating squelching of putrescent flesh answered him. As Micha-El battled the grasping limbs, a horrifying revelation began to dawn upon him. This was no mere impediment—it was a portent. A declaration of eternal warfare.

And for the first time in his unending existence, Micha-El, Yahweh's Warrior, felt the crushing weight of true, abject terror.

His wings thrashed, splattering crimson as he fought against the brutal assault. The hands clawed, scorching like fire. Dragged to the blood-soaked ground, he was pulled deeper still, sinking beneath the earth, trapped by unholy arms.

In a blur of motion, he twisted and writhed, breaking free from the suffocating grasp. His body moved with primal instinct, striking out with fierce blows. Each impact reverberated through him, bones vibrating with the force of his strikes.

The air filled with the metallic tang of blood and the sickening sound of flesh meeting flesh. Grunts and snarls punctuated the chaos as he fought for every breath. Fear surged, sharpening his focus as he pushed back against the relentless onslaught.

With a final burst of energy, he broke through the wall of attackers, gasping for air as he stumbled to freedom. The taste of success was bittersweet, his body battered and bruised from the intense struggle. But he stood tall, a survivor in a world of demonic predators.

"This cannot be," he whispered, his voice trembling. "I am an archangel, I am—"

Another skeletal finger brushed his cheek, and Micha-El recoiled as visions of cosmic horror flooded his mind. He saw worlds devoured by darkness, heard the screams of countless innocents. And beneath it all, Satana's mocking laughter. His battle was not over yet.

"No!" Micha-El cried out, his composure shattering. "I can't let you win!"

But even as he fought, doubt crept in. How could he overcome the Eldar, fulfill his duty to Yahweh, when he could barely protect himself?

With a burst of divine energy, Micha-El tore free from the last grasping arms. His wings unfurled, gleaming gold despite the blood-rain, and he soared upward.

As he ascended, Micha-El's heart ached. Below, Rashford Town lay shrouded in darkness, its inhabitants unaware of the cosmic battle unfolding.

"Forgive me," he murmured, torn between duty and compassion. "I must find another way."

Micha-El's retreat felt like failure, but as he flew, a new resolve hardened within him. He would return, and next time, he would be prepared for Satana's tricks.

Meredith's aged, weathered hands trembled as she wrung out a damp cloth, the scent of calming lavender and soothing chamomile wafting through the quaint farmhouse's cozy kitchen. The delicate fragrance mingled with the lingering aroma of freshly baked bread, filling the air with a sense of comfort and warmth. She turned to Aodhán, who lay unmoving on her well-loved sofa, his ethereal features softly illuminated by the flickering light of the crackling hearth. The dancing flames cast shadows across his slight features, giving him an otherworldly aura.

She softly whispered, "It's okay, my dear," as she carefully wiped the perspiration from his forehead. "You're in a safe place." He had bolted down the stairs from his room, letting out piercing screams of terror. Meredith quickly wrapped her arms around him and attempted to calm him down. After some resistance, he finally settled into her embrace, allowing her to provide comfort and reassurance.

As she tended to him, Meredith's heart ached with a bittersweet mixture of empathy and abject fear. The boy's presence stirred memories of her lost son – a sacrificial lamb to dark forces – yet there was something undeniably otherworldly about him that sent shivers down her fragile spine.

Aodhán's eyes fluttered open, vast and unfathomable as the night sky. "Something... is coming," he mumbled, his voice a breathless whisper.

Meredith's throat felt tight as she tried to swallow. Aodhán was making good progress in learning her language, but he was still vulnerable. "You're safe here, my dear," she insisted. "Nothing will harm you in my home."

As she spoke, the air around them began to shimmer with malevolent intent. The teacup on the side table rose an inch off its saucer, defying gravity and reason. Shadows danced along the walls, twisting into unspeakable forms which terrorized her fragile psyche.

"Oh, dear God," Meredith gasped, her eyes widening in horror. "What is happening?"

Aodhán sat up slowly, seemingly unaware of the supernatural phenomena surrounding him. "I feel... strange," he admitted, his voice wavering with uncertainty and dread. "I am overflowing with the darkest of stars."

A book flew off the shelf with a menacing force, its pages fluttering open like a demonic tome. The flames in the fireplace twisted into serpentine shapes, casting an eerie glow across the room that reflected malevolence itself.

Meredith's heart raced within her chest, threatening to tear itself apart as it beat with equal parts fascination and terror. "Aodhán," she whispered through trembling lips, "are you causing this?"

The boy looked upon her with eyes that swirled like a vortex of cosmic energy – a maelstrom of darkness in human form. "I don't know," he confessed. "Everything feels... alive. Connected. Do you feel it too?"

As Meredith struggled to find words amidst the swirling maelstrom of fear gripping her soul, a vase shattered with unnatural force; its fragments suspended in mid-air like an ominous constellation. She knew she should be afraid – terrified even – but something within Aodhán's innocent wonder tugged at her heart, filling her with a resolve she did not know she possessed.

Together, they would face the darkness.

"No, dear," she said softly, reaching out to touch his hand. "This is something... special. Something only you can do."

The moment Meredith's fingers brushed Aodhán's skin, a jolt of energy surged through her. It was like touching a live wire, but instead of pain, she felt a rush of warmth and an overwhelming sense of... purpose.

"I'll keep you safe," she murmured, her voice thick with emotion. Memories of her lost son flooded her mind, but for once, they didn't bring the usual ache. Instead, she felt a fierce protectiveness welling up inside her.

Aodhán tilted his head, his otherworldly eyes studying her face. "You're afraid," he observed, "but not of me. Why?"

Meredith laughed softly, the sound tinged with hysteria. "Oh, child. I'm afraid of what might happen to you. This world... it's not always kind to those who are different."

As she spoke, the objects in the room slowly settled back into place. The shadows retreated, leaving only the warm glow of the fireplace. Meredith took a deep breath, steadying herself.

"We'll figure this out together," she promised, squeezing Aodhán's hand. "Whatever you are, whatever you can do... you're not alone."

Chapter 5

The farmhouse stood rugged and weathered, surrounded by sprawling fields and woods. The ancient oak loomed nearby, its twisted branches reaching towards the sky. In the shadows, Luke Laufeyson, known to the celestial host as Loki, could be seen, his sinister figure blending in seamlessly with the darkness. His eyes, green and piercing, held a malicious glint as he observed the unfolding events with a twisted smile on his face.

"Oh, this is delicious," he purred, a wicked grin spreading across his face. "An Eldar - still a child - and a mortal woman... what a perfectly chaotic combination."

Luke's mind raced with twisted schemes and cunning possibilities. The boy's immense power, wild and uncontrollable, could be the means to break free from the oppressive chains of Satana and Yahweh. And the woman's maternal instincts... those could be easily manipulated, a tool for his own dark purposes. He was trapped in servitude to both Yahweh and Satana, belonging to both a celestial Master and a demonic Mistress. Perhaps they suspected his deceitful game, but he cared not. For he was Loki, the god of deception, and he would never be a slave to anyone!

"Oh, what a delightful mess we've stumbled into," he murmured as he beheld the raw power of the

Eldar child, his voice a silken purr that sent nearby creatures scurrying for cover. "An Eldar child, a protective mortal, and all those self-righteous angels fluttering about. It's almost too perfect."

The beam of Sheriff Eva Ramirez's flashlight sliced through the inky darkness, revealing twisted tree roots clawing at the earth. A cloying mist clung to her boots as she surveyed the clearing where the boys had been found. The air felt heavy, pregnant with unspoken horrors.

"Jesus," she muttered, her breath forming ghostly tendrils in the frigid night air. "What the hell happened here?"

Her keen eyes scanned for any sign of struggle, any clue to unravel this macabre mystery. But the forest floor remained stubbornly silent, offering no answers to quell the questions racing through her mind.

As Eva crouched to examine a strange pattern in the dirt, a twig snapped behind her. She whirled, hand flying to her holster, heart thundering in her chest. But only shadows greeted her, dancing at the edge of her light. She shook her head, willing away the creeping dread that threatened to cloud her judgment.

"Get it together, Ramirez," she chided herself. "You've got a job to do."

Yet as she resumed her search, Eva couldn't shake the feeling of being watched. Unseen eyes bore into her back, judging her every move. She pushed the sensation aside, focusing instead on the task at hand. Mayor Quinn's son, Jamie, was still missing, and she feared time was running out.

"Let the games begin," Luke whispered, melting into the shadows. As he stood there, the air crackled with a mischievous energy that seemed to promise a storm of chaos on the horizon. The hairs on the back of his neck stood straight, sensing the impending burst of wildness and thrill that was about to unfold. It was as if the very atmosphere was charged with anticipation, waiting for the first flash of lightning to ignite the frenzy within. He couldn't help but feel a surge of excitement and trepidation, unsure of what exactly was about to unfold amidst this electric atmosphere.

Luke slipped away from the farmhouse, his lithe form weaving through the moonlit trees. The forest seemed to bend around him, branches reaching out like grasping fingers, but never quite touching the trickster god.

He paused at the edge of a moonlit clearing, his eyes glinting with malevolent glee. The air shimmered around him, hinting at the power he kept carefully contained.

"But how to play this game?" Luke mused, tapping a long finger against his chin. "Perhaps a whisper in the right ear... or a nudge towards forbidden knowledge."

His laughter, low and melodious, sent a chill through the night air. "After all, what's the fun in letting Yahweh have all the toys?"

As he prepared to depart, Luke cast one last glance towards Meredith's farmhouse. His smile was a knife's edge, promising mischief and mayhem.

"Sleep well, little Eldar," he crooned. "Your destiny awaits... and I'll be there to give it a little push."

With that, Luke vanished into the shadows, leaving behind only the faintest scent of chaos and the certainty that Rashford Town's fragile peace was about to be shattered.

Hours later, Eva sat in her office, the harsh fluorescent lights a stark contrast to the forest's

oppressive gloom. Before her sat Mr and Mrs Quinn, their faces etched with worry and exhaustion.

"Tell me again," Eva commanded, her voice steady despite the turmoil churning within. "Every detail, no matter how small."

Bella Quinn wrung her hands, her voice quavering. "We've told you everything we know, Sheriff. Jamie went out with his friends, like always. Then we got the call..."

"And you're certain he mentioned nothing unusual?" Eva pressed, leaning forward. "No new acquaintances, no strange behaviour?"

Mayor Quinn's eyes flashed with indignation. "Are you implying our son is involved in something nefarious? He's the victim here!"

Eva held up a placating hand, even as irritation simmered beneath her professional demeanour. "I'm simply trying to gather all the facts, Mr Mayor."

As the parents continued their fragmented account, Eva's mind raced. Something about this case felt off, a wrongness that settled in her bones like a bitter chill. The unconscious boys, the missing Jamie, the eerie stillness of the forest – it all pointed to something far more sinister than a simple disappearance.

"We're good people, Sheriff," Bella Quinn pleaded, tears glistening in her eyes. "Our Jamie, he's a good boy. Please, you have to find Jamie. You have to make this right."

Eva nodded, her expression softening even as determination blazed within her. "I give you my word, I will not rest until we uncover the truth. No matter where it leads us."

As the Quinns left, their shoulders slumped with the weight of uncertainty, Eva turned to the evidence board. Her fingers traced the connections between scraps of information, searching for the thread that would unravel this twisted tapestry.

"Where are you hiding, Jamie?" she murmured, her eyes fixed on the smiling face of the Mayor's son.

The silence of her office offered no answers, only the echoing whisper of secrets yet to be revealed.

A soft knock interrupted Eva's reverie. She turned to find Shania Queen standing in the doorway, her vibrant presence a stark contrast to the sombre atmosphere of the sheriff's office.

"Come in, Ms Queen," Eva said, gesturing to a chair. "I appreciate you coming to speak with me."

Shania settled into the seat, her curls bouncing with nervous energy. "I'm not sure how much help I'll be, Sheriff, but what I saw... it wasn't natural."

Eva leaned forward, her keen eyes studying Shania's face. "Tell me everything."

Shania's voice quavered as she began, "I was by the lake, just enjoying the evening, you know? And then I saw them – a man and a woman. But they weren't... they weren't normal."

"How so?" Eva prodded gently.

"The woman, she was breathtaking. Like, literally took my breath away. And the man..." Shania's eyes glazed over, lost in the memory. "He glowed, Sheriff. Like the sun itself was trapped beneath his skin."

Eva's brow furrowed. "Glowed? Ms Queen, are you certain—"

"I know how it sounds," Shania interrupted, her voice gaining strength. "But I swear to you, they were there. A man and a woman, like Greek gods!"

Eva looked up annoyed. "Greek gods? In Rashford? Really?"

Shania nodded emphatically. "They were arguing about something. The man seemed... protective. And she looked scared. Like she was running from something."

As Shania continued her account, Eva's mind raced. Could this be connected to the boys? To Jamie's disappearance? The rational part of her brain rebelled against the notion, but a deeper instinct whispered that Shania's words held the key to unravelling this mystery.

Little did Eva know that across town, in a room bathed in ethereal light, Apollo stood perfectly still, his rusty hair shimmering as he processed the information his keen senses had gathered. The sheriff's investigation posed a threat to everything he had worked to protect.

Time was a merciless executioner, its blade poised to fall. Each breath he took felt like a countdown to disaster, his chest tightening with each one. The fear of discovery gnawed at him, knowing that Aphrodite's reckless actions could bring chaos and destruction to this once peaceful sanctuary. How much longer could they keep their secrets hidden? How many more sacrifices would have to be made to maintain the fragile peace?

His fingers twitched, yearning for the comforting weight of his lyre. But that, like so much else, was lost to him now. All that remained was the bitter taste of desperation on his tongue.

With a deep breath that did little to calm the storm within, Apollo strode towards the Sheriff's office. Each step echoed with grim purpose, a rhythm

that spoke of inevitability. The few townsfolk still awake at this unholy hour shrank from his path, their mortal instincts recognizing the barely contained power that simmered beneath his skin.

The Sheriff's office loomed before him, a bastion of mortal law that seemed laughably inadequate in the face of cosmic upheaval. Apollo's hand hesitated on the door handle, a fleeting moment of doubt.

Is this truly the only way? he wondered, the thought a poisonous whisper in his mind. *To drag another innocent into our eternal dance of betrayal and ruin?*

But the moment passed, resolve hardening his features into a mask of determination. He had to intervene or the secrets of the gods and the safety of Aphrodite would be threatened by the human world. The door creaked open, the sound like the groan of a dying god. Apollo stepped into the dimly lit interior, the silence of the night shattered by his presence.

"Sheriff Ramirez," he called out, his voice carrying the faintest echo of its former divine resonance. "I require your assistance in a matter of utmost urgency."

The words hung in the air, a challenge and a plea intertwined. Apollo's gaze swept the office,

seeking the one mortal who might yet tip the scales in this cosmic game of chess. His heart raced, a staccato beat that whispered of the precious seconds slipping away.

Let her be here, he prayed silently, though to whom, he dared not contemplate. *Let her listen. Let me succeed. Before it's too late for us all.*

Sheriff Eva Ramirez sat hunched over her desk, the harsh fluorescent light casting deep shadows across her furrowed brow.

The creak of the door jolted her from her reverie. Eva's hand instinctively moved to her holster as she looked up, her dark eyes narrowing at the sight of the golden-haired intruder.

"This is a restricted area," she said, her voice clipped and authoritative. "State your business or leave."

Apollo stepped forward, his presence filling the small office with an otherworldly aura. "My apologies for the late intrusion, Sheriff," he began, his voice a melody that seemed to caress the very air. "I couldn't help but notice the dedication with which you pursue justice in these... trying times."

Eva's jaw clenched, her instincts screaming that this was no ordinary man. She stood, her posture rigid. "Flattery won't get you anywhere. What do you want?"

Apollo's eyes, blue as a cloudless sky, locked onto hers. "I merely wish to offer my assistance. These recent events must be... troubling for someone sworn to protect this town."

"Who are you?" Eva inquired, her curiosity piqued.

"I am just a philanthropist," Apollo lied through his teeth. "Someone who wishes this town to remain a safe haven. Safe from shady characters who . . . well, you know . . ."

He knows something, Eva thought, her heart racing. *But can I trust him? Should I?*

"I appreciate the offer," she replied coolly, "but I have everything under control."

Apollo's lips curved into a smile that didn't quite reach his eyes. "Do you, Sheriff? Do any of us truly have control in the face of what's coming?"

The words hung between them, heavy with unspoken truths and barely concealed threats. Eva felt a chill crawl up her spine, the weight of her responsibility pressing down on her like a physical force.

The traitorous voice in her mind whispered, questioning again if she should trust him. Could he truly be right? Could he actually help save Rashford? She felt torn between her doubts and

the desperate need to find a solution for her loved one's perilous situation.

Apollo's gaze flickered to the window, where the moon hung low and bloated in the sky. "I'm sure you've noticed the... peculiarities surrounding the woman at the lake," he said, his voice dropping to a near-whisper. "The chaos that seems to follow in her wake."

Eva's breath caught in her throat. She'd been investigating a series of bizarre incidents—unexplained fires, sudden outbreaks of violence, even reports of spontaneous orgies erupting in the town square. All somehow tied to the enigmatic woman known as the Woman at the Lake.

"What do you know about her?" Eva asked, her professional mask slipping as curiosity and desperation won out.

Apollo's eyes glinted with something dark and ancient. "More than you could imagine, Sheriff. And believe me when I say, the situation is far more dire than you realize."

Eva's fingers twitched towards her holstered gun, an unconscious gesture of self-reassurance. "Explain," she demanded.

Apollo leaned in, close enough that Eva could smell the faint scent of sunlight and honey on his breath. "Her very presence is a threat to this town.

Her... abilities are beyond her control now. Every moment she remains here, the fabric of reality frays a little more."

Eva's mind reeled, trying to reconcile Apollo's words with the world she thought she knew. "And why should I believe you?" she asked, her voice hoarse.

Apollo's frustration flashed across his face, a crack in his ethereal composure. "Because, Sheriff," he hissed, "if you don't, there won't be a Rashford left to protect."

Eva's heart thundered in her chest, each beat a war drum pounding out the conflict raging within her. Apollo's words slithered through her mind, venomous and alluring. She clenched her fists, nails biting into her palms, anchoring her to reality as the world seemed to tilt on its axis. She tried to resist his allure but he was seductive and she was being drawn to him by some force she could not understand. He was beautiful to behold, ageless and yet, menacing.

"Tell me what you know," Apollo whispered, "and I'll let you know what to look for . . . and where."

"You're asking me to betray my oath," she whispered, the words tasting like ash on her tongue.

Apollo's eyes, blue as a cloudless sky yet fathomless as the deepest ocean, bore into her. "I'm asking you to save your town, Eva. To be the shield that protects the innocent from forces beyond their comprehension."

His voice, melodic and hypnotic, wove a tapestry of seduction and doom. Eva felt herself swaying, caught in the undertow of his presence.

"Picture it," Apollo continued, his words painting vivid horrors in Eva's mind. "Streets running red with blood and madness. Families torn apart by uncontrollable lust and rage. The very foundations of reality crumbling beneath your feet."

Eva's breath came in short, sharp gasps. She could see it all too clearly—the chaos, the destruction, the utter collapse of everything she'd sworn to protect.

Apollo leaned closer, his golden hair catching the dim light of the office, creating a halo effect that seemed both divine and demonic. "You stand at a precipice, Sheriff. The fate of Rashford balances on the edge of a knife. Will you let it fall, or will you take my hand and help me save it?"

Eva's world narrowed to Apollo's intense gaze, her duty and desire colliding in a maelstrom of conflicting emotions. The weight of her decision pressed down on her, suffocating in its enormity.

Eva's fingers trembled as she reached for her badge, the cool metal a stark reminder of her oath. Yet, as she traced its contours, doubt seeped into her resolve like poison.

"I..." she began, her voice barely a whisper. "I can't just abandon my responsibilities."

Apollo's lips curved into a smile that didn't quite reach his eyes. "Your true responsibility is to protect, is it not? Sometimes, Sheriff, that means venturing beyond the confines of human law."

He extended his hand, an offering and a temptation. Eva stared at it, her heart pounding a frantic rhythm against her ribs. The air in the office grew thick, charged with an electric tension that made her skin prickle.

"What you're asking..." Eva swallowed hard, her throat suddenly dry. "It goes against everything I've stood for."

"Does it?" Apollo's voice was silk and shadow. "Or does it align perfectly with your deepest desire to truly make a difference?"

Eva closed her eyes, memories of unsolved cases and unexplained phenomena flooding her mind. How many times had she felt powerless, knowing there were forces at work beyond her comprehension?

"You're due to clock off," Apollo went on. "Come with me and accept my help."

When she opened her eyes again, resolve hardened her gaze. "My flat," she said, the words tasting of surrender and possibility. "We'll talk there."

As Eva rose from her chair, her legs unsteady, she felt the weight of her decision settle over her like a shroud. She was stepping into uncharted territory, and the path ahead was shrouded in darkness.

The heavy door of the Sheriff's office creaked shut behind them, sealing away the last vestiges of Eva's carefully constructed world. The night air rushed to greet them, cool and biting, carrying the scent of rain-soaked earth and pine. Eva shivered, unsure if it was from the chill or the electric charge that seemed to emanate from Apollo's very presence.

They walked side by side, their footsteps echoing on the empty street. Eva's mind raced, her thoughts a cacophony of doubt and desire. She glanced at Apollo, his hair catching the dim light of the streetlamps, a halo that mocked her wavering faith.

"You're trembling," Apollo observed, his voice low and melodic.

Eva clenched her fists, willing herself to steady. "It's just the cold," she lied, the words feeling hollow even to her own ears.

Apollo's laugh was a soft, dangerous thing. "We both know that's not true, Sheriff. Your body betrays your inner turmoil."

They reached Eva's car, a nondescript sedan that suddenly felt far too small for the weight of what was transpiring. As she fumbled with the keys, Apollo's hand brushed against hers, sending a jolt of electricity through her body.

Eva hesitated, her instincts screaming at her to run, to retreat to the safety of her known world. But the pull of the unknown, of the secrets Apollo promised to reveal, was too strong to resist.

As they settled into the car, the interior filled with a palpable tension. Eva gripped the steering wheel, her knuckles white, as she navigated the familiar streets that now seemed alien and foreboding.

"What am I doing?" she whispered, more to herself than to Apollo.

His fathomless, blue eyes turned to her. "You're embracing your destiny, Eva. The veil between your world and mine has always been thin in Rashford. You've sensed it, haven't you? The

unexplained occurrences, the whispers in the shadows..."

Eva's breath caught in her throat. Images flashed through her mind: trees that seemed to move of their own accord, blood-red rain that stained the streets, the haunting melody that sometimes drifted on the wind.

"I've tried to rationalize it all," she admitted, her voice barely whisper over the hum of the engine. "To explain away the impossible."

Apollo's hand came to rest on her thigh, a touch both comforting and terrifying. "And now you're ready to see the truth, to step beyond the veil of mortal understanding."

As they neared Eva's flat, her grip on the wheel tightened, each mile bringing them closer to a point of no return. The air in the car crackled with anticipation, thick with unspoken promises and lurking dangers.

"What if I'm not strong enough?" Eva asked, fear and excitement warring within her.

Apollo's smile was both beautiful and terrible to behold. "My dear Eva, you have no idea of the power that lies dormant within you. Tonight, we awaken it."

The car lurched to a stop outside Eva's flat, the engine's sudden silence amplifying the pounding of her heart. Apollo's presence beside her felt like a gravitational force, pulling her inexorably towards a fate she couldn't fully comprehend.

As they approached her door, Eva's hand trembled, fumbling with the keys. Apollo's fingers brushed hers, steadying them, and she felt a jolt of electricity course through her body.

"Allow me," he murmured, his voice a seductive melody that seemed to resonate in her very bones.

The lock clicked open, and they stepped into the darkened hallway. Eva reached for the light switch, but Apollo caught her wrist, his touch gentle yet unyielding.

"Some truths are best revealed in darkness," he whispered, his breath warm against her ear.

The door closed behind them with a finality that sent a shiver down Eva's spine. In the dim light filtering through the curtains, she could see Apollo's eyes gleaming with an otherworldly intensity.

"I... I'm not sure I'm ready for this," Eva stammered, her resolve inexistent.

Apollo's laugh was low and melodious, filled with ancient secrets. "Oh, my dear Sheriff. Readiness

is a luxury afforded to mortals. We gods... we simply are."

As he spoke, the shadows in the room seemed to deepen, whispering secrets that only the night could hear. Eva felt herself teetering on the edge of a vast, unknowable abyss, torn between her duty to protect Rashford and the irresistible pull of Apollo's divine allure.

"What happens now?" she asked, her voice barely above a whisper.

Apollo's smile was both beautiful and terrible to behold. "Now, Eva Ramirez, you take your first step into a world beyond your wildest dreams... or your darkest nightmares."

Eva's mind screamed caution, but her body betrayed her, leaning into his touch. "I shouldn't..." she murmured, even as she found herself rising from her chair.

Apollo's hand cupped her cheek, his thumb tracing her lower lip. "Trust me, Eva," he breathed, the use of her first name sending shivers down her spine. "I can show you truths beyond your wildest imagination."

As their lips crashed together, Eva's last conscious thought was a vague concern for the case. But then Apollo's searing kiss obliterated everything else.

Apollo's mouth blazed a trail down Eva's neck, his touch sparking a wildfire within her that scorched all rational thought into cinders. She gasped, her fingers knotting in his thick hair as he descended before her like some kind of god.

His gaze held hers, his eyes intense blue supernovas that seemed to possess an uncanny, celestial intensity. "Surrender, Eva," he murmured, his warm breath teasing her skin like the promise of raw sexual release. "Let this moment consume you."

As his mouth found that spot, that goddamn sweet spot, Eva's world detonated into pure ecstasy. She bucked against him, a raw, animalistic cry clawing its way out of her throat. As waves of pleasure ravished her senses, memories began to melt away - the disappearance of the boy, the weird occurrences happening around town, her suspicions over Rashford's newcomers - all faded to dust.

Apollo's tongue moved with an unearthly expertise that sent Eva spiralling into heady heights until she teetered on the verge of consciousness. Her legs wobbled dangerously close to collapsing beneath her.

"God," she groaned out through gritted teeth, "don't you fucking stop". As the tsunami of her climax crashed over her in relentless waves, Eva

felt herself plunging into oblivion - her mind purged of everything but raw carnal pleasure.

With gentle hands, Apollo caught her limp form, cradling her against his chest. He laid her carefully on the couch, brushing a strand of hair from her face.

"Forget, my dear Eva," he murmured, his melodic voice tinged with regret. "For your own safety, forget it all."

Apollo's footsteps echoed through the darkened alleys of Rashford as he sought out Hermes, his mind still haunted by Eva's lingering scent. The weight of his actions pressed upon him, a reminder of the mortal complexities he now navigated.

He found Hermes lounging against a brick wall, moonlight glinting off his mischievous eyes. "Brother," Apollo called, his voice low and urgent. "We have a situation."

Hermes straightened, his lips curving into a smirk. "Don't we always? What's got you so worked up this time?"

Apollo's jaw clenched. "A woman . . . Shania Queen. A witness to Aphrodite's actions with that boy. She's becoming a liability."

"Ah, the vivacious one. I know her. I know where she lives," Hermes chuckled. "And here I thought you'd summoned me for something truly dire."

"This is serious," Apollo hissed, his eyes flashing with irritation. "She's seen too much. If she keeps talking..."

Hermes waved a hand dismissively. "Relax, brother. Mortals are fickle creatures. A few well-placed words, and she'll doubt her own memories."

Apollo's frown deepened. "It's not that simple. We can't risk exposure."

As they spoke, the two gods began to move through the streets, their steps silent and purposeful. The moon cast long shadows, transforming familiar surroundings into a landscape of eerie beauty and hidden dangers.

"You worry too much," Hermes said, his tone light but his eyes sharp. "Where's that golden confidence of yours?"

Apollo's mind raced, weighing options and consequences. "It died with our divinity," he muttered. "We're vulnerable now, whether you choose to accept it or not."

They turned down a quiet street, the air growing thick with tension. Shania's house loomed ahead, a beacon of warmth in the oppressive darkness.

"So, what's the plan?" Hermes asked, his earlier levity fading. "Surely you're not suggesting we... silence her permanently?"

Apollo's heart clenched at the thought. "No," he said firmly. " But we need to ensure her silence, one way or another."

As they approached the house, Apollo's senses heightened, every rustle and shadow demanding his attention. He couldn't shake the feeling that they were walking into something far more complicated than they'd anticipated.

"I don't like this," he murmured, more to himself than Hermes. "I should be looking for the Eldar boy not covering up for our sister."

Hermes raised an eyebrow. "Having second thoughts? That's not like you, brother."

Apollo shook his head, unable to articulate the dread building in his chest. "Let's just get this over with," he said, reaching for the door.

As they neared the house, two figures materialized from the shadows, their crisp police uniforms a stark contrast to the inky night. Apollo's heart

raced, his mind calculating the potential ramifications of their presence.

"Evening, gentlemen," one officer called out, his hand resting casually on his holster. "Mind if we ask what brings you here at this hour?"

Apollo's muscles tensed, ready to spring into action. He exchanged a quick glance with Hermes, a silent communication born of millennia of brotherhood.

"Now!" Apollo hissed, launching himself at the nearest officer.

His movements were swift and precise, a dance of violence honed by countless battles. In mere seconds, both officers lay unconscious at their feet, victims of Apollo's ruthless efficiency.

"Help me move them," Apollo commanded, already dragging one limp body towards a nearby hedge.

As they concealed the officers, Apollo's mind whirled with conflicting emotions. The ease with which he'd dispatched the men disturbed him, a stark reminder of the darkness that lurked beneath his golden exterior.

"We need to hurry," Hermes urged, tossing Apollo a police uniform. "Before someone else shows up."

They donned their disguises quickly, the fabric feeling alien against Apollo's skin. He couldn't shake the feeling that with each deception, each act of violence, they were straying further from redemption.

Approaching Shania's front door, Apollo paused, his hand hovering over the knob. The house loomed before them, hosting in it a witness of his sister's deeds.

"Are you sure about this?" Hermes whispered, his usual mischief replaced by uncharacteristic hesitation.

Apollo swallowed hard, steeling himself. "We have no choice," he replied, his voice barely audible. "Can you open the door?"

"I am the god of thieves!" Hermes replied haughtily. "Of course I can! I got pure unadulterated crime running in my veins."

Hermes fiddled with the lock for some moments. "It's open!" he exclaimed, unable to contain his surprise.

The door creaked open, a sound that seemed to echo through the oppressive silence of the night. They stepped inside, enveloped immediately by a darkness so complete it seemed to devour even the faintest glimmer of light.

Apollo's senses went into overdrive, every nerve crackling with tension. The air felt thick, almost suffocating, reminiscent of the crushing void they'd left behind. Each step was a gamble, the unfamiliar terrain a minefield of potential mishaps.

"I can't see a damn thing," Hermes muttered, his voice unnaturally loud in the stillness.

Apollo shushed him, straining his ears for any sign of life within the house. Their goal was clear - find Shania, wipe her memory, ensure her silence - but the darkness seemed to muddy even that simple objective.

As they inched forward, Apollo couldn't shake the feeling that they were being watched, unseen eyes boring into them from the shadows. The weight of their actions, the violence outside, the deception of their disguises, pressed down on him like a physical force.

"We shouldn't be here," he thought, a cold sweat breaking out across his brow. "This isn't who we are... who we're supposed to be."

But it was too late to turn back now. They were committed to this course, for better or worse. As they delved deeper into the house, Apollo silently prayed to whatever powers might still listen to

fallen gods, hoping against hope that they weren't about to make a terrible mistake.

Suddenly, the room exploded with light and sound.

"Surprise!" came a chorus of shouting voices.

Apollo's eyes widened in shock, his heart pounding as he found himself face-to-face with a crowd of laughing, cheering middle aged women.

"Oh my god, they're here!" one woman squealed, her face flushed with excitement. "And just look at them. Such fine specimens!"

Apollo froze, his mind racing. This wasn't part of the plan. He glanced at Hermes, seeing his own confusion mirrored in the younger god's eyes.

"Ladies, ladies," Hermes recovered quickly, his voice smooth as silk. "What's the occasion?"

A voluptuous blonde strutted forward, her eyes smouldering with a devilish gleam. "Shania's birthday bash, baby! You're the main course, ain't ya?" Apollo's gut clenched tight. They'd been mistaken for... what? Exotic dancers? The irony was painfully delicious. Once revered as gods, now reduced to this mindless erotic spectacle.

"Fuck yeah, we are," Hermes replied smoothly, his voice laced with a taunting echo of his former divine audacity. "We wouldn't pass up such a

sinful rendezvous." Apollo shot Hermes a scathing look and the women roared in anticipation.

Apollo felt the creeping slick of sweat down his spine. How in hell had they ended up here? Another woman piped up, "Well, don't just gawk there! Strip off and give us some skin!"

Panicking, Apollo shot a wide-eyed look at Hermes. "What's the play here?" he huffed sharply. Hermes merely shrugged nonchalantly.

Apollo kept looking at his brother for help. Thankfully, he could see a plan forming in Hermes' racing mind.

"Play along to escape suspicion," Hermes whispered. "Or kill them all . . ."

Apollo shot a look laced in horror and surprise. Was this the best plan his would be trickster brother could come up with? It was enough that they had been caught red-handed. But debasing himself this way? He felt a shiver of revulsion crawl on his skin.

"We've forgotten to bring music," he tried weakly, but the woman quickly replied that they had their own.

Donna Summer's "*Hot Stuff*" blared in response from a hi-fi unit.

"Follow my lead," Hermes mumbled, mustering up a smile that was laced with unnecessary enthusiasm.

Amidst the mounting cheers from the boisterous women, Apollo and Hermes found themselves unwittingly entangled in a surprising birthday bash, their divine composure was hilariously tested beyond measure. Despite their lofty origins, they had to shimmy and shake as if their immortal lives depended on it, much to the amusement of the middle-aged revellers.

As Hermes hips ground and swayed seductively while he licked his lips suggestively, Apollo began unbuttoning his shirt inch by inch and let it slip down his arms before throwing it to the floor. Shania Queen burst through the front door — a tornado of effervescent excitement. Her raven curls adorned with glittering clips that sparkled under the light.

"Ladies, what a surprise!" she shouted over the music. "Is this for me?"

"We're almost finished," Apollo tried, stopping his gyrating but Shania simply grabbed him and made him resume dancing.

"No you're not. Ladies get ready to sin!" she announced, her eyes dancing with laughter.

"Keep fucking dancing," he whispered urgently. "We've opened Pandora's box."

Shania's intrigued gaze caught them, her eyebrows arching in amused surprise. "Well, well! Looks like we're in for a treat!"

"Your birthday present, darling!" one of the women hollered. "Two beefcakes, all yours!"

Apollo felt a wave of heat creep up his neck. Beefcakes? Was this how mortals saw them now — titillating playthings? Attempting to regain control, he stammered out, "We're here to... put on a show," the words tasting like sour grapes.

"Then set us on fire, boys! Show us what you've got!" Shania commanded with a flirtatious smile.

As the night progressed and the party's energy ebbed away, Apollo and Hermes took turns spinning and grinding against each other, hands exploring every inch of their respective toned bodies. They slid their hands down their own pants at times, simulating pleasurable sensations.

"Come on, fellas," the voluptuous blonde hollered, "Let's see what you're made of. Take off all your clothes!" Whistles and provocative remarks echoed her command as a chorus of "strip it all off" drowned out the music.

As the last piece of clothing fell to the floor, and the women beheld the glorious sight of the two naked gods' bodies, the laughter softened and the gods' movements became seductive dances. Apollo felt a strange cocktail of relief and anger as he sensed the night drawing to a close.

"We need to beat feet," Hermes murmured sultrily into Apollo's ear, while running his hand over Apollo's chest and pinching his nipple lightly.

Apollo nodded, his gaze sweeping the room one last time. Shania was sprawled across a plush armchair, her eyes half-lidded but still glimmering with mischief. For a moment, he wondered what secrets lay behind that captivating smile.

"Ladies, it's been... an experience," Apollo said, collecting his clothes and getting dressed again, his voice carrying a hint of his former divine resonance. "But we must bid you farewell."

As the two brothers made their daring escape from Shania's unexpected birthday bash turned impromptu strip show, much to Apollo's annoyance, Hermes couldn't help but chuckle to himself.

Outside, the cool night air caressed their skin, a stark contrast to the warmth of the party. Apollo inhaled deeply, tasting the crisp scent of pine and damp earth.

"Well, that was... unexpected," Hermes chuckled, breaking the silence.

Apollo couldn't help but glower. "Indeed. Who would have thought we'd end up as mortal entertainment? Unadulterated crime in your veins indeed!"

"Well, that was one way to really 'strip down' our divine image," Hermes quipped to his visibly annoyed brother under his breath as they tiptoed towards the exit. "Who knew we'd end up as the main course at a middle-aged women's soirée! I guess we can add 'exotic dancers' to our resumes now, huh? Who needs Mount Olympus when you can headline Shania's birthday bonanza?"

As they walked through the deserted streets, Apollo's mind wandered. Their mission had failed, yet he felt strangely lighter. The weight of divinity, of constant vigilance and control, had momentarily lifted.

"You know, brother," Hermes suddenly mused, "perhaps there's more to this mortal existence than we realized."

Apollo raised an eyebrow. "Oh? Do tell, oh wise one."

Hermes laughed, the sound echoing in the empty night. "Their lives are so... unpredictable. Chaotic, yes, but also vibrant. Full of surprises."

"Like impromptu dance parties?"

"Exactly," Hermes nodded. "It's... refreshing."

They walked in companionable silence, their footsteps echoing softly. Apollo felt a warmth in his chest, a strengthening of the bond between them. This shared experience, embarrassing as it was, had brought them closer.

As they reached the edge of town, Apollo paused, looking back at the twinkling lights of Rashford. "We may have failed tonight, Hermes, but I feel... oddly content."

Hermes clapped him on the shoulder. "As do I, brother. As do I."

With one last glance at the sleeping town, they melted into the shadows, two former gods with a newfound appreciation for the chaotic beauty of mortal life.

Chapter 6

As a raven croaked outside his window, Aodhán jolted awake, his heart pounding. The feeling of unseen eyes watching him in the darkness had returned. He glanced around the moonlit room, searching for any sign of an intruder, but found nothing. The farmhouse was silent.

Letting out a shaky breath, Aodhán tried to calm his nerves. How long would these disturbing nights continue? Ever since he had arrived at the farm with no memory of his past, an ominous presence seemed to stalk his dreams. What secrets lurked in his forgotten life?

With a sigh, Aodhán nestled back under the blankets. Tomorrow, he would lose himself in the comfort of routine—caring for the animals, working the fields beside Meredith. For now, he could only hope that sleep would return, undisturbed by whatever malignant force seemed intent on tormenting his unconscious mind.

It was the month the rains returned that things took a turn for the worse. At the stroke of the desolate hour, just as Aodhán found himself jolted from the grasp of slumber, his heart convulsing within his heaving chest.

Every night!

The malevolent sensation of unseen eyes pierced through the cloak of darkness, haunting him every night. A feverish gaze darted through the ill-lit chamber, desperately seeking any trace of a trespasser, yet finding naught but chilling emptiness. The farmhouse lay enshrouded in an unsettling silence.

On a particular night, tremulous breath escaped Aodhán's parched lips as he endeavoured to quell his frayed nerves. Since his arrival at the farm—his past sealed behind a cryptic veil—an ominous presence continued to taunt his dreams like a ravenous vulture stalking its prey. What unhallowed secrets lay buried in the crypts of his forsaken memories?

With a sigh tainted by despair, Aodhán sought solace beneath the tattered quilt—a futile shield against his spectral assailants. He prayed for a fleeting respite in the morrow's routine; tending to the farm animals, and toiling in the fields alongside Meredith, that angel of a woman. For now, he could only cling to the feeble hope that slumber would return, unmarred by whatever malevolent force hungered to ravage his vulnerable mind.

It was upon the harrowing arrival of torrential rains that Aodhán's blissful existence took a dire turn. From his bed, he bore witness to the ghastly sight

of vermillion orbs gleaming with infernal light like cursed emeralds, their venomous glare fixed upon him with unwavering intensity. He sought refuge beneath his meagre blankets, but even there he could not escape the weight of their oppressive scrutiny.

One night, Aodhán jolted awake, his heart pounding like the drums of Hell. The sensation of probing eyes piercing his very soul returned, as though some malevolent force preyed upon him in the darkness. He scanned the moonlit chamber, searching for any wretched sign of an intruder, in the direction of those gleaming eyes in the corridor outside his bedroom. Otherwise, the forsaken farmhouse lay still, enshrouded in a suffocating quietude.

This accursed night, sick with terror, Aodhán dared investigate the source of his torment. He uncovered his head and looked in the direction of the eyes—those foul orbs creeping ever closer. His heart pounded like a wild beast thrashing against its cage. He closed his eyes and fluttered them open again.

Closer still, they had drawn.

He tried to cry out for Meredith, but the words suffocated in his throat. The twisted branches of an old tree outside his window groaned in protest

as he shot a look in its direction, then back at the eyes.

The vile orbs had crept nearer once more.

With trembling hands, he reached for his side lamp—a beacon in the oppressive darkness—and cast forth a feeble amber light that sent those malicious eyes fleeing. He drew a breath heavy with relief and snuffed out the light.

As his gaze settled once more upon the void that had housed those demonic entities, they reappeared. Closer! Aodhán's terror surged as he felt hot urine stream down his leg, soiling the very bed from which he could not escape. Sweat and tears streamed down his cheeks, unable to be contained. Every movement to wipe them away seemed only to bring those accursed eyes nearer yet.

In an eruption of primal fear, he screamed—a wail that echoed through the night like a banshee's lament. The orbs hung before him, their malignant gaze intent on consuming his very soul.

Summoning strength forged from sheer terror, Aodhán reached once more for the switch. As the amber light spilled into the room, banishing shadows and forcing back the encroaching darkness, those detestable eyes finally vanished.

He sank onto the damp pillow behind him, trembling and broken. Surrendering to exhaustion and despair, Aodhán knew that sleep would elude him on this unholy night—as it would for countless nights to come.

Aodhán rose from his sorrowful bed, opened his small window and stood before Meredith's farmhouse's ornate mirror, his reflection glistening with a spectral radiance. The aroma of fresh hay and damp earth invaded his nostrils as he reached out, fingers quivering, to touch the cold glass. Suddenly, the image before him shifted, transforming into a countenance not his own. Luke, the trickster god, sneered at him with wicked delight, eyes gleaming with devilish mischief.

"Well, well, what have we here?" Luke's voice oozed from the mirror, dripping with false sweetness. "A lost little godling, far from home."

Aodhán stumbled backward, his heart pounding. "Who... what are you?" he gasped, struggling to comprehend the impossible scene before him.

Luke's laughter echoed through the room as he stepped out of the mirror, his presence filling the space with an aura of chaos. "Oh, my dear boy," he purred, circling Aodhán like a predator. "I'm the thing that goes bump in the night, the whisper in the dark that makes mortals tremble."

Aodhán's mind raced, trying to make sense of the situation. Was this another test? Another strange human custom he didn't understand? But the power radiating from Luke felt ancient, malignant, in a way that terrified him.

"You're... like me?" Aodhán ventured, his voice barely above a whisper.

Luke's grin widened, revealing too many teeth. "Oh, we're cut from the same cloth, you and I. Eldar gods, beings of immense power. But you," he leaned in close, his breath hot on Aodhán's cheek, "you're just a babe in the woods, aren't you? No idea of the forces you're playing with."

Aodhán felt a chill run down his spine. "I don't understand," he admitted, hating how small his voice sounded. "What forces? What am I supposed to do?"

Luke threw back his head and laughed, the sound sharp enough to cut. "That's the beauty of it, little one. You don't have to do anything. You simply exist, and the world trembles." His eyes glittered dangerously. "But oh, the fun we could have if you embraced your true nature."

The creak of the farmhouse door shattered the tense moment. Meredith's gentle voice called out, "Aodhán? Is everything alright, dear?"

Relief flooded Aodhán's body. Meredith's familiar presence felt like a lifeline in the chaos. He turned, hope blooming in his chest, only to watch in horror as Luke's form blurred with inhuman speed.

"No!" Aodhán cried, but it was too late.

Luke's hand plunged into Meredith's chest with sickening ease. Her eyes widened in shock, a choked gasp escaping her lips. Blood bloomed across her shirt like a macabre flower. For a moment, time seemed to stand still.

Then Meredith's body crumpled to the floor, lifeless.

Aodhán felt his legs give way, collapsing beside her. "Meredith," he whispered, reaching out with trembling hands. "No, please... wake up."

A harrowing sound of nails on wood permeated the air, drawing Aodhán's tear-filled gaze to the wooden wardrobe. There, etched with a sinister hand, these words appeared: "AODHÁN, YOU ARE MINE TO ENJOY!"

Luke's laughter echoed through the room, but Aodhán couldn't tear his eyes away from Meredith's still form.

Suddenly, Meredith's body began to twitch and contort. Aodhán scrambled backward, his heart pounding. "What's happening?" he gasped.

Meredith's features twisted, melting and reforming into something else entirely. Where once there was warmth, now there was only malice.

He stumbled out of his bedroom, heart racing, and frantically searched for a way out. The front door was locked, and he couldn't find the keys anywhere. Heavy footsteps echoed through the hallway, and he froze as he saw Meredith's undead form slowly descending the stairs towards him, letting out an eerie chant that sent shivers down his spine.

"Please, Meredith," Aodhán wept. "It's me, Aodhán!"

Meredith's eyes blazed with lust as she grabbed him by his unkempt hair and yanked him towards her. She stormed up the stairs, dragging him along like a helpless rag doll. Aodhán struggled to break free, but the pain in his scalp was unbearable. Finally, they reached his room, and Meredith flung him onto the bed with a forceful thud. He winced in pain and fear as she stood above him, seething with rage

"Oh, sweet little Aodhán," she purred, her voice like honey laced with poison. "Did you really think your mortal guardian could protect you from us?"

Aodhán's mind reeled. "Us?" he whispered.

Meredith's laugh was low and cruel. "The gods, the demons, the things that lurk in the shadows of your precious world. We've been waiting for you, Aodhán. And now," she reached out, her nails grazing his cheek, "the game truly begins."

Aodhán recoiled from her touch, his skin crawling with revulsion and... something else. A traitorous thrill that made his stomach churn. This was not Meredith. It was some evil being. And yet, he could only see Meredith.

"Stay away from me," he rasped, his voice cracking. His eyes, against his will, traced the curves of her form, drinking in her otherworldly beauty.

Meredith's lips curved into a wicked smile as she too climbed onto the bed. "Oh, but darling," she cooed, "you don't really want me to stay away, do you?" She took a step closer, her presence overwhelming. "I can feel your desire, your curiosity. It's intoxicating."

Aodhán's breath hitched, coming in hard, ragged gasps. "No, I...I can't do this." His voice was but a whisper against the powerful thrumming in his

chest. But even as he attempted to push back, he felt his stubborn will crumbling.

Meredith's slender fingers traced a tantalizing path along the rough line of his jaw, her touch sparking like live wires on his weathered skin. "Shh," she whispered sultrily, her hot breath dancing across his face, intoxicating him. "Let go of your fears. Embrace the raw darkness brooding within you."

Aodhán's mind was ablaze with protests, echoing loudly in his skull. But his body betrayed him. He leaned into her electrifying touch, the heat searing through him and making his eyes flutter closed in helpless surrender.

"That's right," Meredith cooed seductively. Her voice was a smooth melody of temptation that wound around him, pulling tight until he had no escape. "Give yourself over to me."

As Meredith's lips claimed his, a hot surge of desire coursed through Aodhán's veins, igniting every nerve ending in its path. It felt like his soul was splitting apart under her touch, a piece shattering and melting away with their shared heat. The taste of her on his tongue was more intoxicating than any liquor he'd known, an exquisite poison he couldn't refuse.

Her fingers deftly worked at the buttons of his shirt, her nails scraping tantalizingly against his

chest. His heart pounded as his shirt pealed open, revealing his chiselled abs and strong biceps. The sight of him exposed, vulnerable, visibly affected Satana, her breath hitching as she gazed upon his physique.

Her fingers slipped beneath the waistband of his pants, pulling them down along with his undergarments. Meredith knelt before him and took him in her mouth, swirling her tongue around the sensitive tip. Aodhán gasped and clenched his fists as she moved on him, taking him deeper each time. But something felt wrong.

"Please," let me go," he wept. "Please Meredith, I know you're there, I can feel you." He summoned all his strength to push her away, but Meredith reciprocated with equal strength. He laid back, watching as she discarded her own clothing to reveal her seductive form. Climbing onto the bed, Meredith straddled Aodhán, positioning herself above him.

Their gazes locked once more as she slowly lowered herself onto him, engulfing him in her warmth, robbing him of his virginity. Aodhán's entire body tensed at once, overwhelmed by the sensation that mirrored both pain and absolute pleasure.

Meredith began moving on top of him, their bodies melding together in a dance of passion. Aodhán's

hands gripped Satana's hips tightly and in spite of himself, he thrust upwards to meet her. They moved together, rhythmically in sync with every flex of muscle and twist of limb.

As their passion escalated, Aodhán could no longer deny the overwhelming heat that coursed through his veins. He surrendered himself entirely to her control, the intensity of their union blurring the line between lustful desire and a terrifying loss of self. Nothing else existed beyond that moment – it was just them and a connection forged in fire and darkness.

With a final cry that echoed through the room, Aodhán succumbed to the pleasure Meredith had drawn from him. As their breaths mingled in the air above them, a chilling satisfaction settled upon Meredith's visage, and Aodhán knew his life would never be the same.

Meredith's own climax followed, her cries of pleasure mingling with Aodhán's as their bodies trembled together, gripping one another tightly.

Aodhán's heart stopped as Meredith's face began to contort and shift, her features melting away like flesh caught in a fire. In their place, a stunningly beautiful woman emerged - one that Aodhán could only dream of. But he knows better than to trust his eyes. This is no ordinary woman, but a

demon in disguise, her seductive form meant to lure him into her trap.

"Yes," she whispered seductively in his ears. "I am Satana. I have come for you."

In that moment, the world outside ceased to exist - they were consumed by the all-consuming fire of their shared ecstasy.

Goddard, Windsor, Ryan, and Matt returned to the grounds of their school. The once lush green lawn was now withered and brown, a reflection of the weight that had been pressing on their hearts since Jamie's disappearance. The four friends had deliberately avoided each other in the aftermath, too afraid to face the truth of what they could not remember. Vague memories swirled in their minds like fog, but the details were just out of reach. They all hazily recalled encountering a stunningly beautiful woman, her features blurred by a haze that seemed to cloud their thoughts. Her actions and intentions remained shrouded in mystery. Only Goddard retained a clear memory of her, his mind unable to shake the image of her mating with Jamie. But even that information proved useless to the determined local sheriff who was searching for answers.

They all gathered in the school yard by the entrance gate that day.

"How is it possible that none of us can remember her face?" Goddard wondered aloud.

Windsor made a disapproving noise. "Still fantasizing about fucking Jamie, huh?" he sneered.

"Shut up, Windsor," Goddard snapped, but Ryan held him back from going after Windsor.

"We all saw her by the lake," Matt insisted after a moment of silence.

"Maybe it was just a dream," Ryan suggested, but Windsor's snarl indicated that this was not the case.

"We couldn't have all dreamt the same thing," Goddard reasoned after a pause.

As the tension simmered between the friends, Ryan broke the silence with a thoughtful expression. "What if there's some kind of spell or magic at play here? Something that's clouding our memories?"

Windsor scoffed again, crossing his arms defiantly. "Magic? Really, Ryan? We're not in some fairytale, mate. The only fairy around is Goddard."

Goddard's jaw clenched as he shot a pointed look at Windsor. "We can't just ignore what happened to Jamie," Ryan interrupted them. "There was something strange about that woman, something... powerful."

Matt, usually the quiet one of the group, spoke up tentatively. "I keep having these flashes of images in my mind, like snippets of a movie I can't quite remember watching. Maybe if we piece together what each of us remembers, we can figure this out."

Ryan nodded in agreement, his gaze shifting from one friend to the other. "We need to stick together on this. The more we push each other away, the harder it'll be to unravel the truth."

Windsor's stoic expression softened slightly as he reluctantly admitted, "Fine. But if this leads us into some messed up situation again, I'm out."

Goddard nodded in understanding before turning his attention towards the school building looming behind them. "Let's start by retracing our steps from that night. Maybe there's something we missed, something that could jog our memories."

The friends exchanged determined looks before they set off towards the lakeside where it all began, ready to confront the shadows of their

forgotten past and uncover the mysteries that lay hidden within.

As they did, a sleek black SUV screeched to a halt at the school gate, drawing the attention of all who passed by. The driver's window rolled down, revealing the flawless face of Aphrodite, goddess of beauty.

Windsor's heart skipped a beat as he caught sight of her. "There she is," he exclaimed, unable to take his eyes off her. "The woman from the lakeside."

Aphrodite's charm and radiance seemed to have only intensified since their last encounter. She beckoned to the boys with a seductive smile. "Hello again, my darlings. Remember me?"

The boys were in a trance, unable to look away from her hypnotic gaze. They couldn't believe their luck as she began to weave a spell on them once more.

"I can't stand loose ends," Aphrodite muttered to herself as she reapplied her fiery red lipstick in the rearview mirror. Turning back to the boys, she purred, "Would you like a ride, my loves?" Without hesitation, they hopped into the car, completely under her control like obedient puppies following their master's command.

Hermes pounded on the door at Elm Manor with all his might, anticipation fuelling each strike. After what felt like an eternity of agonizing silence, the lock clicked and the door slowly creaked open. Before him stood an old fashioned but large butler, his rigid posture resembling that of a penguin. But Hermes couldn't contain his amusement as he took in the comical sight.

The butler's face contorted in surprise at the unexpected visitor. "Yes?" he finally spoke, his voice laced with suspicion and annoyance.

"I'm here to see Truly," Hermes stated firmly, but a nagging feeling of doubt crept into his mind. Was this all just some elaborate prank?

"Truly?" The butler repeated with raised eyebrows, clearly taken aback.

"This is the residence of Truly Scrumptious?" Hermes clarified, his words dripping with sarcasm. But to his surprise, the butler's expression changed as if recognizing the name.

"Please, do come inside, sir," he gestured towards the grand entrance with a sweeping hand, revealing a room that sent shivers down Hermes' spine. It was like walking into a graveyard at night, the air thick with an unsettling darkness that seemed to press in from all sides. The only source of light came from flickering candles, placed

strategically around a menacing altar that dominated the centre of the room. On top of the altar sat a massive inverted cross, surrounded by three cloaked and hooded figures who seemed to be conducting some sort of ritual. Their low chants reverberated off the walls, adding to the eerie atmosphere of the room. Hermes couldn't help but feel a sense of foreboding as he stepped further into the chilling scene before him.

"What is this?" Hermes exclaimed in disbelief, but any humour was quickly replaced by fear as the hooded figures advanced towards him with ill intent. He realized too late that he had walked right into their trap, cunningly disguised as an innocent meeting. Panicked thoughts raced through his mind as he attempted to escape, but the butler's massive form held him down with surprising strength.

"Let me go!" Hermes begged, terror now coursing through his veins at full force. One of the hooded men emerged from the shadows with a baseball bat in hand, mercilessly striking Hermes on the head. Darkness consumed him as he fell to the ground, unconscious and at the mercy of his captors.

Away from any prying eyes, nestled within a sensually lit love nest of a seedy hotel room,

Aphrodite unabashedly bared herself before an antique mirror. Her raw sexuality was left unhindered by her state of undress; yet a shadow of sorrow lurked in her mesmerizing azure eyes, her full pout set in a captivating frown.

Turning slowly in an enticing dance only she could perform, she met the hungry eyes of three strapping lads sprawled in sinful disarray on the bed. Each one was utterly bewitched, their gazes heavy with unbridled lust and total adoration for the goddess before them. Their hardened bodies told unspoken stories of their physical attraction to her divine allure – virility standing at attention under the weight of their animalistic need.

"My darlings," she murmured, her voice carrying the weight of millennia. "If only you knew the price of loving me."

The door creaked open, and Goddard Greening stepped into the room, his polished oxfords squeaking against the grimy floor. His eyes widened in horror as he took in the scene before him.

"Matt? Ryan? Windsor?" he called out, his refined voice cracking with desperation.

Aphrodite turned to him, her eyes shimmering with unshed tears.

The atmosphere was thick with carnal energy as Matt's trembling hand reached to touch Aphrodite's porcelain skin. The contrast between her cool flesh and his burning desire sent shudders down his spine.

"Join us," she invited him.

Despite his preference for others in terms of sexual partners, he longed to discover every inch of her physique; to experience the smoothness of her breasts, the firmness of her hips - to surrender himself to her alluring embrace. His heart beat faster at the mere idea of their bodies intertwined, each passionate movement bringing them closer to an unforgettable climax.

Matt, always the shy type, caved first to her potent allure. Her lips, full and tempting as ripe fruit, pulled into a grin that suggested sin as her focus shifted to the trembling lad. His self-restraint melted like ice under a scorching sun, and he was all too willing to submit to her physical command. Her otherworldly hands, soft as a lover's secret but cold as the kiss of death glided up his back, leaving in their wake tendrils of chill-inducing delight.

Windsor and Ryan, impervious to the immediate danger they were in, kissed Aphrodite's skin as she focused on Matt. Couldn't break away - they were captivated by the tantalizing scene playing

out before them. Her swaying hips seduced them like a belly dancer's shimmy, drawing them in closer to their ruin, much like flies drawn to a dangerous flame.

Matt's breathing became rough and uneven, his pupils dilating wide with unholy pleasure. Each stroke, each contact was like a blissful burn ripping through his reason. He was adrift in an ocean of raw desire, sinking in the depths of Aphrodite's captivating gaze.

"Oh, Aphrodite," he panted, mouthing her name he'd only seen in musty old books "I... I've never..."

Aphrodite answered with a sultry laugh - pure temptation mixed with impending doom. "No need for words, love," she breathed out, her voice a mixture of sweet honey and lethal poison. "Your body language is telling me everything."

With that final sentence hanging heavy in the air, Matt took the plunge into oblivion. His eyes rolled back in ecstasy while his face spoke volumes about the pleasure coursing through him. Aphrodite bared her fangs as she leaned in closer; her lips were just millimetres from his tender neck.

"This is it for you, Matthew," she whispered, her voice drenched in wicked delight, "Welcome to forever."

As Aphrodite bit into his neck, Matt felt an explosion of pleasure unlike anything he had ever experienced before. It was as if every nerve ending in his body ignited with fireworks of sensations that coursed through him like wildfire. A sweet nectar began to flow into his system, filling him up like an insatiable thirst being quenched for the very first time. He could feel himself beginning to lose control; his body was being overwhelmed by this newfound sensation that was taking him into a realm he could never have imagined possible before now.

Aphrodite's otherworldly hands gripped him tightly as she fed from him hungrily. Her lips were locked onto his skin, sucking deeply and rhythmically as if she were drawing not only his blood but also his very soul into herself. Matt felt her hips move against him in perfect time with her feeding rhythm - it was almost hypnotic how in sync they were together. Each thrust of her hips sent shivers down his spine and made him groan with pleasure - an unpleasure he had never known before today. He knew he was lost forever now; there was no turning back from this moment onwards. He would be hers for eternity now and there was nothing that could change that fact ever again.

In an instant, his body crumbled to dust, scattering across the stained sheets.

"No!" Goddard cried, lunging forward. But it was too late.

Ryan and Windsor, blissfully unaware of their comrade's grim destiny, eagerly pressed their lips against Aphrodite's sensuously soft skin. Their bodies reacted to the electric touch, stiffening with anticipation before succumbing to a wave of unabashed pleasure that rolled over them like a kinky tsunami.

Their heated gazes were firmly locked on the goddess's curvaceous figure. Ryan, with his ruggedly handsome features and piercing hazel eyes, had a smouldering look of desire burning in his eyes. On the other hand, Windsor, with his chiselled abs and sun-kissed skin was practically drooling at the sight of Aphrodite's bare flesh.

"I'll be damned," Ryan muttered under his breath, clasping her hip with a firm grip, his muscular arm rippling with raw masculine power. His gaze never wavered from those hypnotic eyes of hers.

Windsor, silent till now, let out a low whistle as he allowed his fingers to trace lightly over the curvature of her body. "Holy shit," he breathed out, completely captivated by her celestial beauty.

The moment their hips brushed Aphrodite's skin, they were hit with a sensation so intense that it left them gasping for breath. It was akin to being

struck by lightning - shocking yet incredibly exhilarating.

Their bodies responded to the contact in an earth-shattering way; muscles convulsing in ecstasy before they gradually disintegrated into tiny particles that sparkled like scattered stardust, just like Matt before them.

Goddard fell to his knees, retching. "Why?" he choked out, tears streaming down his face.

Acting swiftly, he regained his composure and grabbed the keys to the SUV which had been carelessly left on top of a chest of drawers. He also took the room keys before locking the door behind him and rushing to the vehicle.

As he escaped, he couldn't shake off the haunting screams of Aphrodite, a constant reminder of how mortal life is no match for divine power. Despite being a novice driver, he drove as best as he could in his panicked state.

Back at Meredith's farmhouse, Aodhán stood before Satana, his eyes vacant and hollow. His will had been shattered by the demoness, leaving him vulnerable to her manipulations. She circled him like a predator stalking its prey, her aura radiating with palpable glee at her victory. He had been awakened. Memories of his past life flooded back

into his mind, but they were clouded by the alluring presence of Satana. Despite knowing that giving in to her would lead to his downfall, he found himself unable to resist her seductive powers. The mere thought of being with her again was enough to make him weak in the knees.

"Oh, my sweet, innocent boy," Satana crooned, running her fingers through his hair. "You're mine now, body and soul."

Aodhán's voice was barely a whisper as he replied, "Yes."

Satana threw her head back and laughed, the sound reverberating through the farmhouse. Outside, the sky darkened, and a chill wind howled through the trees.

"Tell me, darling," Satana purred, "what would you do for me?"

Aodhán's lifeless eyes met hers. "Anything. Everything."

The air in the Manor hung thick with the acrid stench of blood and incense. Hermes, once fleet-footed and silver-tongued, now hung limp, nailed upside down against the crude wooden beams of the inverted cross, his wrists and ankles pierced by iron spikes. Crimson rivulets traced paths down

his pale flesh, dripping steadily into a copper bowl beneath him.

Three robed figures circled him, their faces hidden by grotesque masks fashioned from human skulls. One raised a wickedly curved dagger, its edge glinting in the flickering candlelight.

Hermes gasped for air, his once smooth voice now a broken rasp of desperation. He pleaded with wild eyes, his usual charm replaced by raw fear. "No, no, no," he whimpered, trying to claw his way out of the excruciating pain that engulfed his entire body. But he was immobilized, helpless against the torment. "I'm not who you think I am," he choked out between sobs. "I can't give you what you want." The agony intensified as he struggled against invisible restraints, his pleas falling on deaf ears.

The lead priest chuckled, a sound devoid of mirth. "Oh, but you are, godling. Your blood, your essence - it will feed our mistress and hasten her ascension."

As the dagger bit into his flesh again, Hermes screwed his eyes shut. They had discovered his immortality. He was truly in trouble.

"Have you seen Hermes?" Athena asked Apollo, who was sitting at his desk in his opulent palace,

surrounded by the fragrant smoke of exotic incense.

"He could be out and about," Apollo replied nonchalantly, his fingers tapping against the smooth marble surface of his desk. "You know how he is . . ."

Athena's brow furrowed with worry as she paced back and forth in front of the large windows that overlooked the sprawling city below. "Not at this hour," she replied anxiously. "I'm worried."

She left the room, leaving Apollo to his thoughts. The sun god let out an irritated huff, slamming his hand down on his desk. He needed to focus on finding the elusive Eldar, but his mind kept wandering to other matters. "I swear, when I find him, I'll end his immortal life," he grumbled under his breath.

"Have you looked in his room?" he called out to Athena, who was standing at the door of the grand mansion.

"Of course I did," she replied sternly before exiting.

Apollo let out another frustrated sigh before begrudgingly making his way to his brother's room. As much as he resented Hermes' carefree nature and habit of disappearing for days on end, he couldn't shake off the growing concern for his brother's safety.

He knocked gently on the dark wooden door of Hermes' room, receiving no response. Trying the knob, he found that it was unlocked and pushed the door open slowly. The room was shrouded in darkness except for a faint glow coming from Hermes' laptop screen.

"Hermes?" Apollo called out cautiously as he stepped into the room. There was no answer, and the only sound was the soft hum of the laptop's fan. The room felt eerily silent, like a tomb.

With a flick of his wrist, Apollo illuminated the room with a soft golden light. As he scanned the room, his eyes fell upon Hermes' laptop. It was open and still logged onto an online dating site.

Fury boiled up inside of Apollo as he read through his brother's messages with someone named "Truly Scrumptious". Slamming the laptop shut, he couldn't believe that Hermes had fallen for such an obvious prank. But at least now he had an address to track his brother down.

Hermes was still suspended upside down, barely conscious as the priests used a strange dagger to repeatedly pierce his body, igniting waves of searing agony. The priests' eerie chants echo in the background, amplifying his misery to a fever pitch. Each jab of the dagger felt like a malevolent

symphony playing on his nerves, orchestrating his suffering with cruel precision.

Suddenly, the heavy oak doors exploded inward, showering the room with splinters. Apollo strode in, his golden hair seeming to glow with an inner light despite the gloom. His blue eyes blazed with fury as he surveyed the scene.

"Step away from my brother," he commanded, his voice resonating with barely contained power.

The priests, caught off guard, lunged at him with daggers gleaming in the dim light. Apollo moved like a lightning strike, sidestepping their attacks with grace. With a swift motion, he disarmed the closest priest and swiftly silenced him.

The clash of metal echoed through the room as Apollo engaged the remaining priests in a dance of deadly precision. Their movements were frenzied but futile against his calculated strikes. Each blow landed with a resounding impact, sending shockwaves through the room.

"Stay down," Apollo growled, his voice cutting through the chaos. The priests, fuelled by desperation, pressed on with renewed vigour. But Apollo was relentless, his actions speaking louder than words as he swiftly took them down one by one.

The metallic scent of blood filled the air, mingling with the acrid tang of incense. The sounds of struggle and defiance reverberated off the walls, creating a symphony of violence and retribution.

In mere moments, the room fell silent, save for the harsh panting of Apollo and the defeated groans of his adversaries. His gaze met Hermes', a silent promise of protection and vengeance burning bright in his eyes.

The priests redoubled their efforts, chanting in a guttural language that made the air itself seem to thicken. Apollo felt his movements slowing, as if wading through molasses. Drawing on reserves of strength he didn't know he still possessed, Apollo pushed through the magical resistance.

Apollo's eyes blazed with an otherworldly light as he raised his hands, palms outward. The air crackled with energy, and the priests' chanting faltered.

"You sought to harm what's mine," Apollo intoned, his voice echoing with the remnants of his divine power. "Now, become part of this unholy place you revere."

With a sickening lurch, the priests' bodies began to twist and elongate. Their screams of agony filled the chamber as flesh melded with stone, bones cracking and reforming. Apollo watched,

his face a mask of cold fury, as the writhing forms were slowly absorbed into the walls.

"Brother," Hermes gasped, his voice weak but tinged with awe. "That was... impressively horrific."

Apollo strode to the crude altar, his hands gentle as he began to remove the nails pinning Hermes in place. "I won't let them hurt you again," he murmured, his earlier rage replaced by tender concern.

As the last nail was extracted, Hermes collapsed into Apollo's arms. The brothers clung to each other, their shared immortality a cold comfort in the face of such brutality.

"Can you walk?" Apollo asked, supporting Hermes' weight.

Hermes nodded weakly. "Just... give me a moment."

As they made their way towards the exit, Apollo's mind raced. "We need to find a safe place," he said. "This chaos... it's spreading. We need to find the Eldar. We have to put an end to it."

Hermes managed a pained chuckle. "Always the hero, aren't you, big brother?"

Apollo's jaw tightened. "Someone has to be."

As they stumbled out of the chamber, the air grew thick with an oppressive darkness. Apollo's skin prickled, an ancient instinct warning of unseen danger. He tightened his grip on Hermes, scanning the shadows for threats.

"Do you feel that?" Hermes whispered, his voice trembling. "It's like... like the void is reaching for us."

Apollo nodded grimly.

They pressed on through winding corridors, the walls seeming to pulse with malevolent energy. Each step felt heavier than the last, as if the very air resisted their escape.

"Apollo," Hermes said suddenly, his eyes wide with fear. "What if we can't stop this? What if we've already lost?"

Apollo halted, turning to face his brother. "We haven't lost," he said fiercely. "Not while we still draw breath. We've faced worse than this, remember?"

But even as the words left his mouth, doubt gnawed at Apollo's heart. The world was changing, twisting into something unrecognizable. And they were no longer the gods they once were.

A cold laugh echoed through the corridor, sending chills down their spines. "Oh, how the mighty have

fallen," Satana's voice purred from the shadows. "Two broken immortals, clinging to each other like frightened children."

Apollo's fists clenched, golden light flickering weakly around them. "Show yourself, demon!"

But only silence answered. The darkness seemed to deepen, pressing in around them with suffocating intensity.

"We need to move," Hermes urged, his eyes darting nervously. "This place... it's feeding on our fear."

As they resumed their desperate flight, Apollo's mind raced. The pieces were falling into place – the Eldar's mysterious power, Satana's machinations. A cosmic game was unfolding, with all of existence hanging in the balance. He remembered his vision from the blood of the vine. He turned to his brother.

"Hermes, I have seen this in my vision with Micha-El," he murmured. "An Eldar has indeed entered this world and he seems to have fallen to her."

"You mean . . ?" Hermes swallowed weakly.

"Yes, Satana has the Eldar," Apollo admitted reluctantly.

Silence fell between the brothers. Then Hermes offered. "What if we joined forces with her?"

"You don't mean that!" Apollo reacted in surprise.

"Why not?" his brother insisted. "She hates Yahweh, We hate Yahweh. It would be a formidable allegiance to put an end to the Semites."

"No!" Apollo shouted, silencing his brother. "Never consider that again."

They travelled under guise of the night in silence.

"What are we going to do?" Hermes asked after a while, his voice small and uncertain.

Apollo's jaw set with determination. "We fight," he said. "We gather our allies, we find the Eldar, and we face this darkness head-on. It's what we've always done."

But as they finally emerged into the night air, the weight of their task settled heavily upon them. The stars above seemed dim and distant, as if even the heavens were retreating from the encroaching shadows.

Apollo looked out over the sleeping town of Rashford, his heart heavy with the knowledge of the battles to come. The air hummed with an ominous energy, a palpable sense of dread that even mortals could surely feel in their dreams.

"May the Fates have mercy on us all," he murmured, as the darkness continued to gather on the horizon.

Chapter 7

The shadow cast by Marcus Taser's imposing frame seemed to stretch and writhe across the polished mahogany of his desk, a dark extension of his influence. His fingers, adorned with rings that caught the dim light like predatory eyes, tapped out a rhythm of impatience and authority.

Tap. Tap. Tap.

Each sound resonated through the room, a subtle reminder of the power that lay coiled within his corpulent form. Marcus' lips curled into a cold smile as he surveyed his domain.

"How quaint," he murmured, his voice a silken whisper that belied the steel beneath. "To think that simple men believe they control their own destinies."

His gaze, sharp and calculating, swept across the room. It lingered on a shelf lined with ancient tomes, their spines cracked and faded, whispering of forbidden knowledge. A gleaming obsidian statue caught his eye next, its surface reflecting nothing but darkness.

His eyes narrowed, focusing on a framed photograph of his son, Windsor. The boy's arrogant smirk mirrored his own, a testament to the legacy of contempt he had cultivated.

Marcus shifted in his chair, the leather creaking beneath his substantial weight. Despite his size, he moved with a grace that seemed almost preternatural, his bulk flowing like liquid shadow. The fine fabric of his tailored suit strained against his frame, yet he bore himself with an elegance that defied expectation.

"The pieces are falling into place," he murmured, his voice a low rumble that seemed to reverberate through the dim office. "Soon, God Himself will tremble."

His fingers tapped a rhythmic pattern on the armrest, each beat like the ticking of a doomsday clock. In the shadows of the room, something seemed to stir, responding to the dark hunger that radiated from Marcus' very being.

Marcus closed his eyes, rehearsing the conversation with the mayor that would soon unfold. His lips moved silently, shaping words with meticulous precision.

"My dear friend," he began, his imagined voice dripping with honeyed politeness, "I assure you, our interests are perfectly aligned. The prosperity of Rashford is my utmost concern."

A pause, calculated to perfection.

"Of course, I understand your reservations. Change can be... unsettling. But progress demands sacrifice, does it not?"

His internal monologue continued, each word a carefully crafted weapon. "We must look to the future, to the greater good. And sometimes, that means making difficult decisions."

Marcus' eyes snapped open, a predatory gleam flickering within their depths. The formal cadence of his rehearsed speech belied the cold calculation beneath. Every syllable was a chess move, positioning his pawns for the final, devastating play.

His hands came to rest on the desk, fingers steepling in contemplation. The heavy rings adorning his digits caught the dim light, casting fleeting shadows across the polished wood. These dancing silhouettes seemed to take on a life of their own, writhing and twisting like tortured souls.

Marcus watched the play of light and shadow, a visual metaphor for the machinations that consumed his thoughts. Each flicker represented a life to be manipulated, a destiny to be twisted to his will. The shadows danced to his tune, just as the people of Rashford soon would.

A soft chuckle escaped his lips, devoid of mirth. "Oh, how they'll dance," he mused, "when they realize the true nature of the puppet master."

The office around Marcus exuded an aura of opulent menace. A massive desk dominated the centre of the room, its surface gleaming like obsidian in the low light. Behind it loomed a high-backed leather chair, more throne than seat, a silent testament to Marcus' self-appointed position of power.

"How fitting," Marcus thought, running a finger along the chair's smooth surface. "A throne for the true king of this miserable little town."

He paused before a large, ornate mirror, its frame adorned with writhing figures caught in eternal torment. Marcus studied his reflection.

"Soon," he whispered to his image, "soon the veil will be lifted, and all will tremble before the true face of Marcus Taser."

Marcus approached the window, his fingers grazing the heavy drapes. With a slight hesitation, he parted them just enough to peer outside. The world beyond was a blur of muted colours and indistinct shapes, as if viewed through a veil of shadow.

"A fitting barrier," he murmured, his voice barely above a whisper. "Let them remain blind to the truth that lurks in their midst."

As he gazed out, memories of his past began to surface, unbidden and relentless. The faces of those he had used, betrayed, and discarded in his climb to power flickered through his mind like a macabre slideshow.

"Necessary sacrifices," Marcus thought, his expression remaining impassive despite the turmoil of his thoughts. "Each one a stepping stone on the path to true dominion."

As he sat in his darkened study, surrounded by the symbols and artifacts of a secret society, he couldn't help but feel a surge of pride at how easily he had risen through their ranks. He remembered the whispered oaths and hidden ceremonies, the thrill of learning their closely guarded secrets before ultimately betraying them for his own gain. The power he now held was a sweet reward for his deceitful actions.

Marcus turned from the window and returned to his desk.

"The pieces are almost in place," Marcus murmured, his voice barely above a whisper.

Marcus shifted his attention to a map of Rashford Town spread across his desk. Red pins marked

various locations – the church, Elm Manor. Each point represented a thread in the complex web he was weaving. An interesting development had occurred at Elm Manor. "Seems immortals walk among us after all," he mused. He would investigate that report further but now his mind turned to other matters.

"Soon," he said, his tone filled with cold anticipation. "Soon, the barriers between realms will weaken, and I'll be there to seize control."

As he spoke, a predatory gleam flickered in the depths of his eyes, a hunger that seemed to consume the very light around him. The shadows in the room appeared to deepen, as if responding to the darkness within Marcus Taser's soul.

His desk was a messy jumble of papers, scattered pens, and half-empty coffee mugs. He furiously scribbled notes and diagrams on scraps of paper, his mind racing as he planned the takedown of Mayor Quinn. Suddenly, his thoughts were interrupted by the sound of his phone ringing. He answered frantically, hoping it was news about his son Windsor and his friends who had disappeared yet again. Worried lines creased his forehead as he paced around the room, muttering curses under his breath. The clock on the wall ticked mercilessly, each second that passed without word about Windsor feeling like an eternity.

A sharp knock echoed through the room, causing him to tense up in his seat. "Come in," he barked, the steel in his voice enough to make anyone think twice about disturbing him.

The door creaked open and in walked Sheriff Eva Ramirez, her body taut with determination. "Sheriff," he growled, his eyes scanning her for any sign of progress.

Her answer was a disappointing shake of her head.

"What do you mean, no news?" he snarled, his fists clenching tightly.

But before she could respond, Marcus silenced her with a hard glare.

"Do your job and find those boys," he demanded, his tone dripping with venom. "Actually, find my son and to hell with the other two."

The Sheriff held his gaze for a moment before nodding solemnly and swiftly exiting the room.

Marcus sat back in his chair, seething with impatience and an overwhelming sense of dread. He knew time was running out and he would stop at nothing to find his son before it was too late.

He straightened his tailored suit jacket, smoothing non-existent wrinkles as he gathered his composure.

A sudden cold sent a shiver down his spine. He noticed a dark corner of the office growing darker, as if light could not seep through. He decided to investigate. Step by measured step, he approached the corner of the room where the darkness roiled and churned. Shadows danced at the edges of his vision, faces half-glimpsed and quickly gone. Marcus forced himself to ignore them, keeping his gaze fixed on the void before him.

When he spoke, his voice was smooth as silk and cold as the grave. "Who . . . What are you?"

A whisper in his mind came. "I AM WHAT I AM AND NOTHING BUT. I AM THE DARK."

"Do you mean me harm?" Marcus insisted, his voice betraying a twinge of fear for his safety.

He inclined his head in a calculated nod, careful to project confidence while hiding his fear and acknowledging the entity's power. Inside, his heart raced. Everything hinged on this moment, on striking the proper balance between deference and strength.

The darkness pulsed, and Marcus fought to suppress a shudder. He could feel it probing at the edges of his mind, testing for weakness.

I am no simpering fool to be cowed, he reminded himself. *I am Marcus Taser, and I bow to no one.*

Yet even as the thought formed, a tendril of doubt wormed its way into his heart. For all his cunning and influence, what was he before this primordial force of chaos and despair?

The silence stretched, pregnant with possibility and peril. Marcus stood resolute, awaiting the entity's response with outward calm. Inside, his mind raced through contingencies, weighing options should this gambit fail. Still, as the shadows writhed around him, Marcus couldn't quite banish the cold finger of dread that traced its way down his spine.

Suddenly, Marcus' mind exploded with sensation. A cacophony of whispers filled his consciousness, each one promising power beyond mortal reckoning. Visions of chaos and despair flashed before his eyes – cities crumbling, oceans boiling, the very fabric of reality tearing asunder.

For a moment, Marcus faltered. His carefully constructed facade cracked, revealing a flicker of unease in his eyes. The sheer magnitude of what he was dealing with threatened to overwhelm him.

Control yourself, he chided inwardly. Then pushed his voice to mouth, "What do you want from me?"

The Dark's presence intensified, and Marcus felt the weight of its attention bearing down upon him.

When it spoke, it was not with words, but with impressions that seared themselves into his mind.

"SOULS," it demanded. "BRING US SOULS, AND UNPRECEDENTED POWER SHALL BE YOURS."

"What power?" Marcus asked. "What are you talking about?"

"POWER OVER LIFE AND DEATH!" the Dark went on.

Marcus' lips curled into a smile. Seemed to him that Christmas had come early this year. "Of course. I assure you, there will be no shortage of souls in Rashford Town."

The Dark's response was immediate and jarring. "GODS," it hissed. "ELDAR. THEY WALK AMONG YOU. I WANT THEIR SOULS TOO."

Marcus blinked, momentarily thrown. "Gods? The immortal boy at Elm Manor?"

He felt a resentful acknowledgement from within the darkness.

"Can you make me immortal?" Marcus licked his lips.

"YES."

His mind raced, recalibrating his plans. "Well," he said softly, "this does change things, doesn't it?" He considered the offer.

"Let me show you what I have to offer," he purred, his voice a silken whisper that belied the predatory gleam in his eyes. "Each mark represents a soul ripe for the taking. Vulnerable. Isolated. Perfect for our... purposes."

"I WANT GODS!" the Dark hissed in his mind.

"One thing at a time," Marcus replied realising now that this dark entity was indeed in need of his input.

His finger traced a path between the marks, connecting them like a twisted web of fate. "I have cultivated these prospects for years, waiting for the right moment. And now, with your power behind me, we can harvest them all."

Marcus' heart raced, a heady mix of fear and exhilaration coursing through his veins. He had danced with darkness before, but this... this was something entirely new.

The Dark shifted, its amorphous form undulating like oil on water. The shadows in the room seemed to deepen, reaching out with tendrils of inky blackness that caressed the edges of Marcus' consciousness.

"SHOW US," it demanded, its presence growing more oppressive with each passing moment.

Marcus swallowed hard, fighting to maintain his composure. "Of course," he said, gesturing to a cluster of X's near the town's outskirts. "We'll start here, in the poorer districts. No one will miss them, and their desperation makes them easy targets."

The air in the room crackled with an unspoken tension, the weight of their impending agreement hanging heavy between them. Marcus could feel the Dark's consideration, its alien intelligence probing at the edges of his offer.

What have I gotten myself into? he wondered, a flicker of doubt worming its way into his mind. But he quickly quashed it. There was no turning back now.

His eyes gleamed with a predatory hunger as he pressed on, voice low and seductive. "Consider the souls we'll reap together," he purred. "Not just the dregs of society, but the pillars of the community. Imagine the chaos when their masks slip, revealing the rot beneath. And if there be gods in Rashford, I'll bring them to you too."

The Dark pulsed, a silent approval that sent shivers down Marcus' spine. He could feel its anticipation, mirroring his own twisted desire.

"I've spent years building a network of influence," Marcus continued, his words dripping with

calculated charm. "Judges, politicians, even members of the clergy – all with secrets they'd kill to keep hidden. We'll use their fear, their shame, to bend them to our will."

As he spoke, Marcus felt a newfound boldness surge through him. The presence of The Dark, once terrifying, now felt almost... comforting. A perfect symbiosis of ambition and ancient malevolence.

"PROVE YOUR DEVOTION," The Dark's non-voice reverberated through Marcus' mind, a command that sent ice through his veins.

Without hesitation, Marcus reached for a small pocketknife on his desk. "I seal this pact with my own blood," he declared, drawing the blade across his palm. Crimson welled up, and as the first drop hit the floor, the shadows exploded into motion.

Inky tendrils shot out, wrapping around Marcus in a cocoon of absolute darkness. He gasped, feeling the entity seep into his very being. It was pain and ecstasy, terror and exultation, all at once.

What have I become? The thought flickered through his mind as the darkness consumed him, sealing their unholy alliance.

As the darkness receded, Marcus stood resolute, his frame trembling with newfound power. A triumphant smile curved his lips, eyes glittering

with spiteful glee. He flexed his fingers, marvelling at the subtle shift in his demeanour – no longer just a man, but a vessel of The Dark's insidious will.

"Magnificent," he whispered, his voice carrying an otherworldly resonance that sent chills down his own spine.

The shadows clung to the corners of the room, a constant reminder of the pact forged. Marcus turned, his movements fluid and predatory as he approached his desk. Each step exuded a newfound confidence, an authority that seemed to ripple through the very air around him.

How fragile they all are, he mused, settling into his chair with regal poise. *Mere insects compared to what I'll become.*

The Dark's presence pulsed softly in the periphery of his consciousness, a silent observer to his machinations. Marcus ran his fingers over the polished wood of his desk, savouring the texture as if experiencing it for the first time.

"Tell me," he addressed The Dark, his tone dripping with malicious curiosity, "how many souls will it take to bring a god to its knees?"

The entity's response came not in words, but in a flood of terrifying visions that made Marcus' breath catch in his throat. He saw cities engulfed

in shadow, heard the screams of countless victims, felt the intoxicating rush of power that would come with each sacrificed soul.

"AODHÁN! THE ELDAR. HE MUST BE DEFEATED!"

A low chuckle escaped Marcus' lips, growing into a full-bodied laugh that echoed through the room. "Oh, my dear friend," he purred, "we are going to reshape this world in our image, and neither god, mortal or this Eldar thing will stand in our way."

Marcus reached for a pen, its weight familiar yet somehow different in his transformed grip. He began to jot down notes, each stroke precise and deliberate, a roadmap to chaos etched in black ink.

John and David, he mused, a cruel smile playing at the corners of his mouth. *Such convenient pawns.*

The room seemed to pulse with dark energy, shadows writhing at the edges of his vision. Marcus lifted the phone, his fingers dancing across the keypad with practiced ease.

"John? It's Marcus," he said, his voice a study in false concern. "I've had some… developments regarding Matt. Could you come by the office? And bring David with you – I think this concerns Ryan as well."

As he spoke, Marcus' free hand continued to sketch out his plans, intricate webs of deceit and manipulation flowing from his pen.

"Of course, of course," he soothed, responding to the anxious father on the other end of the line. "I understand your worry. That's precisely why we need to meet. I'll see you both soon."

He set the phone down, a sardonic chuckle escaping his lips. "Oh, how they rush to their own demise," he murmured, his words seeming to hang in the oppressive air.

The Dark shifted, a tendril of shadow caressing Marcus' shoulders in what felt like approval. The atmosphere crackled with potential energy, the promise of impending chaos almost tangible.

Soon, Marcus thought, his eyes gleaming with anticipation. *Soon, the true harvest will begin.*

Marcus turned his gaze to the window, the night beyond a vast expanse of inky blackness. The streetlights of Rashford Town flickered weakly, their golden glow seeming to shrink away from the encroaching darkness. His reflection stared back at him, a testament to the power he had always craved.

"What price, this power?" he mused aloud, his voice barely above a whisper. The weight of his choices pressed upon him, a delicious burden

that sent shivers of excitement down his spine. "The souls of the innocent, the blood of the unsuspecting... a small price to pay for divinity."

His mind wandered to Windsor, his son. A pang of something akin to regret flitted through him, quickly smothered by cold ambition. "Even he may need to be sacrificed," Marcus murmured, his fingers tracing patterns on the cool glass. "No attachment can be allowed to hinder our grand design."

The Dark pulsed in response, a wave of wicked approval washing over Marcus. He closed his eyes, savouring the sensation of raw power coursing through his veins. When he opened them again, his reflection seemed changed – darker, more sinister, eyes glinting with an otherworldly hunger.

"We stand on the precipice of a new era," Marcus declared, his voice growing stronger. "The gods themselves will tremble before us. John and David will be here soon. Tell me. What do you intend to do with them?"

As if in response to his proclamation, The Dark shifted once more, its formless mass undulating in the corners of the room. Marcus turned from the window, acknowledging the entity with a slight nod. Their gazes met – or rather, Marcus stared

into the void where eyes should be – and a silent understanding passed between them.

"The challenges ahead are formidable," Marcus said, his tone measured and resolute. "Real gods to dispose of. But we shall strip them of their power, feed on their essence, and reshape reality in our image. I will be a god among mortals!"

The Dark's presence intensified, a tendril of shadow reaching out to brush against Marcus' hand. He didn't flinch, instead welcoming the chill touch as a lover might.

"Together," Marcus whispered, his eyes gleaming with determination, "we shall plunge this world into eternal night."

As if summoned by his very thoughts, the door to his study creaked open. Two men stumbled in, their movements jerky and uncoordinated. Marcus recognized them instantly: John, Matt Holmes' father, a proud businessman, and David, Ryan McDormand's father, a respected doctor.

"Ah! John, David! Welcome," Marcus started but before he could continue he witnessed the power of the Dark. In fact, the moment John and David stepped foot into the office, they were ambushed by the Dark's malicious tendrils. The smoky tendrils slithered around their bodies like hungry serpents, binding them tightly and squeezing the

life out of them. Shadows morphed into skeletal hands that pierced through their sternums, clutching at their hearts before ripping them out in one swift motion. The air filled with the sound of wet tearing as their lungs were torn from their ribcages, leaving gaping wounds that bubbled and frothed with each ragged breath they took.

The smell of blood and viscera filled the room as dark tendrils sliced through veins and arteries like razor-sharp blades through warm butter. The men's screams were deafening as their insides were slowly pulled out through gaping wounds on their backs, leaving long trails of innards dangling from gaping gashes in their flesh. Bones broke and shifted under the men's skin as if they were nothing more than puppets being controlled by an unseen master.

Marcus stood frozen in horror as he watched his friends being brutalized before his very eyes. A sense of helplessness washed over him as he realized there was nothing he could do to save them from this unspeakable torment. Their faces contorted into a mask of agony and fear that chilled him to the bone; their eyes were empty sockets reflecting only darkness and despair.

Finally, when it seemed as though there was nothing left to take from them, the Dark released its hold on their mangled bodies. They lay

motionless on the ground like discarded dolls, their once proud forms reduced to broken shells covered in blood and gore. Marcus could do nothing but stare in disbelief at what had been done to his friends; he felt sick to his stomach knowing that he had witnessed such a brutal display of violence and suffering firsthand.

With a guttural growl, the lifeless bodies of John and David jerked upright, their eyes empty of all humanity as they stood ready to carry out Marcus' every command like mindless drones. Stripped of their souls, they were nothing more than hollow shells, void of any emotion or conscience.

"THEY ARE NOW YOUR OBEDIENT SERVANTS," the Dark hissed in Marcus' mind.

"Ah, gentlemen," Marcus purred, circling them like a predator. "How kind of you to join us."

The men stood motionless, vacant expressions betraying no hint of comprehension. Marcus reached out, running a finger along David's jaw. The skin felt cold, waxy.

"I wonder," Marcus mused, "do you feel it? The darkness consuming you from within?"

As if in response, David and John's bodies began to twitch and convulse. Their skin rippled, as though something beneath was trying to claw its

way out. Marcus watched, transfixed, as the men's features began to twist and warp.

"Fascinating," Marcus murmured, his scientific curiosity warring with a newfound sadistic glee. "The corruption is so... complete."

The transformation reached its horrifying climax. Where two men had stood, there were now monstrosities – skin mottled and grey, limbs elongated and joints bent at unnatural angles. Their eyes, once lifeless, now gleamed with an unholy light.

Marcus felt a surge of dark pride. These were his creations, his first steps towards reshaping the world in his image. He leaned in close, whispering to the zombified remains of Matt and Ryan's fathers.

"You have the honour of being the vanguard of a new era," he said, his voice dripping with malice. "Now, let's put you to work, shall we?"

Marcus' eyes, cold and calculating, swept over the twisted forms before him. A thin smile played on his lips, devoid of warmth or humanity.

"Gentlemen," he intoned, his voice a silken whisper that seemed to absorb the very light from the room. "Your task is simple. Mayor Quinn and his assistant Jeff Greening must be eliminated. Leave no witnesses."

The two zombies' heads jerked in unison, a grotesque parody of understanding. Marcus felt a thrill of power course through him, tinged with a hint of revulsion he quickly suppressed.

How easy it is, he mused internally, *to bend the will of men. Even in death, they dance to another's tune.*

"Go now," Marcus commanded, waving a dismissive hand. "And do try to be... thorough."

As the monstrosities shambled towards the door, their movements jerky and uncoordinated, Marcus found himself pondering the nature of his pact with The Dark. *Have I truly gained control, or merely traded one master for another?*

The zombies' footsteps echoed through the corridors, a dread drumbeat heralding the approach of death. Marcus listened, a chill creeping up his spine despite his best efforts to remain detached. But it was too late for second thoughts. The die was cast, the dark pact sealed. As the last echoes faded, Marcus Taser sat alone in his study, surrounded by shadows that seemed to whisper of power, chaos, and the point of no return.

The night air hung heavy with an unnatural stillness as the zombies lurched towards Mayor

Quinn's residence. Shadows seemed to coalesce around them, their grotesque forms barely discernible in the murky darkness. The usually bustling streets of Rashford Town were eerily quiet, as if the world itself held its breath in anticipation of the horrors to come.

Inside the Quinn household, Bella Quinn lounged on the couch, idly flipping through channels on the television in hope of finding news about Jamie. Her husband, the Mayor, sat at the dining table, poring over documents.

"Don't you ever take a break?" Bella Quinn called out, her voice tinged with both affection and exasperation. "Seems even your son's disappearance can't tear you away from your work!"

Mayor Quinn looked up, a weary smile on his face. "I won't sleep until I find what happened to Jamie, my dear."

Bella's retort died on her lips as an icy tendril of dread slithered down her spine, its glacial touch seeping into her very marrow. Her eyes widened, pupils dilating in primal fear as the air around her thickened, charged with an otherworldly malevolence. "Did you... did you feel that?" she whispered, her voice trembling like a frail leaf in a storm.

Before Mayor Quinn could respond, a deafening crack shattered the silence, the front door exploding inward as if struck by an unseen, monstrous force. Splinters of wood rained down, each shard seeming to whisper dark omens as they clattered to the floor. Through the yawning void where the door once stood, they came.

The two barely recognisable figures of John and David lurched forward, their movements a grotesque parody of life. Pallid, rotting flesh hung from exposed bone, the stench of decay flooding the room like a noxious fog. But it was their eyes that froze the blood in Bella's veins - bottomless pits of emptiness, devoid of all humanity, yet burning with an insatiable hunger that defied death itself.

Mayor Quinn's chair screeched against the floor as he stood, the sound unnaturally loud in the surreal tableau. "What in God's name—" he began, his words faltering as the full horror of the situation crashed over him like a tidal wave of despair. The zombies' gazes locked onto them, a collective rasping moan rising from decaying throats, the sound carrying with it the promise of an agonizing eternity trapped between life and death.

As the undead duo shambled closer, Bella felt her grip on reality start to slip. The walls seemed to

breathe, pulsating with an unholy life of their own. Whispers, too faint to comprehend yet impossibly loud, filled her mind, threatening to drown her in a sea of madness. In that moment, she knew with terrifying certainty that death would be a mercy compared to what awaited them.

Bella's heart raced, her mind struggling to comprehend the nightmarish scene unfolding before her. *This can't be real,* she thought, frozen in terror. *It's like something out of those horror movies I love, but... oh God, it's actually happening.*

The zombies moved with unnatural speed, their actions precise and brutal. Mayor Quinn barely had time to reach for the phone before one of the creatures was upon him, its hands wrapping around his throat with inhuman strength.

"My love!" Bella screamed, finally snapping out of her paralysis. She leaped forward, grabbing a nearby lamp and swinging it at the zombie attacking her husband. The porcelain shattered against its skull, but the creature didn't even flinch.

Why isn't it working? Bella's mind raced. *In the movies, you always go for the head!*

As she desperately searched for another weapon, cold, clammy hands gripped her shoulders.

Bella's scream was cut short as she was thrown across the room, crashing into the bookshelf with a sickening thud.

Through blurred vision, she watched in horror as the zombies tore into her husband with mechanical efficiency. The mayor's struggles grew weaker, his gasps for air becoming more desperate.

"Please," Bella whimpered, tears streaming down her face. "Someone help us!"

But no help came. The night swallowed their screams, leaving only the sound of tearing flesh and breaking bones. As darkness closed in around her, Bella's last thoughts were of the cruel irony – how the horrors she'd once found thrilling on screen had become her terrifying reality.

The Greening estate loomed in the moonlight, its elegant facade belying the horror that approached. Inside, Jeff Greening sat in his study, poring over ancient texts, unaware of the impending doom.

Goddard's heart raced as he burst into his father's study, the taste of fear bitter on his tongue. The flickering candlelight cast long shadows across Jeff Greening's face, etching deep lines of concern as he looked up from the ancient tome before him.

"Father, I've witnessed something horrific," Goddard gasped, his usual eloquence faltering.

Jeff's brow furrowed, setting aside the book. "Calm yourself, son. What's happened?"

Goddard's hands trembled as he gripped the back of a leather chair. "Matt, Ryan, Windsor - they're gone. Dust. I saw it with my own eyes." The words tumbled out, each one heavier than the last. "They were with her, intimately, and then... God!."

His father's eyes widened, a flicker of understanding - or was it fear? - passing across his face. "With who? Are you certain?"

"As certain as the breath in my lungs," Goddard replied, his voice barely above a whisper. The memory of their agonized faces flashed before him, a nightmarish tableau he couldn't shake.

"Goddard?" Jeff looked up, his brow furrowed. "Have you been drinking?"

Goddard's words caught in his throat as a chill crept up his spine. Shadows on the lawn outside the office window... they were moving. Not with

the gentle sway of branches in the breeze, but with a sinister, purposeful writhing. His mind reeled, desperately grasping for a rational explanation, but finding none.

The darkness seemed to pulse, to breathe, as if alive with malevolent intent. Goddard's heart hammered in his chest, each beat echoing in his ears like a drum of doom. He blinked rapidly, willing the nightmarish vision to disappear, but the shadows only grew darker, more defined.

Tendrils of inky blackness began to seep under the window frame, bringing with them a palpable aura of dread. The temperature in the room plummeted, and Goddard's breath came out in visible puffs. He tried to call out, to warn the others, but his voice failed him, reduced to a pathetic whimper.

As the shadows encroached further into the room, Goddard's mind began to fracture. Whispers, barely audible yet deafening in their intensity, filled his head with promises of eternal torment.

"We need to leave. Now." Goddard's voice trembled, his usual eloquence abandoning him in the face of primal fear.

"What are you on about?" Jeff asked, unable to mask his annoyance at his son's gibberish.

A crash from downstairs shattered the night's silence. Jeff sprang to his feet, his eyes widening in realization. "Intruders! How did they . . ? The back door," he whispered urgently. "Go!"

As they rushed through the house, Goddard's mind raced. *This can't be happening. Not here. Not to us.*

They reached the kitchen, but froze at the sight before them. Two figures, once human, now grotesque parodies of life, blocked their escape. In the dim light, Goddard recognized the twisted features of Matt and Ryan's fathers.

"Oh God," Jeff breathed, his calm demeanour cracking. "Goddard, run. Find safety."

"Dad, I can't leave you—"

"You must!" Jeff shoved him towards the pantry. "Remember what I taught you. You are too important for me."

As Goddard stumbled into the pantry, searching frantically for the hidden passage he'd been shown years ago, he heard his father's last words: "I'm sorry, old friend. May your soul find peace."

The sound of tearing flesh filled the air, and Goddard bit back a sob as he finally found the latch. As he slipped into the secret tunnel, the oppressive darkness closed in around him,

whispering promises of power and chaos. But Goddard pressed on, his heart pounding, driven by the need to survive and the desperate hope that somewhere he might find salvation.

In his dimly lit study, Marcus Taser leaned back in his leather chair, a satisfied smile playing across his fat face. The air hung heavy with the scent of aged books and expensive cigars, mingling with the lingering essence of The Dark's presence.

"Well," he mused aloud, his voice a low, cultured rumble, "that was certainly... invigorating."

The shadows in the corners of the room seemed to pulse in response, a faint whisper echoing in the stillness. Marcus' eyes, sharp and calculating, darted to the darkest recess.

Power, he thought, savouring the word. *True, unbridled power at last*.

He reached for a crystal decanter, pouring himself a generous measure of amber liquid. As he raised the glass, he caught his reflection in the polished surface of his desk. For a moment, he thought he saw something lurking behind his own image – a mass of writhing darkness, hungry and insatiable.

Marcus chuckled, taking a long sip. "To new beginnings," he toasted the empty room.

The whispers grew louder, a cacophony of promises and demands swirling around him. Marcus closed his eyes, relishing the sensation.

"Yes, yes," he murmured. "All in good time. We have much work ahead of us, you and I."

He stood, moving to the window. Outside, the night was unnaturally still, as if the world itself held its breath in anticipation of what was to come.

"Tell me," Marcus said, addressing The Dark, "what delicious chaos shall we unleash next?"

The whispers coalesced into a chilling response, filling Marcus' mind with visions of devastation and dominion. He smiled, a cold, predatory expression that never reached his eyes.

"Perfect," he breathed, raising his glass once more. "To the fall of gods and the rise of Taser."

As he drank, Marcus felt The Dark's presence intensify, a reminder of the pact that now bound them. But in his arrogance, he failed to notice the shadows creeping ever closer, hungry for more than just the souls he had promised. In his appetite for power, Marcus had even forgotten Windsor.

Chapter 8

Apollo froze as the iron scent of blood invaded his senses. Blinking rapidly, he scanned the shadowy street, dread pooling in his gut. There, where he had left it, at the base of an ancient oak, lay Hermes' broken body. Apollo's heart seized at his brother's mangled form. Gripping his brother's limp hand, Apollo bowed his head. Justice had been delivered swift and merciless. But still he was concerned for his brother.

Hermes woke up and managed a weak grin, wincing as he probed a bruise on his ribs. "Easy there, big brother. I'm fine. Well, mostly fine. Nothing a few millennia won't heal."

Apollo's jaw clenched, frustration bubbling beneath the surface. "This is intolerable. We're sitting ducks out here, vulnerable to every petty demon and power-hungry mortal."

As if summoned by his words, the air suddenly crackled with ethereal energy. A blinding light erupted before them, forcing Apollo to shield his eyes. When the radiance faded, two imposing figures stood before them – Micha-El and Gabri-El, their wings unfurled and casting long shadows in the moonlight.

Apollo instinctively moved in front of Hermes, his stance defiant despite his mortal limitations.

"Well, well," he said, his voice dripping with sarcasm. "The heavenly host graces us with its presence. To what do we owe this dubious honour?"

His skin prickled as he sensed a shift in the atmosphere, an oppressive weight descending upon them. He turned, still supporting the weakened Hermes, to face the source of this otherworldly presence.

Apollo straightened to his full height, meeting Micha-El's eyes with a mixture of defiance and vulnerability. His heart raced, torn between his lingering affection for the archangel and the knowledge of what was to come.

"Apollo," Micha-El's voice rang out, a blend of divine authority and barely concealed anguish. "What have you done?"

The former god of light clenched his fists, fighting to keep his voice steady. "What I had to do, Micha-El. What you should have done."

Micha-El's wings bristled, his eyes flashing with hurt and betrayal. "You've broken the ancient pact. You've chosen chaos over order, destruction over harmony. You have interfered with human lives."

"And you've chosen blind obedience over compassion," Apollo retorted, his words laced with bitterness. "Tell me, Micha-El, does Yahweh's

love extend only to those who bow before him? Or is there room in his grand design for mercy?"

Gabri-El stepped forward, his voice cold and unforgiving. "You speak of mercy while you make yourself judge and executioner?"

Apollo's mind raced, searching for words that could bridge the chasm between them. He thought of the mortals in Rashford Town, blissfully unaware of the cosmic battle unfolding around them. Of his fellow gods, struggling to maintain their identities in a world that had all but forgotten them.

Apollo's voice trembled with raw emotion, his eyes pleading with desperation. "Don't you understand?" he cried, his words cracking like thunder. "The ancient ways are crumbling, the bonds between realms unravelling. We must change or face certain annihilation."

Micha-El's expression softened for a moment, a flicker of understanding passing across his face. But as quickly as it appeared, it vanished, replaced by resolute determination.

"I'm sorry, my love," Micha-El's voice wavered with indecision as he spoke. "I cannot allow this to continue. It goes against everything I believe in." His eyes flickered with guilt and inner turmoil as he struggled to find the right words.

As the archangels advanced, Apollo braced himself for what was to come. He cast one last glance at Hermes, silently vowing to protect him no matter the cost. In that moment, he felt the weight of his mortal form more acutely than ever before, keenly aware of how vulnerable he had become.

Micha-El's hand trembled as he reached for Apollo, his fingers just inches from the fallen god's golden hair. For a fleeting moment, Apollo saw the anguish in Micha-El's eyes, a reflection of their shared history and unspoken devotion.

"Micha-El, please," Apollo whispered, his voice barely audible. "This isn't you. Remember who we were, what we meant to each other."

The archangel's resolve wavered, his internal struggle evident in the tightening of his jaw and the moisture gathering at the corners of his eyes. "I... I can't disobey Him, Apollo. You know that."

Apollo's frustration surged, mingling with a profound sense of helplessness. "And what of your own will? Your own heart?" he challenged, his blue eyes blazing with intensity.

Before Micha-El could respond, Gabri-El's voice cut through the tension. "Enough of this, Micha-El. We have our orders."

"Leave my brother out of it," he pleaded at last. "I am the one who sinned against Yahweh's laws."

"Brother!" Hermes exclaimed.

"Hermes won't be touched," Micha-El promised. "An ambulance will pick him up. The mortals can tend to his wounds without uncovering the truth."

In a blur of motion, the archangels seized Apollo, their grip unyielding despite his struggles. Celestial chains materialized, wrapping around his limbs and binding him to a weathered wooden pole that seemed to sprout from the very earth.

"No!" Apollo cried out, his muscles straining against the otherworldly bonds. "Micha-El, don't do this!"

Micha-El's expression hardened, his internal struggle hidden behind a facade of determination. He couldn't bear to look at Apollo, the one he was supposed to love and protect but also the cause of all his pain. In a flash of anger, flames engulfed Apollo, the conflicting emotions within Micha-El fuelling the destructive inferno.

The agony was immediate and all-consuming. Apollo's screams tore through the night, a haunting melody of pain and betrayal. As the fire climbed higher, devouring his mortal form, he locked eyes with Micha-El one last time.

"I forgive you," Apollo gasped through the smoke and tears, his voice barely a whisper. "But I fear... the consequences... of this night... will echo... through eternity."

The flames engulfed him fully, and Apollo's world became nothing but searing pain and the distant sound of his own anguished cries.

As the inferno consumed Apollo, his consciousness splintered. Flashes of Aodhán's face, contorted in anguish, seared themselves into Apollo's mind. The boy's eyes blazed with an otherworldly light, pulsing with raw, uncontrolled power.

"No... not this," Apollo gasped, his words lost in the roar of the flames.

"Brother!" Hermes cried out, his voice thick with anguish.

The flames climbed higher, devouring Apollo's flesh. The pain was excruciating, but worse was the realization that he was powerless to stop it. In his mind, he saw flashes of his past glory – the sun chariot, the Oracle at Delphi, the adoration of mortals. All of it reduced to ash.

"Is this what passes for justice in your realm?" Apollo spat through gritted teeth, his skin blistering and blackening.

Micha-El's eyes held a hint of sadness. "This is not justice, Apollo. This is necessity."

As the flames engulfed him, Apollo's mind raced with guilt and fear. He had failed. As he prayed for the survival of his remaining family, he couldn't help but wonder if it was all in vain. The chaos and destruction that consumed his thoughts were a reflection of the turmoil within him.

In his last moments of consciousness, Apollo realized with horror that this was only the beginning of something far worse.

As the flames consumed Apollo's human form, his consciousness fractured into a kaleidoscope of prophetic visions. The Eldar's face, innocent yet terrible, flashed before him - eyes blazing with cosmic power that threatened to tear reality asunder.

The once-charming town twisted and contorted in his mind, morphing into a grotesque scene of horror. The familiar cobblestone streets were now slick with blood, stained by the destruction that had befallen them. Ivy-covered buildings crumbled to dust, their charm replaced by decay and ruin. The air itself seemed to warp and twist, as if reality itself was bending under the immense power of the Eldar. It was a sight that filled him with both awe and dread, a testament to the untamed might of his kind.

Apollo's mind raced with fear and determination as he struggled to find a way to warn his family. The visions that flooded his mind were filled with terror, each one worse than the last. He saw his loved ones torn apart, their once bright divinity fading into darkness. But amidst all the chaos and destruction, there was always the undeniable looming presence of the Eldar, a force beyond his understanding and control. With every passing moment, Apollo felt more conflicted about what course of action to take. How could he protect those he loved without putting himself in grave danger?

As Apollo's consciousness wavered again, teetering on the brink of oblivion, the scene shifted.

Athena stood atop a nearby hill, her grey eyes reflecting the inferno that consumed her brother. Her jaw clenched, fingers digging into her palms hard enough to draw blood.

"Fools," she hissed, her mind racing. "They think this will solve anything?"

She watched as Micha-El and Gabri-El departed, their celestial forms fading into the night. Hermes knelt by Apollo's smouldering form, weeping openly. Athena's heart ached, but she pushed the

emotion aside. There was no time for grief. Not now.

"We need allies," she murmured, her tactical mind already formulating plans. "But who can we trust in this godforsaken realm?"

The weight of responsibility settled heavily on her shoulders. She was Athena, goddess of wisdom and war strategy. If anyone could navigate this treacherous path, it was her. But as she gazed upon the remnants of Apollo's punishment, doubt crept in like a poisonous mist.

"What if I'm not enough?" The thought chilled her to her core.

The crimson sun dipped below the horizon, staining the sky with a macabre hue as Athena stood at the mansion's grandiose balcony. Beneath her, the town of Rashford slumbered, oblivious to the turmoil roiling in her heart. The air was heavy with the scent of rain-soaked earth and the acrid tinge of ozone, heralding a storm both literal and metaphorical.

Athena knew the time for subtlety had passed; she needed allies, and allies meant alliances with those she once swore to oppose. She had heard of the attacks on the houses of the Mayor and his assistant; attacks that were mercilessly executed

by some darkness she yet had to understand. She would have loved to consult her brother about it but now Apollo was beyond her reach, at least for the time being.

With a heavy heart, clad in a tailored suit, her long dark hair tamed into a professional bun, she set out to meet the man she suspected to be at the centre of this maelstrom: Marcus Taser. She had to take matters into her own hands.

Marcus Taser's mansion loomed ahead like a dark beacon of opulence and excess, its gargoyles leering at her as she climbed the steps. The air was thick with the scents of burning incense, sulphur, and the unmistakable tinge of fear.

"Good evening, Ms Pallas," he purred, his oily voice slithering through the air as he ushered her inside. "To what do I owe this... honour?"

Athena's eyes blazed with a banked fury, but she smiled nonetheless, her voice dripping with honeyed venom. "I've heard of your... vision for Rashford," she purred. "And I must say, it intrigues me."

Marcus' eyes narrowed, but he masked his suspicion well, gesturing for her to sit. "Oh, really?"

Their conversation was a delicate dance of words and wit, each trying to gain an advantage over the other. Athena's sharp mind picked up on subtle cues that revealed this man's hunger for power and status, far beyond what his current position allowed. She couldn't help but admire his boldness, if only in another life.

"And what is it that drives you, Marcus?" Athena inquired, her voice steady and calculating.

Marcus smirked, his eyes gleaming with ambition. "I have always sought to better myself. Mediocrity does not suit me, my dear Ms Pallas. I crave influence, respect, and the power to shape the world around me."

Athena arched an eyebrow, a faint smile playing on her lips. "A lofty goal indeed. But tell me, Marcus, do you not fear the consequences of such relentless pursuit?"

Marcus chuckled, a low and confident sound. "Fear is for the weak-willed and timid. I am neither. I will do whatever it takes to achieve greatness, even if it means stepping on a few toes along the way."

Athena's gaze held his, a silent challenge passing between them. "Very well, Marcus. Just remember, in this game of power and ambition, it

is not always the boldest player who emerges victorious."

As the meeting wore on, their conversation continued to ebb and flow like a river winding its way through rocky terrain. Each word spoken was a move in their intricate verbal chess match, where strategy and subtlety were key.

"Tell me," Marcus purred over a glass of amber liquid, "what would you say if I told you that I could make your every desire come true? Rashford, the world... at your feet?"

Athena's heart pounded faster. This was the opening she had been waiting for. "And what would it cost me, Marcus?" she asked, feigning trepidation.

Marcus' smile spread like the stain of rot, his true nature bubbling to the surface. "Oh, just a little allegiance. A small favour here and there. Nothing too... taxing." His laughter echoed through the dimly lit room, mingling with the shrieks of the damned.

In that moment, Athena knew the depths of his depravity, and her decision was made.

With a flash, she shed her mortal guise, wings of glimmering feathers unfurling from her back. "I'm afraid I cannot accept your generous offer, Mr Taser," she said, her voice ringed with the fury of

the heavens. "For you see, I have no intention of supporting a monster."

"Foolish girl!" Marcus hissed, a dark power surging through him. "You underestimate the reach of the one you serve!"

Shadows swirled around him like an evil hurricane, taking shape: a towering silhouette with tendrils of pure Darkness lashing out at the goddess. Athena buffeted against the onslaught, but she remained resolute, her jaw set in determination.

"I have faced greater threats than you," she spat, her voice ringing with divine authority. "In the name of Zeus, I, Athena, cast you out!"

As the words left her lips, the air itself rippled with ancient power. The shadows recoiled, their grip on the mortal plane tenuous under the onslaught of celestial light.

"My powers!" she exclaimed, unable to believe that she had unexpectedly rediscovered her divinity. "They're back!"

But Marcus was cunning, and he was not alone in this fight.

"Ah, a goddess!" he exclaimed. "Yes, I have been searching for your kind!"

Athena eyed him in shock. How did this mortal know about the existence of the gods?

"Strike, my pet!" he commanded, and from the shadows emerged a creature of bone and sinew, its form twisting and contorting like the very stuff of nightmares.

Athena's heart raced as she recognized the abomination before her.

"Apollo's Prophecy," she whispered, dread coiling around her heart. "You've freed it, haven't you?"

Marcus Taser's maniacal laughter echoed through the room, reverberating against the very walls of reality. "The Dark has been patient, biding its time, waiting for a moment such as this. And now, with your meddling, you've sealed Rashford's fate."

The servitor lunged, its bony talons extended, and Athena barely had time to dodge. She rolled across the floor, her wings unfurling to their full, majestic span.

"I won't let you do this," she vowed, inhaled deeply, and unleashed a blast of power.

The room erupted in a cacophony of light and sound, the air itself shimmering under the onslaught of celestial fury. The servitor howled, its twisted form disintegrating under the onslaught,

but the Dark remained, its malevolent presence undeterred.

"You cannot win this fight, Athena," Marcus crooned, his voice echoing in the chaos. "The tide of time is turning, and you are on the wrong side of history."

Athena's brow furrowed as she scanned the room, her eyes narrowing. "Show yourself, coward!"

A sinister chuckle emanated from behind her, and a cold hand clasped her shoulder. She whirled around, her powers at the ready, only to find the room was empty.

"FOOL," a mocking voice hissed in her ear. "I AM THE DARKNESS, THE VERY VOID YOU SEE WHEN YOU CLOSE YOUR EYES. YOU CANNOT ESCAPE ME."

Athena's blood ran ice cold as the Dark began to coil around her, its tendrils like icy fingers caressing her skin. In her mind's eye, she saw the horrors of her past; the battles lost, the lives taken, the ones she had failed to protect. All her doubts and fears swirled together, encased in the suffocating embrace of the shadows.

Athena gritted her teeth, digging her nails into her palms as she struggled to maintain her sanity. "No! I won't let you win!" she growled, drawing on her last reserves of strength.

In a blinding flash of light, the suppressed divinity within her erupted outwards, scouring the Dark from her body and mind. The repelling energies of light and darkness collided, the very fabric of reality itself beginning to fray under the strain.

"You think that will stop me?" Marcus cackled, emerging from the chaos, his form rippling and shifting like the shadows themselves. "I am the Unmaker, the Harbinger of the End. I have seen empires crumble and gods fall before me!"

"Then you know this is not the end," she countered, her voice firm despite the fear gnawing at her heart. "There will always be those who stand against the darkness, who fight for what's right."

"VERY WELL, THEN," the Dark hissed. "IF YOU WISH TO RESIST, THEN YOU SHALL FEEL THE FULL FORCE OF MY WRATH!"

With a roar, the Dark unleashed a torrent of infernal flames at her, the very air searing with heat. Athena braced herself, the light of the Greek Pantheon pulsing around her like a beacon in the encroaching night.

The battle raged on for what felt like an eternity, the two forces of light and darkness locked in a deadly waltz. Shadows writhed and flames

danced, their macabre dance a morbid mirror of the conflict within their hosts' souls.

Athena's strength was waning, her divine power fading as quickly as it had come. The darkness within her clawed at her mind, whispering sweet lies of oblivion and release.

"Join me," Marcus cajoled, his voice a seductive whisper in her ear. "Surrender, and I will end your torment. Together, we can usher in a new era of chaos and despair."

Athena faltered. Her heart pounded in her chest, a traitorous part of her aching for the respite he offered.

"No," she gasped, the word escaping her parched lips like a prayer. "I will not... submit!"

With a primal scream, she summoned every ounce of her remaining strength and threw herself at her foe. Her power flared brighter than ever before, a beacon of hope in the encroaching darkness.

Athena sensed her chance. With a wordless roar, she leaped at Marcus, ignoring the Dark, her blade of starlight arcing through the air like a shining comet.

Two forces collided, light and dark, hope and despair, tangled in an eternal dance.

The blade struck true, cutting through the veil of shadows that cloaked Marcus. A sickening thud echoed through the room as the sword found its mark, sinking deep into his flesh.

Marcus' eyes widened, a mixture of shock and admiration flickering across his face. "Well played, my dear," he gasped, blood trickling from the corner of his mouth. "But this... this is far from over."

Athena watched, her breath ragged, as Marcus began to dissolve into the shadows, taken away by the Dark. The darkness seemed to swallow him whole, leaving nothing but a lingering chill in the air.

"You can't hide forever, Marcus," Athena called out, her voice trembling with exhaustion and barely contained fury. "I'll find you, no matter where you slither off to."

The room fell silent, save for the thundering of Athena's heart. She stood there, sword still raised, scanning the corners for any sign of movement. Her mind raced, replaying the battle, searching for clues.

"What have you become, Marcus?" she whispered to herself, a wave of sadness washing over her. "How did we end up here?"

As the adrenaline began to fade, Athena felt the weight of her actions settle upon her shoulders. She had prevailed, yes, but at what cost? The darkness that had touched her during the battle left an indelible mark on her soul, a constant reminder of how close she had come to falling. But it had not been in vain. She had rediscovered her divine abilities. This was a twist in her favour.

The dimly lit room in the heart of President Helena Boyd's residence cast long shadows across Athena's face as she faced her estranged daughter. The air hung heavy with tension, thick enough to choke on.

"Athena." Helena's voice was cool, controlled. "I didn't expect to see you here."

Athena's grey eyes flickered with barely contained fury. "Desperate times call for desperate measures, Madam President."

As Helena turned, the silvery light caught the worry lines etched deep around her eyes. For a moment, Athena saw not the leader of the free world, but a woman burdened by secrets and regret.

"I suppose they do," Helena sighed, gesturing for Athena to sit. "What brings the Goddess of Wisdom to my door at this ungodly hour?"

Athena remained standing, her fingers tracing the edge of the Resolute desk. "You know why I'm here. The Dark is rising, and we can no longer afford to be at odds."

Helena's jaw clenched. "And whose fault is that? Your kind brought this chaos to our world."

Athena's voice dripped with a searing venom that burned through the air like acid. "Need I remind you, Helena, of your true divine lineage? Or have you conveniently forgotten that you were once my adopted daughter, saved from death by my own godly blood coursing through your veins?" Athena's eyes flashed with furious disappointment and betrayal.

Athena's chest tightened as she stood in front of Helena. The tension between them was palpable, and Athena could feel years of resentment and hurt simmering just beneath the surface. She remembered all the times they had argued about Athena's true identity, and how Helena had ultimately chosen to leave Athena's protective care. But now, as she looked at Helena, Athena couldn't help but feel a sense of pride for what her adopted daughter had achieved. Despite all the

challenges and doubts, Helena had worked hard and carved out a successful life for herself.

Helena's shoulders sagged. "What would you have me do? I'm just one woman trying to hold a nation together."

"You're more than that," Athena said softly, her anger giving way to something like pity. "You're a bridge between two worlds. We need that now more than ever."

As the two women faced each other, the weight of their shared history hung heavy between them. Athena could almost taste the bitterness of old wounds, feel the ache of lost trust.

"Tell me more about the attacks," Helena said at last, her voice barely above a whisper. "What aren't you telling me?"

Athena's lips curved into a grim smile. "It's not what I'm not telling you, Helena. It's what you've refused to see."

Outside the window, a shadow shifted. Luke Laufeyson pressed himself against the cool stone of the White House, his ears straining to catch every word. A wicked grin spread across his face as he listened to the goddesses lay bare their vulnerabilities.

Oh, how the mighty have fallen, he thought, relishing the delicious irony. To think, the fate of the world resting in the hands of these broken deities.

As Athena and Helena continued their tense discussion, Luke's mind whirled with possibilities. Every secret revealed, every fear confessed, was another piece in his grand design. He would use their discord to sow chaos, to bring about the very darkness they sought to prevent.

For in the coming storm, Luke knew, lay his chance to reclaim what was rightfully his. Power. Glory. Vengeance.

And he would stop at nothing to seize it.

Athena's piercing grey eyes narrowed as she leaned in, her voice a low, urgent whisper. "We need allies, Helena. Powerful ones. The kind that can stand against both celestial and infernal forces."

Helena's fingers trembled as she gripped the edge of her desk, knuckles white. "Who do you suggest? The remaining Greek pantheon is scattered, weakened. And I can't exactly put out a call for supernatural aid without raising suspicion that I lost my mind."

A cold smile played across Athena's lips, a glimpse of the ruthless strategist that lurked beneath her mortal guise. "There are... other options. Entities that exist in the shadows between realms. Dangerous, yes, but potentially invaluable."

The president's face paled. "You can't mean—"

"I do," Athena cut her off, her tone brooking no argument. "The stakes are too high for squeamishness, Helena. Marcus Taser's ambitions threaten not just Rashford, but the whole of the world."

As the weight of their decisions hung in the air, suffocating in its intensity, the scene shifted abruptly.

Goddard Greening stumbled through the darkened streets of Rashford, his breath ragged and heart pounding from the recent escape. His mind raced with fragmented images of the zombie attack, each step echoing with the dread of pursuit. The heaviness of the night hung over the town like a suffocating shroud, the oppressive silence compounded by the knowledge of the unseen horrors lurking nearby.

The flickering streetlights cast long, ominous shadows across the deserted sidewalks, the

shadows dancing grotesquely as if imitating the carnage that had just transpired. Every creak of a loose windowpane or rustle of a restless tree branch sent chills down Goddard's spine, his senses heightened to an almost unbearable degree. In the distance, he could swear he heard the distant moaning of the undead, the hairs on his neck standing on end.

Goddard took refuge in a shadowy alleyway, pressing his back against the damp brick wall, his chest heaving as he struggled to catch his breath. He clutched the bloodied letter opener tightly in his trembling hand, the evidence of his recent, violent acts even though against the zombies, weighing heavily upon his conscience. The blood on his hands, the blood of his fallen friends' fathers —literal and metaphorical—would haunt him for eternity.

The cobblestone streets of Rashford, usually bustling with the laughter of children and the chatter of gossiping housewives, were now silent, an eery testament to the darkness that had descended upon the once-peaceful town. Goddard closed his eyes, trying to block out the horrific visions, but they remained etched into his mind's eye, seared into his very soul.

Taking a deep, shaky breath, he emerged from the alley, his steps measured and calculated as he

made his way towards the relative safety of his mansion. The night air was heavy with the scents of the coming storm, the electricity in the air prickling his skin. The rain would wash away the physical evidence of the night's horrors, but not the stain on his own tainted soul.

He reached the iron-wrought gates of a mansion that seemed to be pulling him towards it. He hesitated. In the distance, a pack of zombies shuffled past, their lifeless gazes cast toward the heavens as if in silent prayer. Goddard steeled himself, the weight of the world resting on his shoulders.

He walked past the gates of the mansion and tried the door. It was open. Entering the mansion, he slammed the door shut behind him, the ancient locks clicking into place with a satisfying thud. The grandfather clock in the hallway struck midnight, its mournful chimes echoing through the empty halls. He lit a candle, the flickering flame casting grotesque shadows upon the walls, as if the very house itself was trying to escape the terrors that lurked outside.

"By all that's holy," Goddard murmured, his usually eloquent speech reduced to a breathy whisper. The wind whipped around him, tugging at his once-immaculate suit, now torn and bloodied from his harrowing escape.

As he approached, memories of his father's cryptic warnings about the mansion flooded his mind. The political machinations, the secrets whispered behind closed doors – all of it seemed to converge on this very spot. Goddard's heart raced, torn between the urge to flee and an insatiable curiosity that had always been his weakness.

Upon reaching the mansion's entrance, Goddard hesitated, a battle between curiosity and caution raging within him. The air grew thick with anticipation, charged with an energy that made the hairs on the back of his neck stand on end.

"Come now, Goddard," he chided himself, attempting to summon his usual charm. "Surely this can't be more daunting than facing the board of the Rashford Cultural Society."

But as he raised a trembling hand to knock on the heavy wooden door, adorned with intricate carvings that seemed to writhe in the dim light, Goddard couldn't shake the feeling that he stood on the precipice of something far beyond his understanding. The weight of his family's legacy, his secret love for Jamie, and the horrors he had just witnessed all pressed down upon him, threatening to crush his resolve.

"What secrets do you hold?" he whispered to the imposing structure, his refined accent wavering. "And am I prepared to face them?"

With a deep breath, Goddard steeled himself, his knuckles poised mere inches from the door. In that moment, suspended between worlds, he felt the full weight of his decision. To knock was to invite the unknown, to embrace a destiny he couldn't fathom. To turn away was to condemn himself to ignorance, perhaps dooming not only himself but all of Rashford.

The storm above intensified, as if nature itself held its breath in anticipation of Goddard's choice.

Goddard's knuckles rapped against the door, the sound swallowed by an oppressive silence. Seconds stretched into an eternity as he waited, his heart pounding a frantic rhythm against his ribs. No answer came.

"Curious," he murmured, his refined accent tinged with trepidation. "Perhaps the owners are out for tea."

His attempt at levity fell flat, echoing hollowly in the eerie stillness. With a steadying breath, Goddard reached for the ornate handle, its cold metal sending a shiver through his fingers. To his surprise, it turned easily, the door swinging open

with a plaintive creak that seemed to reverberate through his very soul.

A dimly lit hallway stretched before him, shadows dancing at the edges of his vision. The air was thick with anticipation, carrying a faint scent he couldn't quite place—something ancient and otherworldly.

"Well, Goddard," he whispered to himself, "in for a penny, in for a pound."

As he stepped across the threshold, a wave of serenity washed over him, so sudden and complete that it nearly brought him to his knees. The chaos of the outside world—the zombies, the demise of his friends, the terror that had driven him here—faded like a distant nightmare.

Goddard paused, allowing the tranquillity to envelop him. His senses, usually attuned to the subtle nuances of Rashford's high society, now strained to capture every detail of this mysterious sanctuary. The walls seemed to pulse with an otherworldly energy, whispering secrets just beyond his comprehension.

"What are you?" he breathed, running his fingers along the smooth surface of a nearby pillar. "And why do I feel as though I've come home?"

The question hung in the air, unanswered yet pregnant with possibility. Goddard knew he should

be afraid, should be running from this place that defied all logic. Yet he found himself drawn deeper into the mansion's embrace, his refined tastes and cultural sensibilities awakening to something far grander than he had ever imagined.

Goddard's footsteps echoed softly as he ventured further into the mansion's depths. The intricate architecture captivated him, each corner and shadow seeming to whisper secrets of an ancient past. Ornate carvings adorned the walls, depicting scenes that stirred something primal within him—battles between gods and monsters, love affairs that shook the heavens.

"Extraordinary," he murmured, tracing a delicate finger along a frieze of what appeared to be the ancient Greek god Apollo fleeing from some unseen pursuer. "Is this... history?"

The air shifted, carrying a scent that made Goddard's head swim. It was faintly metallic, like ozone after a lightning strike, but undercut with something warm and inviting. He inhaled deeply, feeling it curl through his lungs and settle in his bones.

Why does this feel so familiar? he wondered, a fragment of memory tugging at the edges of his consciousness.

His exploration led him to a grand room that took his breath away. Flickering light from unseen sources danced across the walls, casting shadows that seemed to move with purpose. In the centre stood a coffee table, its surface gleaming with an otherworldly sheen that both attracted and repelled his gaze.

"My God," Goddard breathed, approaching the table cautiously. "What manner of place is this?"

He circled the table, noting how the light seemed to bend around it, as if reality itself was warping in its presence. A part of him—the practical, refined socialite—screamed to flee, to return to the comfortable world of galas and charity events. But a deeper part, one he'd long suppressed, urged him forward.

"I shouldn't be here," he whispered, even as his hand reached out toward the table's surface. "Jamie would never approve. But then... Jamie isn't here, is he?"

The thought of his unrequited love sent a pang through Goddard's heart, mixing with the intoxicating atmosphere of the room. He felt himself teetering on the edge of some great revelation, the air thick with potential and danger in equal measure.

As Goddard's gaze swept across the table's surface, his breath caught in his throat. There, gleaming in the otherworldly light, lay a dagger of such exquisite craftsmanship that it seemed to defy mortal creation. Its gothic design spoke of ancient secrets and forgotten power, captivating Goddard's refined sensibilities.

"Extraordinary," he murmured, his voice barely above a whisper. "It's as if it were forged from the very essence of night itself."

Goddard's fingers twitched at his sides, longing to trace the intricate patterns etched into the blade. The dagger's hilt was adorned with twisting serpents, their eyes glinting with wicked intelligence. Along the blade, arcane symbols danced and shifted, seeming to pulse with a life of their own.

He leaned closer, his heart racing. "What are you trying to tell me?" he asked, addressing the dagger as if it could respond. "What secrets do you hold?"

The room around him faded into insignificance as the dagger's allure grew stronger. Goddard found himself drawn inexorably closer, his usual caution giving way to an almost hypnotic fascination. The blade seemed to whisper promises of power, of answers to questions he hadn't even known to ask.

This is madness, a part of him thought. But the thought slipped away like smoke, replaced by an overwhelming desire to understand the mysteries before him.

"You're more than just a weapon, aren't you?" Goddard breathed, his eyes locked on the dagger's gleaming surface. "You're a key to something… something beyond my wildest imaginings."

Goddard's hand trembled as he extended it, fingers hovering mere inches above the dagger's hilt. The air around him vibrated with an unseen energy, prickling his skin. A low, melodic hum filled his ears, as if the dagger itself were singing to him in an ancient, forgotten tongue.

"I can feel you," he whispered, his refined accent tinged with awe and a hint of fear. "You're alive, aren't you? In your own way."

The dagger didn't move, yet Goddard sensed an acknowledgment, a connection forming between them. His mind raced with fragmented images: blood-soaked battlefields, secret rituals performed under starless skies, and the haunting visage of a being that could only be described as divine chaos incarnate.

Lord God, he thought, the name bubbling up from the depths of his consciousness. *Is this... your doing?*

A chill ran down his spine as he contemplated the implications. The recent zombie attack, the whispers of dark forces gathering strength, the uneasy memory of the SUV woman disposing of his friends through sex – could this dagger be the thread that tied it all together?

"If I take you," Goddard said, his voice barely audible, "what price will I pay? What will you demand of me?"

The dagger remained silent, but the air around it seemed to pulse with promise and threat in equal measure. Goddard's fingers inched closer, hovering just above the hilt, caught in a moment of exquisite tension.

Jamie, he thought suddenly, the image of the Mayor's son flashing in his mind. *What would he think of this?*

Goddard's hand trembled, then slowly withdrew. He took a step back, his breath ragged, as if he'd run for miles. The dagger's allure still thrummed through his veins, an intoxicating whisper of power and secrets.

"No," he murmured, clenching his fists. "Not like this. Not without understanding."

The room's oppressive silence seemed to close in around him, the shadows deepening in the corners. Goddard's refined sensibilities, honed by years of navigating Rashford's complex social and political landscape, screamed at him to flee. Yet a part of him, awakened by the night's horrors, yearned to seize the dagger and plunge headlong into the unknown.

He turned away, his gaze sweeping the ornate room. "What other secrets do you hold, I wonder?" Goddard mused aloud, his voice carrying a blend of fascination and trepidation.

As if in response, a gust of wind rattled the windows, carrying with it the faint scent of incense and... something else. Something primal and unsettling.

Goddard's heart raced. "I should leave," he said, though his feet remained rooted to the spot. "I should find Jamie, warn the others about what's happening."

But even as he spoke, a newfound determination began to crystallize within him. The dagger had shown him a glimpse of a world beyond the veil of normalcy that shrouded Rashford. A world where Greek gods and dark forces vied for supremacy, where the very fabric of reality seemed to bend and twist.

"I can't simply walk away," Goddard realized, his voice gaining strength. "Not with zombies hunting me."

With a final, lingering glance at the dagger, he squared his shoulders and moved towards the door. The mansion's secrets might remain tantalizingly out of reach for now, but Goddard Greening was no longer content to remain a passive observer in the unfolding drama of Rashford's hidden world.

"I'll be back," he promised the empty room, his words carrying the weight of an oath. "And next time, I'll be ready for whatever truths you have to reveal."

He turned to leave but felt the dagger call to him again. Unable to ignore it, he wheeled round and grabbed it. As soon as it was in his hand, he took it out of the hilt. In that moment, Goddard's fear melted away. He was someone else.

Goddard's hand trembled as he pushed open the mansion's heavy oak door, the wind immediately assaulting him with a ferocity that nearly stole his breath. He stepped out into the maelstrom, the night air thick with the scent of ozone and decay.

"By all the gods," he whispered, his refined accent barely audible over the howling gale. "What have I stumbled into?"

The streets of Rashford, once so familiar, now seemed alien and threatening. Shadows danced at the edge of his vision, twisting into grotesque shapes that vanished when he tried to focus on them. The dagger's image pulsed in his mind, a siren call he couldn't silence.

A nearby streetlight flickered and died, plunging the area into darkness. Goddard's heart leapt into his throat as he heard a low, guttural moan from somewhere in the shadows.

"Who's there?" he called out, trying to keep the tremor from his voice. "Show yourself!"

Only the wind answered, its keening wail seeming to mock his fear. Goddard pressed on, each step carrying him deeper into the heart of a Rashford he no longer recognized. The dagger's memory burned bright in his mind, a beacon of hope—or perhaps damnation—guiding him through the encroaching darkness.

Scared beyond his wits he ran back to the mansion and slammed the door behind him.

Miles away, in a modest suburban home, First Gentleman, Martin Boyd, paced the living room floor. Each step echoed with a foreboding thud, matching the frantic rhythm of his heart. Something was wrong. Terribly, inexplicably wrong.

He paused by the window, peering out into the gathering dusk. The trees seemed to loom closer, their branches reaching like gnarled fingers towards the house. A shiver ran down his spine.

"Dad?" Llewellyn's voice drifted from upstairs. "Is everything okay?" Llewellyn was slender and shorter than most seventeen-year-olds, with delicate features and a slight frame. His dark tousled hair fell in soft waves around his face, highlighting his almond-shaped green eyes. He had a quiet presence, but his thoughts were sharp and clear like the ringing of a delicate wind chime. There was something mysterious about him, a pleasing quality in his movements that seemed to make time stand still.

His father swallowed hard, forcing a calm he didn't feel into his voice. "Everything's fine, son. Just... checking the locks."

But as he turned from the window, a flicker of movement caught his eye. For just a moment, he could have sworn he saw a face peering back at

him – inhuman, hungry, and filled with spiteful glee.

The sound of fragmented glass shattered the uneasy silence. Martin Boyd's blood ran cold as he heard Llewellyn's terrified scream from upstairs.

"Dad! Help!"

With a resolve born from parental instinct and courage drawn from depths unknown, Martin rushed towards the source of terror unfolding upstairs. As he reached the landing, dread gripped him in its icy talons at the sight that awaited him.

Grotesque figures shambled through Llewellyn's shattered window with an otherworldly grace that defied reality. Their decaying forms exuded an aura of malevolence that tainted the very air around them. In that breathless moment, Martin realized they were no mere zombies but harbingers of a darkness that threatened to engulf everything he held dear.

"Stay away from him!" Martin's voice thundered through the chaos, his fists lashing out at their twisted forms with a feral intensity. But for every foe he struck down, two more emerged from shadows unseen.

Llewellyn fought against their clammy grasp with all his might, his eyes wide with primal fear and

resilience born from unfathomable strength. "Dad! Please!" he called out from another room.

Desperation clawed at Martin's heart as he battled against impossible odds. Where was Llewellyn? Why had fate chosen this moment to unleash its wrath upon them? Questions swirled in his mind like ghosts seeking answers in an ever-darkening world.

The zombies converged on him with unyielding determination, their rancid breath suffocating any semblance of hope that remained. With brutal efficiency borne from an ancient malice long forgotten by mortal tongues, they dragged Martin towards an unknown fate—the rooftop looming ominously above them like a judge passing final judgment on guilty souls.

As they ascended towards the cold embrace of night sky above San Francisco's sprawling horizon, Martin's thoughts raced against time itself—a torrent of emotions crashing against stoic resolve in a battle for survival that transcended mere flesh and bone.

At last, they reached the roof's edge where Marcus Taser stood like a shadowy puppet master orchestrating this macabre dance with gleeful evil gleaming in his eyes.

"Ah, Mr Boyd," Marcus purred darkly. "You've played your part well... but all games must come to an end."

Martin's heart hammered within his chest—a defiant drumbeat beneath the cacophony of impending doom.

"Where is my son?" His voice rang out into darkness thick with treachery and deceit.

Marcus chuckled softly—an echo of deranged amusement reverberating through Martin's fragmented reality. "He is safe... for now. As for you..."

With a cruel flicker of his wrist, Marcus sentenced Martin to fate's cruel embrace as though casting off an unwanted cloak. The zombies released their grasp—betrayal writ large upon their lifeless faces—as Martin plummeted into freefall towards uncertainty far below.

In those final moments, suspended between sky and earth—between life and death—a maelstrom of emotions clashed within Martin's mind: fear entwined with defiance; despair mingling with fleeting hope; acceptance embracing rebellion.

The ground raced up to meet him—a yawning abyss hungry for souls lost amidst shadows that danced upon San Francisco's timeless streets—as darkness swallowed him whole and silence

reigned once more over a city haunted by its own secrets and sins.

On the rooftop, Marcus Taser smiled, satisfaction glinting in his eyes. The chessboard was set, the pieces in motion. And in the shadows of Rashford, ancient powers stirred, ready to wreak havoc on the once sleepy town.

Chapter 9

The ceiling loomed above Hermes like a murky ocean, its stark white colour pulsating with the rhythm of his heartbeat. Every breath he took sent tremors through his battered form, a constant reminder of the brutal ordeal he'd endured at Satana's priests' hands. The air was thick with the metallic scent of blood and antiseptic, assaulting his nostrils and filling his lungs with each laboured intake.

The beeping of machines echoed throughout the room, their monotonous chorus drowning out the distant murmurs of worried nurses and doctors. It was a cacophony of sound that threatened to overwhelm him, but he clung to it like a lifeline – a reminder that he was still alive.

His mind wandered through the labyrinth of memories, each one a jagged shard of glass etched into his consciousness. He recalled the ambrosia-scented halls of Olympus, now replaced by this sterile environment that surrounded him. He longed for the comfort of home, for the warm embrace of his loved ones, but they felt worlds away from where he lay.

Hermes clenched his fists, his eyes blazing with frustration. He strained to conjure a single spark of his godly power, but only felt a deep emptiness where his divinity used to reside. A sickening wave

of nausea washed over him, not just from the excruciating pain in his body, but from the overwhelming weight of his newfound vulnerability.

As he laid in his bed, staring up at the ceiling, he bitterly spoke to Aphrodite, the goddess of love. "Look how far I've fallen," he lamented. "I used to be a messenger of the gods, but now I am nothing but a broken shell." He couldn't help but feel conflicted about his current state and how it compared to his past glory.

"Don't you dare try to hide behind your humanity," Aphrodite seethed. "This is all on you and your eternal quest for sex, your reckless pursuit of carnal desires!" Her words were like fiery daggers, piercing through the air with righteous anger.

"I only want a companion," Hermes tried to answer weakly.

"Brother," Aphrodite pressed on. "A girl does not come under the name of Truly Scrumptious and offers you sex without knowing you. Not unless she's a slut or she's laying a trap."

The sharp click of the door opening jolted Hermes from his brooding. His gaze snapped towards the sound, and he was met with the sight of a nurse entering the room. Her steps were light and graceful, as if she were dancing on air. As she

drew closer, Hermes couldn't help but feel his breath catch in his throat. She was breathtakingly beautiful, her dark hair cascading down her shoulders in waves. Her face seemed to have been sculpted by the finest artisans, every feature perfectly proportioned and flawlessly symmetrical. But it was her eyes that truly captivated him - pools of midnight that held secrets darker than Tartarus itself. He found himself lost in their depths, unable to look away from the mysterious allure they held.

"Feeling any better, handsome?" she purred, her voice like a siren's call to Hermes.

"Not as long as I have to be away from you," Hermes replied with a smirk, trying his best to charm her.

The nurse's eyes sparkled with amusement as she checked his vitals. "Well, let me take care of that for you."

Her touch sent sparks flying through his body, and Hermes couldn't help but lean in closer to her.

As she fluffed his pillows and her hand grazed his chest, Hermes felt a tumultuous battle brewing within him. One part of him screamed to push her away, fearing a danger that he could not quite name. But another part - a darker, more primal part - was drawn to her like a moth to a flame,

craving the release and comfort she provided. In this sterile hospital room, Hermes was torn between two paths, each with its own consequences that would shape his destiny.

Aphrodite watched the nurse leave, her eyes narrowing as the door clicked shut. She turned to Hermes, her ethereal beauty marred by a scowl of disappointment.

With venom dripping from her words, she hissed in disdain, leaning dangerously close. The sickly sweet aroma of roses mixed with the stench of decay emanated from her, a reminder of the darkness that consumed her fractured divinity. "You pathetic fool," she sneered, "can't you see an opportunity when it is laid before you?"

Hermes shifted uncomfortably, wincing as pain lanced through his mortal form. "What are you talking about, Aphrodite?"

Her laughter echoed through the room, sharp and brittle like the shattering of glass. "Oh, my dear Hermes. Always so gullible, even after all these years." Her slender fingers caressed his jawline, her touch alternating between seductive and icy. "That nurse... she's completely infatuated with you." As she spoke, her lips curled into a sly smile, revealing rows of perfectly white teeth. The dim lighting cast shadows on her porcelain skin, making her appear both gorgeous and dangerous.

Hermes' mind reeled, caught between desire and confusion. "I don't understand."

"Of course you don't," Aphrodite sighed.

"What would you have me do?" Hermes asked.

"Seize it, Hermes. Claim what's rightfully yours."

Satana glided down the sterile hospital corridor, her lips curled in a wicked smile. The disguise of a nurse melted away, revealing her true form - a vision of dark beauty and spiteful grace. Her eyes, glowing with infernal light, danced with cruel amusement.

"Oh, Hermes," she purred to herself, her voice a silken caress laced with venom. "So eager, so desperate. Like a starving dog begging for scraps."

She paused at a window, admiring her reflection in the glass. Shadows seemed to coalesce around her, drinking in the fluorescent light.

"You poor, pathetic creature," Satana mused, tracing a sharp nail along her lips. "Once a god, now nothing more than a pawn in my game." Her laughter echoed softly, a chilling sound that sent nearby patients into fitful sleep.

As she continued her purposeful stride, Satana's mind whirled with possibilities. "The seeds are

planted," she thought, savouring each word. "Now to watch them grow into a garden of chaos and ruin."

Back in the hospital room, Hermes lay alone, his mind a tempest of conflicting emotions. Aphrodite's words echoed in his ears, mingling with the lingering scent of the nurse's perfume. He closed his eyes, trying to steady his racing thoughts.

"What am I doing?" he whispered to the empty room. The steady beep of the heart monitor seemed to mock him, a reminder of his newfound mortality.

Hermes clenched his fists, feeling a surge of determination. "No," he said, his voice growing stronger. "I won't be powerless any longer. I won't be forgotten."

With a groan, he pushed himself up, ignoring the protest of his aching body. His eyes fixed on the call button, glowing softly in the dim light.

"Time to reclaim what's mine," Hermes muttered, reaching for the button. As his finger hovered over it, he hesitated for a moment, a flicker of doubt crossing his face. But then he remembered the nurse's gentle touch, the promise of power in her eyes.

With trembling hands, he hit the button like it was a game-winning shot. "Game on," he hissed, a hint of determination in his eyes.

Satana, disguised as the nurse, sauntered back into his room.

"Want me to lend you a hand, sweetheart?" Her seductive proposition wrapped around him like velvet chains, her voice dripping with raw sensuality that sparked his primal instincts.

Once again, Hermes was rendered speechless. He wanted to hit himself into dialogue but all his muscles were frozen.

The nurse flashed a flirtatious smile and perched herself on his bed. "It must totally suck," she whispered, "being stuck here like a helpless little kitten... all alone, abandoned."

Hermes flinched at the word. "They haven't abandoned me," he protested, but even to his own ears, the words sounded hollow.

"No?" The nurse raised an eyebrow, her expression a perfect mask of concern. "Then where are they, this family of yours?"

A spark of anger flared in Hermes' chest. "They're busy. And Aphrodite's just been anyway," he muttered, but doubt gnawed at him. Why hadn't

Athena come? Why was he left here, alone and vulnerable?

The nurse leaned closer, her scent intoxicating. "Perhaps," she whispered, "they see you as a liability now. A fallen god, stripped of his powers... what use could you be to them?"

Hermes' throat tightened, tears pricking at his eyes. How did she know of his identity? How did she know he and his family were fallen gods? But above all, he was hurt by what he perceived as truth in her words. He wanted to deny it, to cling to his faith in his fellow deities, but the nurse's words wormed their way into his mind, feeding the resentment that had been simmering there since his fall from grace.

"Who are you?" he asked, his voice trembling.

The nurse's smile widened, revealing teeth that seemed just a touch too sharp. "Someone who understands, dear Hermes. Someone who can offer you so much more than they ever could."

As she spoke, shadows seemed to writhe in the corners of the room, and Hermes felt a chill creep up his spine. Part of him screamed danger, but another part – a darker, more desperate part – yearned to hear more.

Satana's fingers traced a line along Hermes' body, her touch electric, sending shivers cascading

through his body. He couldn't suppress a gasp, his skin tingling where she'd made contact.

"I can give you everything they've taken from you," she purred, her lips brushing his ear. "Power. Respect. Revenge."

Hermes' heart raced, desire and fear intertwining in his chest. "How?" he whispered, hating the weakness in his voice.

Satana's eyes glowed with an otherworldly light. "Embrace the darkness, Hermes. Let it fill the void they've left inside you."

His mind reeled, a maelstrom of conflicting emotions. Anger at his abandonment warred with loyalty to his kin. The allure of power clashed with the remnants of his moral code.

"You . . . you're her! Satana!" Hermes stammered, his resolve wavering. "I don't want your offers . . ."

Satana's laugh was low and seductive. "Oh, but I can see it in your eyes. The hunger. The desperation."

Hermes squeezed his eyes shut, trying to block out her words, but they echoed in his mind. Images flashed before him – the other gods, laughing at his weakness, revelling in their own power while he languished here, forgotten. But mostly, the fall of Olympus at the hands of the

Semite angels, the slaughter of his brothers and sisters and of his beloved father Zeus.

"They deserve to suffer," he muttered, hardly recognizing his own voice and ignoring all of his brother's advice.

Satana's smile was triumphant. "Yes, they do. And with my help, you'll make them pay."

As Satana's lips drew closer, their mouths finally met in a yearning embrace. Her tongue eagerly sought his own, roving and tasting each millimetre as though it were the last morsel of sustenance left in the world. Hermes matched her ardour, their tongues dancing and twining together in a fiery display of passion.

Slowly, she unbuttoned his pyjama shirt, fingers nimbly working the fabric until every inch of his chest was exposed. Her nails raked lightly over his skin, creating tingling trails that demanded possession. As she reached his waistband, her teeth nipped at his sensitive flesh to further assert her dominance.

Now nude before her, Hermes inhaled sharply as he felt Satana's fingertips dance around his areolas, eventually leading her tongue to encircle his taut nipples. She teasingly licked and flicked at them, causing them to harden with a shuddering need for more.

As their eyes locked, Satana undressed and playfully wrapped her fingers around Hermes' hard shaft. She firmly but gently stroked him from base to tip, savouring the feel of his pulsating veins and the wetness of his desires. Each stroke brought him ever further towards the precipice of ecstasy as she maintained a smouldering gaze that seemed to burn straight through to his soul.

Pressing their bodies together, an electric current of heat coursed through their intertwined forms as if they were two magnets drawn towards each other by some unseen force. With one swift motion, Satana hooked her leg behind his thigh, drawing him irresistibly towards her welcoming centre. As Hermes positioned himself under her, at her entrance, they both gasped at the breathless anticipation that coursed through their veins like wildfire.

Seeing the urgency of desire on his face, she reached down and guided him inside her slick entrance. Their bodies moved together in a primal rhythm—her urging harmonizing with her relentless thrusts as she began to pump him with an animalistic ferocity. Her hips rose to meet each thrust, her breasts bouncing wildly with each impact as they moaned and groaned in unison.

Their movements became more frantic, their skin slick with sweat and passion as they struggled to

hold back their climaxes. Hermes' hands gripped tightly onto Satana's hips as he began to thrust harder and faster, their bodies slamming together with an intensity that left them both panting for air. But just as it seemed like they were on the cusp of release, Satana dug her nails into his back and arched her hips upwards, pushing him deeper inside her than he had ever been before.

Hermes grunted and groaned, feeling the sensation of being buried completely inside Satana's tight warmth more overwhelming than anything he had ever experienced before. He felt a sudden rush of heat building up deep within him as he continued to thrust desperately into her with all his might. He could feel every inch of himself sliding in and out of her wetness as she whimpered and moaned above him, urging him on with a fierce intensity that matched his own.

It was then that Satana reached down between their bodies and began to stroke herself in time with his thrusts, pleasure coursing through every nerve ending as she felt herself beginning to near her own peak. As she cried out in delight, Hermes knew that he could hold back no longer; his body tensed up as he felt himself cumming deep inside her.

With a loud cry, he thrust into her one last time before collapsing, all strength syphoned out,

panting heavily as they both revelled in the delicious aftermath of their intense lovemaking session. Their hearts pounded against each other's chests as they lay there for several moments, caught up in the euphoria of their simultaneous climax and the powerful feeling of being one with each other at last.

"Embrace me, Hermes," Satana urged, her voice a velvet caress against his ear. "Let us dance together in the shadows of our desires."

Hermes felt an electric surge course through him, his heart pounding with a mixture of fear and exhilaration. "I am yours," he replied, his voice husky with passion.

Satana's lips curved into a knowing smile as she traced a finger along his jawline, sending shivers down his spine. "Surrender to me completely, my love," she whispered, her gaze piercing into his soul. "Offer me your soul and body to possess. Let Satana be your mistress. I will give you the power to rule over your family and rise against Yahweh."

With a trembling breath, Hermes closed his eyes and gave himself over to her completely. "I am yours completely," he whispered. In that moment, she devoured his soul. As their souls and bodies merged together in raw ecstasy, a profound transformation took place within Hermes. A primal bond formed—sealed with blood and

shadows—bestowing upon him a newfound understanding of the world's inner workings. The surge of power that flowed through his veins was heady and intoxicating, forever binding them together in ways that transcended the physical realm.

Satana's laughter echoed in his mind. "Now, my love. It's time to pay your family a visit."

Hermes grinned, a predatory gleam in his eyes. "With pleasure."

The Mansion loomed before him, once a sanctuary, now a prison to be shattered. As Hermes slinked through the shadowy hallways, his lean, taut frame moved with a predatory grace. His piercing gaze, sharp as a blade, swept over his surroundings with a calculating hunger, ready to strike at any moment. The faint sound of his soft footfalls echoed off the cold stone walls, a haunting rhythm that spoke of danger lurking in the darkness. The air was heavy with the acrid scent of sweat and anticipation, mingling with the metallic tang of hidden weapons concealed beneath his dark cloak. Each breath he took seemed to draw in the very essence of treachery and deceit, infusing his being with an aura of malevolence that struck fear into the hearts of all who dared to cross his path.

The atmosphere became heavy with apprehension, the walls almost seemed to shiver in anticipation of the impending tempest. The acrid scent of his presence lingered in the air, a dark cloud of foreboding that wrapped around the onlookers like a suffocating cloak. The flicker of torches cast eerie shadows on his sharp features, emphasizing the predatory glint in his cold, calculating eyes. Every whispered breath sent chills down the spines of those who dared to witness his menacing presence, a harrowing reminder of the darkness lurking within his very being.

"How the mighty have fallen," Hermes mused, trailing his fingers along a marble bust of Zeus. It toppled with a satisfying crash. "Hide while you can, 'family.' Your reckoning has arrived."

The sound of shattering marble reverberated through the halls, a clarion call of destruction. Hermes' lips curled into a cruel smile as he heard the panicked shuffling of feet and hushed whispers.

"Come out, come out, wherever you are," he sang, his voice dripping with malice.

With inhuman speed, he burst into the grand atrium. Aphrodite screamed, backing away in terror. "Hermes? What are you doing here?"

He cocked his head, studying her like a wolf eyeing its prey. "I've been... enlightened, dear sister. Care for a demonstration?"

Aphrodite scrambled backward, fear prickling her skin. "Hermes, what's gotten into you?"

Hermes smirked, a predator ready to strike. "Time for a lesson, sister." In a flash, he lunged, his strikes hitting hard and fast. Aphrodite's cries rang out as she was thrown against a wall with a resounding thud. The room echoed with the sound of splintering wood.

Their bodies clashed violently, the air thick with the sounds of grunts and crashing furniture. Hermes moved with brutal intent, each strike finding its mark without hesitation. Aphrodite fought back fiercely, her voice cutting through the chaos.

Tension crackled in the air as they circled each other, movements precise and deadly. The fight escalated into a whirlwind of violence and fury, leaving no room for mercy.

"Stop!" Aphrodite's plea was drowned out by the sounds of their battle. But Hermes was consumed by darkness, relentless in his assault.

"You cannot defeat me," Hermes snarled, his voice dripping with venom. "My mistress has granted me back my divine strength...and more."

"Your mistress?" Aphrodite gasped in disbelief.

"I serve Satana," he declared proudly. "I serve the darkness and its alluring power. I am her loyal servant."

Before Aphrodite could even process this betrayal, Hermes lunged at her with a ferocity that shook the very ground beneath them. In a matter of moments, their once grand chamber lay in ruins, the two powerful deities locked in a brutal battle for dominance.

Aphrodite reacted first. She stood up and fled the room, her body in a pain she had not experienced since the fall of the Greek pantheon at the hands of Yahweh and his angels.

Hermes slammed his fists on the table, causing plates and glasses to shake. "Who's next?" he roared, his eyes wild with bloodlust. With a fierce determination, he stormed out of the room, knocking over chairs and shattering vases as he made his way to his bedroom. The sound of splintering wood echoed through the house as he destroyed furniture in his wake.

As chaos engulfed the mansion, Athena watched from the shadows, her grey eyes narrowed in concentration. This was not the Hermes she knew – something sinister had taken hold of him.

"Athena," a sob escaped Aphrodite's lips as she knelt by her sister's side, "What has he done? He's allowed that vile demon to take over him." Tears streamed down her face, mixing with the blood from her battle with her brother.

"We need to contain him," she muttered, her mind racing through strategies. "But how to break this evil influence without harming him?" Her gaze fell upon an ancient urn, its surface etched with symbols of purification. A plan began to form, but she'd need help to execute it.

Her heart raced as she sprinted through the mansion's shadowy corridors, her footsteps echoing off the marble floors. The sounds of destruction grew fainter behind her, but the urgency in her chest only intensified.

"Dari-El!" she called out, her voice tight with desperation. "I need you, now!"

A shimmer of light coalesced before her, materializing into the form of a radiant being. The angel's wings unfurled, filling the hallway with a soft, ethereal glow.

"I sensed the darkness," Dari-El said, his voice resonating with celestial power. "Hermes has fallen under Satana's influence."

Athena nodded solemnly, her expression grave with determination. "We must perform an

exorcism, before it's too late. You are my only friend in the angelic host," she declared, her voice shaking slightly with urgency.

As they hurried back towards the chaos and destruction that had overtaken their once peaceful sanctuary, Athena's mind raced with questions. How had Satana breached their impenetrable defences? What if they couldn't save Hermes, one of their most revered members?

"I fear we may be out of our depth," she confessed to her companion, her usual confidence faltering in the face of such dire circumstances.

But Dari-El's hand on her shoulder was a source of comfort and strength, his touch warm and reassuring. "Have faith, Athena. The light can pierce even the deepest darkness," he reminded her with unwavering belief. And as they braced themselves for the daunting task ahead, Athena couldn't help but feel a glimmer of hope ignite within her once more.

Athena, Aphrodite and the angel Dari-El burst into the corridor leading to Hermes' room, now a battlefield of broken furniture and shattered divinity. Hermes stood in the centre, a dark aura pulsing around him.

"Brother," Athena called out, her voice steady despite her inner turmoil. "We're here to help you."

Hermes turned, his eyes black as pitch. "Help?" he snarled. "I've never felt more alive."

Dari-El stepped forward, his divine radiance casting eerie shadows across the ravaged hall. "Begin the ritual," he instructed Athena, his voice a mixture of urgency and celestial authority.

Athena's hands trembled as she retrieved a vial of holy water from her robes. The weight of their impending failure pressed upon her like a physical force. "Hermes, please," she pleaded, her voice cracking. "Fight this darkness within you."

Hermes merely laughed, a chilling sound that sent shivers down Athena's spine. "Oh sister, you have no idea how liberating this darkness truly is."

As Athena began to recite the ancient Greek incantation, Dari-El's voice rose in a harmonious counterpoint, his angelic tongue weaving intricate patterns of light in the air. The room thrummed with otherworldly energy, the very fabric of reality seeming to warp and bend around them.

Hermes writhed and snarled, his form flickering between his familiar visage and something far more monstrous. "You can't... save me," he growled through gritted teeth. "I don't want to be saved."

Athena's heart raced as she continued the ritual, her words gaining power and urgency. She could

feel the malevolent presence within Hermes resisting, pushing back against their combined efforts. But she could also feel her brother fighting back against her ritual and attempts to free him. Sweat beaded on her brow as she poured every ounce of her diminished divinity into the exorcism.

But something was wrong. The darkness within Hermes seemed to be growing stronger, feeding off their efforts rather than being repelled by them. Athena's eyes widened in horror as she realized their grave miscalculation.

In that moment of realization, Hermes struck. With inhuman speed, he lunged at Dari-El, his fingers elongating into razor-sharp claws. The angel barely had time to cry out before Hermes was upon him, tearing into his celestial form with savage glee.

Athena's screams echoed through the room, but it was in vain. She could only watch in horror as Hermes tore into Dari-El, cannibalizing his very being with a ravenous hunger. The air was filled with a ghastly wailing as Dari-El's form disintegrated, his holy light fading and extinguishing like a flickering flame being snuffed out by a merciless hand.

Athena's mind reeled, unable to fully process the horrific scene unfolding before her. This wasn't just possession – it was something far worse, far

more primal and terrifying. As the last echoes of Dari-El's light faded away, leaving nothing but a faint, ghostly afterimage, Athena felt a part of herself die along with him.

Hermes turned to face her, his eyes now glowing with an unholy light, the angel's blood dripping from his chin. "Oh, sister," he purred, his voice a twisted mockery of his former self. "You have no idea what you've unleashed."

"Hermes, remember our days on Olympus?" she tried. "Remember how we used to dance to the Muses' songs!"

Hermes hesitated for a moment, a distant memory somehow seeping through the darkness clouding his mind. A tear rolled down his cheek but immediately, he was thrown to the floor unconscious by Athena's unforgiving light.

Chapter 10

Athena looked at the form of her dear brother, still unconscious, now chained to his bed. Aphrodite, beside her, had helped her carry him there and secure him with chains at his wrists and ankles.

"What do we do now?" Aphrodite asked her sister.

"As much as I resent admitting it," Athena admitted, "only Apollo can cure him now." But Apollo was beyond her help at the moment.

She approached the body of her brother and whispered his name.

"Hermes, are you there?"

His dilated eyes fluttered open, his gaze vacant and estranged from the world he once knew. He writhed beneath unseen chains, his growls of animalistic rage softening to moans laden with an inescapable longing. His flesh became a battlefield of desire, pulsing with a craving that, though unseen, was irrefutably compelling. It was as if the ghostly figure of a temptress straddled him, her touch both tender and commanding, traversing his soul with waves of both agony and ecstasy.

This spectral intimacy, woven from shadows and whispers of silk against skin, painted a tableau of dark sensuality amid his torturous existence. Each

breath he drew was a gasp of both pain and pleasure, a testament to the complex interplay of suffering and satisfaction. The room around him seemed to pulse with a brooding life of its own—walls echoing with the faint chorus of distant cries, the air thick with the scent of rain-soaked earth and unspoken secrets.

In this realm where despair danced intimately with desire, he was both prisoner and willing participant in his own torment. The ethereal caresses that marked his flesh spoke of a love that was as cruel as it was sweet, forever binding him to this enigmatic enchantress whose presence was felt yet never fully seen. Through this dark seduction, he encountered the profound depths of hurt intertwined seamlessly with comfort—the two existing as one in a dance as old as time itself.

With a mighty tug he freed himself from the chains at his wrists and then tore those at his ankles. He jumped up from the bed, more werewolf than man. Athena's heart pounded in her chest, her mind racing to formulate a plan. But before she could act, Hermes lunged towards the window. The sound of shattering glass pierced the air as he crashed through, his lithe form silhouetted against the night sky for a brief, haunting moment.

"Hermes, wait!" Athena cried out, her voice cracking with desperation. She rushed to the

window, glass crunching beneath her feet, only to see his dark form disappearing into the shadows of Rashford's streets.

A wave of nausea washed over her as the full weight of their failure crashed down upon her. She gripped the windowsill, her knuckles turning white. "By the gods," she whispered, her voice trembling, "what have we done?"

Athena's mind reeled with the implications. The exorcism hadn't just failed; it had made things infinitely worse. Whatever dark force had taken hold of Hermes was now stronger, more dangerous. And it was loose in the mortal world.

As she stood there, paralysed by the enormity of their mistake, a chilling laugh echoed from the shadows across the street. Athena's head snapped up, her eyes narrowing as she caught sight of a familiar figure.

Luke Laufeyson stood beneath a flickering streetlamp, his sharp features twisted in a satisfied smirk. He met Athena's gaze and gave a mocking bow before melting into the darkness.

"Laufeyson," Athena hissed, her fists clenching. Of course he would be here, revelling in their misfortune. She could almost hear his gleeful report to Satana: "My lady, you should have seen

it. The great Athena, brought low by her own hubris. And Hermes? Oh, he's become something truly marvellous in his corruption."

The thought of Luke's treachery ignited a fire in Athena's chest, momentarily burning away her despair. She took a deep breath, steeling herself. The battle wasn't over – it had only just begun.

At the heart of the Darkness, Satana reclined on her obsidian throne, her eyes glowing with infernal delight as Luke finished his report. The air around them crackled with malevolent energy, thick with the scent of brimstone and forbidden incense.

"Oh, my dear Luke," Satana purred, her voice a seductive whisper that sent shivers down even the trickster's spine. "You've outdone yourself this time. The chaos we've sown... it's simply delicious."

Luke's lips curled into a wicked grin. "I live to serve, my lady. Though I must admit, watching Athena's face as her precious plan crumbled was a personal highlight."

Satana laughed, the sound like shattered glass. "I can only imagine. Now, tell me, how does our young Aodhán fit into this delightful web we're weaving?"

Luke's eyes gleamed with mischief. "Ah, the Eldar's bastard. He's the perfect pawn, isn't he?

So much power, so little control. I've been... nudging him, shall we say? Planting seeds of doubt, of rebellion."

"Mmm," Satana murmured, her fingers tracing patterns in the air. "And how does he respond to your... nudges?"

"Oh, he resists," Luke chuckled. "But the cracks are there. His faith in his own destiny – it's all so fragile. One good push, and it'll all come tumbling down."

Satana's eyes narrowed, a cruel smile playing on her lips. "And when it does, we'll be there to catch him. To mould him into something truly... magnificent."

As they spoke, the shadows in the Darkness seemed to deepen, writhing with anticipation. Luke felt a thrill of excitement mixed with a hint of fear. He'd allied himself with forces beyond even his comprehension, and part of him wondered if he'd gone too far this time.

But the allure of power, of chaos unleashed, was too strong to resist. He pushed aside his doubts and raised an imaginary glass. "To Aodhán, then. May he burn brightly before he falls."

Satana's laughter echoed through the Darkness, a promise of obscure and evil things to come. "Oh, my dear Luke. This is only the beginning. The stage

is set, the players are in motion. And when the curtain falls..." She trailed off, her eyes distant, seeing visions of a world remade in her image.

Luke suppressed a shudder. For a moment, he almost pitied Aodhán and the others caught in their web. Almost. But the die was cast, and there was no turning back now.

As the night deepened outside, Satana and Luke continued to plot, their alliance growing stronger with each passing moment. And somewhere in Rashford, blissfully unaware, Aodhán slept – dreaming of power and destiny, while darker fates gathered around him like storm clouds on the horizon.

Chapter 11

Llewellyn's wrists throbbed in agony as they were bound above the scorching fire, his fragile body exposed and helpless against the daily beatings from Marcus Taser's army of soulless zombies. But that was only a fraction of the horror. After lunch each day, Taser himself would join in on the torture, relishing in the anguish he inflicted by pressing lit cigarettes into Llewellyn's tender flesh and dousing him with searing hot oil. The young man could do nothing but scream and sob, barely given enough sustenance to survive. He pleaded for an explanation, but none was ever given. It seemed that Taser took pleasure in causing him pain without rhyme or reason.

The shadows in Meredith's farmhouse danced and writhed, cast by no earthly light source. Aodhán stood in the centre of the room, his boyish face a mask of wonder and trepidation. His fingers trembled as he extended his hand, wisps of ethereal energy coiling around his fingertips.

"Incredible," he whispered, watching as the shadows bent to his will, stretching and contorting into impossible shapes. The air crackled with potential, heavy with the scent of ozone and something older, more primordial. Satana was a formidable teacher, terrible but efficient. She had

helped him muster his powers and regain his memories. He was an Eldar from the realm of Nahomy in Elya. He had seeped through to this reality where everything was at his and his mistress' mercy.

Aodhán's heart raced. He could feel the power coursing through his veins, intoxicating and terrifying in equal measure. *Is this what it means to be an Eldar?* he wondered, a mixture of awe and fear churning in his gut.

From the darkest corner of the room, a silky voice purred, "Don't hold back, my dear. Let it flow through you."

Satana emerged from the shadows, her eyes gleaming with predatory intensity. She glided towards Aodhán, every movement a calculated seduction.

"I... I don't know if I should," Aodhán stammered, his innocence palpable. "It feels... dangerous."

Satana's laugh was like broken glass. "Of course it's dangerous. That's what makes it exhilarating." She circled him, her words a poisonous caress. "You have so much potential, Aodhán. Why constrain yourself?"

Aodhán's brow furrowed. "But Meredith said—"

"Meredith was a simple mortal," Satana interrupted, her voice dripping with disdain. "What could she possibly understand about your true nature? About the legacy you carry?"

The shadows pulsed, responding to Aodhán's conflicted emotions. He closed his eyes, trying to centre himself. "I don't want to hurt anyone," he said softly.

Satana's smile was razor-sharp. "Oh, my sweet boy. Don't you see? With power like yours, you could reshape the world. End suffering. Create paradise to your own liking." She leaned in close, her breath hot against his ear. "All you have to do is embrace who you truly are."

Aodhán's eyes snapped open, pupils dilated with a heady mixture of fear and temptation. The shadows surged, threatening to engulf the room entirely.

"I... I don't know," he whispered, his voice trembling.

Satana's eyes glittered with triumph. She had planted the seed. Now, she would watch it grow.

The mansion's silence enveloped Goddard Greening as he slumped in a secluded corner, his usually impeccable posture now a crumpled

testament to his grief. Shadows danced across his face, accentuating the haunted look in his eyes as he stared unseeing at the ornate patterns on the worn carpet.

His fingers twitched restlessly, longing for the comforting touch of his father's hand. But Jeff Greening was gone, along with so many others. Goddard's chest tightened, a suffocating weight of loss pressing down on him.

The creak of the door startled Goddard from his reverie. He looked up, his heart racing, only to freeze in horror at the sight of Aphrodite gliding into the room. Her ethereal beauty was marred by the memory of what she had done to his companions.

"Stay back!" Goddard cried, scrambling to his feet, his eyes wild with fear. With one swift motion, he unsheathed the dagger and pointed it towards Aphrodite. "Don't... don't touch me!"

Aphrodite halted, her expression softening with sorrow. "Goddard," she said, her voice a melody tinged with remorse, "I mean you no harm. That . . . that dagger . . . that is the dagger of Ares. It is a mighty weapon, one that does not allow anyone to touch it. You must be Ares' chosen."

"What are you on about?" Goddard seethed, keeping the dagger pointed firmly at Aphrodite.

"You're just trying to lure me as you lured the others."

"That hunger has passed, for now," Aphrodite replied, her tone exasperated.

Goddard pressed himself against the wall, his breath coming in ragged gasps. "How can I trust you? I saw what you did to them... their bodies just... just..."

"Disintegrated," Aphrodite finished, her own voice heavy with guilt. "I know. And I will carry that burden for eternity. But right now, Goddard, we have a greater threat to face."

Despite his fear, Goddard found himself riveted by her words. He swallowed hard, torn between his instinct for self-preservation and the pull of his innate sense of duty.

"What... what do you mean?" he asked cautiously.

Aphrodite took a slow step forward, her movements deliberate and non-threatening. "The darkness that threatens Rashford grows stronger by the moment. We need allies, Goddard. We need your keen mind and your unwavering spirit."

Goddard's eyes narrowed, suspicion warring with hope. "And how do I know this isn't some trick? Some ploy to lure me in?"

A sad smile graced Aphrodite's lips. "You don't. But look into your heart, Goddard. You know the truth of what's coming. Can you truly stand aside and do nothing?"

The weight of her words settled over Goddard like a shroud. He closed his eyes, remembering his father's lessons on duty and sacrifice. When he opened them again, there was a flicker of resolve amidst the fear.

"Who are you?" he asked at last. "Really."

Aphrodite smiled. "We are what remains of the Hellenic Pantheon after the war with Yahweh's host of angels."

"You're gods!" Goddard gulped in disbelief.

"Yes," Aphrodite replied seductively. "We know secrets that transcend the human mind. And right now, we are facing a new struggle. Do you want to know what's going on?"

"Tell me," he said softly, "tell me everything."

The inferno roared around Apollo, a relentless onslaught of pain that threatened to consume him. But it was not just his physical body that burned; his mind was ablaze with terror and protective instinct as he fought against the inevitable.

"No!" he roared, his voice hoarse from screams. "I won't let it happen. I won't."

Through the flames, visions of Aodhán flickered before his eyes. The innocent boy's face twisted into a dark entity, his eyes blazing with malicious power. Apollo's heart constricted.

"He's just a boy," he gasped, struggling against his restraints. "But one with the power to destroy worlds."

In an instant, the fire coalesced into a vortex, revealing a realm of chaotic darkness beyond. At its centre stood a figure, both familiar and otherworldly.

"Who... what are you?" Apollo breathed, transfixed by the sight.

The figure turned, its features shifting and writhing like liquid shadows. When it spoke, its voice echoed with an unfathomable weight that shook Apollo to his core.

"I AM WHAT YOUR PRECIOUS AODHÁN WILL BECOME," it declared. "I AM THE DARK, THE EMBODIMENT OF AN ELDAR'S POWER AND PURPOSE."

Fear seized Apollo's entire being. "No... it can't be."

The Dark's laughter was a cacophony of madness that sent chills down Apollo's spine. "OH, BUT IT IS. AND SOON, AODHÁN WILL JOIN ME IN THIS EXQUISITE OBLIVION."

Rage surged within Apollo. "I won't let you take him," he growled, straining against his bonds. But beneath his defiance, doubt began to creep in. Could he truly stand against such overwhelming power?

The Dark rippled with amusement. "YOU? A FALLEN GOD, BOUND AND BURNING? YOU ARE NOTHING BUT ASH IN THE WIND OF WHAT IS TO COME."

With closed eyes, Apollo fought back tears of frustration and fear. When he opened them again, a steely resolve burned in their depths.

"You underestimate the power of the pantheon," he declared.

The Dark's response was cut short as the vision faded, leaving Apollo alone once more with the engulfing flames. But now, armed with the knowledge of what truly threatened Aodhán, his determination hardened like forged steel.

Aodhán's fingers trembled as he traced patterns in the air, wisps of ethereal energy dancing at his fingertips. The farmhouse creaked and groaned around him, as if straining under the weight of his burgeoning power. A sudden pulse of energy rippled through the room, causing the shadows to writhe and contort.

"Did you feel that?" Aodhán whispered, his eyes wide with a mixture of awe and trepidation. "It's like... like the world just shifted."

Satana's silky laugh sent shivers down his spine. "Oh, my dear boy," she purred, her eyes gleaming with malevolent delight. "That's just the beginning. Imagine what you could do if you truly embraced your potential."

Aodhán's heart raced, torn between the intoxicating rush of power and the nagging voice of conscience. "But I... I don't want to hurt anyone," he stammered, even as tendrils of darkness curled lovingly around his wrists.

"Hurt?" Satana scoffed, her voice dripping with disdain. "You speak of harm when you could reshape reality itself. Why limit yourself to the petty morality of lesser beings?"

As she spoke, Aodhán felt a deep, primal hunger stirring within him. It whispered of untold wonders, of worlds reshaped by his will. Yet

beneath the seductive promises lurked a terrifying void, threatening to consume all he held dear.

"I'm not sure I'm ready for this," Aodhán murmured, his voice barely audible. But even as the words left his lips, he felt the addictive pull of power coursing through his veins.

Satana's smile was razor-sharp. "Oh, but you are, my dear. You were born for this. Why deny your true nature? You yearn to reshape the universe to your will. To make life your subject and bring the light to its knees before the darkness so that there will be peace for all."

Aodhán closed his eyes, fighting against the conflicting emotions raging within him. When he opened them again, there was a new resolve in his gaze. "I need time," he said softly. "To understand, to learn."

"Of course," Satana cooed, her voice a venomous lullaby. "Take all the time you need. I'll be here, waiting to show you the true depths of your power."

As Aodhán grappled with his inner turmoil, elsewhere, Apollo found himself ensnared in a dream unlike any other...

The dream enveloped him like a shroud, transporting him to a realm neither here nor there. The fire faded, replaced by a fireplace in a cozy bedchamber he quickly recognised. Around him, he felt the familiar, comforting embrace of Micha-El's arms. The archangel's wings unfurled around them, casting the shadows of a thousand eons on the bedchamber's walls.

"It's time to react, pet," Micha-El's voice came behind him.

As the celestial chains round Apollo's wrists splintered into thin air. his lips met Micha-El's, his favourite celestial plaything, in a searing kiss that ignited a wild heat. Micha-El traced a trail of tantalizing kisses from Apollo's neck to his chest, sending shudders of pleasure coursing through his body. Apollo gasped as their rigid cocks brushed against each other, the sensation too overwhelmingly potent, leaving him gasping for more.

As Micha-El teased and licked at Apollo's nipples, he felt a surge of ecstasy wash over him when their hardened shafts pressed against one another. The archangel took his time, savouring every gasp and shudder from the god beneath him. His hands roamed down to cup Apollo's ass cheeks, pulling him closer into the intense

embrace. Their pelvises ground together in rhythm with their desire-driven breathing.

Apollo moaned softly into Micha-El's mouth, lost in the throes of passion as the archangel pushed him against the wall behind them. He felt himself being lifted off the floor by an unseen force as if weightless, carried by divine power alone. With each thrust against his entrance, Apollo could feel himself sinking deeper into a pleasure so intense it bordered on painful bliss.

Micha-El bit down lightly on Apollo's shoulder before growling low in his ear, "I need you, my love." His hips snapped forward again, claiming what was his with unrestrained desire. Apollo whimpered at the feel of Micha-El's fingers digging into his hips possessively while thrusting harder into him. The god arched back as waves of pleasure crashed over him with each forceful entry from behind.

Micha-El's skilled hands explored Apollo's increasingly wet entrance with lustful intent before positioning himself at the gateway to Apollo's submission. With one determined thrust, Micha-El buried himself deep inside Apollo's writhing body - their cries joining in an intimate symphony. The memory of their first, forbidden encounter blazed to life in his mind—the shock of

Micha-El's celestial flesh against his own, the taste of ambrosia and eternity on their lips.

Their bodies collided in a sultry dance that defied the ages, each thrust a sin-riddled testament to the wild lust they were damned not to devour. Micha-El's worn fingers gripped Apollo's hips tightly as he drove into him, each movement leaving an imprint on his heated skin. Their eyes met, as old as the cosmos yet teeming with juvenile hunger, holding a hot cocktail of raw desire and sweet agony.

Micha-El's pace quickened, driving Apollo closer to the edge until they both hurtled over it together—cries of ecstasy shattering the silence of the ethereal realm.

In the throbbing pulse of his erotic dreamscape, Apollo knew this was nothing but a wicked tease, a deliciously sinful break from the frigid grip of reality and that Micha-El would never make himself flesh and blood for him. But hell, in that stolen moment of blistering tenderness, he gave in to the raw carnal pleasure of feeling Micha-El's sculpted body grinding against his own; their limbs tangled in a feverish dance.

As their shared lust surged towards its fiery peak, Micha-El moved closer. His hot breath grazed Apollo's earlobe like a sultry secret shared

between lovers. "Apollo, it's time to rise and shine."

Apollo's eyes snapped open, reality crashing down upon him with merciless force. The eternal fire that had consumed him for what felt like eons suddenly extinguished, leaving him gasping and disoriented. He collapsed to the ground, his flesh raw and blistered, smoke still curling from his ravaged form. His shackles reformed round his wrists and he writhed in response.

"You must free yourself," Micha-El whispered in his ear.

Apollo looked around but the archangel was nowhere to be seen.

"I can't free you myself," Micha-El's whispers came again. "It's something you must do – can do yourself. I've taken out the fire. But you must undo the chains."

Apollo took a deep sigh then concentrating all his remaining powers on the chains, reached for the power of the pantheon and smashed the chains to fragmented light.

Apollo fell to his knees. "Micha-El," he croaked, his voice a ragged whisper. The archangel's name tasted like ash on his tongue, a bittersweet reminder of their forbidden union and the salvation it had brought.

Struggling to his feet, Apollo's trembling hand reached for the windowsill as he struggled to stand. He caught a glimpse of his naked reflection in the thick, dusty glass and gasped at the sight. His once-handsome face was now barely recognizable, marred with deep scars and patches of melted flesh. The distorted features stared back at him, a grotesque mask that elicited a strangled sob from his throat. Reality hit him hard as he realized he may never again show his true face to the world, and his heart clenched with despair.

"What have I become?" he whispered, tracing the contours of his ruined face with trembling fingers.

The sound of heart wrenching sobs drew attention. Townspeople scattered before him, their eyes wide with horror and revulsion. Apollo felt a surge of shame and anger, his heart aching with the weight of their fear.

"Please," he called out, reaching towards a fleeing woman. "I mean you no harm!"

But his words fell on deaf ears. The crowd's terror was a palpable force, driving them away from the fallen god they once revered.

With each agonizing step, Apollo made his way towards the Mansion, his sanctuary in this mortal realm. The pain of his transformation was nothing

compared to the ache in his heart, the crushing loneliness that threatened to consume him.

As he approached the Mansion's ornate doors, Apollo's gaze fell upon a discarded mask lying in the shadows. Without hesitation, he snatched it up, securing it over his ravaged features.

"How fitting," he mused bitterly. "The god of light, hiding in darkness."

Stepping into the mansion's oppressive silence, Apollo felt a chill run down his spine. Something had changed in his absence, a malevolent presence seeping into the very foundations of the mansion. Some evil had been there, something that had destroyed the gods' sanctuary and brought it to its knees from its once majestic and gothic beauty.

"What new horror awaits us?" he wondered aloud, his voice echoing through the empty halls.

As if in answer, a cold wind swept through the mansion, carrying with it whispers of impending doom. Apollo shuddered, sensing the gathering storm of darkness that threatened to engulf them all. He remembered the vision he had received after drinking the Blood of the Vine. It was a warning. To him. And he had failed. He had not found the Eldar boy and now the boy had fallen to

darkness. And there was this Dark that hunted him like a vulture, ready to devour him and make him darkness itself. When that happened, not even Yahweh's host would be enough to fight the darkness.

A sudden realization washed over him, a wave of dread that threatened to drown him. "We are not prepared," he whispered weakly, his voice filled with despair. He stumbled to his room, the weight of his burden heavy on his shoulders. In the dim light of the candle, he beheld himself in the cracked mirror and recoiled in horror. He was but a shadow of what he once was, his body scarred and battered from burning in the eternal fire. His once-beautiful face now marred with deep lines, seared flesh and haunted eyes. He knew he could not allow anyone to see him like this.

With trembling hands, he donned a dark cloak and loose track suit trousers, trying to hide the evidence of his ordeal. But when he looked at himself again, he saw only a broken man staring back at him. Desperate to conceal his new image, he reached for a full-face mask from his bedside drawer. It was plain and unadorned, nothing like the majestic masks he used to wear at the Olympian festivities. As he pulled it over his features, he felt a surge of sadness and anger.

"This is who I am now," he muttered to himself as he fought back tears. "No one will be terrified at beholding me again." And with that thought, he resigned himself to hiding behind this mask forevermore.

Outside, the sky darkened ominously, as if nature itself cowered before the approaching evil. In the distance, a lone raven croaked ominously, its mournful cry a harbinger of the battle to come.

Apollo clenched his fists, determination warring with fear. "Let them come," he growled, his scarred lips curling into a defiant snarl beneath the mask. "I will face this darkness together with my brother and sisters or perish in the attempt."

He sat on his bed and closed his eyes. He reached for the power of the pantheon within. He felt it, still there and strengthening. In spite of his state, he grinned. He was still Apollo, a god of the Greek pantheon. Then a vision swept over him, pulling him into a short coma.

As night fell over Rashford, an insidious hunger stirred in the shadows, ravenous for power and souls. The stage was set for a confrontation that would shake the very foundations of reality itself.

Llewellyn's body hung in the darkness, his skin melted and dripping like candle wax. He writhed in agony as the flames licked at him, never relenting in their torture. The smoke that billowed around him took on a sinister form, twisting into grotesque figures that taunted and jeered at his pain.

But it was the voice of the Dark that truly terrified Llewellyn. Its chilling whisper promised to consume his very soul, using his powerful abilities for its own nefarious purposes. He fought against the chains that bound him, only managing to sear his skin even more.

And then Marcus Taser appeared, his eyes gleaming with sadistic pleasure as he revelled in Llewellyn's suffering. But as he drew nearer, a newfound power surged through Llewellyn, burning bright and blinding in its intensity. With one mighty burst of light, he repelled the Dark and sent Taser stumbling back.

Llewellyn gritted his teeth against the searing pain, his eyes blazing with defiance as he locked gazes with Marcus Taser. "You will never break me," he growled through clenched jaws, his voice laced with determination despite the agony coursing through his veins.

Taser's twisted smile widened at Llewellyn's words, a sick delight dancing in his eyes as he

regained his composure. "Oh, but I intend to," he hissed, the red-hot metal still clutched in his hand as he leaned in closer to the tortured figure hanging before him. "I will strip you of your power and watch as you beg for mercy."

The sinister figures formed by the smoke around them seemed to echo Taser's malevolent intentions, their eerie whispers taunting Llewellyn from all sides. But amidst the darkness and torment, a spark of resilience ignited within Llewellyn's soul.

"I won't be broken," Llewellyn declared, his voice ringing with an inner strength that seemed to shake the very foundations of the chamber.

Taser's laughter cut through the air like a jagged blade, sharp and cruel. "And yet here you are, chained and broken before me. I will break you and then feed you to my pet," he sneered, pressing the searing metal against Llewellyn's flesh once more, relishing in the renewed cries of anguish that pierced the oppressive silence.

As Llewellyn's body contorted in agony, a brilliant light began to emanate from within him, pushing back against the encroaching darkness with a force that seemed to defy all reason. In that moment of blinding radiance, Llewellyn's eyes blazed with a newfound resolve as he faced his tormentor head-on.

"My mother will have you thrown in jail for the rest of your miserable life," the surprised Llewellyn proclaimed, his voice resolute and unwavering

Marcus came back to himself and smiled maliciously. "Your mother will play her part soon enough," he smiled. "Why do you think I keep you alive?"

Chapter 12

The Pelian Forest of Elya was alive with the sounds of clashing steel and the grunts and chuckles of the two combatants. Turan's wings, jet black and menacing, unfurled dramatically as he deftly deflected Adnan's attack. The sunlight filtered through the leaves, casting an onyx glow on the glistening feathers. Beads of sweat dotted Adnan's brow, his lithe form moving with a fluidity that could easily be mistaken for a dance. Every movement was precise and graceful, a deadly choreography in this fierce battle among the trees.

"Looks like time's catching up with you, huh?" Adnan needled, his eyes dancing mischievously.

Turan's smirk was as sharp as his blade. "Oh, forgive me for not having your boundless energy, young prodigy."

As Turan gracefully dodged another strike, he couldn't help but quip, "Well, at least my wings haven't forgotten how to fly, unlike some people's feet around here!"

He lunged forward, his blade a silver blur. Adnan danced away, but not before Turan's sword nicked his arm. A thin line of crimson bloomed.

"First blood," Turan said, lowering his weapon. Concern creased his noble features. "Are you alright?"

Adnan waved him off, grinning. "It's nothing. You worry too much."

But Turan was already at his side, examining the wound with gentle hands. Adnan sighed, allowing the fussing. He knew it came from a place of love, even if it chafed at times. Still, a restlessness stirred in his chest, an itch that couldn't be scratched.

"We should head back to camp," Turan said. "Get this cleaned up."

Adnan's eyes were drawn to the dark, foreboding forest. He couldn't help but wonder what secrets and mysteries lurked within its ancient boughs. Part of him yearned to explore, to uncover the unknown wonders hiding in the shadows. But another part of him was hesitant, a sense of fear and uncertainty creeping up his spine. The conflicting desires left Adnan feeling both exhilarated and uneasy at the same time.

"Actually," he said, "I was thinking we could explore a bit further. Who knows what we might find?"

Turan's brow furrowed, his wings rustling uneasily. "It could be dangerous. We don't know what's out there."

"Exactly!" Adnan's eyes gleamed with excitement. "Where's your sense of adventure?"

Turan grumbled, "I must have misplaced it with my common sense." But Adnan could see the inner turmoil brewing within Turan's eyes and his longing for adventure. He knew this was his moment to pounce and exploit the situation.

"Come on, just a quick look. What's the worst that could happen?"

Turan sighed, a sound heavy with foreboding. "I have a feeling I'm going to regret this."

He trailed behind Adnan as they plunged into the undergrowth, leaves rustling and whispering secrets as they passed. The forest grew thick and dense, the sunlight filtering through the canopy above in dappled patterns. Shadows stretched and shifted despite the early hour, lending an eerie atmosphere to their journey. Somewhere in the distance, a bird cried out with a haunting call, its sound echoing through the trees and sending shivers down their spines. It almost sounded like a human cry, adding to the mysterious aura of the forest.

Adnan's heart raced, not with fear but with anticipation. What lay ahead? What marvels awaited them? He glanced back at Turan, saw the tension in his friend's shoulders, the way his hand hovered near his sword hilt.

"Relax," Adnan said. "We're perfectly safe."

But as the words escaped his trembling lips, a frigid shiver crept down his spine. His heart raced erratically as he thought he heard... something. A sinister whisper carried by the wind, beckoning for him to come closer. The hairs on his neck stood on end as a voice, barely audible, whispered his name in a haunting tone that sent chills down his entire body.

"Did you hear that?" he asked, voice hushed.

Turan shook his head, eyes scanning the forest. "Hear what?"

Adnan frowned, straining his ears. But the sound, if it had ever existed, was gone. He shrugged, pushing aside the faint unease. "Never mind. Must have been my imagination."

They trudged forward, oblivious to the piercing gazes that stalked them from the darkness. Little did they know, a malicious force was creeping closer, ready to ensnare them in its deadly grip.

The murmur of voices grew louder as they approached the lake, a vast expanse of dark water that seemed to swallow up the fading daylight. Adnan's skin prickled with goosebumps, whether from the biting cold in the air or the unsettling aura surrounding the lake, he couldn't tell. The surface of the water was like a mirror, reflecting the deepening shades of purple and orange in the sky

above. As they drew closer, Adnan could make out faint ripples on the water's surface, as if something unseen was lurking just beneath. A chill ran down his spine and he couldn't shake off the feeling that they were being watched by some otherworldly presence.

"Adnan," Turan's voice was low, tinged with worry. "Perhaps we should turn back. Something doesn't feel right here."

Adnan's mind was in a frenzy as he stood between his friend's worried gaze and the seductive whispers that lured him with promises of forbidden knowledge and irresistible temptations. He fought against the grip of curiosity, desperately trying to clear his head of the hypnotic whispers. But they persisted, whispering in his ear like a siren's call, until he could feel his resistance weakening with each passing moment.

"It's just a lake, Turan," he said, forcing a laugh that sounded hollow even to his own ears. "And I'm filthy from our sparring. A quick dip won't hurt."

Before Turan could protest further, Adnan boldly began peeling off his layers of clothing. The crisp air tickled his exposed skin, causing a wave of goosebumps to rise. He strolled into the water, its icy embrace encircling his calves and then gripping his thighs with an almost painful chill

"Be careful!" Turan called from the shore, wings rustling nervously.

Adnan's hand trembled as he raised it in a hesitant wave, his eyes fixated on the murky water. He could sense an eerie presence, as if the water itself was alive and watching him. The whispers intensified, transforming into sinister voices that seemed to beckon him closer. Adnan's heart raced as he struggled to make out the words, fearing what they might reveal about the mysterious force lurking beneath the surface.

"Come closer," they seemed to say. "Let us show you wonders..."

Adnan took a deep breath and dived into the cool, murky lake. He kicked his legs and pushed through the water with strong strokes. As he went further into the lake, he felt something brush against his legs. Something that felt like . . . hands? His heart pounded as he turned around, but there was nothing there.

Just as he started to relax, the surface of the lake began to ripple in front of him. A face emerged – stunningly beautiful, with eyes that seemed to hold an entire universe within them. Adnan's mouth fell open in awe as he gazed at this otherworldly being before him.

"Who-" he began, but the word was cut off as invisible hands grabbed his ankles and yanked him under.

The last thing he heard was Turan's desperate cry as the dark waters closed over his head.

Turan's heart dropped into his stomach as he watched Adnan disappear under the dark, icy water. Without a moment's hesitation, Turan dived in after him, his wings slowing his descent but making it difficult to swim. The water stung his skin like knives and he frantically scanned the murky depths for his friend

"Adnan!" he bellowed, his voice muffled by the water. The murky depths obscured his vision, panic rising in his chest like bile.

Suddenly, a haunting melody filled his ears, and the water around him began to glow with an ethereal light. Through the eerie luminescence, Turan saw her – the nymph, her otherworldly beauty both terrifying and mesmerizing. In her arms lay Adnan, pale and lifeless.

Turan lunged forward, but invisible tendrils of water held him back. "Release him!" he demanded, struggling against the magical bonds.

The nymph's laughter echoed like crystal bells. "Oh, sweet guardian," she cooed, her voice

somehow clear despite the watery realm. "Your friend is safe with me."

With a gentle touch, she pressed her palms against Adnan's chest and breathed deeply. As she exhaled, vibrant green energy flowed from her hands into his body. He gasped for air as his eyes slowly opened to meet hers, filled with awe and gratitude for the nymph who had saved him

"Turan," Adnan whispered, his voice dreamy. "Isn't she magnificent?"

Turan's relief at seeing Adnan alive quickly gave way to horror. The nymph's eyes glittered with triumph as she stroked Adnan's cheek.

Turan's thoughts were in a frenzy, his mind struggling to process the situation. "Is this even real?" he wondered. He knew he needed to protect Adnan, but how could he possibly fight against such a formidable force? The weight of responsibility and fear weighed heavily on Turan's shoulders as he searched for a way to save them both.

As if sensing his thoughts, the nymph turned her attention to Turan. With a flick of her wrist, she propelled him back towards the shore, where he landed in a soggy, trembling heap.

"Adnan, please," Turan called out weakly. "Don't trust her. We need to leave!"

But Adnan seemed entranced, floating blissfully in the nymph's embrace. "Why would I ever want to leave?" he replied, his voice thick with infatuation. "I've never felt so... complete."

Turan's heart sank. He had sworn to protect Adnan, but how could he save his friend from a danger the Eldar couldn't even see?

The nymph's eyes gleamed with otherworldly light as she caressed Adnan's face. "My love," she purred, her voice a haunting melody, "will you stay with me? Forever?"

Adnan's gaze locked onto hers, his expression one of utter devotion. "Yes," he breathed, the word hanging in the air like a death sentence. "I love you. I'll never leave your side."

Turan's wings rustled anxiously, his feathers damp and heavy. He struggled to his feet, fighting against the dread that threatened to consume him. "Adnan, please," he pleaded, his voice cracking. "Think about what you're saying. This isn't you!"

But Adnan seemed beyond reason, lost in the nymph's enchanting gaze. He turned to Turan, his eyes glazed with an unnatural sheen. "You don't understand, Turan. This is where I belong. This is my destiny."

Turan's mind raced, searching for a way to break the spell. He thought of the stern lessons from his

father, the weight of responsibility that had been drilled into him since childhood. How could he face his father if he failed to protect Adnan?

Turan's voice wavered as he spoke, torn between his duty to protect and his own desires. "I'll stay," he finally relented with a hint of reluctance, "but only to ensure your safety." Despite his words, his heart was in turmoil, unsure if he could truly keep his feelings for them in check.

The nymph's laughter rang out, cruel and beautiful. "Oh, loyal guardian," she mocked. "You think you can protect him from me?"

Turan squared his shoulders, his wings unfurling to their full span. "I swore an oath," he said, his voice low and dangerous. "I will not abandon my friend, even if it costs me my life."

As the sun began to set, casting long shadows across the mystical lake, Turan resigned himself to a vigil he feared would end in tragedy.

* * *

Miles away, in the heart of the Elfin Camp, Yrus paced anxiously, his brow furrowed with worry. Tamara watched him, her own concern etched deeply in her face.

"They should have returned by now," Yrus muttered, his fingers fidgeting with the hilt of his

sword. "Something's wrong. I can feel it in my bones."

Tamara nodded, her eyes scanning the darkening forest. "Adnan's always been reckless," she said softly, "but Turan... he knows better than to stay out after nightfall."

The tranquil surface of the lake shattered as the elf king Eldarion emerged from its depths, his ebony hair plastered to his face, eyes wild with the knowledge of what he'd seen. The nymph materialized before him, her ethereal beauty a stark contrast to the dread pooling in his gut.

"You've seen it, haven't you?" Her voice was a melodic whisper that sent chills down his spine. "The fate that awaits us all."

Eldarion's breath came in ragged gasps. "Adnan... his child... The Dark." The words tumbled out, fractured and disjointed.

The nymph's lips curled into a cruel smile. "Yes, the child. The one who will tip the scales."

Visions flashed before Eldarion's eyes: armies clashing, brother against brother, the very fabric of their world tearing apart. And at the centre of it all, a child born of Eldar and nymph, radiating power beyond comprehension.

"This civil war," Eldarion choked out, *"it will destroy us all."*

"Perhaps," the nymph mused. *"Or perhaps it will forge a weapon strong enough to pierce the heart of the Dark itself."*

Eldarion shuddered, torn between hope and horror. "And Adnan? Turan?"

The nymph's eyes glittered with malice. "They have their parts to play, as do we all."

* * *

In the secluded grove, Adnan lay entwined with the nymph, his once-vibrant eyes now glazed and distant.

In the shimmering glow of the moonlight, Adnan lay on the mossy ground, his body entwined with the nymph's. Her pale, ethereal skin contrasted with his own sun-kissed complexion as their bodies moved together in a primeval dance. The nymph's delicate hands caressed Adnan's shoulders, tracing patterns that set his skin afire. His fingers dug into the soft moss beneath him, frustration and lust warring within him.

"It's time," she purred, *her voice as intoxicating as honey-mead.*

Adnan's arousal betrayed him, throbbing against her thigh as she straddled him. "No... I... I don't...

want to die." His words came out ragged and breathless, at odds with his swelling desire.

Undeterred, the nymph leaned in and captured his lips in a deep kiss, her tongue invading his mouth with practiced finesse. Her hand closed around his erection, stroking him to full hardness. With a moan of surrender, Adnan gave in to the pleasure consuming him.

The nymph pressed herself against him, sliding her slick folds along his length, teasing them both with their impending union. Their hips rocked together in a primal rhythm as they became lost in each other's embrace. Her soft moans filled the clearing, spurring him on to greater heights of arousal.

As he felt himself approaching climax, Adnan tried once more to resist.

Hunched behind a thick oak tree, Turan peered through the leaves at the happy couple frolicking in the meadow. His chest tightened with every passing day, and finally, he couldn't take it anymore. He burst out of his hiding spot and stumbled towards them, trembling with uncertainty and dread.

"He's fading," Turan whispered, his voice hoarse with grief. "What are you doing to him?"

The nymph caressed Adnan's cheek, her touch both tender and possessive. "I've given him ecstasy beyond mortal comprehension," she purred. "His transformation is nearly complete."

Turan's wings rustled with agitation. "Transformation? Into what?"

"Into something... more," she replied enigmatically. "A vessel worthy of carrying our child."

Adnan stirred, his skin taking on an otherworldly shimmer. "Turan," he murmured, reaching out a hand.

Turan fought back tears, grasping his friend's hand. "Adnan, please. Fight this. Come back to us."

But Adnan's eyes were already drifting closed, a beatific smile on his face. The nymph's laughter echoed through the grove, triumphant and terrible.

"It won't be long now," she said, her hand resting on her swelling belly. "Our child stirs, eager to greet this world."

In that moment, Adnan reached the pinnacle of ecstasy. His lithe, muscular body was filled with an intensity that bordered on supernatural. It was akin to a sexual voltage, cascading through every fibre of his being like a potent wave of pleasure.

His skin glistened with sweat, highlighting every chiselled contour of his physique under the dimly lit room. His chest heaved as if he'd run a marathon, each breath laced with exhaustion and satisfaction.

His eyes, now glazed with post-coital bliss, fell upon his friend, an elf whose rugged good looks were accentuated by his barely concealed desire. The raw attraction between them was palpable; it hung heavy in the air like an unsaid confession.

Adnan let out a low, throaty chuckle, one laden with satisfaction and mischief. His gaze drank in his friend's ruffled appearance - tousled hair, flushed cheeks and those darkened eyes filled with lustful intent.

"Turan," Adnan murmured, the corner of his mouth quirking up into a roguish smile. It was practically sinful how good he felt. Then with a final look of peaceful surrender coupled with an exhilarating sense of fulfillment, he succumbed to the intense pleasure coursing through him and drifted into oblivion.

Turan sank to his knees, wings drooping in defeat. He had sworn to protect Adnan, but how could he protect him from a fate he had willingly embraced?

As night fell, Turan kept his vigil, haunted by the ghost of the friend he had failed and the looming spectre of a future bathed in shadow.

The grove trembled, ancient trees shuddering as if in pain. Turan's wings unfurled instinctively, his senses on high alert. The nymph's face contorted, a cry of agony tearing from her throat.

Turan watched, mesmerized and horrified, as the nymph's body began to dissolve. Adnan's lifeless form sank into her shimmering essence, both of them merging into a pulsating orb of light.

"What's happening?" Turan demanded, his voice cracking with fear.

The orb pulsed, growing brighter. "The birth of a god," the nymph's voice echoed, fading even as it spoke.

A piercing wail split the air, and the orb exploded in a shower of starlight. At its centre, a newborn child floated, eyes closed, skin glowing with an otherworldly radiance.

Turan's breath caught in his throat. "Aodhán," he whispered, the name coming to him unbidden.

As if in response to his name, the child's eyes fluttered open, revealing depths that seemed to contain entire galaxies. Turan reached out, cradling the infant in his arms.

"I will protect you," he vowed, his voice thick with emotion. *"With my life, I promise."*

A bone-chilling laugh echoed through the grove, and the shadows began to coalesce. Turan's blood ran cold as he recognized the oppressive presence of The Dark.

"HOW QUAINT," the Dark hissed. *"A BASTARD ELFLING AND A BABY ELDAR."*

Turan tightened his grip on the precious bundle in his arms.

"GIVE ME THE CHILD AND YOU WILL BE SPARED," the Dark hissed again.

The air crackled with tension as Turan shielded the infant Eldar from The Dark's malevolent advance. Shadows whipped around them, lashing out in a deadly dance. Turan gritted his teeth, his wings beating furiously to protect Aodhán.

"I won't let you near him!" Turan's voice rang out, a vow of defiance cutting through the chaos.

The Dark surged forward, a dark tempest of hate and power. Turan ducked and weaved, narrowly avoiding the tendrils of shadow seeking to ensnare them both. With a primal roar, he pushed back, his resolve steeling against the encroaching darkness.

Aodhán stirred in his arms, a silent encouragement spurring Turan on. The ground trembled beneath their feet, nature itself recoiling from the clash of light and shadow.

In a blur of motion, Turan struck out, each movement fuelled by a fierce determination to protect the child. The clash echoed through the grove, a symphony of battle ringing in their ears.

"Back off!" Turan's voice thundered, his words a challenge to the encroaching darkness.

The fight raged on, a whirlwind of blows and shadows colliding in a deadly ballet. Turan's muscles burned with exertion, his every instinct honed towards keeping Aodhán safe.

And then, with a final push of strength born from love and duty, Turan unleashed all he had in one swift strike that sent The Dark reeling back into the depths from whence it came. The grove fell silent once more, save for the soft babbling of the newborn god cradled in Turan's arms.

***

Aodhán's adrenaline surged as he soared through the air on his dragon, Drogon. The beating of the massive wings sent a rush of wind that threatened to knock him off, but he held on tightly, revelling in the raw power beneath him. With every beat of Drogon's wings, Aodhán could feel the ancient

energy pulsating through his own veins. He leaned forward, pressing his body against the dragon's armoured scales, fully immersed in the exhilaration of flight. He had inherited his father's recklessness and longed to embody the legendary Adnan, spoken of so fondly by his grandfather.

"Now, Drogon!" Aodhán shouted, his voice carrying a hint of childlike wonder.

As they banked for another dive, Aodhán's eyes widened. A writhing mass of darkness rose from the centre of the camp, tendrils lashing out at fleeing soldiers.

"The Dark," he whispered, a chill running down his spine. "It's here."

Aodhán's searching gaze swept across the darkened sky, but he saw no sign of Turan's powerful wings. He couldn't help but recall his friend's tales of being born in the midst of a battle between light and darkness, and how the forces of evil had relentlessly pursued him ever since. And now, as he felt the looming presence of the Dark once again, there was no one to shield him from its grasp without Turan by his side.

Drogon growled, sensing his rider's unease. Aodhán patted the dragon's neck, trying to calm them both. "We can do this," he murmured, though doubt gnawed at him. "We have to."

They dived, Aodhán's hands glowing with ethereal light. As they neared the ground, he unleashed a blast of pure energy at The Dark. It recoiled, hissing in pain and fury.

"FOOLISH CHILD," The Dark's voice slithered into Aodhán's mind. "YOU CANNOT HOPE TO DEFEAT ME. I AM YOUR DESTINY."

Aodhán gritted his teeth, fighting back the fear that threatened to overwhelm him. "No," he declared, his voice stronger than he felt. "I make my own destiny."

The battle raged on, dragon fire and divine light clashing against suffocating darkness. Aodhán could feel his strength waning, but he refused to give up. Too much depended on him, or so he was daily told. He couldn't allow the Dark to capture him.

As The Dark surged forward once more, a battle cry rang out. Elven archers appeared on the hillside, their arrows tipped with glowing runes. Eldarion's warriors charged from the forest below, their weapons gleaming with enchanted light.

Aodhán's heart swelled with hope and determination. He was not alone in this fight. With renewed vigour, he channelled his power, ready to face his greatest challenge yet. He looked round but still no Turan.

The world erupted in chaos as light and darkness clashed. Aodhán felt his power surge, intertwining with the combined strength of his allies. For a moment, victory seemed within reach.

Then, without warning, reality itself began to fracture.

"What's happening?" Aodhán cried out, his voice barely audible above the deafening roar of colliding forces.

The Dark's laughter echoed in his mind. "YOU'VE OPENED A DOOR YOU CANNOT CLOSE, LITTLE ELDAR."

Cracks of blinding light split the air around Aodhán. He felt himself being pulled in multiple directions, his very essence threatening to tear apart.

"No!" he screamed, desperately reaching out to Drogon, to his allies, to anything solid. But his hands grasped only empty air.

As Aodhán's form began to fade, he caught a final glimpse of the battlefield. Elves and warriors alike stared in horror, their faces etched with disbelief and anguish. And then he finally saw Turan flying up to him

"I'm sorry," Aodhán whispered, a tear sliding down his cheek. "I failed you all."

With a blinding flash, Aodhán vanished, leaving behind a vacuum of stunned silence.

***

Apollo's eyes snapped open from his coma and he jolted upright, his heart pounding in terror. He frantically scanned the room, finding his two sisters hovering over him with worried looks on their faces. His gaze then fell upon the young boy, the only other survivor from Aphrodite's grasp.

Apollo's words came out in desperate gasps as he collapsed into Athena's arms. "The Eldar," he whispered, fear etched on his face. "He didn't come alone. Something else is here, hunting him." The weight of his body against her felt like a warning from beyond, and Athena's heart raced with unease at the thought of what other dangers could be lurking nearby.

Chapter 13

The town hall's worn wooden rafters creaked ominously as President Helena Boyd gripped the edges of the podium, her knuckles white with tension. The room, thick with the scent of fear and stale coffee, fell into an uneasy silence as she cleared her throat.

"Citizens of Rashford," Helena began, her voice steady despite the tremor in her hands, "I stand before you today to declare a state of emergency."

A collective gasp rippled through the crowd, followed by hushed whispers that scratched at the air like desperate fingernails on a coffin lid.

"We face an unprecedented threat," she continued, her eyes scanning the sea of pale, frightened faces. "One that requires our immediate action and unwavering unity."

As she spoke, Helena's mind reeled with images of Llewellyn – his tousled hair, his bright, inquisitive eyes. Where was he now? What horrors might he be facing?

"Rest assured," she said, her voice catching slightly, "that every resource at our disposal is being utilized to ensure the safety of our town and its people."

Inwardly, Helena's thoughts spiralled into a maelstrom of panic and guilt. 'My son,' she agonized, 'my beautiful, curious boy. What have I done by bringing him into this world of shadows and secrets?'

The weight of leadership pressed down on her shoulders like a leaden cloak, threatening to suffocate her. Yet she stood tall, her face a mask of determination.

"I understand your fear," Helena said, her voice softening. "But we must stand together in the face of this darkness. We, as a nation, have weathered storms before, and we will weather this one."

As the words left her lips, Helena felt the bitter taste of doubt coating her tongue. How could she protect an entire town when she couldn't even protect her own child?

The room buzzed with a mixture of fear and restless energy, a powder keg of emotions waiting to ignite. Helena took a deep breath, steeling herself for the questions, the demands, the accusations that were sure to follow.

'Forgive me, Llewellyn,' she thought, her heart aching. 'I swear by all that is holy, I will find you. No matter the cost. But there are other matters I also must tend to.'

The streets of Rashford erupted into a frenzy of activity as government forces swarmed the town like a hive of agitated hornets. Armoured vehicles rumbled down the once-quiet roads, their thunderous engines drowning out the whispers of dread that hung thick in the air. Soldiers, their faces grim and resolute, moved with practiced precision, securing perimeters and establishing checkpoints at every major intersection.

Sheriff Eva Ramirez stood at the centre of the maelstrom, her eyes dark and focused as she barked orders to her deputies. The chaos swirled around her, but she remained an island of calm, her voice steady and authoritative.

"Johnson, I want roadblocks on every street leading out of town," she commanded, her words sharp and precise. "Ramirez, coordinate with the National Guard. We need eyes on every inch of this place."

As her deputies scrambled to obey, Eva felt a chill crawl up her spine. The air itself seemed to pulse with malevolent intent, as if the very shadows were watching, waiting to strike.

"Sheriff," one of her younger deputies approached, his face pale with fear, "what exactly are we up against here?"

Eva paused, considering her words carefully. How could she explain the unexplainable? The horrors that lurked just beyond the veil of normalcy in Rashford?

The words of President Boyd echoed in her mind as she listened to the Helena Boyd's warning. She didn't want to believe it, but her recent experiences in Rashford had shaken her belief in what was real. Part of her wanted to run and hide, but another part felt compelled to stay and fight this unknown threat. The conflicting voices in her head left her feeling paralysed and uncertain of what to do next. "Something... not of this world," the sheriff continued, "stay alert, trust your instincts, and for God's sake, don't go anywhere alone."

As Miller nodded and hurried away, Eva's mind raced. She'd grown up in Rashford, witnessed the strange and terrible things that happened here. But this... this felt different. Worse.

'I swore an oath to protect this town,' she thought, her jaw clenching. 'Even if it means staring into the abyss itself.'

The air grew heavier, charged with an otherworldly energy that made Eva's skin crawl. She watched as her officers moved through the streets, their flashlights cutting through the encroaching

darkness like feeble blades against an endless void.

"Whatever's out there," Eva muttered to herself, her hand instinctively tightening on her holstered weapon, "it's not taking this town without a fight."

The ancient oak doors of the town hall groaned open, revealing a chamber bathed in flickering candlelight. Helena Boyd stepped inside, her heart pounding beneath her composed exterior. Before her stood her adoptive mother, Athena. . .

Athena fixed Helena with a piercing gaze.

Helena swallowed hard, acutely aware of the weight of her next words. "Rashford faces a threat beyond my comprehension. My son... Llewellyn is missing. I—we—need your help."

Athena stepped forward, her owl-like eyes narrowing. "And you come to me after all these years because Llewellyn has been kidnapped?"

"Don't you care about your grandson?" Helena snapped back.

The room crackled with tension as Helena's mind raced.

"What would you ask of me?" Athena asked at last, in a softer tone.

Helena's stomach churned at the thought, bile rising in her throat. She clenched her fists, struggling to maintain her composure. 'For Llewellyn,' she reminded herself. 'I'd tear the world apart.'

"I... I cannot sacrifice my people," Helena said, her voice barely above a whisper. "But my own life? My position? If that's what it takes to save my son and protect Rashford, then so be it."

Athena's eyes flashed with interest. "Your devotion is... admirable. But power, Helena, comes at a price. Are you truly prepared to pay it?"

Helena's mind whirled with possibilities and consequences. The weight of her decision pressed down upon her, threatening to crush her very soul.

'What have I done?' she thought, a chill running down her spine. 'What horrors might I unleash in my desperation?'

"Call Sheriff Ramirez," Athena finally said softly. "She is a formidable woman and we can spare her from the battlefield to look for my grandson."

Unsure of what to do, Helena looked to her mother for guidance. Athena's suggestion to call Sheriff Ramirez brought a sense of relief, but also a twinge of guilt at sending someone else to do their dangerous work. And yet, the fact that Athena

referred to Llewellyn as her grandson caused a wave of conflicting emotions in Helena - acceptance from her mentor, but also reminders of past arguments and jabs. As she mumbled a quiet "thank you," Helena couldn't help but feel torn between gratefulness and apprehension for what was to come.

Sheriff Eva Ramirez gritted her teeth as she strode down Main Street, her boots echoing on the cracked pavement. The goddess Aphrodite glided beside her, an otherworldly aura shimmering around her perfect form.

"We should start at the town square," Eva said gruffly, her hand resting on her holstered pistol. "That's where Llewellyn was last seen."

Aphrodite's laugh sent shivers down Eva's spine. "Oh darling, mortal methods won't suffice. We need to follow the threads of desire."

Eva's jaw clenched. "This isn't about desire. It's about finding a missing child."

"Everything is about desire," Aphrodite purred, her eyes glowing in the darkness. "Even a mother's love."

As they turned onto South Street, shadows seemed to writhe and pulse along the edges of

Eva's vision. The air grew thick, tasting of ash and decay. Eva's heart hammered in her chest, every instinct screaming danger.

'Focus,' she told herself. 'You've faced worse than some fallen deity and creepy shadows.'

"Do you feel it?" Aphrodite whispered, her voice tinged with longing. "The hunger in the air? It calls to me, even now."

Eva suppressed a shudder. "I feel something alright. But hunger isn't the word I'd use."

A distant scream pierced the night, sending ice through Eva's veins. She drew her weapon, scanning the darkened streets.

"What the hell was that?" she hissed.

Aphrodite's eyes gleamed with an unsettling mix of fear and excitement. "The beginning, dear Sheriff. The beginning of something beautiful and terrible."

The flickering candlelight from an old streetlamp cast grotesque shadows across Marcus Taser's pudgy face, his eyes glinting with a predatory gleam. Eva stood her ground, her posture rigid as she faced the man who held her fate in his bloated hands.

"Sheriff Ramirez," Marcus purred, his voice a silken caress that made Eva's skin crawl. "I trust you understand the gravity of our situation."

Eva's nails dug into her palms, drawing blood. "Get to the point, Marcus. What do you want?"

A slow smile spread across Marcus' face, revealing teeth too white, too perfect. "It's quite simple, really. Tell the President to surrender control of Rashford Town and her presidency to me, and I'll ensure young Llewellyn's safe return."

"You have the boy," Eva exclaimed, his words confirming her most dreaded suspicions.

The street seemed to tilt beneath Eva's feet. She could hear her heartbeat thundering in her ears, feel the weight of impossible choices pressing down on her shoulders.

"And if we refuse?" Aphrodite asked behind her, her voice barely above a whisper.

Marcus leaned forward, his bulk dwarfing the shadows between them. "Then I'm afraid I can't guarantee the President's son's safety. These are... dangerous times, after all. But I am a reasonable man and can negotiate. Take me to President Boyd."

Helena's mind raced, images of Llewellyn flashing before her eyes. Her son's laughter, her tears, the way he'd curl up in her arms after a nightmare. And now, this living nightmare threatened to tear them apart forever.

"You're asking me to betray everything I've sworn to protect," Helena said, her voice wavering. "The town, its people, the very fabric of our society."

Marcus' eyes glittered with triumph. He knew he held all the cards. "Am I? Or am I merely asking you to choose between your duty and your heart? You've always known this day would come, Helena. The price of power is steep, and now it's time to pay."

Helena closed her eyes, feeling the weight of motherhood and leadership warring within her. Athena's voice echoed in her mind, a reminder of the greater forces at play. But all she could see was Llewellyn's face, scared and alone in the darkness.

"I need time," she whispered, hating the weakness in her voice.

Marcus' smile widened, revealing too many teeth. "Of course, Madam President. But remember, time is a luxury your son may not have."

As Taser turned to leave, the candles guttered, plunging the room into momentary darkness. In

that instant, Helena could have sworn she saw something ancient and terrible lurking behind Marcus' eyes.

In the shadows of the room, Aodhán pressed himself against the wall, his ethereal form barely visible in the flickering candlelight. His eyes, pools of cosmic depth, watched the exchange between Helena and Marcus with a mixture of fascination and horror. The raw emotions emanating from the humans crashed over him in waves, threatening to drown his senses.

Satana's whispers slithered through his mind, a sibilant caress. "See how weak they are, my sweet child. How easily manipulated by fear and love. They deserve our rule, our guidance."

Aodhán's fingers curled against the rough stone, his nails scraping softly. "But they feel so deeply," he murmured, his voice barely a breath. "Their pain, their hope... it's beautiful and terrible."

Away from the room, a woman's sob echoed from somewhere in the building, piercing Aodhán's heart. He felt an overwhelming urge to comfort her, to ease her suffering. But Satana's influence held him back, a dark tendril of doubt coiling around his compassion.

"You are not one of them," Satana hissed. "You are above their petty concerns. Remember who you are, what you are meant to be."

Aodhán closed his eyes, memories of his homeland now flooding his mind. The cosmic vastness, the serene detachment, the pure power coursing through his veins. Yet here, in this mortal realm, everything felt so immediate, so visceral.

"I don't know who I am anymore," he whispered, a single tear tracing a luminous path down his cheek. "I feel... torn."

The weight of his otherworldly origins pressed down on him, isolating him from the very beings he longed to understand. The heavy oak door creaked open, drawing Aodhán's attention back to the vision of the dimly lit chamber. He watched as Helena left the room, her shoulders bowed with the burden of an impossible choice. In that moment, Aodhán felt a kindred spirit in her struggle.

"Perhaps," he thought, defying Satana's influence for a fleeting instant, "we are not so different after all."

Helena re-entered, her face a mask of grim determination. The air grew thick with tension as

she approached Marcus, who lounged in his chair like a bloated spider at the centre of its web.

"I've made my decision," Helena declared, her voice steady despite the slight tremor in her hands.

Marcus leaned forward, his eyes glinting with predatory interest. "And?"

Helena took a deep breath, her gaze unflinching. "I'll surrender control of Rashford, but not the Presidency. That's my final offer."

A low chuckle rumbled from Marcus' chest, sending chills down Aodhán's spine. "Oh, Helena. You misunderstand. This isn't a negotiation."

Helena's jaw clenched, her composure cracking. "Then what is it?"

"An ultimatum," Marcus purred, rising to his feet with surprising grace for his bulk. "You give me everything, or I take it by force."

Aodhán watched as Helena's mind raced, weighing impossible choices. He could almost taste her anguish, her desperation to protect both her town and her son.

"You're a monster," Helena spat, her voice trembling with rage and fear.

Marcus smiled, revealing teeth unnaturally sharp in the flickering candlelight. "Perhaps. But I'm the monster who holds your son's life in his hands."

Aodhán felt a palpable sense of dread settle over Rashford. The air itself seemed to pulse with malevolent intent, shadows stretching and writhing along the walls. Unresolved conflicts hung like a miasma, promising further turmoil to come.

In that moment, Aodhán realized that the true horror wasn't Marcus or his threats. It was the creeping, insidious darkness that had taken root in the very heart of this town – a darkness that threatened to consume everything in its path.

Aodhán wasn't the only one watching the unfurling of these events. From the shadows, Luke watched with unprecedented glee. He left the shadows and quickly materialised in the Celestial Realm, where he was immediately stopped by Gabri-El.

Undeterred, Luke turned away the archangel's grasp and calmly proposed. "I have news Yahweh needs to hear."

"What news could a villain like you possible bring to Yahweh that he doesn't already know?" Gabri-El challenged him.

"My words are for Yahweh alone," Luke grinned.

"Let him come in front of me," boomed Yahweh's voice behind them.

Luke looked at Gabri-El victoriously and moved to bow before Yahweh. "My Lord, there is a Darkness ready to invade the balance you created. Satana and a Darkness from out of this reality have invaded the small town of Rashford and now threaten to envelop the whole world, throwing it into chaos."

Silence ensued.

"And why do you come to me with this news?" Yahweh said at last.

"I come because even I can't operate in the chaos Satana proposes to bring."

Silence ensued again.

"Micha-El!" Yahweh called out at last. "Prepare the angels. We attack Rashford Town immediately. We must restore balance. The chaos must not spread."

Chapter 14

The sky above Rashford Town darkened, as if night had fallen prematurely. A host of angels, led by Archangel Micha-El, descended upon the quaint Ohio settlement like a tempest of divine wrath. Their wings cast ominous shadows that slithered across cobblestone streets and ivy-covered facades, extinguishing the warm glow of streetlamps.

Athena stood amidst the growing chaos, her eyes glowing despite the unnatural gloom. Her piercing grey eyes scanned the faces of her allies – Apollo, Aphrodite, and Helena Boyd's most loyal soldiers. The air crackled with tension, thick enough to choke on.

"My friends," Athena's voice rang out, sturdy yet tinged with desperation. "Our sanctuary stands on the precipice of destruction. We may be diminished, but we are not defeated."

Athena's grey eyes met Apollo's, reflecting a steely resolve. Aphrodite's haunting gaze betrayed inner turmoil, her ethereal beauty a stark contrast to the impending violence.

Athena's mind raced. How could she inspire them when they knew nothing of her divinity until a few hours ago?

"I know you fear what comes for us," she continued, as she turned to the small army of human soldiers. "But remember who you are – you are the last guardians of humanity, the last to take a stand against oppression."

A soldier near her whispered, "But how can we stand against angels?"

Athena turned to him, a flicker of her old radiance burning in her eyes. "With the same courage that has sustained us through millennia. We may bleed now, but our spirits remain unbroken."

As she spoke, Athena caught sight of Micha-El descending, wings unfurled in terrible majesty. "To arms!" she cried, pushing aside her anguish. "For Rashford, for our future!"

The air hummed with anticipation as his allies readied themselves. Athena's hand tightened around her weapon, mortality be damned. She would defend this sanctuary or die trying. She strode forward, her grey eyes flashing with fierce determination. The chaos of the impending battle swirled around her, but she remained a pillar of calm authority.

"Aphrodite," she commanded, her voice cutting through the din, "use your charms to sow confusion among the lesser angels. Distract them, divide them."

Aphrodite nodded with a wicked smile playing on her lips. Her beauty seemed to shine even brighter amidst the chaos. "With pleasure, darling."

Athena turned to Apollo, her gaze softening for a moment. "You know Micha-El best. Can you draw him away from the main force?"

Apollo's jaw tightened. "I'll do what I must."

"Good," Athena said, then addressed the mortal soldiers. "Form a perimeter. Protect the townspeople at all costs."

Athena barked orders, her mind calculating strategies in a split second. The weight of her newly found responsibility pressed on her, but she didn't falter. The clash began.

Angels and mortals clashed in a storm of steel and blood. Swords clashed, shields shattered. A sword arced towards Athena; she parried, countering with a swift strike that sent her opponent staggering back.

The acrid scent of sweat and iron filled the air as warriors grunted and cursed. Athena spun, landing a kick that sent one foe sprawling. Adrenaline surged through her veins, every nerve alive with the thrill of combat.

"Is that all you've got?" she taunted, her voice cutting through the chaos. The enemy surged

forward, their battle cries drowned out by the clash of weapons.

Athena fought with skill and fury, every movement honed to deadly precision. She struck fast and hard, her blows finding their marks with lethal accuracy.

In the heat of battle, there was no room for hesitation or doubt. Only the fight mattered, only survival in this brutal dance of blades and blood.

Aodhán's gaze fell upon the visions of the terrified faces of the townspeople seeking shelter. A wave of empathy washed over him, accompanied by a gnawing guilt. Was this destruction wrought in part because of his presence here?

"You should be revelling in this chaos, little one," Satana's silky voice whispered in his mind. "This is the true nature of the world – violence and fear."

Aodhán shuddered, torn between his loyalty to the demoness who had guided him and the innocents caught in the crossfire. "But they've done nothing wrong," he murmured.

"Wrong? Right? Such mortal concepts," Satana's voice dripped with disdain. "Power is the only truth that matters."

As the first clashes of battle erupted, Aodhán felt his heart constrict. The scent of ozone and blood filled the air, and he longed for the gentle fragrances of Meredith's farm.

"I... I don't know if I can do this," he whispered, his voice lost in the growing cacophony of war.

The sky split with a thunderous crack. Light clashed with steel, shaking Rashford Town to its core. Angels descended, searing flesh with divine radiance.

"Hold the line!" Athena shouted, soldiers falling around her. Energy crackled, illuminating the chaos. Blood sprayed, mingling with angelic essence.

Screams filled the air as the battle raged on. Blades clashed, metal ringing in fierce combat. Athena dodged and struck, every move calculated for survival.

"Fight on!" she bellowed, his words drowned out by the sounds of war. Adrenaline surged through him as he fought for every breath.

In the midst of carnage, Apollo pressed forward, facing the relentless onslaught with grim determination. The clash of forces echoed

through the battlefield, a symphony of violence that painted the earth in hues of red and gold.

Amidst the chaos, he glimpsed a chance to turn the tide. With a primal roar, he charged into the fray, his mind focused solely on the fight at hand.

Apollo's heart clenched at the sight of his former lover turned nemesis, Micha-El, directing his celestial army with cold precision. Their shared history flashed before Apollo's eyes, memories threatening to overwhelm him.

But there was no time for nostalgia or regret. As he surveyed the battlefield, Apollo steeled himself. This was a fight for survival, for their home and each other.

The clash of angelic and mortal forces reverberated through the air, each blow resonating with cosmic power. Apollo moved with grace and precision, his movements a testament to the ancient art of war.

Micha-El locked eyes with Apollo amidst the chaos, recognition and pain flickering in those ancient depths. "Apollo... this isn't personal. You know I have no choice."

Apollo's jaw tightened, anger simmering beneath the surface. "There's always a choice," he retorted, his hand tightening on his weapon. "We made ours long ago."

The Archangel's face hardened, resolve etched on his features. "Then let us finish what was started in the heavens," Micha-El declared, raising his own weapon.

Lovers turned enemies, their passion twisted into violence. The weight of their shared history pressed down on him, threatening to crush his resolve.

But as screams of the dying filled the air and the ground shook beneath their feet, Apollo steeled himself. This was no time for nostalgia or regret. The fate of Rashford Town – and perhaps the world – hung in the balance.

"So be it," Apollo growled, his voice carrying a fierce determination. "Let's dance one last time, old friend."

Their weapons clashed, sending sparks flying in all directions. The air crackled with the clash of their powers, each strike reverberating through their bodies.

Apollo's mind raced, his thoughts a whirlwind of strategy and survival. He evaded Micha-El's blows with fluid grace, countering with strikes fuelled by millennia of combat experience.

As the battle raged on, the surroundings transformed into a nightmarish tableau. Buildings

crumbled under the weight of celestial energy, creating a landscape of ruin and devastation.

Apollo's heart pounded in his chest, adrenaline fuelling his every move. His movements became a blur as he unleashed a flurry of attacks against Micha-El, his weapon slashing through the air with deadly precision.

But Micha-El was no easy opponent. He parried and dodged Apollo's strikes with supernatural speed and agility. Each clash of their weapons sent shockwaves rippling through the battlefield, as if the very fabric of reality trembled under their power.

As they fought, memories of their love and shared past tugged at Apollo's heart. But he pushed them aside, focusing solely on the battle at hand. This was not a fight driven by personal vendettas or lost love. It was a fight for survival, for the future of Rashford Town and all they held dear.

With each strike and parry, Apollo felt his resolve strengthening. He knew that victory would come at a steep price, but he was willing to pay it if it meant protecting those he cared for.

The battle around them raged on, allies fighting side by side against the angelic forces. Apollo caught glimpses of Athena's unwavering presence

in the midst of chaos, her strategic mind guiding their every move.

Apollo drew strength from her courage, channelling the immense power of his divine heritage. His strikes grew fiercer, his movements more fluid. He fought not just for himself, but for the hope that Rashford Town could rise from the ashes and find a new beginning.

With a surge of determination, Apollo pressed his advantage. He unleashed a barrage of attacks on Micha-El, forcing him back with each strike. Their weapons clashed with an explosion of energy that sent shockwaves rippling through the air.

As their battle reached its climax, Apollo found himself consumed by a mixture of emotions – anger at what had been lost, sorrow for what could never be regained, and a glimmer of hope for what lay ahead.

With one final strike, Apollo sent Micha-El crashing to the ground. The Archangel lay there, wounded and defeated, his former glory now tarnished by the choices he had made.

Apollo stood over him, his weapon still raised. Sweat dripped from his brow as he caught his breath. The weight of their shared history pressed heavily upon him, threatening to overwhelm him with its magnitude.

Breathing heavily, Apollo met Micha-El's gaze one last time. Amidst the chaos and devastation, a flicker of understanding passed between them. They were no longer lovers, but they still shared a bond forged in the fires of battle.

"I'm sorry," Micha-El whispered, his voice tinged with regret. "I never wanted it to come to this."

Apollo's grip on his weapon tightened, conflicting emotions swirling within him. "We all make choices," he replied, his voice filled with a mix of sorrow and determination. "And we must face the consequences."

With those words, Apollo lowered his weapon. He turned away from Micha-El, leaving him on the battlefield to contemplate his choices. The fight was not over, but this battle was won. He surveyed the scene before him – a town torn apart by war, its people battered and bruised but still standing. Rashford Town had endured unimaginable pain and suffering, yet there was hope in the air.

As he rejoined his allies to regroup and tend to the wounded, Apollo felt a renewed sense of purpose. The road ahead would be long and treacherous, but with their spirits unbroken and their resolve undimmed, they would rebuild and find a new beginning.

The battle for Rashford Town had left scars that would never fully heal, but it had also brought forth a resilience and strength that could not be extinguished. And as Apollo looked out upon the smouldering ruins of their home, he knew that their fight was far from over.

For Rashford, for their future – they would prevail.

Athena's eyes blazed with fierce intelligence as she surveyed the chaos of battle, her mind whirring like a celestial clockwork. The fallen goddess stood atop a crumbling bell tower, her raven hair whipping in the wind, a beacon of calm amid the storm.

"Aphrodite!" she barked, her voice carrying over the cacophony. "Take your acolytes to the eastern flank."

The goddess of love nodded grimly, her once-radiant beauty now a weapon of war.

Athena's gaze swept the battlefield, cataloguing every skirmish, every potential weakness. "Soldier!" she called to the mortal commander. "Your archers to the rooftops. Aim for their wings!"

As Helena's troops scrambled to obey, Athena felt a pang of bitter nostalgia. How different this was

from the epic battles of old, when she'd led armies with the full might of Olympus at her back.

"We're outmatched," Apollo muttered, appearing at her side, his golden hair matted with blood and ichor.

Athena's lips curled into a predatory smile. "Perhaps in raw power," she conceded. "But not in cunning. We'll turn their righteousness against them."

She pointed to a group of townspeople cowering in a nearby church. "Herd the mortals into the sacred spaces. The angels will hesitate to desecrate their own holy ground."

Apollo nodded, a spark of his old fire returning to his eyes. "Clever as always, owl-eyed one."

As he dashed off to implement her strategy, Athena allowed herself a moment of grim satisfaction. They might be fallen, diminished, but the wisdom of ages still flowed through her veins.

"Come then, Micha-El," she whispered to the sky. "Let's see if your heavenly host can outmanoeuvre the goddess of strategy."

Meanwhile, on the fringes of the battle, young Aodhán found himself drawn inexorably toward the heart of the conflict. His otherworldly senses

reeled from the onslaught of sights, sounds, and emotions bombarding him.

"Why?" he murmured, his ethereal eyes wide with confusion and growing horror. "Why must they fight?"

A nearby explosion sent a shower of debris raining down. Aodhán instinctively raised his hand, a shimmering barrier of Eldar energy deflecting the shrapnel from a group of terrified children huddled in a doorway.

The gratitude in their eyes stirred something deep within him, a protective instinct that clashed violently with Satana's whispered promises of power and dominion.

"This isn't right," Aodhán said, his voice trembling. "Satana said we would bring order, but this... this is chaos."

He watched as an angel's flaming sword cut down a mortal soldier, the man's agonized scream echoing in Aodhán's mind. The Eldar god felt sick, his cosmic nature recoiling from the brutality.

"I have to do something," he decided, his childlike features hardening with determination. "But what? How can I stop this madness?"

As Aodhán stood there, torn between action and indecision, he felt the weight of choice pressing

down upon him. In that moment, he began to understand the true burden of godhood – and the price of remaining innocent in a world drenched in blood.

The air crackled with divine energy as Apollo rallied his diminished army. Sweat glistened on his brow, his mask matted with blood and grime. His once-resplendent form now bore the marks of mortality, yet his eyes blazed with an indomitable fire.

"Stand fast!" he bellowed, his voice carrying over the din of battle. "We may be weakened, but we are not defeated!"

Nearby, Aphrodite loosed a volley of arrows, each shaft finding its mark with deadly precision. But for every angel that fell, two more seemed to take its place. The goddess grimaced, fatigue etching lines across her face.

"Brother," she called out, voice strained, "our strength wanes. How much longer can we hold?"

Apollo's jaw clenched. He could feel the desperation mounting among his troops, their mortal essence stretched thin by the relentless assault. The weight of their struggle pressed down upon him, a crushing burden that threatened to suffocate his resolve.

"As long as we must," he replied, willing conviction into his words. "Rashford is our home now. We cannot—we will not—abandon these people."

A flash of celestial light drew Apollo's gaze skyward. There, descending through the smoke and chaos, was a figure that sent a jolt of recognition through his very being. Micha-El, resplendent in angelic glory, his wings spread wide as he touched down on the blood-soaked earth.

Time seemed to slow as their eyes met across the battlefield. Apollo felt a surge of conflicting emotions—anger, longing, betrayal—all swirling together in a maelstrom of confusion. He took a step forward, drawn by an irresistible pull.

"Micha-El," he whispered, the name both a curse and a prayer on his lips. "Why must we fight again?"

The archangel's expression was unreadable, a mask of divine purpose. But for a fleeting moment, Apollo thought he saw a flicker of something else—regret? Pain? Whatever it was, it vanished as quickly as it had appeared.

"It doesn't have to be this way," Apollo found himself saying, even as he raised his weapon. "We can find another path."

Micha-El's response was lost in the cacophony of battle, but the set of his shoulders spoke volumes.

As they closed the distance between them, Apollo's heart raced with the terrible knowledge that one way or another, everything was about to change.

Their weapons clashed with a resounding clang, sparks flying as divine steel met celestial bronze. Apollo's muscles strained against the weight of Micha-El's assault, his mortal form trembling with the effort.

"Why?" Apollo hissed through gritted teeth, his voice raw with anguish. "Why did you forget us? Forget me?"

Micha-El's piercing gaze bore into him, a tempest of emotions swirling in those otherworldly eyes. "I serve a higher purpose, Apollo. As once did you."

They broke apart, circling each other like predators. Apollo's heart hammered in his chest, each beat a reminder of his newfound mortality. He couldn't help but marvel at Micha-El's grace, the fluid movements that spoke of eons of celestial power.

"And what of love?" Apollo challenged, his voice barely above a whisper. "Was that not purpose enough?"

A flicker of pain crossed Micha-El's face, so brief Apollo almost missed it. "Love..." the archangel

murmured, his grip on his sword tightening. "Love is a luxury we cannot afford in this war."

Their blades met again, the clash reverberating through the war-torn streets of Rashford. Apollo felt a surge of bitterness rise within him. "So you would sacrifice everything we had for your blind obedience?"

As they exchanged blows, Apollo's mind raced. How had it come to this? Lover against lover, divinity against mortality, all hanging in the balance of this one moment.

Suddenly, a scream pierced the air—a mortal cry of terror that cut through the din of battle. Both Apollo and Micha-El faltered, their attention drawn to the chaos around them. In that instant of distraction, Apollo saw an opening and lunged forward.

His blade stopped mere inches from Micha-El's throat, trembling with the weight of indecision. Micha-El's eyes widened, a mixture of surprise and something else—was it admiration?—flickering in their depths.

"What now, Apollo?" Micha-El breathed, not daring to move. "Will you strike down your beloved in the name of these mortals?"

Apollo's hand shook, his resolve wavering. The fate of Rashford Town, of the diminished gods, of

everything he had come to cherish in his mortal life, hung on this moment. Yet as he stared into Micha-El's eyes, he saw not just an adversary, but the echo of countless shared eternities.

The battle raged on around them, a symphony of destruction that threatened to engulf them both. Apollo's blade remained poised, the tip just grazing Micha-El's skin, as the weight of their shared history and the uncertain future pressed down upon them.

In that suspended moment, with the world crumbling around them and the line between love and duty blurred beyond recognition, Apollo made his choice—

Chapter 15

The cobblestones beneath Marcus Taser's feet seemed to writhe, pulsing with an otherworldly energy that mirrored the gleam in his eyes. He stood at the heart of Rashford Town, his corpulent form a dark silhouette against the eerie glow that had descended upon the once-quaint streets.

"My children," Marcus' voice rolled across the gathered crowd, a sonorous cadence that sent shivers through the air. "The time has come for us to claim our rightful place."

The corrupted townspeople pressed closer, their eyes glazed with an unnatural fervour. Marcus' lips curled into a sinister smile as he surveyed his disciples.

"For too long, we've cowered beneath the tyranny of false gods and sanctimonious angels," he continued, his words dripping with honey-coated venom. "But The Dark offers us true salvation, true power."

A murmur of assent rippled through the crowd. Marcus raised his arms, his suit stretching taut across his frame as he embraced the palpable darkness swirling around him.

"March with me," he commanded, his voice dropping to a seductive whisper. "March against

those who would deny us our destiny. The Dark will consume all, and we shall be its harbingers."

With Marcus' dark visions in his mind, he triggered the release of his zombie horde on the unsuspecting army of Helena Boyd. The first wave crashed through their lines with unnatural strength, driven by an insatiable hunger for flesh. Limbs were torn from sockets, rib cages were splintered, and heads rolled beneath the feet of the ravenous undead.

The soldiers of Helena Boyd put up a valiant fight, but they were no match for the macabre efficiency of the zombies. Gunfire and screams echoed through the bloodied streets as the living fought desperately against their inevitable destruction. The air was thick with the coppery stench of freshly spilled blood as fist-sized chunks of rotten flesh were torn from torn open sternums and ground between gnashing teeth.

Despite their best efforts, the soldiers could do little to stop the zombie tide from sweeping them away like so much rubbish in a flood. Pairs of blackened, sunken eyes would suddenly lock onto a soldier and he would be dragged beneath a sea of grasping hands and clawing fingers that tore into him without mercy. Skin was shredded,

muscles were torn, and bone splinters were shoved deep into gaping wounds.

The zombies lunged ferociously at the angelic host amidst the backdrop of Rashford's sprawling townscape, their rotten flesh tearing and crumbling with every strike. The Archangel Ari-El clashed with a snarling undead, their blades clashing in a deafening crescendo that mingled with the distant hum of traffic. The stench of decay mixed with the breeze from the lake, filling the air as they battled for supremacy under the shadow of the city's skyline.

"Is this all you've got, foul creature?" Ari-El taunted, his voice echoing through the fog that rolled in from the Pacific Ocean.

The zombie hissed in response, its movements wild and unpredictable like the ever-shifting mist. It swung its decaying limbs with surprising agility, forcing Ari-El to dance around the blows with expert precision on the cobblestone streets of Rashford Town. The ground trembled beneath their feet, echoing the intensity of their clash against a backdrop of neon lights and bustling crowds.

Gabri-El joined the fray at town centre, his wings slicing through the air as he dived into the heart of

the horde under the gaze of the full moon. His celestial light blazed against the darkness of the undead, illuminating their twisted faces contorted in rage against the backdrop of the historic prison walls. The deafening roars of battle mixed with the unearthly cries of the angels, creating a symphony of conflict that reverberated through the town's hills.

"Stay back, filth," Gabri-El commanded, his voice cutting through the chaos like a blade through fog.

But the zombies cared not for his warnings as they staggered up Lombard Street, their insatiable hunger driving them forward relentlessly. Limbs were torn asunder in North Beach Road, and ichor splattered across the wharf as the two forces clashed in a savage dance of death amidst cable cars ringing their bells. The ground beneath them shook with each impact, fog swirling around them like a shroud.

As the battle raged on, Ari-El found himself surrounded by a horde of undead closing in on him from all sides against a backdrop of glittering city lights. His heart raced with adrenaline as he fought with unmatched skill and determination, shadows dancing around him in an intricate waltz. The screams of his fallen comrades urged him on from Haight-Ashbury, fuelling his resolve to stand

against this tide of darkness that threatened to engulf their vibrant city.

"Is this truly all you can muster?" Ari-El shouted, his voice defiant amidst the chaos that echoed down Market Street.

The zombies pressed closer, their moans growing louder as they sensed victory within reach. But just as all hope seemed lost, a blinding light erupted from the skies above. A host of angels descended upon Town Square, their radiant forms striking fear into the hearts of the undead amidst cries seagulls.

The tide turned in an instant as Rashford's foghorn sounded its mournful cry over the town. The angels rallied behind Ari-El and Gabri-El at the town centre, forming a shield of divine light that pushed back the encroaching darkness. The zombies wailed in agony as they were smote down one by one by Town Hall's glowing dome before finally dissipating into nothingness amidst cheers by the remaining mortal onlookers. But the zombies were yet to be defeated.

Marcus watched impassively from atop a pile of writhing bodies as his horde consumed its prey whole. He took perverse pleasure in their suffering and couldn't wait for the entire town to experience

his brand of hellish agony. For now, he let his minions continue their grisly feast while he plotted further conquests under The Dark's baleful gaze.

Miles away, on a blood-soaked battlefield, a different scene unfolded. Apollo, his mask matted with sweat and grime, locked eyes with Micha-El. In that moment, he made a decision that would alter the course of their eternal struggle.

With trembling hands, Apollo began to peel away his Armor. Each piece that clattered to the ground felt like a shackle being removed, revealing not just his contorted physical form but the vulnerability of his soul.

"What are you doing?" Micha-El's voice was barely above a whisper, his sword arm lowering unconsciously.

Apollo stood naked before his eternal love and adversary, his disfigured skin glowing with an ethereal light that seemed to push back the encroaching darkness.

"I surrender," Apollo said, his voice cracking with emotion. "Not to heaven or to The Dark, but to us—to this love that has outlasted empires and defied the very fabric of creation."

Micha-El's eyes widened, a tempest of emotions swirling in their depths. Slowly, reverently, he too began to remove his armour.

As the last piece fell away, Micha-El stepped forward and embraced Apollo. Their lips met in a kiss that seemed to still the very air around them, a moment of perfect union amidst the chaos of war.

When they finally parted, Micha-El turned to the assembled forces, his voice ringing out with divine authority.

"The battle with the mortals is over," he declared. "Let there be peace with Rashford Town. We fight the undead horde together with the Olympians and the mortals."

As the sounds of conflict died away, Apollo leaned against Micha-El, his thoughts a tumultuous whirlpool. What have we done? he wondered. We are in direct conflict with Yahweh's will but will it be enough to save Rashford from the darkness that threatens to consume it?

"You're injured," Micha-El whispered in his ear, holding him on his feet.

"I need to rest," Apollo sighed. "Unlike you, I bear a mortal frame. Take me to the mansion."

Goddard Greening's voice thundered across the town square, his words a defiant roar against the encroaching darkness. He stood atop the worn steps of Rashford's town hall, his tailored suit a stark contrast to the crumbling façade behind him.

"Citizens of Rashford," he bellowed, his youthful voice carrying the weight of centuries, "we stand on the precipice of oblivion. Marcus Taser would have you believe that salvation lies in surrender to The Dark. But I ask you, what price are we willing to pay for such a poisoned promise?"

Goddard's eyes swept over the crowd, a sea of fear-stricken faces. He could feel their terror, taste their desperation on the air. His heart ached, but he steeled himself. They needed more than comfort now; they needed a beacon of hope.

"I've walked these streets for less years than most of you," he continued, his voice softening. "But I've seen the strength that lies within each of you. The darkness may seem insurmountable but remember – we are the light that pushes it back."

From the crowd, a familiar sneer cut through the tension. Marcus Taser, his face twisted in contempt, called out, "Pretty words from a man who couldn't even protect his own father. Why should they listen to you?"

Goddard's jaw clenched, the old wound of racial prejudice threatening to derail his purpose. But he wouldn't let it. Not now. Not ever again.

"Because, Mr. Taser," Goddard replied, his voice steady and sure, "this town – our home – knows no colour, no creed. The Dark cares not for your bigotry. It will consume us all equally if we let it."

A murmur rippled through the crowd. Goddard could see the flicker of understanding in their eyes, the first embers of resolve kindling in their hearts.

"We are not helpless," he urged, his passion building. "Our faith, our love for one another – these are weapons the Dark cannot comprehend. Stand with me now, and we will push back this tide of corruption!"

As his words echoed across the square, Goddard watched the transformation begin. Fear gave way to determination. Isolation crumbled in the face of unity. The people of Rashford, battered but unbroken, began to stand taller, their eyes shining with newfound purpose.

In that moment, as hope blossomed in the most unlikely of places, Goddard allowed himself a small smile. The battle for Rashford's soul had only just begun.

From the shadows of an abandoned alleyway, Luke Laufeyson watched the scene unfold, his eyes glittering with a mixture of contempt and desperation. The old trickster god's fingers twitched nervously, his mind racing with possibilities and pitfalls.

"Pathetic mortals," he muttered, scanning the crowd. "So easily swayed by pretty words and false hope."

But beneath his scorn, a seed of doubt had taken root. The Dark's growing influence threatened to consume even him, a prospect that sent icy tendrils of fear crawling up his spine. Luke's gaze settled on a distant figure – Micha-El, the archangel, standing apart from the masses.

A plan began to form in Luke's mind, as treacherous and slippery as his own nature. He straightened his back, a sardonic smile playing at the corners of his mouth.

"Well, well," he mused. "Perhaps it's time for the trickster to play his greatest trick yet."

With fluid grace, Luke slipped from shadow to shadow, approaching Micha-El. His heart raced, a cacophony of desperation and cunning. As he drew near, he carefully schooled his features into a mask of earnest concern.

"Micha-El," Luke called out, his voice a honeyed melody. "My old friend, I fear we face a common enemy."

The archangel turned, his piercing gaze settling on Luke with calm intensity. "Luke Laufeyson," Micha-El replied, his tone measured. "What brings you slithering out of the darkness?"

Luke suppressed a flinch at the barb, forcing a rueful chuckle instead. "Ah, ever the wit, aren't you? But surely you can see the gravity of our situation. The Dark threatens us all – even one such as myself. We need balance, but you have set the celestial army against the mortals at a time when we need to be united."

He stepped closer, his eyes wide with feigned sincerity. "I've seen the error of my ways, Micha-El. I want to help. To fight alongside you against this... abomination."

Micha-El's expression remained impassive, but Luke pressed on, desperation lending fervour to his words. "Think of what we could accomplish together! My cunning, your strength – we'd be unstoppable!"

As Luke spoke, he felt a flicker of hope. Perhaps this time, his silver tongue would win the day. But then he saw it – a flash of something in Micha-El's

eyes. Understanding. Pity. And worst of all, dismissal.

"Oh, Loki," Micha-El said softly, shaking his head. "Did you truly believe I would fall for such transparent deception?"

Luke's mask slipped, revealing a snarl of frustration. "You fool!" he spat. "Can't you see I'm offering you a chance at victory?"

Micha-El's voice hardened. "What you offer is poison, wrapped in lies. I see through you, Laufeyson. As I always have."

With a gesture of celestial power, Micha-El cast Luke aside. The trickster god stumbled, his carefully crafted plan crumbling to dust.

As he retreated into the shadows once more, Luke's mind reeled. He had gambled everything on this ploy and lost. Now, alone and exposed, he faced the terrifying prospect of confronting The Dark with no allies to shield him.

For the first time in eons, Luke Laufeyson felt truly, utterly afraid.

Marcus Taser strode through the streets of Rashford, his footsteps a thunderous cadence echoing off cobblestones slick with an oily sheen. Behind him, a sea of corrupted townspeople

surged forward, their eyes vacant and gleaming with an unnatural light. The air grew thick with a cloying miasma, suffocating hope with each laboured breath.

"Behold, my children," Marcus' voice boomed, rich with malevolent charisma turning now to his troop of zombies. "The Dark embraces us, granting strength to the worthy!"

As he spoke, tendrils of inky blackness crept along building facades, devouring warm lamplight and leaving only yawning shadows in their wake. Marcus watched with perverse satisfaction as a woman stumbled, her form engulfed by creeping darkness. When she rose, her eyes shone with the same eerie glow as his zombies.

How easily they fall, Marcus mused, a cruel smile twisting his lips. *Like dominoes toppling into oblivion.* With that, he left the battleground to return to his chained prisoner.

Apollo halted as Taser's procession reached the town square. Here, the corruption seemed to coalesce, swirling and roiling like a sentient fog. Apollo knew he had to take another stand. As he watched, transfixed, the darkness began to take shape.

At first, it was amorphous, a writhing mass of shadow. But then, with agonizing slowness, features emerged. A youthful face, eyes deep as the cosmos, an aura of ancient wisdom.

Apollo felt his breath catch. "Aodhán?" he whispered, momentarily shaken.

But no, this was not the Eldar child. This was something far more sinister, wearing Aodhán's form like an ill-fitting suit. The Dark's approximation of Aodhán tilted its head, regarding Apollo with eyes that held nothing but endless, consuming void.

"What game are you playing?" Apollo demanded, his usual composure slipping. "Why take this form?"

The Dark-Aodhán's lips curled into a smile that never reached its eyes. When it spoke, its voice was a cacophony of whispers, each syllable dripping with malice.

"WE ARE BOUND, THE BOY AND I," it hissed. "TWO SIDES OF A COIN, LIGHT AND SHADOW, CREATION AND DESTRUCTION. DID YOU THINK YOUR PETTY MACHINATIONS WERE THE ARCHITECT OF THIS GRAND DESIGN?"

Apollo felt a chill race down his spine, doubt gnawing at the edges of his confidence. He had

believed himself the master of this dark bargain, but now... now he wasn't so sure.

"What are you saying?" he asked, hating the tremor in his voice.

The Dark-Aodhán's smile widened, revealing teeth like shards of obsidian. "OH, PHOEBUS," it purred, "YOU'RE BUT A PAWN IN A GAME FAR OLDER AND DEEPER THAN YOU COULD EVER COMPREHEND. AODHÁN AND I... WE ARE INEVITABLE. BUT YOU CAN JOIN ME. SURRENDER TO MY WILL AND YOU WILL TASTE VICTORY."

As the words faded, so too did the apparition, dissolving back into formless shadow. Apollo stood frozen, the implications of what he'd witnessed crashing over him like a tidal wave of dread.

The dungeon cellar's oppressive darkness was broken only by the sickly flicker of a single oil lamp, casting grotesque shadows that danced across Llewellyn's battered form. Today, he hung again limply from his rusted chains, his once-vibrant eyes now sunken and hollow, staring vacantly at the blood-stained floor beneath him.

"Still with us, my dear boy?" Marcus' silky voice slithered through the gloom, accompanied by the deliberate click of expensive shoes on stone.

Llewellyn's cracked lips parted, a whimper escaping before he could stifle it. "Why?" he croaked, his throat raw from screaming. "Why are you doing this?"

Marcus chuckled, the sound devoid of warmth. He reached out, cupping Llewellyn's bruised cheek with a tenderness that belied the cruelty in his eyes. "Oh, Llewellyn. So pure, so... deliciously naive. Don't you see? The Dark can't devour you. But it feeds on your suffering. Yes. Your suffering feeds The Dark. And The Dark... well, it feeds me."

As if to demonstrate, Marcus' hand suddenly tightened, fingers digging into Llewellyn's flesh with inhuman strength. Llewellyn cried out, feeling as though his very essence was being drained away. Marcus started releasing the boy, whose body fell to the ground once free of the chains.

"Please," Llewellyn gasped, tears mingling with blood on his face. "I don't understand. I've never done anything to you."

Marcus leaned in close, his breath hot against Llewellyn's ear. "It's not about what you've done, my boy. It's about what you are. A beacon of light in this miserable town. And I'm going to snuff you out, one agonizing moment at a time. I can't kill you, no. But I can snuff out your light."

As Marcus' words sank in, Llewellyn felt a wave of despair wash over him. He closed his eyes, desperately trying to cling to memories of warmth and love, even as The Dark threatened to consume him entirely.

Llewellyn's mind drifted, seeking refuge from the relentless torment. He imagined his mother's gentle touch, her soothing voice. But even these comforts were tainted now, twisted by The Dark's influence.

"Your mother can't save you," Marcus whispered, as if reading Llewellyn's thoughts. "No one can."

A sob caught in Llewellyn's throat. "You're wrong," he managed, his voice barely audible. "There's always hope."

Marcus chuckled, his eyes gleaming with malice as he unbuttoned his fly. "Hope? Oh, you poor, foolish child."

With a sudden, violent motion, Marcus grabbed Llewellyn by the hair and yanked him across the damp stone floor. Llewellyn screamed in agony as his battered body was wrenched forward, the hard stone scraping against his raw skin. Marcus stomped on the boy's right leg, snapping it like a matchstick. Each blow from Marcus' muscular arms landed on the boy's frail body with bone-shattering force, leaving behind a trail of blood

pleading eyes met his own, reflected in their terrified depths the full extent of his helplessness.

"That's it," Marcus purred, running a finger along Llewellyn's jawline. "Take it."

Llewellyn followed Marcus' orders without question, but as soon as the man's shaft was in his mouth, he snapped his teeth down on it with a viciousness that surprised even himself. Marcus howled in agony and tried to pull away, but Llewellyn held on tight, clamping down harder until blood filled his mouth. Infuriated beyond reason, Marcus backhanded Llewellyn across the face, sending him crashing to the floor with a sickening thud. Llewellyn's nose exploded into a burst of pain, but he didn't let go of his attacker until he was thrown off by another powerful blow. As he lay on the ground, spitting blood and gasping for air, Llewellyn couldn't help but grin at Marcus' furious expression. But his amusement was short-lived as Marcus continued to rain down brutal kicks and punches on him, causing black spots to dance before his eyes and darkness to close in around him.

Determined to break Llewellyn's spirit, Marcus grabbed a bucket of freezing cold water and doused him with it, making him jolt awake with a scream. "I need you conscious," Marcus growled, grabbing Llewellyn by the hair and forcing him to

sit up. "Now, you will please me," he threatened through clenched teeth, "without any more resistance or I will do the same to your mother." Llewellyn could only nod weakly, his body trembling with fear and pain as Marcus once again forced himself upon him with cruel satisfaction.

Defeated, Llewellyn took his captor's member in his mouth and gagged but dared not defy the order. Tears streamed down his cheeks as he tentatively parted his trembling lips and enveloped the head of Marcus' cock. The wet heat of Llewellyn's mouth was almost enough to make Marcus climax on the spot.

"That's it," Marcus jeered, grabbing Llewellyn by the back of his head and forcing himself deeper into his mouth. Llewellyn gagged again, but Marcus was relentless in his thrusts, plunging in and out of the boy's unwilling mouth.

Marcus' shaft touched Llewellyn's tongue, and Marcus grunted with pleasure. "I know you like it too," he hissed, revelling in the power he held over the sobbing boy at his feet.

The taste of salt and sweat flooded Llewellyn's senses as he tried not to think about what he was doing. His body revolted against the invasion, but he knew better than to stop.

Marcus groaned with each bob of Llewellyn's head. He grabbed onto Llewellyn's hair more forcefully, angling himself deeper into the reluctant boy's mouth. "Oh, yes," Marcus snarled. "Let's see how much hope you have left after this." Then he pressed the boy's back firmly against the wall, holding Llewellyn's wrists above his head. His other hand slid down to cup the firm curve of his backside, spreading the cheeks apart. The boy shivered in shame and horror, his eyes wide and pupils dilated, as he felt the head of the Marcus' thick erection press against his entrance.

Marcus locked his gaze with the Llewellyn's, watching and enjoying the discomfort and fear as he began to push forward. He nodded wickedly, his breath hitching as he felt the tight warmth suddenly envelop him, inch by slow inch.

Llewellyn bit his lip, trying to keep his sobs at bay and trying to adjust to the intrusion, focusing on taking deep breaths and relaxing around him as best as he could. It was a struggle he could never win. His shattered leg exploded with agony, but it paled in comparison to the searing humiliation and torment of Marcus violating him.

Marcus continued to bury himself deeper inside of him until they were completely joined together. He leaned in close, chest to chest, their sweat-slicked bodies pressed tightly together. As he

slowly pulled back out and then pushed in again with increased force, he began to hum the National Anthem under his breath; a twisted sense of patriotism fuelling his lust.

Their breathing grew ragged, every gasp, sob and moan harmonizing with the haunting melody. Once he reached his climax, Marcus resumed beating the boy, driving him unconscious. As consciousness faded, Llewellyn's last thought was a defiant whisper: "Why?"

Marcus looked pitilessly at Llewellyn's broken body. He had broken the boy's body but could still feel the light inside him. His spirit remained undeterred. Acknowledging defeat, Marcus sought to turn the tide in his favour. He still had the boy. His mother would do anything for him. He held the cards and would play them to his advantage. The boy was anathema to the Dark and he could break him no further. He was tempted to finish him off, but a malicious idea formed in his thoughts. He would return the boy to his mother, as a warning of what he was capable of.

Back at the mansion, Apollo's heart pounded as he heard the screeching of tyres and saw a white mini van come to a sudden stop outside his window. In horror, he watched as a pale and bloodied naked body was thrown out before the

van sped away. Without hesitation, he bolted towards the door and ran to the body, recognizing it as Helena Boyd's missing son.

"Help!" Apollo cried out, desperately hoping someone would hear him. "Athena!"

But no one came. His sisters were still engaged in battle and Athena had given him the full account of Hermes' fate. Fuelled by adrenaline and fear for the boy's life, Apollo lifted the unconscious body and rushed inside to one of the guest bedrooms. The sight of the boy's injuries made Apollo's stomach retch, but he pushed his emotions aside and began tending to the wounds, gently wiping away the blood from his pale skin.

Despite the severity of the boy's injuries, Apollo couldn't help but be captivated by his handsome and innocent appearance. His soft features had a stirring effect on Apollo, evoking a sense of tenderness and protectiveness within him. The way his dark hair framed his face and the way his tortured expression shone with hope despite the pain were like a ray of sunshine amidst the darkness. Even in his weakened state, the boy radiated an undeniable charm that was impossible to ignore.

Apollo's piercing blue eyes, shining like the sun itself, bore through his dull mask and into Llewellyn's unconscious form. He traced the

constellation of scars etched across the boy's pale skin, each one telling a story of horrors endured and a resilience that both awed and haunted the fallen god. The weight of Apollo's gaze felt heavy upon Llewellyn's chest, as if he could will the boy back to consciousness through sheer force of will. It seemed as though the god himself was pleading for Llewellyn to return to the land of the living, his eyes full of sorrow and longing. As if in response, a faint twitch crossed Llewellyn's features, a glimmer of life returning to his still body.

A thin, jagged line caught Apollo's attention - a scar at the corner of Llewellyn's lips. As he watched, those lips twitched upwards in a fleeting smile, a bittersweet expression that sent a twinge through Apollo's immortal heart.

"Even in sleep, you find joy," Apollo murmured, his voice tinged with sorrow. "What dreams comfort you now, I wonder?"

He reached out, fingers hovering just above Llewellyn's face. The urge to touch, to heal, to protect surged within him - an echo of his diminished divinity. But Apollo held back, acutely aware of his current limitations.

Llewellyn's smile faded, replaced by a grimace of pain. A soft whimper escaped his lips, and Apollo's fists clenched at his sides.

"Hush now," he soothed, though he knew Llewellyn couldn't hear. "You're safe here. No one will harm you again."

The words felt hollow, a promise Apollo wasn't certain he could keep. How could he protect this fragile mortal when he could barely protect himself? The thought sent a chill down his spine, a creeping dread that threatened to consume him.

No, Apollo steeled himself. *I may not be a god, but I am still Apollo. I will find a way.*

He leaned closer, studying the minute details of Llewellyn's face. The boy's features were a canvas of contradictions - youthful innocence marred by the harsh strokes of suffering. It stirred something within Apollo, a feeling both foreign and achingly familiar.

Despite knowing it would drain him of his power, he couldn't just leave the boy lying there, broken and helpless. As he cradled Llewellyn's injured form in his arms, a strange sensation washed over Apollo - one that had been missing from his life for centuries. But as quickly as it appeared, it disappeared, leaving him torn between helping the boy and protecting his own strength. With a heavy heart, Apollo gently returned Llewellyn to the bed, unsure of what to do next.

"What have you done to me, Llewellyn Boyd?" he whispered, voice barely audible. "What spell have you cast that I, once worshipped by thousands, now find myself utterly enthralled again by a single mortal boy?"

The question hung in the air, unanswered. Apollo's gaze lingered on Llewellyn's lips, that thin scar a testament to all the boy had endured. Without thinking, he traced it with a gentle finger, feeling the slight pull as Llewellyn's mouth twitched into another unconscious smile.

The touch sent a jolt through Apollo, again a spark of something he hadn't felt in eons. His breath caught in his throat as realization dawned, terrifying and exhilarating all at once.

Apollo traced the contours of Llewellyn's body, a silent elegy to the boy's suffering. The once vibrant form had been whittled down to a harrowing silhouette of survival. Ribs protruded like the bars of a cage, sharp collarbones jutting out as if trying to escape the confines of his skin.

"By the gods," Apollo murmured in sorrow. "What horrors have you endured?"

His gaze lingered on the boy's right leg, noting the unnatural bend that spoke of a poorly healing fracture. Apollo's hand hovered over it, trembling slightly.

"This imperfection," he said softly, "it's a testament to your strength, isn't it? A reminder of your resilience in the face of unspeakable cruelty."

Apollo's mind raced with dark possibilities, each more horrifying than the last. The weight of his powerlessness crashed down upon him, a crushing reminder of his fall from divinity. "Your ankle . . . mortal medicine cannot heal it . . ."

The words hung in the air, loaded with unspoken implications. Apollo's hand finally came to rest on Llewellyn's ankle, a gentle touch that belied the storm of emotions within him.

Apollo's fingers trailed upward, tracing the contours of Llewellyn's battered form until they reached his hair. Once vibrant and full of life, it now hung limp and matted, streaked with dried blood—a grotesque tapestry of the boy's ordeal.

With infinite tenderness, he brushed the hair back from Llewellyn's face. The action revealed a constellation of bruises marring the delicate skin of his neck, their mottled hues a stark contrast to the pallor of his flesh.

Apollo's breath caught in his throat. "They tried to silence you, didn't they? To choke the very life from you."

His mind reeled, conjuring images of Llewellyn gasping for air, clawing at unseen hands. The

former god of light felt darkness creep into his heart, a vengeful fury that threatened to consume him.

"Tell me," Apollo whispered, leaning close. "If I could smite your tormentors with but a thought, would you want me to?"

The unconscious boy gave no reply, but Apollo imagined he saw a flicker of pain cross Llewellyn's features. It was enough to douse the flames of his wrath, leaving only ash and sorrow in their wake.

"No, of course you wouldn't," Apollo said, a bitter smile twisting his lips. He placed his hand softly on Llewellyn's chest, feeling the weak heartbeat of the boy. "Your heart remains pure, even now. It shames me, how easily I succumb to darker impulses."

He closed his eyes, allowing himself a moment of vulnerability in the stillness of the room. When he opened them again, they shimmered with unshed tears and renewed determination.

"I vow to heal you, Llewellyn," Apollo declared, his words carrying the weight of an immortal's promise. "Not just your body, but your spirit. I will be the light that guides you from this darkness, even if it means rekindling the very essence of my divinity."

Apollo's hand hovered over Llewellyn's brow, trembling slightly. The former god of light felt a peculiar warmth blooming in his chest, an unfamiliar ache that both exhilarated and terrified him.

"What is this?" he murmured, his voice barely audible. "This... mortal sensation?"

His eyes traced the delicate curve of Llewellyn's jaw, lingering on the boy's slightly parted lips. A surge of protectiveness washed over him, intertwined with something deeper, more primal.

"Could it be...?" Apollo's breath caught in his throat. He shook his head. "No, surely not. I am a god, fallen though I may be. And you... you're but a mortal boy."

Yet even as he spoke the words, Apollo knew they rang hollow. The tightness in his chest, the quickening of his pulse – these were not the reactions of a detached deity.

"Love?" he whispered, testing the word on his tongue. It tasted of honey and ash, sweet and terrifying. "Is this what mortals call love?"

Llewellyn stirred slightly, a soft moan escaping his lips. Apollo froze, his hand still suspended above the boy's face.

"What have you done to me, Llewellyn Boyd?" Apollo asked, his voice a mixture of wonder and fear. "You've awakened something I thought long dead, buried beneath millennia of divine indifference."

With a trembling voice, he uttered the words that weighed heavy on his heart. "I should have been by your side, protecting you...but what good is my immortality if it couldn't save those I hold dear?" The thought tore at him as he struggled with the conflicting feelings of guilt and helplessness.

Apollo's vow echoed through the air, the weight of his promise pressing down on him like a heavy burden. He knew it was a bold claim to make, swearing by the sacred River Styx, but he couldn't help but feel conflicted. Part of him was determined to find a way to heal Llewellyn, body and soul, but another part feared the consequences of such a powerful oath. It was a risk he was willing to take, but one that left him torn and unsure.

He leaned closer, his lips nearly brushing Llewellyn's ear. "I swear by the fading light of Olympus, I will protect you. From the darkness that hunts you, from the cruelty of this world... and from the consuming fire of my own newfound emotions."

Ignoring the inner voice telling him to not to interfere with the plight of this human child, Apollo bent down and pressed his lips to the boy's forehead, knowing that this healing ritual was his last chance to save him. Doubts swirled in his mind, wondering if he was making a mistake or if it was even worth risking his own life for this boy. But deep down, he couldn't bear the thought of failing and losing someone else he cared for. His determination battled with his fears as he poured all of his energy into the ritual, unsure of what the outcome would be. He kissed Llewellyn's brow softly and started his healing ritual.

As Llewellyn opened his eyes, he saw the opulent bedroom come into focus. The smell of polished marble and fresh flowers filled his nostrils. His mother, Helena, stood at the foot of the bed, her hands covering her mouth in shock. The Greek deities, adorned in signature dark robes, surrounded him with grim expressions. He tried to sit up, but pain shot through his body as he realized he was naked and covered in bandages.

Athena nearby handed Helena a letter with trembling hands, and she read it aloud - an ultimatum from their enemies delivered with a brutal warning: Llewellyn's beaten and battered body had been thrown outside their mansion

gates as a sign of their power and cruelty. Panic rose within her as she understood the gravity of the situation.

Helena Boyd's heart thundered in her chest as she knelt beside Llewellyn's battered form. Her fingers trembled as she reached out, barely grazing his bruised skin.

"My son," she whispered, her voice thick with anguish. "What have they done to you?"

Apollo stepped forward, his piercing eyes blazing with fury under his mask. "This is Taser's doing. The Dark keeps growing stronger by the day."

Helena looked up, her gaze sweeping across the assembled gods. "We can't let this stand. We must act now."

Athena, her grey eyes sharp with calculation, spoke. "We must be cautious. The Dark feeds on chaos and rash decisions."

"Caution be damned!" Aphrodite bellowed, slamming her fist against the wall. "I say we march on Marcus' stronghold and tear it apart!"

Athena shook her head, her resolve hardening. "No. We can't fight darkness with more darkness. We need a plan."

As the gods brooded in silence, Helena's mind raced. She thought of the town she'd sworn to protect, of the innocents caught in this celestial crossfire. The weight of her responsibility pressed down on her, threatening to crush her spirit.

Staring at Llewellyn's bruised and bandaged face, she couldn't help but feel a sense of anger towards their enemies. Yet, as she gazed into his smirking expression, she also felt a wave of determination. "We have to find a way." Her declaration shattered the heavy stillness that enveloped them, but it only added to the weight of doubt already weighing her down. How could they possibly find a way out of this? A million fears and uncertainties flooded her mind, but she refused to let them betray her composure. They had to succeed, or else everything would be lost.

Outside the mansion, an unnatural twilight descended on Rashford. Shadows lengthened, stretching like grasping fingers across the town. In the distance, a dog's mournful howl was cut short, replaced by an eerie silence.

The Dark was coming, and Rashford would never be the same.

Chapter 16

The shadows in the dimly lit room seemed to writhe and pulse, their inky tendrils reaching out as if to caress Aodhán's pale skin. He stood motionless, his young face a mask of confusion and longing. The air around him crackled with untapped power, a raw energy that startled him.

Satana's approach was silent, her movements liquid and predatory. Her eyes, burning with hellfire, locked onto Aodhán's, and when she spoke, her voice was a silken whisper that seemed to coil around his very soul.

"My sweet, innocent Aodhán," she purred, her lips curving into a smile that promised both pleasure and pain. "You've been so lost, haven't you? So confused by this mortal realm and its petty concerns."

Satana's laugh was like shattering glass. "You're awakening to your true nature. To the power that courses through your veins."

As she drew closer, her form began to shift. Her skin darkened to a deep crimson, her fingers elongating into wicked claws. Wings, black as pitch and gleaming like oil, unfurled from her back. Her eyes, now twin pools of liquid fire, bored into Aodhán's.

"You feel it, don't you?" she whispered, reaching out to trace a claw along his jawline. "The potential within you. The ability to reshape reality itself."

Aodhán shuddered at her touch, equal parts repulsed and enthralled. His mind raced, memories of Meredith's kindness warring with the intoxicating promises Satana whispered. "But... but the people of Rashford," he protested weakly. "Why should I harm them?"

Satana's laugh was cruel. "Mortals are fleeting, my dear. Their lives are but a blink compared to beings like us. Why constrain yourself to their pitiful existence when you could rule alongside me?"

Her words resonated within Aodhán, striking a chord of long-buried desire. He felt his powers surge, the Darkness around them beginning to warp and twist.

Satana's smile widened, revealing rows of razor-sharp teeth. "Embrace it, Aodhán," she urged, her voice thick with dark promise. "Let go of your doubts and fears. Take my hand, and I'll show you wonders beyond imagination."

The seductive words of Satana swirled around Aodhán like a hypnotic trance. Apollo and Athena,

watching from their divine mansion, felt the unsettling shifts in the realm as Aodhán started succumbing to her manipulations. Urgency laced their voices as they frantically discussed how to save him from his imminent downfall.

"We must act before it's too late," Apollo exclaimed, his frustration mounting. "The Eldar is teetering on the edge."

Athena's brow furrowed with determination as she weighed their limited options. "We cannot allow him to be claimed by that serpent."

"But what can we do?" Apollo asked, feeling helpless.

Athena's eyes sparked with a sudden idea. "We could seek aid from the archangels."

Apollo hesitated, knowing that involving Yahweh's angels would come at a steep price. "It may mean forfeiting the Eldar to Yahweh in the end."

"But it's better than losing him to Satana," Athena argued fiercely.

With a silent prayer, Apollo reached out to the angelic host. In a blinding flash, Gabri-El and Micha-El materialized before them.

Apollo's voice quivered with urgency as he spoke. "The situation is dire, my friends. We cannot stand

by and watch as Satana gains control through the Eldar."

Gabri-El's eyes flashed with anger as he snapped back, "We are well aware, Apollo. But make no mistake, this will not be an easy battle. The Eldar is a willing pawn in her twisted game."

Athena's voice rang out clear and unwavering, "We must act swiftly before it's too late. The Eldar must not fall to her dark influence."

Apollo's voice grew even more urgent as he continued, "If we fail, she will become a tyrant, ruling over all realms and dominating even the power of Yahweh himself."

As the gravity of the situation sunk in, Micha-El's commanding voice filled the room. "Gather round. We must unite our astral powers and pray that we can save the Eldar before it's too late." The archangels joined hands, their combined strength pulsating through the air as they prepared for battle against the forces of darkness.

Apollo's and Gabri-El's astral forms materialised in front of Aodhán.

"Do not heed the temptress, Eldar child," Apollo's image whispered.

"You will be remembered," Gabri-El's image whispered. "But how?"

Aodhán's mind reeled, torn between Satana's seductive whispers and the urgent cries of those reaching out to him. The Darkness began to distort around him, reality bending to the turmoil in his soul. He found himself in his room at Meredith's farm as the Darkness forced its way around him. Furniture lifted off the ground, swirling in lazy circles. Shadows danced along the walls, taking on grotesque, nightmarish forms.

"They seek to chain you," Satana hissed, realising what was happening, her words dripping venom. "To make you their puppet, afraid of your true potential."

Aodhán clutched his head, overwhelmed by the cacophony of voices both internal and external. "I don't... I can't..." he stammered, his eyes wild with confusion and pain.

The air crackled with energy, sparks of raw power arcing between floating objects. A mirror shattered, its fragments suspended in midair like a constellation of broken stars.

"Please," Gabri-El begged, his form fading because of the maelstrom. "Do not become her pawn, young Eldar!"

Apollo's voice too cut through the chaos, sharp and clear. "You have the power to protect, young Eldar. To nurture, not destroy. Don't throw that away for empty promises."

Aodhán's heart raced, his breath coming in ragged gasps. The room continued to warp and twist, a physical manifestation of his internal struggle. He looked at Satana then to Apollo and Gabri-El inside his soul, torn between two paths, two destinies.

"I... I don't know what to do," he whispered, his voice barely audible above the supernatural storm raging around them.

Satana's eyes flashed with hellfire, her alluring form rippling as she sensed Aodhán's wavering resolve. She glided towards him, her movements liquid and predatory.

"Sweet, naive Aodhán," she purred, her voice a silken caress that sent shivers down his spine. "Why cling to such feeble hopes when I offer you the unbridled power?"

Her fingers, now tipped with obsidian claws, traced the contours of his face. Aodhán's breath caught in his throat, desire and terror warring within him.

"I can give you freedom beyond your wildest dreams," Satana whispered, her lips brushing his ear. "Power to reshape reality itself."

As she spoke, the room around them shimmered and twisted. Aodhán saw visions of himself ruling over vast, shadowy kingdoms, mortals cowering at his feet.

"I will make you as beautiful as the morning sun," Satana continued. "You will be able to forge mortals in your own image and they will look upon you with awe and despair."

"Yes," he gasped, his will wavering. "It's what I want."

Satana was relentless. In one fluid motion, she pulled him close, guiding his lips to her breast. "Then drink," she invited him, her voice resonating with otherworldly power. "Drink and claim your destiny."

"Aodhán, don't," Apollo's image called out. "If you drink from the demoness' breast, you will be her thrall forever. There is no breaking that pact."

Aodhán recoiled at the thought, but Satana continued enticing him.

"Remember your homeland," Satana continued. "Remember your friend Turan, your grandfather and your grandmother. "

Aodhán looked at her in surprise. How did she know about his secrets and his former life?

As if understanding his questioning gaze, Satana slithered around him like a serpent. "Yes, I have been in your mind. I know what you truly want."

Aodhán bit his lips, fighting back tears of confusion.

"Drink my milk and you will be powerful enough to return to them. Our powers will unite and we will be able to destroy the Dark that haunts you and also supplant Yahweh and end his rule. You will be the ultimate power in the multiverse, more potent than your own father and ancestors. Think of what we could do together."

Unable to resist any further, Aodhán's lips surrendered to her will, parting in a silent plea for more intimacy – for a connection that would tether their fates together. The first sinfully sweet drop of Satana's milk laced his taste buds, and his world detonated into a firework of sensation. It tasted of taboo desire, deliciously dark secrets, and the intoxicating allure of infinite possibilities. He drank hungrily, each decadent gulp tethering him tighter to her intoxicating command.

Their attraction was an explosive collision of two stormy souls. Their first touch was electric, skin tingling as if some unseen force had been

unleashed. His soft hands were a contrast to her hard body as they moved to caress her waist, pulling her closer with an urgency that spoke volumes. Her sultry gaze never left his as she leaned in for a kiss, igniting the fire between them again.

"Yes," Satana crooned, tilting his head gently. "Together, we'll watch the world burn and dance in its ashes."

She cradled his head in a soft, silky hand, guiding it towards her bare breast. Her other hand traced the contours of his wiry back as he eagerly latched on, hungrily drinking in her sweet milk. A current of raw desire and carnal love swept over him as she watched him greedily suckle with contentment.

"It is done," she purred. "All that remains for you to give me a son. A new Eldar to rule by my side and to do my bidding."

Aodhán looked at her in shock. "I will die!"

"I can support your life system," she reassured him. "Trust me, and you and your son will rule by my side and will annihilate all that tries to stand against our will."

With that she guided him to an altar and made love to him. He did not fight back, completely seduced by her assurances.

Satana's lips were a promise of unrelenting passion, intermingling with Aodhán's own desires, and together they found themselves locked in a dance of lustful abandon. Their breaths mingled as Satana guided Aodhán's hand to the curve of her breast, allowing him to feel the undeniable weight and warmth within his grasp.

Aodhán's response was visceral – his own body reacting instinctively to her touch, his hardness pressing against her leg as she straddled him. Together they explored the recesses of one another's bodies – tasting and touching with deliberate intent, every movement pushing them closer towards their inevitable union.

Complete surrender came when their bodies finally merged together – an explosion of sensation that rocked both the heavenly and infernal realms. Aodhán's powerful thrusts were met by Satana's eager hips, their bodies colliding with primal intensity. The sounds of their pleasure filled the room as they clawed at each other, seeking solace in their physical connection.

To look upon them was to witness two souls entwined – a sinful encounter that would be forever imprinted upon both heaven and hell. The moment would never be forgotten – for it marked a turning point in their fates when they embraced

both darkness and desire in their pursuit of a love that would defy the very fabric of their existence.

Yet, once he reached his climax and Satana crowed in victory, he was still alive. Breathless, but alive.

"Now, Aodhán dear," Satana purred in his ear. "Go forth and reshape this reality to our image."

As reality trembled and altered, Aodhán must have seen a blur of colours and shapes before finding himself back at Meredith's farmhouse. Then, with a flick of his arm, the farmhouse vanished and, in its place, stood a towering structure, ominous and imposing against the grey sky. Its sharp edges were hewn from dark rocks, giving off an eerie aura of evil. Aodhán grinned with content at the extent of his powers.

"You can do better," Satana pushed him. "Bring Hell on Earth. Unleash the darkness."

Aodhán nodded, his long hair brushing against his naked collar. Suddenly, the ancient tower began to throb with a supernatural energy, as if the very stone and material that made it up had come alive. With swift movements, Aodhán summoned a dense mist that encircled the tower, serving as a shield from any outside forces and even his own powers. It was a powerful mist, capable of distorting reality and driving even the strongest

minds to madness. The tower had no openings or exits, designed in a way that anyone who entered would never find their way out unless Aodhán allowed it. This would be his fortress, from where he would conquer other realms and rule over the multiverse. As he stood inside, the walls and floors took on the shape of his thoughts and desires. He knew that within these walls, he was invincible and unstoppable - for the tower itself was impregnable and obeyed only his will. Using his powers, he created a bridge between realities that stretched over the tower, giving him access to other worlds to conquer and control as he pleased.

The circle of gods and archangels fell to the floor. They were defeated. Apollo looked at the archangels and Athena in horror. They had failed. Satana had claimed the Eldar and he had brought her kingdom to reality.

Aodhán fashioned himself a large throne inside the tower and sat in it triumphantly. He cloaked himself in tendrils of darkness from the mist outside the tower, his eyes gleaming in the dark, wondering who to subject first to his will.

Suddenly, a new presence filled the throne room. The door burst open, revealing the astral form of Llewellyn Boyd. His eyes shone with an intensity Aodhán had never seen before, a newfound vitality coursing through his lithe frame. The chaos in the room seemed to pause, the floating objects trembling in mid-air as if uncertain.

Llewellyn's gaze locked onto Aodhán's, and for a moment, Eldar god cowered and covered his eyes. How had this presence entered the tower?

"Aodhán," Llewellyn said, his voice soft yet unwavering. "I see you. I know you."

The simple words pierced through the veil of confusion clouding Aodhán's mind. He blinked, his chaotic powers momentarily stilled.

"What do you mean?" Aodhán asked, his voice a hiss of a serpent.

Llewellyn's shape took a step forward, seemingly unafraid of the supernatural forces swirling around them. "I see the light within you, the goodness that's always been there."

"Capture him," came Satana's unforgiving voice."

Aodhán nodded. He willed Llewellyn's form to be shackled in chains of dark smoke that snuffed the boy's light out. He fashioned a torture room

purposely for this being that dared interfere with his plans.

"Now we'll have some fun," he grinned and transferred Llewellyn inside this room.

"Find a way out," he hissed in Llewellyn's mind, "And I will release you. Fail to do so, and I will turn your light to darkness and you will serve me forever."

Chapter 17

Apollo was rushed to Llewellyn's room only to find that the boy had once again dropped in a coma. He tried reaching out to him to pull him back but Llewellyn's consciousness was not within the body or the mind. He looked over to Helena and shook his head.

"There is nothing I can do," he stammered. "Llewellyn has been captured and is not here."

"What do you mean?" Helena gasped. "He's here in front of us."

"His body is," Apollo pursed his lips, "but his spirit is elsewhere."

Helena Boyd covered her mouth and fought back some tears. "Is there no hope then?"

"He must fight his way back," Apollo replied quietly. He looked at the door as Athena entered the room, and then straight into his sister's eyes.

"Back from where?" Helena interrupted his thoughts.

Apollo shifted his eyes from Athena to Helena, but could not bring himself to reply.

"From hell," came Micha-El's voice behind Athena. "There is a new problem. The Eldar has fallen to the demoness Satana and has brought

Hell on Earth in the form of a dark tower. We do not know what lies within the tower as it is impregnable to us. But we do know that it is protected by a power that exceeds our own and that rivals Yahweh's Himself."

Athena approached her adopted daughter and took her in her arms. "Llewellyn found a way round the defences of the tower, we felt it," she whispered softly to Helena. "But once within, he was lost to us."

"Can't we siege this tower?" Helena asked, tearing herself away from Athena's arms.

Athena shook her head. "It is too dangerous. We do not have the power to rival that of the Eldar."

"My brother is in the Celestial Realm to ask Yahweh for support," Micha-El tried to reassure here. "But it seems Yahweh is reluctant to intervene as this would lead to all out war between Heaven and Hell and this time, Satana has tipped the scales. Better lose one mortal than the whole of reality."

Llewellyn stood up in the room in the tower. He was surrounded by darkness but at least was no longer shackled. He tried to reach out to Aodhán once more, hoping to negotiate sense with him but his light was extinguished, and his astral form

would not materialise. For the first time in his life, he despaired.

Aodhán's voice echoed ominously in Llewellyn's mind as the boy found himself hopelessly lost in the labyrinthine corridors of the tower's torture room. His heart pounded against his ribcage, each beat sending a jolt of adrenaline through his veins, while sweat trickled down his spine, chilling him to the bone.

Suddenly, the lights flickered on, revealing a grisly sight that froze Llewellyn's blood. The room was filled with rows upon rows of eyeless sockets staring back at him, their lifeless bodies dangling from thick ropes that disappeared into the darkness above. The ceiling, if there even was one, seemed to stretch out endlessly into an abyss of dread and despair.

As Llewellyn tentatively took a step forward, he felt a tug on his shirt sleeve. Whipping around in terror, he saw nothing but the empty space around him - or so he thought. One of the corpses lurched towards him, its lifeless fingers grasping desperately at his ankles. Panicking, he shrieked and tried to run but found himself rooted to the spot as another corpse reached out for him from the shadows.

The eyeless sockets seemed to pierce his very soul as they gazed unblinkingly at him, sucking

away what little remained of his sanity. He felt himself being pulled towards them against his will; it was as if some unseen force was draining him of his life force and replacing it with their own malevolent energy.

Before he knew what was happening, one of the corpses reached up and yanked the noose tight around his neck. With a gurgling cry of horror, Llewellyn felt himself lifted off his feet as the rope tightened around his throat, cutting off his air supply and sending waves of agony coursing through his trachea and cortex.

More corpses freed themselves and approached Llewellyn's suspended body. They reached out at him pulling him down, robbing him of his last breaths. Then when he felt his final breath escape him, he was freed of the noose round his neck and fell to the floor to face the animated corpses that populated the room with him.

"Join us," came Aodhán's voice inside his mind. "Embrace the darkness and be free."

"Aodhán," Llewellyn stammered, catching his breath. "There is good in you still. You are not what you have become!"

Aodhán's laughter echoed in the corridors of the room. Slowly the corpses approached Llewellyn

with ill intent. Llewellyn prepared to defend himself as the first corpse reached for him.

Back on the streets of Rashford, Marcus Taser's eyes smouldered with barely contained rage as he watched from the shadows, his massive form hidden behind a gnarled oak tree. The flickering torchlight cast dancing shadows across Goddard's face as he addressed the gathered citizens of Rashford, his voice rising above the anxious murmurs of the crowd.

"We will not bow to tyranny!" Goddard proclaimed, his fist raised in defiance. "Rashford stands united against the darkness that threatens to consume us all!"

A chorus of cheers erupted from the assembled townsfolk, their faces alight with hope and determination. Marcus felt his lip curl in disgust, bile rising in his throat.

Fools, he thought, his mind seething with contempt. *They dare to challenge me? To resist the inexorable tide of The Dark?* His fingers dug into the rough bark of the tree, splintering it beneath his grip. *I will make them suffer for their insolence. I will crush their pathetic rebellion and watch as their hope withers and dies.*

As Goddard continued his impassioned speech, Marcus retreated deeper into the shadows, his heart pounding with anticipation. The time had come to unleash the full fury of The Dark upon these miserable mortals.

With practiced precision, Marcus began the ritual, his corpulent frame swaying in an otherworldly dance. He raised his arms to the starless sky, feeling the oppressive weight of The Dark pressing down upon him. A chill wind whipped through the trees, carrying with it the faint whispers of countless tormented souls.

"Hear me, oh Great Void," Marcus intoned, his voice a guttural rasp. "I call upon your infinite hunger, your insatiable appetite for destruction. Grant me the power to bend these mortals to my will, to crush their feeble resistance beneath the weight of your terrible might!"

As he spoke, Marcus felt the cold tendrils of The Dark's power seeping into his very being, filling him with an intoxicating sense of invincibility. His eyes rolled back in his head, revealing only milky white orbs as he continued the incantation.

"Rise, oh servants of shadow! Emerge from your earthen tombs and feast upon the flesh of the living! Let your hunger know no bounds, your thirst for vengeance never be quenched!"

The air grew thick with malevolence, a palpable miasma of dread that seemed to smother all light and hope. Marcus' words echoed through the night, a chilling symphony of despair that sent shivers down the spines of all who heard it.

As the final syllables of the incantation fell from his lips, Marcus felt a surge of dark energy course through his veins. A twisted smile spread across his face, his eyes gleaming with malicious triumph.

"Now," he whispered, his voice dripping with sadistic glee, "let the slaughter begin."

The earth beneath Rashford shuddered, a deep groan emanating from its depths. Cracks spider-webbed across the once-peaceful streets, widening into gaping maws that belched forth a noxious, putrid stench.

Llewellyn, struggling to breathe, prepared to defend himself from the onslaught of decaying flesh. His heart raced as he readied himself for the impact of the first corpse's fist. With a grunt, he swung his fist forward, aiming for its sternum. The rotten flesh gave way beneath his knuckles, sending a wave of nausea through him. The stench of decay was overpowering, coating his tongue and filling his nostrils.

But even as he hit the first corpse, more of them closed in around him. Their bony fingers dug into his shoulders and waist, holding him in place as they rained down blows upon him. Llewellyn wheezed, feeling the air being forced from his lungs. Blood filled his mouth as he tried to scream, the taste of copper burning on his tongue.

One particularly vicious blow landed square on his ribcage, causing him to gasp for breath. He felt a hot wetness spread across his shirt, knowing it was more than just sweat or blood. His vision started to blur as he struggled against the onslaught. The corpses seemed to sense their prey was weakening; they pressed in harder, grabbing handfuls of hair and skin as they tried to rip him apart.

With a final desperate effort, Llewellyn lashed out with his foot, connecting with the shinbone of one of the creatures. There was a sickening crunch as bone gave way under pressure. The corpse let out an eerie moan before collapsing onto its neighbour in a pile of rotten flesh and broken bones.

But it was too late; Llewellyn couldn't catch his breath any longer. His trachea burning from the constant assault on his airways. He felt himself slipping into darkness as he was pulled down into the abyss of unconsciousness by the remaining

corpses - their fingers clutching at what remained of his torn body and ruined face.

Llewellyn felt his skin being ripped away, exposing his glistening bones, starting from his chest and then moving up to his face, the pain excruciating as he could see every bloody detail of his body.

Then, at the climax of his pain, the corpses vanished. He fell to the floor with a thud, agonising in pain but his spirit still intact.

"Aodhán," he called in a voice that gurgled with blood. "Stop this charade!"

And with that, he drifted into unconsciousness.

"I'm going to attack the tower," Helena said at last. "However strong this Eldar being is, I doubt he can withstand a direct assault of my military."

"Don't do this," Athena warned her. "It will only cost lives and increase the despair. It is what Satana feeds on."

"I have to save my son," Helena insisted.

"You have a duty to your country," Athena stopped her again. "You must defend your country. You must defend Rashford."

"And the best way I can do it is by saving my son," Helena insisted. With that she called on her

generals to initiate an air attack on the dark tower and left the mansion for the streets.

"Helena!" Athena barked behind her.

"Call me if Llewellyn returns," was her dry reply.

When Llewellyn returned to his senses he was in his bed at home. He was all bandaged again and could feel someone tending to him. With great difficulty he opened his eyes to find the form of his father tending to his bruises.

"Hush, Llewellyn," he heard his father whisper comfortingly, as stabs of pain etched through him like daggers each time Martin Boyd attended to his bruises.

"Dad?" Llewellyn whispered in pain. "Is that really you?"

"Yes son," came Martin's answer.

Tears came to Llewellyn's eyes. "I thought you were dead. Taser said his minions pushed you off the roof."

"Well here I am, son," Martin reassured him.

Llewellyn wanted to believe his father but knew something was off. "I saw your body tumble down the building," he whimpered.

"Aodhán brought me back from the abyss and save me," Martin replied in a hushed tone. "We can be together now, safe from Taser and his minions. Just you, me and mum."

"But mum," Llewellyn started, then stopped. "Where is mum?"

"She'll be joining us soon," Martin answered, trying to reassure his son.

Llewellyn closed his eyes as his father's comforting hands continued to tend to his injuries. He felt safe and content, wrapped in some sort of cocoon that was keeping the madness he had just experienced, both at the tower and also at the hands of Marcus Taser, away. He savoured the moment for an instant then gritted his teeth to fight back his tears.

"No," he wept, "I know you are dead."

"Aodhán saved me," his father replied. "All he asks is that you stop fighting him and serve him, and we'll be together forever as a family, safe under his protection."

"No," Llewellyn shouted, overcoming his pain. "My dad would never ask me to sell my soul." He pushed away Martin Boyd's hand that was tending to a scar on his face and tried to sit up.

Suddenly, his father's form caught fire.

"Llewellyn, please," Martin pleaded. "I am trapped in the circles of Hell. Only you can set me free and extinguish the eternal flames around my soul."

"How can I do that?" Llewellyn asked through his tears.

"Embrace Aodhán," Martin replied. "Accept him as your friend and Master."

"I can't," Llewellyn wept. "I just can't."

"Llewellyn, don't you love me?" his father writhed in the flames.

"Yes, dad, I do," Llewellyn replied, his tears rolling down his cheeks. There was a sincerity in his father's plea and Llewellyn doubted his resolve.

"Then please, accept Aodhán!"

Llewellyn closed his eyes. He sensed that this was an offer that Aodhán himself was offering. His soul for that of his father. Only he could save his father. He was about to accept the bargain but a voice inside him made him reconsider.

"My father would not want this," he cried.

"The offer is still on the table," came Aodhán's voice in his mind.

Llewellyn took a deep breath. "No," he said at last. "I refuse."

Martin's body shrieked in the flames. It launched itself at Llewellyn beating him with its fists.

"You could have saved me," he cried. "Only you could save me. Now I am cursed in hell for all eternity, thanks to you. I hope you know that I hate you and curse you. I disown you as my son and hope the eternal flames consume you too."

More blows from his father's flame ravaged arms rained on Llewellyn. He knew he could not change his mind, but the torment was unbearable. He let out a desperate cry from the bottom of his heart. The cry echoed throughout the tower over Llewellyn's sobs but Martin's arms would not stop.

But in the apex of darkness, Llewellyn rediscovered the light.

From these fissures, pale, gnarled hands clawed their way to the surface. Decaying flesh sloughed off bone as corpses, long buried and forgotten, dragged themselves into the moonlight. Their eyes, milky and unseeing, somehow burned with an unholy hunger.

"Dear God," whispered one of President Helena Boyd's soldiers, his rifle trembling in his hands. "What manner of hell is this?"

Helena stood at the edge of the misty forest that had spontaneously grown in front of the Dark Tower. She had watched helplessly as fighter planes had tried to break the tower only for them to fall down as dead flies once they flew within distance of the tower. Seeing the futility of the fighter planes, she had ordered them to stop flying and concentrated her forces on a ground assault. But the moment her soldiers entered the misty forest, they were drained of skin and blood only to fall down as lifeless skeletons to the ground. In frustration, she again ordered a halt to the assault but no sooner she did, the skeletons of the fallen soldiers awoke and started attacking the living. The ground in front of the tower became a killing ground as the skeletons fought the soldiers effortlessly, unable to die. Helena herself stood at the forefront, her composure a stark contrast to the horror unfolding before her. "Stand your ground," she commanded, her voice steady despite the fear gnawing at her insides. "We are the last line of defence for our people."

As the words left her lips, another wave of undead surged forward. The stench of decay filled the air, accompanied by the sickening squelch of rotting flesh and the rattling of bones.

"Open fire!" Helena ordered, her own weapon raised.

The night erupted in a cacophony of gunfire and inhuman shrieks. Bullets tore through desiccated bodies, yet the skeleton horde pressed on, driven by an insatiable hunger for the living.

"They just keep coming," a young soldier cried out, his face pale with terror. "How can we stop them?"

Helena's mind raced, searching for a strategy, a way to turn the tide. But as she watched her soldiers fall, overwhelmed by the sheer numbers of the undead, a chilling realization settled in her gut.

"We can't stop them," she thought, her heart heavy with the weight of impending doom. "We can only hope to survive."

The streets of Rashford descended into chaos, a nightmarish tableau of terror and desperation. Screams pierced the air as citizens fled from the advancing horde, their faces contorted in primal fear. The once-peaceful town now reeked of decay and despair, an oppressive miasma that clung to every surface.

Amidst the pandemonium, Sheriff Eva Ramirez's voice cut through the cacophony. "This way! Move towards the town hall!" Her words carried the weight of authority, a beacon of hope in the darkness.

Goddard Greening appeared at her side, his usual air of sophistication replaced by grim determination. "Sheriff Ramirez, we need to get these people to safety. The basement of the library might hold."

Eva nodded, her eyes scanning the scene. "Agreed. But we can't leave anyone behind." She paused, considering their options. "Goddard, can you lead the first group? I'll bring up the rear, make sure we don't lose stragglers."

As they moved through the streets, Eva's mind raced. How had it come to this? The town she'd sworn to protect was crumbling around her. She pushed the thought aside, focusing on the task at hand.

"Keep moving!" she shouted, her voice carrying over the din. "Stay together!"

Goddard's smooth voice joined hers, his words laced with a calm that belied the horror surrounding them. "This way, everyone. Quickly now, but don't panic. We'll get through this together."

Eva watched as he guided a group of terrified citizens, his presence seeming to steady them. She felt a flicker of admiration, quickly suppressed by the urgency of their situation.

"Sheriff!" A panicked voice caught her attention. A young woman, tears streaming down her face, clutched at Eva's arm. "My brother, he's trapped in the grocery store. Please, you have to help him!"

Eva's heart clenched. Every instinct screamed at her to keep moving, to focus on the group. But she couldn't abandon anyone. "Goddard!" she called out. "Keep them moving. I'll catch up."

As she turned back, Eva couldn't shake the feeling that this night would haunt her forever, regardless of its outcome. The weight of her duty pressed down on her, a constant reminder of the lives at stake. With a deep breath, she steeled herself and plunged back into the chaos, praying she wasn't making a fatal mistake.

Marcus Taser stood atop the crumbling bell tower, his corpulent frame silhouetted against the blood-red sky. A cruel smile played upon his lips as he surveyed the carnage below, his eyes glinting with malevolent satisfaction. The screams of the dying, the sickening crunch of bone, and the wet tearing of flesh formed a symphony of destruction that sent shivers of pleasure down his spine.

"Look at them scurry," he murmured, his voice thick with disdain. "Like ants beneath my boot."

As he watched, a group of soldiers made a valiant stand against his horde of zombies, their weapons flashing in the eerie light. For a fleeting moment, Marcus felt a twinge of... something. Not quite doubt, but a nagging sensation that tugged at the edges of his consciousness.

"What if—" he began, but quickly shook his head, banishing the thought. "No. This is my destiny. My triumph."

He raised his hands, channelling the dark energy that coursed through his veins. The air around him crackled with malevolent power.

"More," he commanded, his voice a guttural growl. "Give me more!"

On the blood-soaked streets below, the undead surged forward with renewed vigour. Rotting hands clawed at the soldiers' armour, tearing through steel as if it were paper. The clash of sword against putrid flesh filled the air, accompanied by the agonized screams of the fallen.

A young soldier, barely more than a boy, swung his blade wildly, decapitating one of the shambling horrors. "We can't hold them!" he cried, his voice cracking with fear.

His sergeant, a grizzled veteran with haunted eyes, gripped the boy's shoulder. "Stand your ground, lad. We die here if we must, but we die fighting."

With a chilling roar, a horde of ravenous zombies descended upon their helpless group. The sergeant's screams were immediately silenced as decaying jaws ripped into his flesh, tearing through muscle and bone with a sickening crunch. Blood sprayed in all directions, adding to the already chaotic scene. The stench of death and decay filled the air, overpowering all other senses. The once brave and confident soldier was now nothing but a lifeless, mangled corpse at the mercy of the bloodthirsty zombies.

Marcus watched the slaughter with growing excitement, his earlier moment of hesitation forgotten. "Yes," he hissed, his eyes burning with an unholy light. "Let it all burn. Let them all fall before me."

He raised his arms once more, ready to unleash another wave of destruction upon the beleaguered town. In that moment, Marcus Taser felt like a god—terrible, unstoppable, and utterly without mercy.

Amidst the chaos, Goddard Greening and Sheriff Eva Ramirez stood back-to-back, facing down a horde of shambling corpses. The stench of decay assaulted their nostrils, a nauseating reminder of the horror they faced.

"On your left, Eva!" Goddard shouted, his voice strained but resolute. He swung his makeshift weapon—a broken street sign—connecting with a sickening crunch against a rotting skull.

Eva spun, her service pistol barking twice. Two undead dropped, dark ichor oozing from the holes in their foreheads. "I'm running low on ammo," she growled, her eyes darting from one threat to the next.

Goddard's usually immaculate suit was torn and splattered with gore. "We can't keep this up forever," he panted, his refined accent incongruous with the brutality surrounding them.

As they clashed, the images of those they had lost bombarded their minds. Eva's vision was filled with the gruesome sight of Deputy Johnson's torn and lifeless body, still fresh in her memory from evacuating helpless civilians. Goddard's thoughts were consumed by the haunting screams of his father, Jeff Greening, as he fell victim to the first wave of zombies.

"We have to push through," Eva insisted, her voice thick with determination and barely suppressed grief. "There are still people counting on us."

Goddard nodded, swallowing hard. "Indeed. Though I fear the cost may be higher than we can bear."

They pressed forward, cutting a swath through the undead horde. Each face they saw—whether friend or foe—etched itself into their minds, a grim reminder of the town they were fighting to save.

High above, Marcus Taser's triumphant grin began to falter. His eyes narrowed as he watched Goddard and Eva's determined stand. "How?" he snarled, his earlier confidence giving way to frustration. "How are they still fighting?"

He reached out with his dark powers, probing for weakness, searching for a chink in their psychological armour. But their resolve, bolstered by shared purpose and the weight of responsibility, proved stronger than he'd anticipated.

Marcus' fists clenched, nails digging into his palms until blood flowed. "I will not be denied," he hissed, his eyes darting from one defender to another, seeking any sign of faltering will or flagging strength. "There must be a way to break them."

As the battle raged on, Marcus' frustration grew, his carefully laid plans unravelling before his eyes. The sweet taste of victory he'd savoured moments ago now turned bitter in his mouth, leaving him hungry for a triumph that seemed to be slipping from his grasp.

The cacophony of battle faded to an unsettling silence. Eva Ramirez stood amidst the carnage, her chest heaving, her blood-slicked hands trembling. The acrid stench of death clung to her nostrils, a visceral reminder of the horror surrounding them.

Her gaze swept over the survivors huddled nearby, their eyes wide with terror. A young woman cradled a child, rocking back and forth, lips moving in a silent prayer. An elderly man stared blankly at his blood-stained hands, his mind seemingly untethered from reality.

"Sheriff," Goddard's voice cut through the eerie calm, "do you think it's over?"

Eva's jaw clenched. "No," she whispered, her voice hoarse. "This is just the eye of the storm."

As if summoned by her words, a low moan echoed across the battlefield. The undead were regrouping, their relentless hunger undiminished.

"We can't keep this up," a soldier muttered, his face ashen. "There's too many of them."

Eva felt the weight of their despair, threatening to crush her resolve. She closed her eyes, memories of fallen comrades flashing behind her eyelids. The faces of those she'd failed to protect haunted

her, their silent accusations a torment worse than any physical pain.

"We have to hold," she said, her voice stronger than she felt. "For Rashford. For each other . . . For humanity."

The undead surged forward, their decaying bodies moving with unexpected speed. Eva and Goddard fought back-to-back, their weapons slicing through rotten flesh.

Eva's gun barked, the sound echoing through the chaos as she aimed for headshots. Goddard swung his makeshift weapon in a deadly arc, breaking bones and skulls with each strike.

The stench of death filled the air, mixing with the metallic tang of blood. The ground trembled beneath their feet as the zombies pushed closer, their moans drowning out all other sounds.

"We need to hold the line!" Eva's voice cut through the din, urging them to stand firm against the relentless onslaught.

Goddard's reply was drowned out by another surge of undead, forcing them to fight harder, faster. They moved as one, a deadly dance of survival amidst the chaos.

Their movements were swift and precise, calculated strikes aimed to incapacitate their

foes. Each blow landed with lethal accuracy, buying them precious moments in the frenzied battle.

As they fought on, exhaustion threatened to slow their movements, but adrenaline pushed them forward. The fight raged on, a brutal symphony of violence and desperation as they fought tooth and nail for every breath, every step gained in the deadly dance of survival.

Eva's gaze swept across the battered faces of the survivors, their eyes wide with fear but still burning with a desperate hope. She knew she had to tap into that hope, to fan its flames before it was extinguished forever.

"Listen to me!" she bellowed, her voice cutting through the cacophony of battle. "We are Rashford! We've faced angels and monsters, and we're still standing!"

She parried a lunging corpse, its putrid breath washing over her as she drove her blade through its skull. "Each of us carries the strength of those we've lost. Their memory fuels us, their love shields us!"

The survivors rallied around her words, their strikes becoming more focused, more determined. Eva felt a surge of pride, but it was

tinged with a gnawing dread. How many would she lead to their deaths today?

As she fought, memories of her father flooded her mind. His unwavering dedication to justice, his compassion in the face of chaos. What would he do in this moment?

"We fight not just for ourselves," Eva continued, her voice hoarse but unyielding, "but for the very soul of our humanity. For every child who deserves a future untainted by this darkness!"

She locked eyes with a young woman, barely more than a girl, wielding a makeshift spear with trembling hands. In that moment, Eva saw herself, years ago, stepping into her father's shoes, the weight of responsibility nearly crushing her.

"Hold the line!" Eva roared, throwing herself back into the fray with renewed vigour. "For Rashford!"

The chant was taken up by the survivors, a defiant cry against the encroaching darkness. But as Eva fought, her heart heavy with the burden of command, she couldn't shake the feeling that their stand might be their last.

Apollo sat by Llewellyn's comatose body. "There has to be a way to bring him back," he kept saying to himself.

Micha-El sat by his side. "Yahweh has called off the angelic forces from Rashford," he confided. "We are alone now."

"We?" Apollo asked, turning to the archangel.

"I will stand with you," Micha-El replied, "but I fear the worst is yet to come. It is unlike Yahweh to call off an attack before the end of a battle."

Apollo turned back to Llewellyn's body. "Somehow I suspect that this boy is the key to undo the darkness."

"Why?" Micha-El asked. "Why do you keep faith in these mortals?"

"We need them just as much as they need us," Apollo whispered.

"And why such faith in this boy?" Micha-El inquired.

Apollo stood still for a moment and measured his words. "Because the moment we were cut off from the Eldar, I felt his presence. This boy is with the Eldar. He is probably being tormented but he has found a way to reach him."

"Do you really think so?" Micha-El asked suspiciously.

"Yes," came Apollo's abrupt answer. "The boy must find the light to fight the Eldar's darkness. He is our only hope now."

Micha-El pursed his lips. "Then help him," he muttered. "You may be god of light and protector of life, but you are one foolish godling, my love!"

"What do you mean?" Apollo asked, as he turned back to Micha-El, his heart missing a beat.

"You proclaim to prefer the human body to the cosmic entity of your being," Micha-El explained, "And yet you forget that hearing is the last sense to abandon the human soul. Make him listen to you. Remind him who he is. You have cured him once so there is a connection between the two of you."

Apollo turned back to Llewellyn, his heart racing. Micha-El's suggestion was wild but it held truth. Slowly, he began singing a ditty from the old days, a ditty of love he used to sing to Hyacinthus before the wind killed the youth.

"In the quiet glow of moonlit skies,
Two boys meet with hearts unwise.
Their laughter spills like ocean's song,
A bond that's fierce, unyielding, strong.

Their fingers touch, a tender spark,
A flame that brightens shadows dark.
In a world that whispers, "Not for you,"
They build a love, both bold and true.

No walls could cage their boundless art,
For love knows only open hearts.
Two souls entwined, they rise above—
A simple truth: love is love."

Martin Boyd's fists landed on his face and body with brutal force, the sharp sting of each hit punctuated by a distant, melodic voice. Despite the pain and fear consuming him, Llewellyn couldn't help but listen to the hypnotic tune. As he hummed along, Apollo's soothing voice grew louder, filling him with a spark of hope. But his father became enraged by this defiance and continued to unleash his rage upon him. Yet Llewellyn felt a glimmer of light inside himself, fuelled by Apollo's empowering melody. As Llewellyn hummed and learned the words to the tune, light started filling his soul. Then, summoning all his strength he stood up and faced his father.

Martin Boyd's image cowered and withdrew from the light his son was emanating. But as the image faded away, so did the darkness around him, revealing a small demon sitting on a throne. He was naked of clothing and defences, no mist to protect him. The demon screamed in agony as it tried to shield itself from Llewellyn.

"Aodhán," Llewellyn whispered as he extended his hand, "come with me."

The demon turned to face him. "Yes. Aodhán. That was my name." Slowly the demonic features faded and Aodhán stood before him, defeated.

"Leave me," Aodhán requested, his voice broken. "This is a place of darkness, no place for you," but Llewellyn only approached and hugged him.

"Come with me," he repeated. "Save me too."

"I have fallen," Aodhán sobbed.

"There's goodness in everyone, Aodhán," Llewellyn's voice echoed, both in the vision and in reality. "Even in those who've lost their way. It's a spark that can never truly be extinguished."

Aodhán felt something stir within him, a warmth that pushed back against the seductive darkness of Satana's promises. "But how can you be so sure?" he whispered, torn between hope and despair.

Llewellyn's smile was gentle, yet it held an unshakeable certainty. "Because I've seen it, even in the darkest moments. In acts of kindness, in the courage to stand up for others, in the ability to change and grow."

The vision began to fade, reality seeping back in. But Llewellyn's words lingered, creating a flicker of

doubt in Satana's allure. Aodhán looked at his hands, remembering not the destruction they could cause, but the life they could nurture.

"I... I want to believe that," Aodhán murmured, his voice barely audible above the din of the room. His mind reeled, torn between the intoxicating darkness and the fading light of his humanity. What should he choose? Power or compassion? Chaos or peace? As Satana's milk coursed through him, the decision seemed to slip further from his grasp with each passing moment.

The conflicting forces within Aodhán reached a fever pitch. His eyes blazed with an otherworldly light, and the air around him began to crackle and hum. The walls of the room shuddered, ancient wood groaning under the strain of his unleashed power.

"What's happening?" Aodhán cried out, his voice distorted by the maelstrom of energy swirling around him. Objects lifted from surfaces, suspended in a chaotic dance. Shadows writhed on the walls, taking on monstrous forms that leered and gibbered. Aodhán stood up, a demonic half man-half serpent, hissing with evil intent. With a wave of his hand, the lava exploded from the Dark Tower into the misty forest below, but whereas the forest resisted the heat of the lava's march, the human and earthly environment was

battered into a molten landscape. Blood rain fell again over Rashford as skeletal demons emerged from the floor and bowed to him.

Satana's laughter rang out, triumphant and cruel. "Yes, my beautiful chaos-bringer! Let it all out! See how powerful you've become."

The lava spread from the Dark Tower to cover Rashford, burning and consuming everything in its path. It inadvertently consumed the skeletons finishing off Helena's soldiers and ground battalions.

Helena's ground forces seized their chance and retreated to the town centre to provisional safety.

But even as the demonic entity revelled, a small, clear voice cut through the cacophony. "Aodhán!" It was Llewellyn Boyd, still inside the tower by Aodhán's side. He took Aodhán's hand into his, undeterred by the moaning of the demonic skeletons around him and ignoring the presence of the demoness Satana.

Aodhán's mind raced. Why isn't he afraid? How can he stand there, so small and fragile, in the face of this... this madness?

"I know you're in there, Aodhán," Llewellyn called out, his hand outstretched, still holding Aodhán's.

The sincerity in the boy's voice made Aodhán's heart clench. "Stay back!" he warned, terrified of what his uncontrolled power might do. "I don't want to hurt you!"

But Llewellyn took another step forward, his eyes never leaving Aodhán's. "You won't," he said simply, with the unshakeable conviction of youth. "Because that's not who you are."

Aodhán's breath caught in his throat. In that moment, Llewellyn's unwavering faith pierced through the veil of chaos, illuminating a path forward. The maelstrom of energy surrounding him began to slow, objects gently descending to the floor. Aodhán's eyes were drawn to the raging maelstrom before him, a scene of chaos and destruction. But amidst the terror, a warm light from Llewellyn enveloped him, stirring up memories and emotions he thought he had buried long ago. Part of him wanted to embrace it, but another part resisted, unsure if he was ready to face his past.

Satana hissed, her beautiful form flickering to reveal something monstrous beneath. "No! You are mine, Aodhán. Remember the power I've shown you, the pleasures I've promised!"

But her words rang hollow now. Aodhán closed his eyes, focusing on the warmth of compassion he'd felt from Llewellyn, from Meredith, from the

people of Rashford Town. When he opened them again, his gaze was clear and resolute.

"I choose them," he said softly, his voice gaining strength. "I choose hope."

The Darkness shuddered one final time as Aodhán's power coalesced, no longer a chaotic storm but a focused beam of pure, radiant energy. It struck Satana squarely in the chest, sending her reeling back with an inhuman shriek.

"This isn't over," she snarled, her form already beginning to dissolve into inky shadows. "You may think you've won, but I've tasted your essence, little god. You'll come crawling back to me when the weight of their pitiful lives becomes too much to bear."

As Satana's last words faded, so too did the oppressive darkness that had filled the tower. Aodhán looked at Llewellyn and nodded. By willing it, both were out of the Dark Tower and in the mansion. Aodhán stumbled, suddenly exhausted and back to his human form. *What have I done?* he wondered, both exhilarated and terrified by the choice he'd made. The demoness's final threat echoed in his mind, a chilling reminder of the path not taken.

He looked around him to find the terrified looks of Apollo and Micha-El gazing at him. Then he turned

to Llewellyn's body and touched his brow. The boy gasped back into consciousness and embraced Aodhán.

The silence that followed Satana's departure was deafening, broken only by the ragged breaths of those who remained. Aodhán's legs trembled, threatening to give way beneath him. He felt a hand on his shoulder, steadying him, and looked up to see Apollo's face, etched with relief and pride.

"You did well, young one," came Apollo's voice, rich with emotion. "The path you've chosen is not easy, but it is right."

"We will stand with you, Aodhán," Micha-El promised, his tone resolute. "Whatever challenges lie ahead, you will not face them alone."

Aodhán's chest tightened, overwhelmed by their support. He wanted to speak, to thank them, but words failed him. Instead, he nodded, swallowing hard against the lump in his throat.

"But... what if she comes back?" he whispered, voicing the fear that gnawed at his insides. "What if I'm not strong enough next time?"

Llewellyn moved closer, his youthful face bearing an expression of wisdom beyond his years. "Strength isn't always about power, Aodhán," he said softly. "Sometimes, it's about having the

courage to choose kindness, even when darkness seems overwhelming."

Aodhán met Llewellyn's gaze, finding comfort in the unwavering belief he saw there. A tentative smile tugged at his lips. "I'm glad you're here," he admitted, reaching out to clasp Llewellyn's hand. "I don't think I could have resisted her without remembering what your strength is like."

As their fingers intertwined, Aodhán felt a surge of warmth, a connection that seemed to transcend the physical. For a moment, the horrors they'd faced faded, replaced by a sense of possibility, of hope.

But even as he embraced this newfound camaraderie, a part of Aodhán's mind whispered treacherously, reminding him of the intoxicating power he'd tasted at Satana's breast. Would he truly be able to resist if she called to him again?

Aodhán gently disentangled his hand from Llewellyn's, the phantom sensation of Satana's touch still lingering on his skin. He moved towards the window, drawn by an inexplicable pull. The night beyond the glass was a tapestry of shadows, broken only by the faint glow of distant streetlamps.

As he gazed out at Rashford Town, Aodhán's breath caught in his throat. The quaint buildings,

once merely picturesque, now seemed fragile, vulnerable. Each flickering light represented a life, a soul he had nearly betrayed in his moment of weakness.

"It's so... terrible," he murmured, pressing his palm against the cool glass. "But I can feel them out there. All of them."

Apollo's voice came from behind him, tinged with curiosity. "What do you sense, young Eldar?"

Aodhán closed his eyes, focusing on the myriad sensations flooding his consciousness. "Their dreams," he whispered. "Their fears. Their hopes. It's... overwhelming."

A cold sweat broke out on his brow as the weight of responsibility settled upon him. "How can I protect them all?" he asked, his voice cracking. "What if I fail?"

Aodhán turned to Michale and Apollo, his eyes wide with a mixture of gratitude and lingering doubt. "But Satana... she's still out there. And a part of me..." he trailed off, shame colouring his cheeks.

"A part of you still yearns for what she offered," Apollo finished gently. "It's natural, Aodhán. The allure of power is not easily forgotten. But we will help you. Stay with us at the mansion. Join our family and we will stand together."

He nodded, relief washing over him at her understanding. "Yes, I choose this," he said, gesturing to the town beyond. "I choose them."

Aodhán felt something shift within him. A resolve, as delicate as a new sprout yet as unyielding as ancient roots, took hold in his heart. The path ahead might be fraught with danger, but he would face it. For Rashford Town. For the mortals who had shown him kindness. For the friends who stood beside him now.

And perhaps, in protecting them, he might find the strength to resist the darkness that still whispered in the recesses of his mind.

Chapter 18

Aodhán's chest rose and fell in the soft candlelight of the mansion of the gods, his delicate features peaceful in repose. Gossamer curtains billowed gently around his humble bed, casting dancing shadows across his face. In sleep, he looked every bit the innocent child-god he was, unaware of the malevolence gathering at the edges of his consciousness.

As Aodhán's mind drifted through tranquil dreamscapes, wisps of darkness began to seep into the corners of his subconscious. At first, they were barely perceptible - wisps of shadow that dissipated when he tried to focus on them. But gradually, insidiously, they took form.

My sweet, guileless Aodhán, a silken voice purred. *So much power, so little wisdom to wield it.*

Aodhán stirred restlessly, his brow furrowing. "Who's there?" he called out in the fog of his dream.

A throaty chuckle resonated through the ether. *Who indeed? I am everything you fear, everything you desire.*

The shadows coalesced, taking on a feminine silhouette of terrible beauty. Satana's eyes glowed with infernal light as she regarded the sleeping god-child.

Such delicious innocence, she mused. *How I long to corrupt it again.*

A chill crept over Aodhán's skin. Even in sleep, he sensed a wrongness invading his dream. "Leave me be," he murmured, tossing fitfully.

But the demoness only laughed, the sound like shards of glass in his mind. *Oh, but we've only just begun to play, little one.*

As she spoke, the very air around Aodhán seemed to thicken and darken. An oppressive weight settled on his chest, making each breath a struggle. The shadows writhed and pulsed with unnatural life, hungry voids seeking to devour all light.

YES, the Dark whispered, its voice the hiss of wind through dead leaves. FEED US YOUR FEAR, YOUR DESPAIR. LET US HOLLOW YOU OUT UNTIL NOTHING REMAINS BUT AN EMPTY HUSK FOR US TO INHABIT.

Aodhán whimpered, trying to retreat from the encroaching darkness. But there was nowhere to hide from the horrors invading his mind. "Please," he begged, "I don't understand. What do you want from me?"

Satana's laughter mingled with the susurrations of the Dark, a discordant symphony of dread. *Everything, sweet child. We want everything you*

are, everything you could be. And we will have it, one way or another.

The young Eldar's face contorted in anguish as nightmarish visions assaulted him. Cities burning, oceans of blood, the screams of countless souls in torment. And through it all, Satana's cruel smile and the endless hunger of the Dark.

"No," Aodhán moaned, fighting against the grip of sleep. "This isn't real. It can't be real."

But as hard as he struggled, he couldn't break free from the nightmare's grasp. The malevolent presence of Satana and the Dark had sunk its hooks deep into his psyche, and they were not about to let their prey escape so easily.

Aodhán's eyes snapped open, his chest heaving as he gulped in ragged breaths. The once-comforting darkness of the mansion's chamber now felt oppressive, alive with malice. Shadows writhed on the walls, twisting into grotesque shapes that seemed to leer at him with eyeless faces.

"It was just a dream," he whispered, trying to calm his racing heart. But even as the words left his lips, he knew it was a lie. The chill that permeated the air was unnatural, seeping into his bones and making him shiver uncontrollably.

Aodhán sat up, hugging his knees to his chest. "What's happening to me?" he asked the empty room, his voice trembling. "Why do I feel so... tainted?"

The shadows seemed to pulse in response, growing darker and more substantial. One particularly dense patch of darkness began to take shape, forming into a vaguely humanoid figure with elongated limbs and razor-sharp claws.

Panic gripped Aodhán's heart. He scrambled backward, pressing himself against the headboard of his bed. "Stay away!" he cried out, his eyes wide with terror.

The shadow creature tilted its head, regarding him with an air of cruel amusement. When it spoke, its voice was like gravel scraping against metal. "Poor little Eldar-child," it rasped. "Did you think you could hide from us forever?"

Aodhán's mind raced, searching for an explanation, a way to make sense of the horror unfolding before him. "This can't be real," he muttered, squeezing his eyes shut. "I'm still dreaming. I have to be."

But when he opened his eyes, the nightmare hadn't faded. If anything, the shadows had grown more numerous, more menacing. They danced at

the edges of his vision, always just out of focus, waiting for the moment to strike.

A sultry laugh cut through the oppressive silence, sending a shiver down Aodhán's spine. The air shimmered, and suddenly Satana stood before him, her beauty as terrifying as it was alluring.

"Oh, but this is very real, my dear," she purred, her eyes glowing with infernal light. "And you're right where you belong."

Aodhán felt a pull towards her, an inexplicable desire to bask in her presence. He shook his head violently, fighting against the compulsion. "No," he said, his voice barely above a whisper. "I don't belong here. This isn't right."

Satana's lips curved into a cruel smile. "But it could be," she whispered, her voice a seductive melody. "Think of the power you could wield, Aodhán. The pleasure you could experience. All you have to do is embrace the darkness."

Images flashed through Aodhán's mind – visions of himself wielding unimaginable power, bending reality to his will. The temptation was overwhelming, threatening to consume him.

"I... I can't," Aodhán gasped, clutching his head. "It's not who I am."

As if angered by his resistance, the shadows surged forward. They engulfed Aodhán in a suffocating embrace, their touch icy and invasive. He tried to scream, but no sound escaped his lips as the darkness poured into his mouth, choking him.

Aodhán's vision blurred, his lungs burning for air. In his mind, he cried out for help, for someone to save him from this nightmare. But only the mocking laughter of Satana answered, echoing in the void that threatened to swallow him whole.

Panic seized Aodhán's heart as he tore himself from the suffocating shadows, his bare feet slapping against the cold stone floor of the mansion. Each step sent shockwaves of pain through his body, but he didn't dare stop. The walls seemed to pulse and writhe, closing in on him with malevolent intent.

"Where am I?" he gasped, his wide eyes darting frantically from one twisted corridor to another. "This can't be real... it can't be..."

His mind raced, trying to make sense of the nightmare he'd found himself in. The mansion of the gods, once a sanctuary, had become a labyrinth of terror. As he stumbled around a corner, Aodhán's foot caught on an unseen obstacle, sending him sprawling onto the unforgiving floor.

Satana's laughter pierced the air, a haunting melody that sent chills down his spine. "Oh, sweet innocent Aodhán," her voice cooed, seeming to come from everywhere at once. "Your futile attempts to flee are so... delicious."

Aodhán scrambled to his feet, his heart pounding. "Leave me alone!" he cried out, his voice cracking with fear. "I don't want your power or your promises!"

"But don't you see?" Satana's voice whispered, now right beside his ear. "You're already mine. A puppet on my strings, dancing to my tune."

As if to prove her point, Aodhán felt his body move against his will, taking a step towards the deepening shadows. He fought against it, his muscles straining, but the pull was undeniable.

"No," he whimpered, tears streaming down his face. "This isn't me. I won't let you control me!"

But even as he spoke the words, doubt crept into his mind. How long could he resist? How long before the darkness consumed him entirely?

Aodhán's bare feet slapped against the cold stone as he forced himself forward, each step a battle against the invisible force pulling him back. The entrance loomed ahead, a rectangle of fading light in the encroaching gloom.

"Just... a little... further," he gasped, his lungs burning with exertion.

But as he reached the threshold, a tidal wave of shadow surged forward. The Dark, formless and all-consuming, crashed over him with relentless force. Aodhán's legs buckled, and he collapsed to the ground, his strength sapped by the overwhelming power of his adversaries.

"No... please," he whispered.

The world around Aodhán began to fade, colours bleeding into an inky blackness. His consciousness slipped away, the Dark consuming everything in its path. As the void closed in, a final, fleeting thought of resistance flickered in his mind.

I am Aodhán, heir of the Eldar. I will not be extinguished.

But even as he clung to that defiant spark, it too was swallowed by the darkness. Aodhán's last sensation was of falling, endlessly, into a pit of absolute nothingness.

"He's gone," Athena broke into Apollo's room. "Aodhán has disappeared."

Apollo sat up and swore. "This boy is becoming too much trouble," he spat. "Any idea where he might be?"

Athena shook her head. "No one left by the door," she whispered. "I was at the front room all the time. He must . . ."

"He's been kidnapped again," Apollo interrupted her. "Right from under our noses."

He looked at his sister with concerned eyes. They had to get Aodhán back but did not have the powers to do so.

"We must inform the Celestials," Athena said at last.

"No!" Apollo stopped her.

"If Satana's taken him," Athena started, "we need to get him back. Only they have the power to invade her realm."

"Yahweh will probably kill him," Apollo growled through gritted teeth.

"There is no other way," Athena insisted.

"There is one," came a small voice behind them. They turned to find Llewellyn supported on a crutch. "I've found him once, I can do that again."

Apollo shook his head. "When you did that your spirit was scarred," he replied.

"Aodhán is my friend," Llewellyn insisted.

"He was your tormentor," interjected Athena. "Llewellyn, sweetheart, these are powers you don't comprehend. Satana and Aodhán won't be so forgiving this time."

"I can't just stand here doing nothing," Llewellyn insisted.

"No!" Apollo decided. "It is too risky."

"But," Llewellyn started, but he was quickly silenced by Athena.

"Go to your room, honey," she said soothingly, as if implying she had all the answers. "We'll find a way."

Llewellyn turned in a sulk. He wanted to find Aodhán again badly but the gods were not permitting it. Then he grinned. A little plan started forming in his head. It was time to see whether Pardon was easier obtained than Permission.

Consciousness returned like a cruel tide, dragging Aodhán from the depths of oblivion. His eyes fluttered open, only to be greeted by an oppressive darkness that pressed against his naked skin like a living shroud. The air, thick and viscous, cloyed in his lungs with each laboured breath.

"Where...?" he gasped, his voice cracking.

As his senses slowly returned, Aodhán became acutely aware of his predicament. Cold chains of pitch-dark smoke bit into his wrists, suspending him upright within a cage so small he could barely shift his weight. Every muscle screamed in protest, forced into an unnatural rigidity.

How long have I been here? he wondered, panic rising in his chest. *Minutes? Hours? Eternities?*

The silence that enveloped him was absolute, save for a distant, unsettling whisper that seemed to emanate from everywhere and nowhere at once. It was the voice of the Dark, he realized with a shudder, its malevolent presence seeping into his very bones.

"I am Aodhán," he murmured, desperate to cling to some shred of his identity. "I am... I am..."

But the words felt hollow, swallowed by the void. Exhaustion weighed heavily upon him, threatening to drag him back into unconsciousness. Yet a spark of defiance still burned within his core, refusing to be extinguished.

"You cannot break me," Aodhán whispered, his voice trembling. "I am more than this... more than flesh and bone."

The whispers intensified, as if in mocking response to his feeble resistance. Aodhán squeezed his eyes shut, trying to block out the

insidious sound, but it only grew louder in his mind.

What if I'm wrong? a traitorous thought wormed its way into his consciousness. *What if this is all there is... forever?*

Aodhán's eyes snapped open, his breath coming in ragged gasps. He tugged at the chains binding his wrists, ignoring the searing pain as the metal bit into his flesh. Blood trickled down his arms, warm rivulets that stood in stark contrast to the cold, unyielding darkness surrounding him.

"No," he growled through gritted teeth, his voice hoarse. "I won't accept this."

The shadows around him seemed to writhe in response, their erratic patterns mocking his futile efforts. Aodhán's eyes darted frantically, trying to make sense of the ever-shifting void.

"Is anyone there?" he called out, his voice cracking. "Please... someone..."

But only the whispers answered, a cacophony of unintelligible murmurs that sent chills down his spine. Aodhán's thoughts turned to his friends, their faces flickering in his mind like fading embers.

"Apollo? Micha-El?" he whispered, a desperate plea. "Can you hear me?"

The darkness seemed to thicken, pressing in on him from all sides. Aodhán's chest tightened, each breath a struggle against the oppressive weight. "Llewellyn," he tried more out of desperation than conviction.

They can't hear you, a sinister voice hissed in his mind. *You're alone. Forever alone.*

"No," Aodhán whimpered, tears stinging his eyes. "That's not true. They'll come for me. They have to."

But as the words left his lips, doubt crept into his heart. How could they find him here, in this realm beyond mortal comprehension? The realization hit him like a physical blow, and a sob escaped his throat.

"Please," he begged, unsure if he was addressing his friends, the darkness, or some higher power. "Don't leave me here. I can't... I can't..."

The chains bit into his flesh as Aodhán slumped against them, his strength failing. Hope, that fragile lifeline, began to slip through his fingers like sand.

Aodhán's head lolled forward, chin resting on his chest. The darkness pulsed around him, a living entity feeding on his despair. He closed his eyes, seeking refuge in memories of light and warmth.

"I am... I am more than this," he whispered, his voice barely audible. "I am Eldar. I am... strength."

The shadows seemed to recoil slightly, as if stung by his words. Aodhán felt a flicker of something deep within – not hope, not yet, but a spark of defiance.

You are nothing, the darkness hissed. *A child playing at godhood.*

Aodhán's eyes snapped open, a faint glow emanating from their depths. "No," he said, his voice steadier now. "I am Aodhán, son of Elya. And I will endure."

He straightened as much as the chains would allow, ignoring the burning in his wrists. The air around him shimmered, the barest hint of his divine essence pushing back against the void.

"You cannot break me," Aodhán declared, each word gaining strength. "I have seen wonders beyond your comprehension. I have felt the love of friends. And I will not let you extinguish that light."

The darkness writhed and coiled, its whispers rising to a crescendo of rage and frustration. But Aodhán stood firm, his spirit flickering like a candle in the wind – small, perhaps, but unquenchable.

A soft glow pierced the darkness, and Llewellyn's form materialized before him, ethereal and shimmering. The boy's presence brought a warmth that seeped into Aodhán's very being.

"Llewellyn," Aodhán whispered, his voice cracking. "How... how are you here?"

Llewellyn's smile was gentle, untouched by the horrors unfolding around them. "I'm not really sure," he admitted. "But I knew you needed me."

Aodhán's chest tightened with a mix of gratitude and despair. "Everything's falling apart. I don't know if I can stop it."

"You don't have to do it alone," Llewellyn said, reaching out to touch the cage. His hand passed through the bars as if they were mist. "Remember we are all connected."

Aodhán closed his eyes, memories of a simpler time washing over him. "I remember."

"We're connected too," Llewellyn continued. "All of us in Rashford. And you're part of that now."

As Llewellyn spoke, Aodhán felt something stir within him. The raw power of his Eldar heritage surged, intertwining with the warmth of human connection. The chains began to crack, hairline fractures spreading like spider webs.

"I'm scared," Aodhán confessed, his voice barely a whisper.

Llewellyn's eyes shone with unwavering faith. "Don't be. I believe in you, Aodhán."

The cage shattered, fragments of metal and shadow dissolving into nothingness. Aodhán stood free, cosmic energy crackling around him like lightning. With a thought, he reached out across dimensions, grasping Llewellyn's essence.

Reality bent and twisted, and suddenly they were standing side by side in a field in the shadow of the Dark Tower. Lava still poured from the tower and the evil mist still surrounded its essence maliciously, but this field stood up to the darkness as if to say that Hope was never dead. The scent of hay and wildflowers filled the air, a stark contrast to the oppressive void of moments before.

Aodhán's legs trembled, overwhelmed by the sudden shift and the weight of his power. Llewellyn steadied him, his touch grounding in its simple humanity.

"What now?" Aodhán asked, his voice small against the looming threat.

Llewellyn's response was cut short by a bone-chilling howl that echoed across Rashford. The sky outside darkened, and an unnatural wind began to howl.

Aodhán's eyes widened in terror. "It's coming," he whispered. "The Dark... and something else. Something ancient and terrible."

As the boys witnessed the ravage of Aodhán's earlier exertions, the storm of undead horror descended upon the town, Aodhán clung to Llewellyn's unwavering optimism like a lifeline. He knew that the choices he made in the coming moments would shape the fate of not just Rashford, but of reality itself. Scared out of his life, Aodhán longed to find refuge in his Dark Tower. *That's what I built it for,* he told himself. But he quickly dropped the thought knowing that in building it, he had given the tower a life and will of its own. He had poured in it his fear and his ill intentions and returning to it now would mean he embraced Satana again.

Aodhán's heart raced, his breath coming in short, ragged gasps. The weight of responsibility crashed down upon him, threatening to crush his spirit. But as he looked into Llewellyn's eyes, he found the strength to stand tall.

"Stay with me, Llewellyn," Aodhán breathed to the astral form of his friend. Llewellyn nodded although strains in his expression were becoming obvious.

"I have to protect them," Aodhán whispered, his voice trembling. "All of them."

With a shaky exhale, he stepped outside. The air crackled with malevolent energy, and the sky above churned like a sea of nightmares. Aodhán raised his hands, feeling the raw power of creation surging through his veins.

"Please," he pleaded to no one in particular, "let this work."

Cosmic energy erupted from his fingertips, weaving an intricate tapestry of light and shadow around Rashford Town. The barrier took shape, a shimmering dome that pulsed with otherworldly radiance. Aodhán's body convulsed with the effort, every fibre of his being stretched to its limit.

As the last threads of the barrier fell into place, Aodhán collapsed to his knees, gasping for air. The world spun around him, reality itself seeming to waver.

"What have I done?" he whispered, staring at his trembling hands.

Screams erupted from the town. Aodhán watched in horror as panic spread like wildfire through the streets of Rashford. People poured out of their hiding places, pointing at the sky in terror and confusion.

"It's the end times!" a woman wailed, clutching her child to her chest.

"We're trapped!" a man shouted, pounding his fists against the shimmering barrier.

Aodhán's heart sank. He had meant to protect them, but instead, he had become the source of their fear. The weight of his actions threatened to crush him.

"I didn't mean to frighten them," he said, his voice barely audible. "I only wanted to help."

Llewellyn placed a comforting hand on Aodhán's shoulder. "Sometimes, the right path isn't always clear. But you acted out of love, Aodhán. That's what matters."

As chaos continued to unfold below, Aodhán struggled with the realization that good intentions didn't always lead to good outcomes. The barrier he had created to save Rashford might very well become its tomb.

The summit room crackled with tension as Micha-El, Apollo, and Helena Boyd stared out the window at the shimmering barrier enveloping Rashford Town. The ethereal dome pulsed with an otherworldly energy, casting an eerie glow across their faces.

"This changes everything," Apollo muttered, his golden eyes narrowing. "The boy's power... it's beyond anything we anticipated."

Helena pressed her palm against the cool glass, her reflection a mask of concern. "We can't let fear cloud our judgment. Aodhán's intentions are pure, even if his methods are... extreme."

"He almost killed your son," Micha-El snapped.

"He was under the influence of that demon," Helena retorted.

Micha-El paced the room, his wings rustling with each step. "Pure intentions pave the road to damnation," he growled. "We must act now, before—"

The archangel's words died on his lips as reality itself began to warp and bend. The air grew thick, charged with an ancient, terrible power that made even Micha-El's divine essence quiver.

"No," he whispered, his face pale with dread. "He wouldn't dare..."

But even as the words left his mouth, the sky above Rashford Town split open. A blinding light poured through the rift, searing the eyes of all who beheld it. The very foundations of the earth trembled as Yahweh, in all His terrible glory, descended upon the town.

Micha-El lunged forward, his voice raw with desperation. "Father, wait! We can still—"

But his pleas were drowned out by the deafening roar of creation unravelling. Buildings warped and twisted, defying the laws of physics. The barrier Aodhán had crafted with such care shuddered and cracked under the weight of divine presence.

As Yahweh's form took shape above the town, Micha-El felt his heart sink. The battle for Rashford's soul had begun, and he feared they were all woefully unprepared for what was to come.

Helena Boyd stood transfixed, her eyes wide with a mix of awe and terror. The air around her crackled with static electricity, making her hair stand on end. She swallowed hard, her throat dry as sandpaper.

"Dear God," she whispered, her voice barely audible over the cacophony of reality bending to Yahweh's will. "What have we done to deserve this?"

Beside her, Apollo's face was ashen, his usual radiance dimmed by the overwhelming presence of the Almighty. "This... this is beyond anything I've ever witnessed," he murmured, his voice trembling. "Even at the height of Olympus' power, we never..."

The god's words trailed off as a wave of divine energy washed over them, nearly bringing them to their knees. Helena gritted her teeth, fighting to maintain her composure.

"We can't just stand here," she said, her voice gaining strength as she spoke. "Our people—Rashford—they need us now more than ever."

Micha-El nodded grimly, his wings unfurling in preparation for battle. "You're right. But against Him... I fear our efforts will be futile."

As if in response to Micha-El's doubts, a bone-chilling laugh echoed through the air. Satana materialized from the shadows, her eyes gleaming with malevolent glee.

"Oh, how the mighty have fallen," she purred, her voice dripping with cruel amusement. "Tell me, Micha-El, does it hurt to see your Father turn against you?"

The archangel's face contorted with rage and pain. "You know nothing of His ways, demon," he spat.

Satana laughed cruelly as she disappeared before the archangel could apprehend her.

But even as he spoke, doubt gnawed at Micha-El's heart. What if Satana was right? What if Yahweh had truly abandoned them?

As the divine and infernal forces clashed above Rashford Town, Helena felt a chill run down her spine. The air grew heavy with the scent of ozone and brimstone, a palpable reminder of the cosmic powers at play.

"We need to evacuate the town," she said, her mind racing. "If this turns into an all-out war..."

Apollo nodded, his eyes darting nervously between Yahweh's blinding light and the encroaching darkness that heralded The Dark's arrival. "But where can they go? Is anywhere truly safe from this?"

Helena's heart sank as she realized the truth of Apollo's words. There was nowhere to run, nowhere to hide from the impending doom that loomed over them all.

As if sensing her despair, The Dark's tendrils began to seep into the edges of her vision, whispering promises of oblivion. Helena shuddered, fighting against the creeping hopelessness.

"We stand and fight," she declared, her voice steady despite the fear coursing through her veins. "For Rashford, for humanity, for everything we hold dear."

But even as the words left her lips, Helena couldn't shake the feeling that they were all

merely pawns in a cosmic game far beyond their understanding. The fate of Rashford Town—and perhaps the entire of humanity—hung in the balance, teetering on the edge of annihilation.

Chapter 19

The night shattered like black glass as divine radiance erupted over Rashford. Yahweh's arrival tore the sky asunder, casting down beams of searing light that scorched the earth and sent townspeople scrambling for cover. Trees bent and swayed as if bowing before their creator, leaves rustling in a cacophonous whisper of devotion and terror.

Aodhán shielded his eyes, the celestial brilliance threatening to blind him even through his ethereal form. He felt the air crackle with divine energy, raising the hairs on his neck and sending tremors through his spectral body.

"By all the gods," he breathed, awe and fear mingling in his voice. "What have we wrought?"

As if in answer to his unspoken dread, shadows began to coalesce at the edges of Yahweh's light. Inky tendrils of darkness crept across the landscape, devouring the divine radiance and leaving an oppressive void in their wake. The Dark had come.

Aodhán's heart raced as he watched the two cosmic forces faced each other, light and shadow locked in an eternal struggle. The air grew thick, heavy with anticipation and the promise of violence. He could feel the weight of destiny

pressing down upon him, threatening to crush his very essence.

"Shadow," he whispered, a part of him still yearning for the familial connection even as revulsion twisted his gut. "Why have you come?"

The Dark offered no response, its amorphous form roiling and churning like a storm of pure malevolence. Aodhán could sense its hunger, its insatiable desire to consume all of existence. He shuddered, remembering the tales of the Dark's origins - once an Eldar god like himself, now a maddened void seeking only destruction.

As the two primordial forces squared off, Aodhán felt a surge of protective instinct for the cowering townspeople. They were innocents caught in a war beyond their comprehension, pawns in a cosmic game. He steeled himself, drawing upon his newfound powers and the wisdom of his Eldar heritage.

"I won't let you destroy this place," he declared, his voice carrying more conviction than he truly felt. "Whatever the cost, I'll stand against you both if I must."

But even as the words left his lips, Aodhán knew the truth. He was woefully unprepared for the cataclysm about to unfold. As Yahweh's light clashed with the Dark's endless shadow, he could

only watch and pray that something of Rashford would survive the coming storm.

The heavens split asunder as Yahweh's wrath descended upon Rashford. Pillars of searing light pierced the night, each beam a javelin of divine fury that scorched the earth where it struck. The air itself seemed to ignite, crackling with celestial energy that made Aodhán's skin prickle and his hair stand on end.

"No!" Aodhán cried out, his voice lost in the deafening roar of battle.

The Dark retaliated with horrifying efficiency. Tendrils of shadow, blacker than the void between stars, lashed out to meet Yahweh's assault. Where light and darkness collided, reality itself seemed to warp and twist. Grotesque shapes bloomed in the air - nightmarish amalgamations of light and shadow that defied comprehension.

Aodhán's breath caught in his throat as he witnessed the sheer scale of destruction. "This... this is what true divinity looks like?" he whispered, awe and terror warring within him.

A stray bolt of divine energy struck a nearby building, reducing it to rubble in an instant. The screams of trapped townspeople pierced Aodhán's heart, reminding him of his duty.

"I have to do something," he muttered, hands trembling as he reached out with his nascent powers. "But what can I possibly do against forces like these?"

As he stood there, doubts consumed him like a swarm of insects, gnawing at his every thought and action. How could he, a mere child in the grand scheme of things, be expected to fight in this battle of titans? The weight of responsibility crushed down on him, making it hard to breathe. He wanted to run away, but he also couldn't bear to leave the fate of the world in the hands of others.

"Focus," Aodhán told himself, closing his eyes and drawing upon the lessons of Elya. "Remember who you are. What you are."

As he centred himself, a faint shimmer of ethereal energy began to coalesce around him. It was a mere whisper compared to the maelstrom above, but it was a start.

"I may not be able to stop them," Aodhán realized, a grim determination settling over him. "But perhaps I can shield the innocent, just a little."

With that thought, he poured his will into enforcing the protective barrier over Rashford, even as the battle of cosmic forces raged on.

As Aodhán strained to maintain his fledgling shield, a sudden hush fell over the chaotic scene. A figure descended from the heavens, his arrival heralded by a soft golden glow that cut through the darkness like a blade of hope.

Micha-El, the archangel, alighted between the warring entities with preternatural grace. His wings, shimmering with celestial light, folded behind him as he stood tall, a bastion of calm amidst the storm.

"Enough," Micha-El's voice rang out, clear and commanding. "This ends now."

Aodhán felt a surge of relief at the archangel's presence. "Micha-El," he breathed. "Can you stop this madness?"

Micha-El's piercing gaze met Aodhán's, a flicker of compassion softening his otherwise stoic features. "I will try, young one. But brace yourself. The worst is yet to come."

As if in response to Micha-El's warning, Yahweh's wrath intensified. A blinding pillar of light crashed down, splitting the earth and sending tremors through Rashford's very foundations. Buildings groaned and crumbled, their structures unable to withstand the divine onslaught.

The Dark retaliated with renewed vigour, its inky tendrils lashing out and engulfing entire streets in

suffocating shadows. The air grew thick with the stench of decay and despair.

Aodhán's heart shattered as he stood in front of the smouldering remains of the once-beautiful homes he and Meredith used to admire during their peaceful walks on the farm. He couldn't believe what his eyes were seeing - charred walls, twisted metal, and piles of rubble where families had once lived. His mind raced with confusion and grief: how could something meant to bring salvation result in such devastation?

Micha-El stood firm, his presence a buffer between the cosmic forces and the town. But even he seemed to struggle against the sheer magnitude of power being unleashed.

"Please," Aodhán pleaded silently, his heart aching for the innocent lives caught in the crossfire. "There must be another way."

Aodhán's empathy surged, overwhelming him with the collective fear and anguish of Rashford's inhabitants. Their terror coursed through him like a poisonous flood, threatening to drown him in despair. Yet, amidst the chaos, a fierce determination ignited within his core.

"I can't let them suffer," he thought, gritting his teeth as he channelled his ethereal energy into the protective shield enveloping the town. The strain

was immediate and excruciating, like molten lead flowing through his veins.

Micha-El's voice cut through the maelstrom, a beacon of reason in the tempest of divine wrath. "Father, I beseech you! Spare these mortals, for they know not what transpires here!"

Yahweh's response was a thunderous roar that shook the heavens, causing Aodhán to stumble. The young Eldar steadied himself, his adolescent frame trembling with exertion as he poured more of his essence into the shield.

"Micha-El," Aodhán gasped, sweat beading on his brow, "why won't he listen?"

The archangel's wings unfurled, a dazzling display of celestial light. "His anger blinds him," Micha-El replied, his voice heavy with sorrow. "I fear my words alone may not be enough."

As another wave of destruction washed over Rashford, Aodhán felt his resolve waver. The weight of his cosmic heritage pressed down upon him, a crushing burden that threatened to break his spirit. Yet, with each scream of terror from the townspeople, his determination rekindled.

"I won't give up," he whispered, his eyes gleaming with an otherworldly light. "Even if it costs me everything."

The sky above Rashford suddenly ignited with a blinding radiance, as if the very fabric of reality had been torn asunder. Yahweh's divine power surged forth, a torrent of celestial energy that crashed against the Dark's amorphous form. The air crackled with raw power, sending shockwaves through the town that shattered windows and toppled chimneys.

Aodhán watched in awe and terror as the Dark writhed under the onslaught, its inky tendrils recoiling from the searing light. "It's retreating," he breathed, his voice a mixture of relief and dread.

Micha-El's expression remained grim. "This battle is far from over, young one. The Dark may flee, but its taint lingers."

As if in response to Micha-El's words, the Dark began to dissolve, its essence seeping into the shadows of Rashford. Buildings, streets, and even the very air seemed to darken, as if a veil of despair had been drawn over the town.

"What's happening?" Aodhán asked, his voice trembling.

Micha-El's wings folded tightly against his back, his otherworldly eyes scanning the landscape.

"The Dark leaves its mark, a cancer that will fester in the hearts of mortals."

The retreat of the Dark brought no respite, for Yahweh's wrath now turned fully upon Rashford. The divine light intensified, becoming a searing, all-consuming force that threatened to obliterate everything in its path.

"No," Aodhán whispered, his heart racing. "He can't... He wouldn't..."

But the young Eldar could feel the change in the air, the shift from battle to judgment. The townspeople, emerging from their shelters, looked to the sky with expressions of abject terror.

"Why?" Aodhán cried out, his voice lost in the rising storm of divine fury. "They're innocent!"

Micha-El's face was a mask of anguish. "In his eyes, they are tainted by the Dark's presence. He sees only the need to cleanse, to purify through destruction."

The air grew thick with tension, charged with the impending doom that loomed over Rashford. Aodhán could hear the prayers of the faithful, their desperate pleas for mercy rising like smoke from a pyre.

"We have to do something," Aodhán said, his voice cracking with desperation. "We can't let this happen!"

Llewellyn, who hadn't left his side, put his hand over Aodhán's shoulder. "Let's do it together," he offered. "But I'm not sure I know how to use the Light as a weapon. Help me."

Aodhán's eyes flickered with an otherworldly light as he reached deep within himself and his friend, drawing upon the cosmic wisdom that flowed through their veins. With trembling hands, he began to weave strands of ethereal energy, his fingers dancing in intricate patterns.

"I won't let them die," he murmured, sweat beading on his brow.

The shield over Rashford shimmered into visibility, a gossamer-thin barrier of iridescent light. Aodhán poured every ounce of his power into it, his young frame shaking with the effort.

Micha-El watched, his golden eyes wide with awe and concern. "Aodhán, be careful. You could burn yourself out."

"I don't care," Aodhán gritted through clenched teeth. "These people... they're not just mortals. They're lives, dreams, hopes. I can feel them all."

As Yahweh's wrath bore down upon the town, Aodhán's shield flickered and strained. The young Eldar's knees buckled, but he refused to yield.

"Please," he whispered, tears streaming down his face. "I can't... I can't let them die."

Micha-El's heart was torn between his allegiance to Yahweh and his empathy for the beings he had been tasked to protect. He gazed at Aodhán, then up at the sky, unsure of what decision to make. After a long moment of agonizing inner turmoil, he summoned all his courage and took flight, uncertain of where his loyalties truly lay.

"My Lord!" Micha-El's voice rang out, clear and resonant above the chaos. "I beg you to stay your hand!"

The divine light paused, as if listening. Micha-El pressed on, his words carrying the weight of millennia.

"These mortals... they are your creation, flawed but worthy of mercy. And this child," he gestured to Aodhán, "he shows us the very compassion you once taught us to embody."

Aodhán, still straining to maintain the shield, looked up at Micha-El with a mixture of gratitude and fear. He could feel Yahweh's presence, a crushing weight of judgment and power, considering Micha-El's words.

The air crackled with tension as all of Rashford held its breath, awaiting divine judgment.

"The Eldar is tainted with Satana's darkness. He has fallen," Yahweh's voice boomed.

"Even so," Micha-El insisted, "he persevered in defending the innocent. Please let it end."

The oppressive light began to recede, its intensity dimming like a dying star. Aodhán felt the pressure ease, his shield no longer straining against an unstoppable force. He collapsed to his knees, exhausted and trembling.

Yahweh's voice boomed with a finality that shook the earth. "I entrust it to you and your comrades to put an end to this darkness," he declared, his eyes blazing with righteous fire. With that, he disappeared back into the celestial realm.

Aodhán stood tall, his body glowing with an otherworldly energy. He raised his hand and summoned a powerful gust of wind, causing the zombies to crumble to the ground. The soldiers and townsfolk of Rashford watched in awe as their saviour defeated the undead with just a whisper. The air was still as Aodhán turned to face them, his eyes blazing with determination. "It ends here," he declared, his voice echoing through the silent streets.

A deafening silence fell over Rashford, broken only by the occasional whimper or sob from the terrified townspeople. Slowly, hesitantly, they began to emerge from their hiding places, blinking in the aftermath of divine fury.

Llewellyn was the first to approach Aodhán, his young hands gently touching his shoulders. "You saved us, Aodhán," he whispered, his voice thick with emotion.

Aodhán looked up at him, his eyes brimming with tears. "I... I don't understand. Why would he want to destroy you all?"

Llewellyn shook his head, a sad smile on his face. "The ways of the divine are often beyond our comprehension, my friend."

As the townspeople gathered, their murmurs grew louder, a cacophony of relief, fear, and confusion. Aodhán struggled to his feet, his ethereal form shimmering weakly.

"What now?" he asked, his voice barely audible. "The Dark... it's still out there. And Yahweh..."

Micha-El descended, his wings folding behind him. "Yahweh has withdrawn, for now. But this reprieve comes at a cost, Aodhán. The balance has shifted."

Aodhán felt a chill run down his spine. "What do you mean?"

Micha-El's eyes were grave. "In sparing Rashford, Yahweh has created an opening. The Dark will not waste this opportunity."

As if summoned by Micha-El's words, a shadow seemed to pass over the moon, plunging the town into momentary darkness. When it passed, the air felt colder, heavier with foreboding.

Aodhán shuddered, remembering the suffocating void of the Dark's presence. "It comes from my world, but I don't know how to fight it," he breathed, his voice small and uncertain.

Micha-El placed a hand on Aodhán's shoulder. "We must prepare. The battle for Rashford—and perhaps for all of creation—has only just begun."

"Now," the archangel continued, "do as Yahweh bid. Stop the undead."

Aodhán's eyes narrowed as he raised his hand, fingers slightly curled.

"How can I... what am I supposed to do?" he whispered, his voice lost in the cacophony of divine warfare.

Suddenly, a golden light cut through the chaos. Apollo's voice, clear and commanding, rang out across the town square. "To arms, my brothers

and sisters! The darkness encroaches, and we must stand firm!"

Aodhán turned, witnessing Apollo and Athena as they rallied the human forces. The Greek god's hair shimmered like spun sunlight, his piercing blue eyes blazing with determination. Beside him, Athena stood tall and resolute, her athletic form poised for battle.

"Apollo, take the eastern flank," Athena ordered, her voice steady despite the apocalyptic scene unfolding around them. "I'll coordinate our aerial defence with the angels."

As the gods and celestial beings took their positions, forming a living barrier against the encroaching shadows, Aodhán felt a surge of... something. Not quite hope, but a flicker of possibility amidst the despair.

"Perhaps... perhaps I'm not meant to understand," he mused, watching the coordinated movements of the divine beings. "But to act, to choose, even in the face of incomprehensible forces..."

The thought was left unfinished as another tremor shook the town, a stark reminder of the battle raging above and the choices that lay ahead.

As the tremor subsided, a chill swept through the air, carrying with it the scent of brimstone and decay. From the deepest shadows, a figure

emerged, her presence a perversion of beauty that made Aodhán's skin crawl.

Satana, the fallen demoness, stepped into the fray. Her raven hair writhed like living shadows, framing a face both alluring and terrifying. Her eyes, burning with infernal light, swept across the battlefield, a cruel smile playing on her lips.

"My, my," she purred, her voice like poisoned honey. "What a delightful party you've thrown. But it seems you've forgotten to invite the guest of honour."

With a graceful flick of her wrist, Satana unleashed a wave of malevolent energy. The air itself seemed to warp and twist, carrying whispers of madness and despair. Aodhán watched in horror as the wave crashed against the defensive line of gods and angels, sowing confusion and chaos in its wake.

"No!" Aodhán cried out, his voice lost in the maelstrom. He staggered, overwhelmed by the suffocating darkness that threatened to consume everything.

Through the chaos, he caught glimpses of two figures moving with purpose amidst the panicked crowds. Sheriff Eva Ramirez's stern voice cut through the din, her words sharp and authoritative.

"Everyone, remain calm! Head towards the evacuation points!" She turned to the man beside her, her eyes reflecting a mix of determination and barely contained fear. "Goddard, we need to get these people out of here. Now."

Goddard Greening nodded, his refined features set in grim resolve. "The situation grows dire by the moment." He raised his voice, addressing the terrified civilians. "This way, everyone! Follow the sheriff's instructions. We shall weather this storm together!"

Aodhán watched as Eva and Goddard worked in tandem, their shared sense of duty palpable even from a distance. Eva's no-nonsense demeanour provided a steadying influence on the panicked masses, while Goddard's charisma and eloquence seemed to inspire hope in even the most despairing faces.

"They're... they're saving them," Aodhán murmured, a flicker of admiration cutting through his fear. "In the face of all this..."

His thoughts were interrupted by Satana's mocking laughter. "Run, little mortals," she crooned. "Your fear is delicious."

As the demoness advanced, leaving chaos in her wake, Aodhán felt a weight settle on his shoulders. The clash between light and dark,

order and chaos, raged around him, and he knew that soon, he would have to make a choice that could alter the fate of everything.

In the shadows of a crumbling building, Marcus Taser watched the unfolding pandemonium with glittering eyes. His corpulent frame was rigid with anticipation, meaty fingers twitching as he surveyed the chaos like a chessboard.

"Perfect," he murmured, his voice a silken purr. "Let them exhaust themselves in this futile struggle."

Marcus' gaze darted between the battling forces, his mind racing with calculations. He reached into his tailored suit, withdrawing a small, obsidian orb that pulsed with an unholy light.

"Now, my dear Dark," he whispered, "let us tip the scales."

As Marcus began to chant in an eldritch tongue, tendrils of inky blackness seeped from the orb, coiling around his arms. But something was wrong. The darkness grew, spreading faster than he anticipated, engulfing his body in a writhing mass of shadows.

"No!" Marcus gasped, his eyes widening in horror. "This isn't... I command you to stop!"

But The Dark paid no heed to his pleas. It was angry and seething at the defeat at Yahweh's hands. It consumed him, growing stronger with each passing moment, its influence expanding beyond the confines of Marcus' control. The Dark screamed and disappeared, taking with it the armies of the undead.

Across the streets, Aodhán felt a shift in the air. The young Eldar's eyes, filled with cosmic mysteries, scanned the ravaged landscape of Rashford Town. Bodies lay strewn across the once-peaceful streets, buildings crumbled, and the sky itself seemed to bleed with otherworldly energies.

"So much suffering," Aodhán whispered, his voice trembling. "Is this... is this what my power brings?"

A surge of energy coursed through him, making his skin tingle and his heart race. He clenched his fists, torn between the urge to unleash his full potential and the fear of causing more destruction.

"I have to do something," he said, taking a hesitant step forward. "But what if I make it worse? What if I'm not strong enough?"

The ground shook beneath his feet, and Aodhán stumbled, catching himself on a nearby lamppost.

As he steadied himself, he saw a young child crying amidst the rubble, reaching for a teddy bear just out of reach.

Without thinking, Aodhán rushed to the child's side, scooping up both the child and the toy in one fluid motion. As he held the trembling form close, he felt a surge of clarity.

"I may not understand everything," Aodhán said, his voice growing stronger, "but I know I can't stand by and watch this happen. Whatever the cost, I have to try."

With newfound determination, Aodhán stepped forward, ready to face the cosmic battle that raged around him, even as the weight of his choices threatened to crush his young soul.

Satana's laughter cut through the chaos like a poisoned blade, her silken voice dripping with malice. "Oh, how the mighty have fallen," she purred, her obsidian eyes gleaming with wicked delight as she faced Apollo and Athena. "Tell me, darlings, how does it feel to be so... mortal?"

Apollo's jaw clenched, his mask matted with sweat and grime. "Your words are as empty as your soul, Satana," he spat, his once-melodious voice now hoarse with exertion.

Athena stood beside him, her grey eyes narrowed in concentration. "We may be diminished, but our

resolve remains unbroken," she declared, her words carrying the weight of ancient wisdom.

Satana's lips curled into a cruel smile. "Oh, how adorable. Still clinging to your precious nobility." With a flick of her wrist, she sent a wave of darkness hurtling towards the gods. "Let's see how long that lasts when you're writhing in agony!"

Apollo and Athena moved in perfect synchronization, their remaining divine energy coalescing into a shimmering shield. The darkness crashed against it, sending tremors through their bodies.

"We can't keep this up forever," Apollo muttered, his muscles straining.

Athena's mind raced, searching for a strategy. "We need to redirect her energy, use it against her."

As the gods struggled against Satana's relentless assault, Aodhán felt a sudden warmth in his chest. His connection to Llewellyn pulsed with newfound intensity, flooding his senses with a kaleidoscope of emotions and memories.

"Llewellyn," Aodhán whispered, his eyes widening with realization. "Our bond... it's more than just friendship. It's a bridge between worlds."

Llewellyn nodded and offered his hand to Aodhán. Aodhán took it hesitantly, for a moment fearing

what this might do to his friend. Then he closed his eyes, focusing on the ethereal thread that linked him to his friend. As he did, he felt a surge of power unlike anything he'd experienced before.

"I can feel it," Aodhán gasped, his voice filled with wonder and trepidation. "The cosmic divide... I can see it, touch it."

With trembling hands, Aodhán reached out, both physically and metaphysically, drawing upon the strength of his connection with Llewellyn. As he did, he felt the very fabric of reality bend to his will.

"Rally to me!" Aodhán called out, his voice carrying across the chaos with unexpected authority. "We can push them back!"

As the defenders rallied around Aodhán, a bone-chilling laugh cut through the air. Satana materialized from the shadows, her eyes blazing with infernal light. The demoness's raven hair whipped around her like snakes, and her voice dripped with venomous sarcasm.

"How adorable. The little god-child thinks he can save them all," she purred, her lips curling into a cruel smile. "Let me show you true power, darling."

Satana raised her arms, and the sky above Rashford Town split open. A deluge of blood-red rain poured down, sizzling as it touched the earth.

The air grew thick with the stench of sulphur and decay.

Aodhán's heart raced as he watched civilians scream and scatter. "I have to do something," he thought, his mind reeling. "But what can I possibly do against this?"

The demoness's laughter echoed as she wove her hands in intricate patterns. The blood-rain coalesced into writhing, serpentine forms that lunged at the defenders.

"Come now, Aodhán," Satana taunted. "Embrace your power. Show me what an Eldar can really do."

Aodhán felt a surge of energy coursing through his veins. The Eldar Mysti responded to his turmoil, begging to be unleashed. He could feel the raw potential crackling at his fingertips.

"I could end this," he thought, his heart pounding. "But at what cost?"

Images flashed through Aodhán's mind: the destruction he could cause, the lives he could snuff out with a mere thought. The power was intoxicating, terrifying.

He looked at Llewellyn again. He realised that if he joined his power to his, it would mean the end of his friend. Quickly he freed his hand of Llewellyn's grasp.

Llewellyn tried to grasp his arm again. "Do it," he cried. "I'm not afraid to die."

"No," he whispered, tears streaming down his face. "There has to be another way."

In that moment of hesitation, Satana struck. A tendril of darkness lashed out, wrapping around Aodhán's throat. He gasped, struggling to breathe as the demoness pulled him close.

"Poor, sweet child," she hissed, her breath hot against his ear. "So much power, and you're too afraid to use it. How disappointing."

As Satana's grip constricted like a vice around his throat, Aodhán's world fragmented into a smudge of distortion and shadow. Time stretched, pulling at the edges of reality until each second felt like an eternity aching to break free. The air quivered with tension, charged with anticipation.

And then—an unholy scream split the frozen silence, so sharp it might have cleaved the fabric of the night itself. It was a sound that clawed at your soul, leaving ragged marks of dread in its wake. Collapsing onto her knees with all the clumsiness of despair unveiled, Satana dropped her relentless facade.

The obscuring fog cleared for just an instant, allowing Aodhán to glimpse Goddard Greening rising from behind her like a spectre born of

nightmares—his features muddied by soot and smoke that still lingered acridly in the cool midnight air. In his grasp was the obsidian dagger from the mansion, oozing gory ink-like blood that seeped into the earth beneath their feet—a landscape painted in horror's palette.

In this tableau of chaos and corporeal ruin, awareness came crashing down on Aodhán like icy water on feverish skin. Clarity sharpened his senses until every detail stood out with unnerving precision, sending tremors through his resolve; his past sins weaving into this present moment as he faced shadows casting none but dark hues upon them all.

"I choose... balance," he choked out, his eyes meeting Satana's with newfound resolve.

A blinding light erupted from Aodhán's body, searing away the darkness that held him. The demoness recoiled, her screech of pain piercing the air. Aodhán felt the Eldar Mysti flow through him, not as a weapon, but as a conduit for healing.

"What are you doing?" Goddard called out, his voice a mix of awe and concern.

Aodhán didn't respond. His focus was entirely on the task at hand. Tendrils of light spread from his fingertips, weaving through the town like gossamer threads. Where they touched, wounds closed,

buildings reformed, and the very air seemed to purify.

"Impossible," Satana snarled, her form beginning to dissolve. "You can't... you can't just..." She fell to the ground, her lifeless form covered in shadow. But even if weak, nobody dared approach her. At last, she disappeared into shadow leaving only the form of a raven where she had fallen. The raven looked around, then flew off into the night.

As the light receded, Aodhán collapsed to his knees, exhausted. The town around him was transformed. The scars of battle remained, but hope blossomed in their wake.

Eva's heart raced as she cautiously approached Aodhán, her eyes wide with a mixture of fear and wonder. "Aodhán...what have you done?" she asked, her voice trembling.

He looked up at her, his face twisted into a weary smile. "I've remembered who I truly am," he replied, his eyes burning with determination.

"But how?" Eva pressed, unable to comprehend the sudden strength in him.

Aodhán's gaze shifted to Goddard, his saviour. He took in two deep breaths, feeling a surge of gratitude wash over him. "Thank you," he whispered hoarsely, his voice filled with emotion.

Chapter 20

Aodhán's legs buckled, his ethereal glow flickering like a dying star. He fell into Llewellyn's waiting arms, the boy's youthful face etched with concern.

"Aodhán! Are you alright?" Llewellyn's voice quavered, his arms tightening around the Eldar god's frail form.

Aodhán's eyes, once radiant with cosmic mysteries, now dulled with exhaustion. He managed a weak smile, his voice barely a whisper. "I... I've never felt so... mortal."

Llewellyn's brow furrowed, his innate curiosity bubbling to the surface despite the chaos around them. "But you're a god, aren't you? How can you be tired?"

A dry chuckle escaped Aodhán's lips, followed by a wince. "Even gods have limits, it seems. Especially when they're... not quite sure what they are."

The air was thick with the acrid stench of smoke and something more sinister - the lingering taint of The Dark's presence. Llewellyn glanced around, taking in the devastation. Buildings lay in ruins, the streets littered with debris and... things he'd rather not identify.

"We should get you somewhere safe," Llewellyn said, his optimism shining through the grime on his face.

Aodhán's hand grasped Llewellyn's arm, stopping him. "No... we can't leave. There's still work to be done."

As if on cue, a commanding voice cut through the smoky air. "Everyone able to stand, gather here! We need to organize our efforts!"

President Helena Boyd stood atop a pile of rubble, her tailored suit torn and stained but her composure unshaken. Her eyes, sharp and determined, scanned the survivors as they stumbled towards her.

"Llewellyn," Aodhán whispered, "help me up. We need to join them."

The boy nodded, his face set with a resolve beyond his years. As they made their way towards the gathering crowd, Aodhán couldn't help but marvel at the resilience of these mortals. Even in the face of cosmic horror, they clung to hope.

But deep within, a nagging doubt gnawed at him. Had he truly banished The Dark, or merely delayed the inevitable?

Athena emerged from the haze, her regal bearing a stark contrast to the chaos surrounding her. Her piercing grey eyes swept over the devastation, cataloguing every broken beam and shattered stone. In her hand, a piece of charcoal scratched feverishly across a scrap of parchment.

"The layout is all wrong," she muttered, her voice low and intense. "We'll rebuild, but stronger. Smarter."

Aodhán watched as she knelt, spreading her makeshift map on a slab of fallen concrete. Her fingers, once adorned with the glow of divinity, now bore the grime of mortality. Yet there was power still in those hands – the power of a mind that could reshape worlds.

"What do you see?" Llewellyn asked, his curiosity overwhelming his fatigue.

Athena's gaze snapped up, a ghost of a smile touching her lips. "The future, my dear. A Rashford that can withstand the storms to come."

A blur of motion caught Aodhán's eye. Hermes, his lithe form little more than a streak of colour, darted through the ruins. The young god's

movements were erratic, desperate – a far cry from his usual grace.

"Something's wrong," Aodhán whispered, his heart clenching. "Llewellyn, stay here."

He pushed himself up, ignoring the protests of his battered body. As he stumbled forward, he saw Hermes skid to a stop before Apollo. The messenger god's eyes were wild, his chest heaving.

"Help... me..." Hermes gasped, his voice a strangled plea.

Apollo's face hardened, recognition and sorrow warring in his eyes. "Oh, brother," he murmured, "what has she done to you?"

Aodhán watched, transfixed, as Apollo placed his hands on Hermes' temples. Golden light, a mere echo of Apollo's former glory, pulsed between them. Hermes screamed, a sound of both agony and release.

In that moment, Aodhán saw it – the writhing, oily tendrils of Satana's corruption fleeing Hermes' body. The young god's form shimmered, the taint of demonic influence melting away.

Then, as suddenly as it began, it was over. Hermes collapsed, his now-unmarred face peaceful in

unconsciousness. Apollo sagged, exhaustion etched in every line of his being.

Aodhán approached slowly, his mind reeling. "How did you...?"

Apollo looked up, a weary smile on his lips. "Some tricks," he said softly, "you never forget."

Apollo's hands trembled as he cradled Hermes' head, his touch gentle as a whisper. The masked god's eyes shimmered with unshed tears, a mix of relief and anguish etched across his face.

"I should have protected you," Apollo murmured, his voice cracking. "I failed you, little brother."

Aodhán knelt beside them, his own chest tight with empathy. "You saved him," he offered, struggling to find words of comfort.

Apollo's laugh was hollow. "Did I? Look around us, Aodhán. The Dark's taint lingers like a disease."

As if summoned by his words, shadows seemed to writhe at the edges of Aodhán's vision. He shivered, suddenly aware of an oppressive weight in the air. The rubble-strewn street took on a sinister cast, jagged edges of broken buildings reaching towards a sky that felt too close, too suffocating.

"Can you feel it?" Apollo whispered, his eyes darting to the deepening shadows. "The corruption seeps into the very stones."

Aodhán nodded, his skin crawling. "How do we fight something so... insidious?"

Apollo's fingers absently stroked Hermes' hair. "I don't know," he admitted, his voice laced with frustration. "My power is a fraction of what it once was. And yet..."

He trailed off, his gaze distant. Aodhán leaned closer, drawn by the god's intensity.

"And yet?" he prompted.

Apollo's eyes refocused, blazing with a fierce determination. "And yet, I refuse to let The Dark claim another of my family. We will find a way, Aodhán. We must."

Around them, the ruins of Rashford buzzed with activity. Humans and gods alike worked side by side, clearing debris and tending to the wounded. The air was thick with dust and the metallic tang of blood, yet beneath it all, a current of determination pulsed.

"Look," Llewellyn said, pointing to where Helena Boyd directed a group of volunteers. "Everyone's working together. We're not beaten yet."

Aodhán watched, a glimmer of hope flickering in his chest. The collaboration before him was a testament to the strength found in unity, a stark contrast to the isolation he felt in that moment.

"You humans never cease to amaze me," Aodhán murmured, his voice tinged with both admiration and envy. "Even in the face of such devastation, you find the will to rebuild."

Llewellyn beamed, his optimism infectious. "That's because we know that together, we can overcome anything. Even the darkest night gives way to dawn, right?"

Aodhán nodded, trying to draw strength from the boy's unwavering faith. But as he surveyed the scene of destruction and rebirth, a chilling thought crept into his mind: What kind of dawn would Satana's unholy offspring bring?

Apollo stood amidst the wreckage, his once-radiant form now dulled by the grime of mortality. His hands trembled as he lifted a fallen beam, muscles straining against the weight. A bead of sweat trickled down his temple, a stark reminder of his newfound limitations.

"Curse this mortal flesh," he hissed through gritted teeth, his melodic voice tinged with frustration.

Yet as he glanced around at the determined faces of those working alongside him, a flicker of purpose ignited within his chest. Apollo drew a deep breath, steeling himself against the ache in his muscles.

"Take heart, friends," he called out, his words carrying a hint of his former divine resonance. "Though our bodies may falter, our spirits remain unbroken. Each stone we clear paves the way for Rashford's rebirth."

A nearby volunteer, her face streaked with dirt and tears, looked up at Apollo with renewed vigour. "Thank you," she whispered, her voice choked with emotion. "Sometimes I forget we're not alone in this."

Apollo's chest tightened, a mix of pride and sorrow washing over him. He was no longer a god to be worshipped, but perhaps... perhaps he could still be a beacon of hope.

As he bent to lift another piece of debris, a commanding voice cut through the air like a blade.

"Apollo! I need you to organize a team," Athena's authoritative tone brooked no argument.

He turned to see her striding through the chaos, her regal bearing a stark contrast to the devastation around them. Her piercing grey eyes

scanned the scene, cataloguing every detail with ruthless efficiency.

"Of course, Athena," Apollo replied, straightening despite the protest of his aching back. "What's our priority there?"

Athena's lips thinned as she gestured towards a partially collapsed building. "That structure houses vital medical supplies. We need it cleared and secured within the hour."

As Apollo nodded and moved to gather volunteers, he couldn't help but marvel at Athena's unwavering focus. With the return of her divine powers, she commanded respect and obedience with ease.

"How do you do it?" he murmured, more to himself than to her. "How do you maintain such... purpose?"

Athena's gaze softened for a moment, a flicker of understanding passing between them. "We adapt, Apollo. It's what we've always done. Now, more than ever, Rashford needs our strength – mortal or otherwise."

With those words ringing in his ears, Apollo strode towards the eastern quadrant, his voice rising in a rallying cry. For the first time since their fall from grace, he felt the stirrings of true hope – not for

godhood restored, but for a new kind of strength forged in the crucible of adversity.

The once-quaint streets of Rashford now thrummed with a feverish energy, the air thick with sawdust and the metallic tang of fresh paint. Aodhán wandered through the labyrinth of scaffolding and half-finished structures, his ethereal presence a stark contrast to the gritty, mortal toil surrounding him.

"It's... remarkable," he murmured, his cosmic eyes wide with wonder as he watched a team of workers hoist a gleaming steel beam into place. The cacophony of hammers and power tools formed a discordant symphony that both thrilled and unsettled him.

Goddard Greening appeared at his side, his refined features etched with a mixture of pride and weariness. "Indeed it is, my young friend. Rashford may have been brought to its knees, but its spirit remains unbroken."

Aphrodite turned to the man, tilting her head in curiosity. "You've changed, Goddard. There's a... weight to you now. A gravity I didn't sense before."

Goddard's lips quirked in a rueful smile. "Adversity has a way of stripping away pretence, doesn't it? I find myself reevaluating my priorities, my very

purpose in this world." Aodhán stepped by his side, placing his arm on the human's shoulder.

As they spoke, Llewellyn Boyd bounded up to them, his youthful exuberance a stark counterpoint to the sombre mood. "Aodhán! Goddard! Have you seen the new community centre plans? It's going to be amazing!"

Aodhán felt a pang of envy at Llewellyn's unbridled enthusiasm. "Your optimism is... admirable, Llewellyn. How do you maintain it in the face of such destruction?"

Llewellyn's smile faltered for a moment, a shadow passing across his features. "I guess... I have to believe things can get better. Otherwise, what's the point of all this?" He gestured at the rebuilding efforts around them.

Goddard placed a gentle hand on Llewellyn's shoulder. "It's that very belief that will see us through the dark times ahead, my boy. Never lose it."

As they stood there, surrounded by the cacophony of rebirth, Aodhán felt a curious tightness in his chest. These mortals, with their fragile bodies and fleeting lives, possessed a resilience that both awed and terrified him. He wondered, not for the first time, if he truly belonged among them.

A chill wind swept through the streets, carrying with it the acrid scent of smoke and something darker, more insidious. Aodhán's ethereal senses prickled, his gaze drawn to the shadows that seemed to lengthen and writhe at the edges of his vision.

"Do you feel that?" he murmured, his voice barely above a whisper.

Goddard frowned, his refined features creasing with concern. "I'm afraid I don't possess your otherworldly perception, Aodhán. What troubles you?"

Llewellyn, his earlier enthusiasm dampened, looked between the two with wide eyes. "Is it... is it The Dark? Has it returned?"

Aodhán closed his eyes, reaching out with his diminished powers. The taint was there, subtle but unmistakable. "Not returned, precisely. It never truly left. The Dark lingers, like a cancer in remission, waiting for the opportune moment to strike."

As if summoned by his words, a woman's laughter echoed faintly on the wind – sultry, seductive, and laced with malice. Satana's presence, though distant, sent a shiver down Aodhán's spine.

"And she's not alone," he added grimly. "Satana carries within her a seed of chaos, one that I...

that we..." He trailed off, unable to voice the horror of his unwitting role in The Dark's plans.

Goddard's jaw tightened. "We've weathered one storm. We'll face whatever comes next."

But Aodhán could see the doubt in his eyes, the tremor in his hands. The mortal's bravado was admirable, but ultimately futile against the cosmic forces arrayed against them.

Llewellyn, ever the optimist, squared his shoulders. "We're stronger together. We've learned from our mistakes. Next time, we'll be ready."

As the young man spoke, Aodhán felt a flicker of something dangerously close to hope. Yet even as it bloomed, he ruthlessly crushed it. Hope was a luxury they could ill afford in the face of the encroaching darkness.

The sun dipped below the horizon, painting the sky in hues of blood and ash. In the gathering gloom, Aodhán could almost see the threads of fate tightening around them all, drawing them inexorably towards a confrontation that would shake the very foundations of reality.

"Ready or not," he whispered, more to himself than his companions, "the reckoning approaches. And this time, I fear, there will be no resurrection for those who fall."

Chapter 21

The grand celestial chamber shimmered with an otherworldly radiance, its walls pulsing with a soft, golden light that seemed to breathe. Apollo stood before Yahweh, his golden hair gleaming despite the suffocating tension that hung in the air like a shroud. Beside him, Athena's piercing grey eyes bore into the omnipotent being before them, her jaw set in grim determination.

Apollo's voice carried a ragged edge as he addressed Yahweh. "We come seeking peace, not as conquered subjects, but as equals." His fingers tightened around the tattered scroll at his side, knuckles whitening. "The blood spilled between our realms has stained the cosmos for too long."

Yahweh's presence loomed, vast and terrible, His voice a rumble that shook the very fabric of reality. "And what makes you think, Fallen One, that I would entertain such a notion?"

Athena stepped forward, her crippled frame taut with barely contained energy. "Because the alternative is mutual annihilation." Her words cut through the air like a blade. "Surely even You can see the folly in that."

As the gods parlayed, Aodhán watched from the periphery, his heart thundering in his chest. The

weight of worlds pressed down upon his shoulders, threatening to crush him. He was an Eldar, yes, but also so terribly, achingly mortal. How could he possibly bear the burden thrust upon him?

His father's legacy burned within him, a constant reminder of the power that coursed through his veins. Yet with that power came a price – the knowledge that his very existence could tear reality asunder.

"I never asked for this," Aodhán thought, his mind reeling. "To be a fulcrum upon which the fate of realms balances." He watched as Apollo and Athena, once proud deities, now stood humbled before Yahweh. Their determination was palpable, but so too was their fear.

The air crackled with divine energy, making Aodhán's skin prickle. He could feel the threads of fate tightening around them all, weaving a tapestry of destiny that he could neither fully comprehend nor escape.

As Yahweh's gaze swept the chamber, it lingered for a moment on Aodhán. In that instant, he felt laid bare, every secret and doubt exposed to that terrible, omniscient scrutiny. He shuddered, fighting the urge to flee.

"You carry a heavy burden, young one," Yahweh's voice resonated within Aodhán's mind. "The choices you make in the coming days will shape the very fabric of existence."

Aodhán swallowed hard, his throat suddenly dry. "And if I'm not strong enough?" he whispered, the words barely audible even to himself.

The silence that followed was deafening, filled with the weight of unspoken possibilities and the looming shadow of annihilation.

Suddenly, Yahweh's thunderous voice shattered the tense silence. "Llewellyn Boyd, step forward."

A collective gasp rippled through the assembly as all eyes turned to the slender, youthful figure standing near the edge of the grand chamber. Llewellyn's eyes widened in shock, his heart pounding so loudly he was certain even the divine beings could hear it.

With trembling legs, he approached the centre of the celestial gathering. The weight of countless immortal gazes pressed upon him, making each step feel like wading through molasses.

"Your contributions have not gone unnoticed, mortal," Yahweh intoned, His voice resonating with power that made Llewellyn's bones vibrate.

Llewellyn bowed his head, overwhelmed by a mixture of pride and humility. "I... I only did what I thought was right, Lord," he stammered, his voice barely above a whisper.

Apollo stepped forward. "It is precisely this spirit of righteousness that we must nurture," he declared, his melodic voice carrying to every corner of the chamber. "Too long have we dwelled in conflict, allowing ancient grudges to fester and poison the very fabric of existence."

Llewellyn watched in awe as Apollo's words seemed to weave a tapestry of light in the air, each syllable pulsing with divine energy.

"We stand at a crossroads," Apollo continued, his piercing blue eyes sweeping across the assembly. "The path of continued strife leads only to mutual destruction. But there is another way – a way of peaceful coexistence and mutual respect."

Athena moved to stand beside Apollo, her grey eyes flickering with tactical calculations. "Consider the strategic advantages of unity," she added, her voice sharp and clear. "Our combined strengths could face any threat, our united wisdom solve any problem."

As the two former deities spoke, Llewellyn felt a surge of hope. Yet beneath it all, a creeping dread gnawed at his heart. He couldn't shake the feeling

that this moment of potential harmony was balanced on a knife's edge, with unspeakable horrors waiting in the shadows should they fail.

The celestial chamber fell into a tense silence as Yahweh's brow furrowed, His luminous form seeming to dim as He contemplated the proposal. The air grew thick with apprehension, each breath a struggle against the weight of countless millennia of conflict.

Apollo's eyes darted to Athena, a flicker of uncertainty crossing his face. She met his gaze, her own resolve unwavering. In that silent exchange, volumes were spoken - of shared battles, of lost glory, of desperate hope.

"The risks..." Yahweh's voice rumbled, each word resonating with the power of creation itself. "The wounds of the past run deep, Apollo. Can they truly be healed?"

Apollo's throat tightened, memories of his murdered son threatening to overwhelm him. He swallowed hard, forcing the words past the lump in his throat. "They must be, Lord Yahweh. For all our sakes."

As the tension in the chamber reached a fever pitch, Aphrodite stood apart, lost in her own tormented thoughts. Her ethereal beauty seemed dimmed, overshadowed by the weight of her sins.

She gazed at her hands, once instruments of passion and love, now stained with the blood of innocents.

"What have I become?" she whispered, her melodic voice cracking. Memories of countless liaisons flashed through her mind, each one a desperate attempt to cling to her fading youth and power. The faces of those she had inadvertently destroyed haunted her, their agonized screams echoing in her ears.

Aphrodite closed her eyes, a single tear tracing a path down her perfect cheek. "There must be a way to make amends," she thought, her heart aching with the enormity of her transgressions. "But how can one atone for an eternity of selfish indulgence?"

The goddess of love stood alone, wrestling with the demons of her past as the fate of the cosmos hung in the balance mere feet away.

The air in the celestial chamber crackled with electric anticipation. Apollo's heart thundered in his chest, each beat a silent plea to the Almighty. Yahweh's eyes, bottomless wells of cosmic wisdom, bore into him with unfathomable intensity.

"Very well," Yahweh's voice resonated, shaking the very foundations of reality. "I shall agree to these terms."

A collective exhale rippled through the assembly. Apollo felt his knees weaken, relief flooding his immortal veins. He glanced at Athena, her stoic facade cracking to reveal a glimmer of hope.

"Thank you, Lord," Apollo breathed, his voice barely above a whisper. "This covenant will usher in a new era of peace."

As the weight of the moment settled, a familiar figure materialized at the edge of Apollo's vision. Hermes, once cocksure and mischievous, now approached with uncharacteristic hesitation.

"Apollo, Athena," Hermes began, his silver tongue now leaden with remorse. "I... I've made grievous errors."

Apollo studied his brother, noting the haunted look in those once-playful eyes. "We all have, Hermes," he replied, a hint of warmth creeping into his tone.

Hermes swallowed hard, his Adam's apple bobbing. "I was a fool, driven by base desires. I've learned the cost of such recklessness." His gaze darted between Apollo and Athena. "If you'll permit me, I wish to make amends. To earn back your trust."

Apollo felt the weight of millennia press upon him. Could he truly forgive Hermes' betrayal? The memory of his half-brother's duplicity during their darkest hour still burned.

"Trust," Apollo mused aloud, "is a fragile thing, Hermes. Once shattered..."

He trailed off, leaving the ominous implication hanging in the air between them.

As the final words of the covenant echoed through the celestial chamber, Micha-El stood rigid at Yahweh's side, his golden wings trembling imperceptibly. The archangel's sapphire eyes, usually brimming with unwavering devotion, now held a storm of conflicting emotions.

How many eons have I served without question? Micha-El pondered, his gaze flickering to Apollo's radiant form. *And yet, these fallen gods show more compassion than we've offered in millennia.*

The rigid hierarchy of heaven suddenly felt suffocating, its unyielding structure a prison rather than a bastion of righteousness. Micha-El's fingers twitched, longing to reach out and bridge the chasm between realms.

"It is done," Yahweh's voice boomed, causing ripples in the very fabric of reality.

Micha-El inclined his head, a gesture of respect masking his internal turmoil. "As you will it, Lord," he murmured, the words tasting of ash on his tongue.

Across the chamber, Apollo caught Micha-El's eye. The fallen god's gaze held understanding, perhaps even a flicker of affection that made Micha-El's heart constrict painfully.

As the divine assembly began to disperse, Apollo found himself drawn to a quiet alcove where Llewellyn stood, wide-eyed and trembling. The mortal's presence was a balm to Apollo's weary soul.

"It's... it's really happening, isn't it?" Llewellyn whispered, his voice quavering. "A new covenant between realms?"

Apollo reached out, his fingers ghosting along Llewellyn's jaw. "Indeed, my dear boy. A new dawn approaches, fraught with both promise and peril."

Llewellyn leaned into the touch, his breath hitching. "I'm afraid, Apollo. What if it all falls apart?"

"Fear not," Apollo murmured, drawing closer. "We've weathered greater storms."

The air between them crackled with unspoken desire, a tension as old as time itself.

The chamber, once bustling with divine energy, now settled into an uneasy calm. Celestial beings drifted apart, their faces etched with a mixture of hope and trepidation. The air thrummed with potential, as if the very fabric of reality held its breath.

Hermes, his winged sandals barely touching the ground, flitted from group to group, his eyes darting nervously. "A new age," he muttered, more to himself than anyone else. "But at what cost?"

Yahweh stood apart, his beard crackling with suppressed lightning. His gaze swept the room, lingering on each face as if committing them to memory. The weight of eons pressed upon his shoulders.

Amidst the dispersing crowd, Aodhán remained rooted in place, his youthful face a mask of concentration. The enormity of what had transpired threatened to overwhelm him.

"Are you alright, young one?" a gentle voice inquired.

Aodhán looked up to see Athena, her warm eyes filled with concern.

"I... I'm not sure," he admitted, his voice barely above a whisper. "Everything's changing so fast."

Athena nodded sagely. "Change is the nature of existence, dear Aodhán. Even for us immortals."

Aodhán's brow furrowed. "But what if I'm not ready? What if I fail?"

"Doubt is the shadow of greatness," Athena replied, her voice carrying the wisdom of ages. "Embrace it, learn from it, but do not let it consume you."

As Athena drifted away, Aodhán closed his eyes, feeling the cosmic energies swirling around him. The weight of his destiny pressed down, suffocating yet exhilarating.

"I am Aodhán," he whispered to himself, his resolve solidifying with each word. "I am of the Eldar. I will not falter."

The chamber seemed to pulse in response, as if acknowledging his declaration. Aodhán opened his eyes, a newfound determination glinting in their otherworldly depths. The path ahead was shrouded in darkness, but he would face it head-on.

Athena stood at the chamber's edge, her steel-grey eyes scanning the dwindling assembly. The air crackled with potential, a fragile hope hanging by gossamer threads. Her fingers unconsciously traced the outline of her shield, now nothing more than a mortal adornment.

"Quite the spectacle, wasn't it?" Apollo's voice cut through her reverie, tinged with exhaustion and relief.

Athena's lips curved into a wry smile. "A necessary one. But our work has only just begun."

She watched as Hermes slunk away, shame and regret etched into his once-carefree features. The fall from grace had changed them all, but some wounds ran deeper than others.

"Do you truly believe this covenant will hold?" Apollo asked, his golden hair dulled in the chamber's fading light.

Athena's jaw clenched, her voice low and fierce. "It must. For all our sakes."

She closed her eyes, memories of celestial battles and mortal suffering flooding her mind. The scent of otherworldly incense mingled with the metallic tang of spilled blood – divine and human alike.

"I won't let it be in vain," she whispered, more to herself than to Apollo. "Not after everything we've sacrificed."

Apollo placed a hand on her shoulder, his touch a reminder of their shared burden. "We stand with you, Pallas. Always."

Athena nodded, her gaze fixed on the retreating form of Aodhán. The boy – no, the Eldar – carried

the weight of worlds on his young shoulders. She vowed silently to guide him, to protect him from the darkness that lurked at the edges of their fragile peace.

"The threads of fate are tangled," she murmured, her tactician's mind already weaving strategies. "But we will unravel them, Apollo. Whatever the cost."

Chapter 22

Eva Ramirez stood motionless, her dark eyes scanning the chaotic web of reports pinned to the bulletin board. Crimson strings connected seemingly unrelated incidents – blood rain in the town square, spectral sightings at the old church, unexplained fires erupting from still water. The air in her office felt thick, oppressive, as if the weight of these supernatural occurrences had become tangible.

She reached out, fingertips brushing a photo of a tree that had reportedly given birth to a being of light. The image blurred as memories of her father flooded her mind – his unwavering resolve, his quiet strength in the face of Rashford's peculiarities.

"What would you do, Papa?" Eva whispered, her voice barely audible. The silence that answered felt like a void, sucking the air from her lungs.

A knock at the door jolted her from her reverie. Deputy Johnson's anxious face appeared. "Sheriff, there's a crowd gathering in the square. They're... unsettled."

Eva's jaw clenched, steeling herself. "I'll handle it."

She strode out of the station, each step echoing on the cobblestones like a metronome counting down to an unknown fate. The murmur of voices

grew louder as she approached the square, a cacophony of fear and confusion.

"It's not natural, I tell you!" an elderly woman's voice rose above the din. "The sky turned green last night, green as sin!"

Eva's mind raced, cataloguing possible explanations, searching for words that could quell the rising panic. The weight of her badge felt heavier than ever, a physical reminder of the responsibility she carried.

"Listen to me," she called out, her voice cutting through the noise. The crowd turned, a sea of worried faces seeking reassurance. "I know you're frightened. But we've faced strange times before, and we'll face these together."

A man near the front, his eyes wild with fear, stepped forward. "But Sheriff, how can we protect ourselves from... from things we don't understand?"

Eva met his gaze, forcing calm into her voice even as doubt gnawed at her insides. "By staying vigilant, by looking out for each other. We are Rashford – we've weathered storms both natural and... otherwise."

As she spoke, Eva's eyes scanned the crowd, noting familiar faces twisted with worry. She thought of the secrets that lay beneath Rashford's

quaint exterior, of the ancient powers that walked among them. How long could she maintain this delicate balance between truth and necessary illusion?

"I promise you," she continued, her voice carrying a strength she didn't entirely feel, "that I will do everything in my power to keep this town safe. But I need your help. Stay calm, report anything unusual, and above all – trust in each other."

The crowd murmured, a mix of reluctant acceptance and lingering fear. Eva felt the weight of their expectations pressing down on her, threatening to crush her beneath their collective dread. She wondered, not for the first time, if she was truly equal to the task before her.

As the gathering slowly dispersed, Eva's gaze was drawn to the distant tree line. For a moment, she could have sworn she saw a flicker of something – a shadow deeper than the surrounding darkness, watching with hungry eyes. She blinked, and it was gone.

Eva suppressed a shudder, her hand unconsciously moving to rest on her holstered gun. Whatever was coming, whatever dark tide threatened to engulf Rashford, she would stand as

the bulwark between her people and the encroaching chaos. Even if it cost her everything.

Goddard Greening stood at the edge of the crowd, his keen eyes absorbing every nuance of the scene before him. The air thrummed with a palpable tension, fear and uncertainty radiating from the gathered townspeople like a miasma. He felt it seep into his bones, a familiar ache that spoke of ancient conflicts and cosmic upheavals.

With a practiced grace, Goddard stepped forward, his polished shoes barely making a sound on the worn cobblestones. He approached a cluster of familiar faces – Mrs. Abernathy, the librarian; old Mr. Finch from the hardware store; and young Sarah, who worked at the diner. Their eyes turned to him, a flicker of hope kindling in their haunted gazes.

"My friends," Goddard began, his rich baritone carrying a warmth that seemed to push back the encroaching shadows. "These are trying times, indeed. But we mustn't forget that our strength lies in our unity."

He paused, allowing his words to sink in. In that moment, Goddard felt the weight of his father's legacy, the whispered secrets of gods and mortals

that had shaped his understanding of this precarious world.

"I propose we form a support group," he continued, his voice dropping to a more intimate tone. "A place where we can share our experiences, our fears, and find solace in each other's company."

Mrs. Abernathy's eyes widened. "You mean... talk about the things we've seen? The... impossible things?"

Goddard nodded, a sad smile playing at his lips. "Sometimes, naming our monsters is the first step to defeating them."

As he spoke, Goddard's mind raced. How much could he reveal without shattering the fragile veil that protected Rashford's mortal inhabitants from the full truth of their situation? The memory of his father's warnings echoed in his mind, a constant reminder of the delicate balance he must maintain.

"We've all been touched by these events," Goddard continued, his words weaving a tapestry of hope and solidarity. "But together, we can face whatever comes. We are not alone in this darkness."

The crowd around him began to nod, murmurs of agreement rippling through the gathering.

Goddard felt a surge of warmth in his chest, tinged with a bittersweet ache as he had a vision of Jamie, the Mayor's son, on the periphery of the group. He thought their eyes met for a brief, electric moment before Jamie looked away and disappeared in thin air.

Goddard pushed down the familiar pang of longing, focusing instead on the task at hand.

"Who among you would be willing to join me in this endeavour?" he asked, his gaze sweeping across the assembled faces.

Hands began to rise, tentatively at first, then with growing confidence. As Goddard looked upon the determined faces of his neighbours, he felt a glimmer of hope. But beneath it all, a cold dread coiled in the pit of his stomach. For he knew, better than most, the true nature of the storm that was gathering on Rashford's horizon.

The heavy oak doors of Rashford's town hall creaked open, releasing a gust of stale air tinged with the faint scent of brimstone. President Helena Boyd strode into the dimly lit chamber, her heels clicking ominously against the worn floorboards. The local leaders, gathered around a long mahogany table, fell silent as she

approached, their eyes reflecting a mixture of hope and trepidation.

Helena's gaze swept across the room, taking in the worried faces before her. She could feel the weight of their expectations pressing down upon her, a burden she had borne since her adoption by Pallas Athena. With a deep breath, she centred herself, drawing upon the strength that coursed through her veins.

"Gentlemen, ladies," she began, her voice carrying a quiet authority that commanded attention. "We stand at a crossroads. The veil between our world and the divine has grown thin, and we must navigate this treacherous path with care."

As she spoke, Helena's mind raced, calculating the risks of each word. How much could she reveal without endangering the delicate balance they had maintained for so long?

Mayor McMore leaned forward, his brow furrowed. "Madam President, with all due respect, how can we possibly reintegrate with the outside world? The things we've seen... the blood rain, the trees giving birth to... to those things. They'll think we're mad!"

Helena met his gaze, her expression softening. "I understand your fear, Brian. But isolation is no longer an option. You must find a way to bridge the

gap between Rashford and the wider world, or risk being consumed by the darkness that threatens to engulf us all."

She paused, allowing her words to sink in. The room was thick with tension, the air itself seeming to pulse with the unspoken fears of those present.

"What do you propose?" asked Councilwoman Rivera, her voice barely above a whisper.

Helena's lips curled into a smile that didn't quite reach her eyes. "A gradual reintroduction. We'll start with controlled visits from select outsiders – researchers, perhaps, or journalists looking for a quaint human interest story. We'll show them the face of Rashford we want them to see, while keeping our true nature hidden in plain sight."

As she outlined her plan, Helena felt the familiar ache of deception in her chest. How long could they maintain this charade? How long before the gods' presence in Rashford became impossible to conceal?

"And what of the... incidents?" Sheriff Ramirez interjected, her face etched with concern. "How do we explain away the inexplicable?"

Helena turned to the sheriff, her voice taking on a soothing cadence. "We'll craft a narrative, Eva. One that speaks to the unique geological and

atmospheric conditions of our region. It won't be a perfect explanation, but it will buy us time."

As the meeting progressed, Helena deftly navigated the concerns raised by each leader, her words a delicate dance between truth and obfuscation. She could feel the tension in the room slowly dissipating, replaced by a cautious optimism.

Yet even as she spoke words of reassurance, a part of Helena recoiled at the web of half-truths she was weaving. How long before this fragile construct came crashing down around them all?

The crunch of gravel under Eva Ramirez's boots echoed in the still night air as she patrolled the outskirts of Rashford. Her hand instinctively rested on the holster at her hip, fingers twitching with each rustle in the undergrowth. The trees loomed overhead, their branches reaching out like gnarled fingers, casting long shadows that danced in the moonlight.

A shrill scream pierced the silence, sending a jolt through Eva's body. She sprinted towards the sound, her heart pounding in her ears. As she rounded a bend in the path, she came upon a group of teenagers huddled together, their faces ashen with terror.

"What happened?" Eva demanded, her eyes darting around for any sign of immediate danger.

A girl with tear-streaked cheeks stepped forward, her voice trembling. "We... we saw something by the river, Sheriff. It wasn't human."

Eva's stomach clenched. "Tell me everything," she said, fighting to keep her voice steady.

As the teenagers recounted their tale, Eva felt a cold dread seeping into her bones. They spoke of a tall, shadowy figure with glowing eyes and limbs that seemed to stretch and contort unnaturally. It had emerged from the water, they said, bringing with it a suffocating darkness that extinguished their flashlights.

"And then it... it spoke," a boy added, his face pale. "But not with words. It was like... like it was inside our heads."

Eva listened, her mind racing. How could she protect her town from something she couldn't even begin to comprehend?

"Alright," she said finally, forcing a calm she didn't feel into her voice. "I want you all to go straight home. Lock your doors and stay inside. I'll investigate this further."

As the teenagers nodded and turned to leave, Eva called out, "And stay vigilant. If you see anything

else unusual, anything at all, you call me immediately. Understood?"

They murmured their assent and hurried away, leaving Eva alone with the oppressive darkness of the forest. She stared out at the river, its surface deceptively calm in the moonlight. What horrors lurked beneath those placid waters?

Eva's hand tightened on her gun, even as she acknowledged its likely uselessness against whatever had frightened those kids. She was a sheriff, trained to uphold the law and protect the innocent. But how could she protect anyone from forces that defied the very laws of nature?

A twig snapped behind her, and Eva whirled around, her heart in her throat. Nothing but shadows greeted her. Yet as she stood there, gun drawn and senses on high alert, she couldn't shake the feeling that something was watching her from the darkness, waiting for its moment to strike.

The warmth of Café Lumière enveloped Goddard Greening like a comforting embrace as he stepped inside, the scent of freshly ground coffee and cinnamon pastries a stark contrast to the chill that had settled over Rashford. He paused, surveying the cozy corner he'd reserved for the support

group meeting. Soft, amber light from vintage Edison bulbs cast a gentle glow over the mismatched armchairs and plush sofas arranged in an intimate circle.

Goddard's fingers trembled slightly as he adjusted his silk cravat, a nervous habit he'd never quite shaken. "Deep breaths," he murmured to himself. "They need you calm."

As the attendees began to filter in, Goddard greeted each with a warm smile and a gentle touch on the arm. He noted their haunted eyes, the way they startled at sudden movements. These were people pushed to the brink by forces beyond their comprehension.

"Welcome, everyone," Goddard began, his rich voice carrying easily through the café. "I'm glad you've joined us tonight. Please, make yourselves comfortable."

As the group settled in, clutching steaming mugs like lifelines, Goddard leaned forward, his dark eyes radiating empathy. "We're here to share, to listen, and most importantly, to remind ourselves that we're not alone in facing these... unusual circumstances."

A middle-aged woman with silver-streaked hair spoke first, her voice barely above a whisper. "I... I

saw my dead husband in our garden last night. But when I blinked, he was gone. Am I going mad?"

Goddard's heart ached at the raw pain in her voice. He'd seen similar occurrences, knew the gut-wrenching hope and subsequent despair they brought. "You're not mad, Margaret," he assured her gently. "Many of us have experienced things that defy explanation. It's why we're here."

As the evening progressed, Goddard guided the conversation with practiced ease, encouraging participants to voice their fears while subtly steering them away from hysteria. He drew upon his knowledge of Rashford's hidden truths, offering comfort without revealing too much.

"Remember," he said, his voice low and intense, "in times of darkness, it's our connections to each other that give us strength. We may not understand everything that's happening, but together, we can face it."

The meeting concluded on a cautiously optimistic note, with plans to reconvene the following week. As the last attendee departed, Goddard sank into an armchair, exhaustion washing over him. He closed his eyes, allowing himself a moment of vulnerability.

"Oh, Jamie," he whispered, his unrequited love for the former Mayor's son a dull ache in his chest. "If only you knew the burdens we carry."

The café's warmth suddenly felt stifling. Goddard loosened his cravat, fighting the creeping dread that threatened to overwhelm him. He was a pillar of the community, yes, but even pillars could crumble under enough pressure. And the pressure in Rashford was building to a fever pitch.

The town square thrummed with nervous energy as Helena Boyd ascended the makeshift stage. Twilight cast long shadows across the cobblestones, and the air hung heavy with the scent of rain-soaked earth and barely contained fear. Helena's eyes, sharp as flint, scanned the crowd before her. Their faces were a tapestry of anxiety and hope, each gaze a silent plea for salvation.

"Citizens of Rashford," Helena began, her voice carrying a weight that belied her mortal form. "We stand at a crossroads, your town besieged by forces beyond mortal comprehension."

A murmur rippled through the crowd. Helena felt the weight of her adoptive mother's legacy press upon her shoulders. Athena's wisdom, tempered

by millennia of divine existence, now flowed through her veins.

"But we are not helpless," she continued, her tone hardening. "We have faced adversity before, and we will do so again. Our strength lies not in denial, but in unity and action."

As she spoke, Helena's mind raced with memories of her childhood — lessons learned at Athena's knee, stories of gods and monsters that now walked among them. She pushed those thoughts aside, focusing on the task at hand.

"I have implemented new security measures," Helena declared, her voice rising. "Increased patrols, enhanced communication systems, and a task force dedicated to investigating the... unusual occurrences plaguing our town."

A man near the front, his face etched with worry, called out, "But how can we fight against things we don't understand?"

Helena's gaze locked onto him, her eyes blazing with an intensity that made him flinch. "Understanding is not always a prerequisite for survival," she replied, her words resonating with an otherworldly wisdom. "Sometimes, faith and perseverance are our greatest weapons."

As she continued outlining her plans, Helena felt a familiar presence at the edge of her

consciousness. Athena, watching from the shadows, a silent guardian. The connection strengthened her resolve, even as it reminded her of the impossible tightrope she walked between two worlds.

"In times of crisis," Helena intoned, her voice taking on a lyrical quality that echoed her divine upbringing, "we must look to the wisdom of those who came before us. To draw strength from their triumphs and learn from their failures."

The crowd hung on her every word, their fear slowly giving way to a tentative hope. Helena felt the weight of their trust, a burden both exhilarating and terrifying. She knew the path ahead was fraught with danger, but in that moment, standing before her people, she felt a surge of determination that would have made Athena proud.

As she concluded her speech, the first drops of rain began to fall, cool and cleansing. Helena raised her eyes to the darkening sky, a silent prayer on her lips. The battle for Rashford's soul had only just begun.

Eva Ramirez stood in the dimly lit sheriff's station, her eyes burning as they scanned the maps and reports spread before her. The flickering

fluorescent light cast grotesque shadows across her face, deepening the lines of exhaustion etched there. Her fingers traced the outline of Rashford, lingering on areas marked with ominous red circles.

"What am I missing?" she muttered, the words tasting bitter on her tongue. The air felt thick, oppressive, as if the weight of the town's supernatural occurrences had condensed into a suffocating miasma.

A report fluttered to the floor, and as Eva bent to retrieve it, a chill ran down her spine. The paper trembled in her hand, not from the non-existent breeze, but from the tremor in her own fingers. She stared at the words, willing them to reveal their secrets.

"Blood rain in the east quadrant... trees birthing otherworldly beings near the old mill..." Eva's voice trailed off, her mind racing. "There has to be a pattern, a reason."

She pinned the report back on the board, her movements sharp with frustration. The cork gave way too easily, as if even the inanimate objects in the room were conspiring against her. Eva's fist clenched, nails biting into her palm.

"Papa, what would you do?" she whispered, her voice barely audible. The ghost of her father's

presence seemed to linger in the corners of the room, a constant reminder of the legacy she bore.

Eva's gaze fell on her badge, the metal dulled by the weak light. She picked it up, its weight familiar yet suddenly overwhelming. "I swore to protect this town," she murmured, "even if it means facing down gods and monsters."

A knock at the door jolted her from her reverie. Deputy Johnson stood in the doorway, his face ashen. "Sheriff, there's been another incident at the river. They're saying the water... it's turned to blood."

Eva's heart sank, but her voice remained steady. "Grab your gear, Johnson. We're heading out."

As she holstered her gun, Eva cast one last look at the cluttered board. The pieces of the puzzle swam before her eyes, refusing to align. But she would make them fit, she vowed silently. For Rashford. For her father. For herself.

Meanwhile, in the hushed confines of the town hall, Goddard Greening and Helena Boyd sat across from each other, their faces illuminated by the warm glow of a single lamp. The room seemed to pulse with unspoken tension, the air heavy with the weight of their responsibilities.

"The town is teetering on the edge, Madam President," Goddard said, his usually smooth voice rough with concern. "I can feel the fear, the uncertainty. It's like a living thing, feeding on their doubts."

Helena nodded, her eyes distant. "I know. But we can't let it consume us. We must be the pillars they lean on, even as we grapple with our own uncertainties."

Goddard leaned forward, his gaze intense. "And what of the divine aspect? Your... unique perspective must surely offer some insight?"

A shadow passed over Helena's face, a flicker of something ancient and unknowable. "The gods are restless, Goddard. Their powers chafe at them, and the threat of a reprise of Yahweh's wrath looms ever closer. We're caught in the crossfire of a war beyond mortal comprehension."

"Then what hope do we have?" Goddard asked, his voice barely above a whisper.

Helena reached across the table, her hand finding his. The touch was electric, a spark of shared purpose igniting between them. "Hope lies in unity, in the strength of the human spirit. We may not be gods, but we have something they lack – the ability to adapt, to evolve."

Goddard nodded, drawing strength from her words and touch. "Then we stand together, come what may."

As they sat in companionable silence, the shadows seemed to deepen around them, as if the very darkness was listening, waiting to strike. But in that moment, their resolve burned bright, a beacon against the encroaching night.

Apollo's lips curled into a bittersweet smile as he watched Aodhán, Hermes, Goddard, and Llewellyn take turns singing at the karaoke bar. The sound of their off-tune voices and unfamiliar tunes pierced his heart with longing for his home country and the festivals where he would sing for his father, Zeus, in front of adoring crowds. But amidst the joyous atmosphere, a sense of foreboding gripped Apollo's mind. These boys were in grave danger - Aodhán and Hermes had given themselves over to Satana, Goddard had dared to strike her with a sacred weapon, and Llewellyn possessed a power that could unravel Satana's plans. Apollo knew that the demoness would seek revenge on them soon, and he clenched his fists in frustration at not being able to protect them. When the time came, he vowed to be their unwavering shield against the darkness that threatened to consume them all.

Chapter 23

Aodhán stood in the heart of Rashford, his eyes flickering with a mix of wonder and trepidation. The town had transformed, its quaint streets now thrumming with an otherworldly energy that set his nerves on edge. Shadows danced at the corners of his vision, whispering of ancient powers and cosmic battles.

He closed his eyes, inhaling deeply. The scent of rain-soaked earth mingled with something else—a subtle, electric charge that made the hairs on the back of his neck stand up. When he opened his eyes again, the world seemed to shimmer, reality bending at the edges.

"It's... beautiful," Aodhán murmured, his voice barely above a whisper. "And terrifying."

A surge of power coursed through him, unbidden and wild. Panic gripped his chest as he struggled to contain it, his hands trembling with the effort.

"Focus, Aodhán," Apollo's firm voice cut through his rising fear. The former god of light stood before him, his head sheltered by his mask from the overcast sky. "Remember what we practiced. Channel the energy, don't let it control you."

Aodhán nodded, sweat beading on his brow. He reached out with his mind, trying to grasp the elusive threads of power that danced just beyond

his reach. A warm, calming presence enveloped him—Yahweh, lending his silent support.

"I can't—" Aodhán gasped, his body shaking with effort. "It's too much. I'm not strong enough."

Apollo's eyes flashed with a mixture of frustration and concern. "You are stronger than you know, Aodhán. Your power comes from a place beyond mortal comprehension. Embrace it."

Aodhán closed his eyes again, focusing on the ebb and flow of energy around him. He could feel it now—the delicate balance between divine and mortal, light and shadow. With trembling hands, he reached out, grasping at the threads of power that swirled around him.

For a moment, everything stilled. Then, with a rush that left him breathless, the energy surged through him, filling every fibre of his being. Aodhán's eyes flew open, glowing with an otherworldly light.

"I... I did it," he breathed, staring at his hands in awe. "But what now? How do I control this?"

Apollo's lips quirked in a small smile. "That, my young friend, is where the real work begins."

As Aodhán stood there, caught between exhilaration and terror, he couldn't shake the feeling that this was only the beginning. Something dark lurked at the edges of his

consciousness, a looming threat that sent shivers down his spine. He pushed the thought away, focusing instead on the warmth of Apollo's pride and Yahweh's steady presence.

But deep down, Aodhán knew the truth. The battle for Rashford—and perhaps the world—had only just begun. He looked at Apollo. He longed to tell him that he had sired a son in Satana and that he had strangely survived the ordeal. He wanted to tell him that his son was due within months. But every time, the words stuck in his throat.

Llewellyn Boyd strode through the cobblestone streets of Rashford, his youthful face a beacon of hope amidst the town's surreal transformation. Ethereal mist clung to his ankles, a constant reminder of the divine energies now permeating the once-ordinary town.

"Mr. Boyd!" called out Mrs. Fitzgerald, her wrinkled face a map of worry. "The apples in my orchard... they're glowing. Is this... normal now?"

Llewellyn's bright eyes sparkled with a mix of curiosity and reassurance. "Nature's adjusting, just like us, Mrs. Fitzgerald. Those apples might just be the sweetest you've ever tasted."

He placed a comforting hand on her shoulder, feeling the tremor of fear beneath her skin. The

weight of his role as mediator pressed heavily upon him, but Llewellyn's voice remained steady, belying his inner uncertainty.

"How do you do it?" Mrs Fitzgerald whispered. "How can you be so calm when the world's gone mad?"

Llewellyn's laugh was tinged with a hint of darkness. "Mad? Perhaps. But there's beauty in the chaos, if we're brave enough to look for it."

As he continued his walk, Llewellyn's thoughts churned. Am I truly qualified for this? Or am I just another pawn in a game beyond my comprehension?

The newly established pantheon loomed before him, its marble columns seeming to pierce the very heavens. Inside, voices echoed off the cavernous walls.

"We must establish clear boundaries," Athena's authoritative voice rang out. "The mortals need structure, a framework to understand their new reality."

Apollo nodded. "Agreed. But we must be careful not to overwhelm them. Too much, too soon, and we risk panic."

An angel - Micha-El, Llewellyn recalled - spread his wings in agitation. "And what of the balance between our realms? We cannot simply coexist without rules."

Hermes, lounging on a marble bench, chuckled darkly, turned to the Archangel. "Rules? In a town where trees birth beings and blood rains from the sky? Good luck with that, feathers."

Athena's grey eyes flashed dangerously. "This is no laughing matter, Hermes. The fragile peace we've established hangs by a thread."

Llewellyn lingered in the shadows his right leg still plastered, holding a crutch under his right arm, heart pounding. The fate of Rashford - of worlds beyond - balanced on a knife's edge. And he, a mere mortal, stood at the precipice of it all.

The sun dipped low on the horizon, casting long shadows across the river's surface as Aodhán, Llewellyn, Goddard, and Hermes gathered on its banks. The water whispered secrets, its gentle lapping a stark contrast to the weight of their unspoken fears.

Aodhán skimmed a stone across the water, watching it dance before sinking into the depths. "Sometimes I wonder," he mused, his voice tinged with melancholy, "if I'm just like that stone -

skimming the surface of my power, never truly grasping its depths before I... disappear."

Llewellyn held his crutch under one shoulder and placed a comforting hand on Aodhán's shoulder, his touch warm and grounding. "You're more than your power, Aodhán. You're our friend, our anchor in this storm."

Goddard nodded, his refined features softened by the fading light. "Indeed. Though I must admit, the concept of divine offspring still boggles my mortal mind. Do you suppose the little tyke will have wings, or perhaps a glowing halo?"

Hermes snorted, a mischievous glint in his eye. "With any luck, he'll inherit his father's dashing good looks and his uncle Hermes' unparalleled wit."

They laughed, the sound echoing across the water, momentarily lifting the veil of dread that hung over them. But Aodhán's smile faded quickly, his cosmic eyes clouding with worry.

"And what if... what if he inherits something darker?" Aodhán whispered, voicing the fear that gnawed at his core. "Satana's influence..."

The mood shifted, a chill wind rustling through the trees. Llewellyn shivered, not entirely from the cold. "We'll face it together, whatever comes," he

said, his voice steady despite the tremor in his hands.

Goddard nodded solemnly. "United we stand, divided we fall. A trite saying, perhaps, but no less true for its repetition."

Hermes' usual smirk faltered, replaced by a rare look of vulnerability. "You know," he said softly, "in all my centuries, I've never felt quite so... mortal. So fragile. It's terrifying, and yet... exhilarating."

As night fell, casting the river in shades of inky black, Aodhán couldn't shake the feeling that somewhere in the darkness, something wicked was brewing.

Miles away, in a shadowy alley that reeked of decay and despair, Satana emerged from the gloom. Her swollen belly pulsed with unholy life, each movement a promise of chaos to come. She traced a clawed finger along the grimy wall, leaving a trail of smouldering embers in its wake.

"My precious acolytes," she purred, her voice a seductive whisper that wormed its way into the minds of the huddled figures before her. "You hunger for power, for meaning in this pathetic mortal coil. I offer you both, and so much more."

A woman stepped forward, her eyes gleaming with desperate hope. "What must we do, mistress?"

Satana's lips curled into a cruel smile, revealing teeth sharp as razors. "Embrace the darkness, my dear. Let it consume you, fill you, transform you. For in the coming storm, only those who have tasted true power will survive."

She placed a hand on her distended abdomen, feeling the kick of the abomination growing within. "My son," she hissed, "will usher in a new age of glorious chaos. And you, my faithful, will be his harbingers."

The alley filled with fevered whispers and pledges of loyalty, the air thick with the stench of corruption. As Satana basked in their adoration, she felt a flicker of something almost like love - a twisted, possessive hunger for the child she carried.

"Soon, my little monster," she crooned. "Soon, we'll paint this world in beautiful shades of suffering."

The streetlights of Rashford flickered ominously, casting writhing shadows across the once-quaint storefronts. A chill wind whispered through the empty streets, carrying with it fragments of half-heard voices that made the skin crawl.

Eva Ramirez strode down Main Street, her boots echoing on the cracked pavement. Her hand

rested on her holstered pistol, a useless comfort against the supernatural horrors that now plagued her town. She paused, catching sight of her reflection in a shop window - the bags under her eyes a testament to sleepless nights spent patrolling.

"Everything alright, Sheriff?" called out old Mrs Hendricks from her porch, voice quavering.

Eva forced a reassuring smile. "Just keeping an eye out, ma'am. Best head inside for the night."

As the door clicked shut behind the elderly woman, Eva's smile faded. *How can I protect them from something I can barely comprehend?* she thought, a gnawing dread settling in her gut.

A streetlight above her sputtered and died, plunging the corner into darkness. Eva's breath caught in her throat as she glimpsed a writhing mass of shadows coalescing in the alley beside her. Her fingers tightened on her gun, knowing it was useless against this formless evil.

"I won't let you have this town," she growled, more to steady herself than anything else. The darkness seemed to pulse in response, a silent laugh that chilled her to her core.

Eva backed away slowly, her mind racing. *I need to find Aodhán, or one of the others. They'll know*

what to do. But even as she thought it, a traitorous voice whispered: *And what if they don't?*

The shadows retreated, melting back into the night. But Eva knew they were still there, waiting. Always waiting. She squared her shoulders and continued her patrol, duty warring with the primal urge to flee.

"Stay strong," she muttered to herself, to the town, to anyone who might be listening. "We've survived worse."

But as the wind carried another chorus of unearthly whispers, Eva wondered if that was still true.

In the shadow of an ancient oak, Hermes slouched against gnarled bark, his once-radiant form now dimmed by mortality. His eyes, usually alight with mischief, were clouded with a tempest of emotions as he absently twirled a fallen leaf between his fingers.

"Foolish, arrogant child," he murmured, his voice tinged with self-recrimination. The leaf crumbled in his grip, its decay a stark reminder of his own diminished state.

A cool breeze rustled through the branches, carrying with it the faint scent of ambrosia – a

cruel taunt of the divinity he'd lost. Hermes closed his eyes, memories of celestial glory warring with the harsh realities of his new existence.

"What use is a messenger without wings?" he asked the indifferent night. "A trickster without tricks?"

The sound of approaching footsteps jolted him from his reverie. Instinctively, he melted into the shadows, old habits dying hard. A figure emerged into the moonlight – Goddard Greening, his sketchbook clutched to his chest like a talisman.

Hermes watched as the young man settled on a nearby bench, opening his book with trembling hands. Goddard's pencil flew across the page, capturing the ethereal beauty of Rashford's transformed landscape with feverish intensity.

Curiosity piqued, Hermes stepped forward. "Quite the artist, aren't you?" he remarked, his voice carefully modulated to mask his inner turmoil.

Goddard startled, nearly dropping his sketchbook. "H-Hermes," he stammered, eyes wide. "I didn't see you there."

The former god smiled wryly. "Old habits," he said, gesturing vaguely. His gaze fell on the open page, where Goddard had captured the twisted, dreamlike quality of the town's new reality with

unsettling accuracy. "You have a gift for seeing the truth of things."

Goddard's fingers tightened on the pencil. "Sometimes I wish I didn't," he admitted, his voice barely above a whisper. "The things I've seen... they haunt me."

Hermes nodded, understanding all too well. "And so you seek to exorcise them through art?"

"It helps," Goddard said, his eyes distant. "To make sense of it all. To try and find beauty in the chaos."

A heavy silence fell between them, pregnant with unspoken fears and fragile hopes. Hermes found himself envying the mortal's ability to process trauma through creation. What outlet did a fallen god have for his regrets?

Athena stood at the centre of the town square, her presence a beacon of strength amidst the swirling uncertainty. A small crowd had gathered around her, their faces etched with worry and confusion. The air was thick with the scent of ozone and decay, a constant reminder of the supernatural forces at play.

"We stand at a crossroads," Athena's voice rang out, clear and authoritative. "The world as you

knew it has changed, but that does not mean all is lost."

A woman with greying hair stepped forward, her eyes brimming with tears. "But how can we go on? Everything feels... wrong."

Athena's gaze softened, though her posture remained unyielding. "Change is often painful, but it can also bring growth. We must adapt, learn to see with new eyes."

As she spoke, tendrils of mist curled around her feet, seeming to pulse with an otherworldly energy. The townspeople shifted uneasily but remained transfixed by her words.

"What about the... things we've seen?" a young man asked, his voice cracking. "The shadows that move when they shouldn't, the whispers in the night?"

Athena's eyes flashed, a reminder of the divine power that once coursed through her veins. "Knowledge is your shield," she said firmly. "Understanding will be your sword. I am here to guide you through this new reality."

As the conversation continued, Athena felt a familiar ache in her chest. How long could she maintain this facade of strength when her own doubts gnawed at her constantly?

Miles away, at the forest's edge, Aodhán stood alone, his young form dwarfed by the ancient trees. The wind whispered through the leaves, carrying with it the faint scent of decay and rebirth. His eyes, filled with the weight of cosmic mysteries, gazed unseeing into the depths of the woods.

"What am I?" he murmured, his voice barely audible above the rustling foliage. "A god? A child? Both? Neither?"

The forest offered no answers, only the creaking of branches and the occasional scurrying of unseen creatures. Aodhán closed his eyes, feeling the pulse of life around him – mortal, divine, and something... other. The responsibility of it all threatened to crush him.

"I never asked for this power," he thought, a wave of despair washing over him. "How can I protect them when I can barely understand myself?"

As if in response, a cold wind gusted from the forest, carrying with it the faintest hint of sulphur. Aodhán's eyes snapped open, a chill running down his spine. Something was coming, something dark and hungry. And he, this child-god with powers he couldn't comprehend, stood as

the only barrier between it and the fragile world he had come to love.

The sky above Rashford began to bleed, deep oranges and purples seeping across the horizon like an open wound. Aodhán turned from the forest, his heart heavy as he made his way back to town. The air grew thick with anticipation, a palpable tension that seemed to hum in his very bones.

As he entered the outskirts, the young Eldar caught sight of Helena Boyd standing on her porch, her eyes fixed on the surreal sky. She noticed him and offered a wan smile.

"Beautiful, isn't it?" she said, her voice steady despite the worry lines etched around her eyes. "And terrifying."

Aodhán nodded, unable to find words. How could he explain the dread coursing through him, the certainty that this beauty heralded something unspeakable?

"Do you think we're ready?" Helena asked softly. "For whatever comes next?"

The question hung in the air, heavy as lead. Aodhán's mind raced, images of Satana's malevolent grin and the writhing darkness that haunted his dreams flashing before his eyes. He

wanted to reassure her, to be the pillar of strength this town needed. But the lie stuck in his throat.

"I don't know," he admitted, his voice cracking. "I'm... I'm afraid, Helena."

She reached out, squeezing his shoulder gently. "We all are, child. But fear doesn't make us weak. It makes us human."

The irony of her words wasn't lost on Aodhán. Human. Is that what he was? Or something else entirely? As the last rays of sunlight bled from the sky, leaving Rashford bathed in an otherworldly twilight, he couldn't shake the feeling that they were all standing on the precipice of a nightmare from which there would be no waking.

Chapter 24

The grand hall of the cosmic council in the Heavenly Realm stood magnificent, emanating a brilliant light and an overwhelming aura. It towered over Aodhán, its otherworldly design beyond human understanding. Pillars of celestial stardust spiralled upwards, holding up a ceiling that glimmered like the swirling depths of a black hole. The atmosphere was charged with palpable energy, thick enough to make one feel suffocated. Every sense was heightened in this sacred space, where the very fabric of reality was inexistent and light created substance.

Yahweh sat at the head of the table, his form a blinding radiance that hurt to look upon directly. To his right, Micha-El's wings twitched nervously, golden feathers rustling in the oppressive silence. Across from them, Apollo's once-lustrous hair hung lank from beneath his mask onto his shoulders. Athena's piercing grey eyes darted between the gathered deities, her fingers drumming an anxious rhythm on the crystalline surface before her.

As Aodhán approached, Apollo's gaze locked onto him. "The boy arrives," he heard Gabri-El mutter, voice dripping with barely concealed disdain. "Our supposed saviour."

Aodhán's stomach churned. He could feel the crushing weight of their expectations, their desperation. His palms grew slick with sweat as he took his place at the table, acutely aware of how young – how mortal – he appeared next to these ancient beings.

"I'm not here to save anyone," Aodhán said, his voice steadier than he felt. "I'm here because we need each other. All of us."

Yahweh's light dimmed slightly, allowing Aodhán to make out the weary lines etched into his ageless face. "And what would you have us do, child of the Eldars?" he asked, his voice a whisper that echoed like thunder. "Our powers wane. The darkness grows. How can we stand united when the very fabric of reality frays around us? How can we stand united with you when you have built a Dark Tower that threatens Heaven and Earth?"

Aodhán closed his eyes, drawing upon the well of ancient wisdom that resided within him – a legacy of his Eldar heritage. When he opened them again, there was a quiet confidence in his gaze that belied his youthful appearance.

"We start," he said softly, "by acknowledging our shared vulnerability. Our shared humanity."

Aodhán raised his hands, palms upturned. The air around him began to shimmer, tiny motes of light

coalescing into intricate patterns. The deities leaned forward, their eyes widening as the swirling energies took shape.

"Behold," Aodhán whispered, his voice carrying an otherworldly resonance. "The threads that bind us all."

The cosmic forces danced between his fingers, a tapestry of light and shadow, order and chaos. Athena gasped, her hand unconsciously reaching out as if to touch the ethereal display.

"There is nothing we can do about the Tower for now. It has a will and life of its own and I cannot undo what I have done. But that's all the more reason to stand united," Aodhán continued.

"Impossible," Micha-El muttered, his brow furrowed. "Such harmony... it defies all we've known."

Gabri-El's scepticism wavered, a flicker of hope igniting in his eyes. "Perhaps," he mused, "we've been blind to the greater design."

Yahweh remained silent, his gaze inscrutable as he watched the interplay of energies.

"But something else is coming," he swallowed at last, his voice trembling.

The divine beings looked at him, recognising horror in his eyes.

"What is it, Aodhán?" Apollo asked at last.

Aodhán swallowed again. He felt a bead of sweat trickle down his forehead. "I have sired a son to Satana," he replied.

"That's impossible," Yahweh boomed.

"I survived the ordeal," Aodhán went on. "But Satana is pregnant with my son - an Eldar and Demon combined. In her hands he will be a formidable enemy."

Silence fell over the grand hall.

"Why didn't you tell us earlier?" Apollo asked, disappointment weaved in his tone.

Aodhán's heart raced, the effort of maintaining the delicate balance draining him rapidly. "I was scared." Sweat beaded on his brow as he struggled to hold the cosmic forces in harmony. Just as his concentration began to slip, a gentle hand touched his shoulder.

Llewellyn Boyd's astral body intruded the meeting, his youthful face alight with wonder. "May I?" he asked softly.

Aodhán nodded, gratefully relinquishing control. Llewellyn addressed the council, his voice trembling with earnest passion.

"Forgive my presumption," he began, "but I've witnessed something profound here. We speak of divinity and humanity as separate entities, yet are they not intertwined?"

The deities shifted uncomfortably, exchanging uneasy glances.

"Young man," Athena said, her tone gentle but patronizing, "you cannot fathom the complexities of—"

"Can't I?" Llewellyn interrupted, his eyes flashing. "I've seen gods bleed. I've seen mortals perform miracles. The line between us blurs with each passing day."

The grand hall of the cosmic council thrummed with an undercurrent of tension, the air thick with the scent of ozone and ancient power. Yahweh's brow furrowed as he leaned forward, his voice resonating with barely contained frustration.

"We cannot simply discard millennia of tradition," he growled, eyes flashing with divine fire. "Our ways have maintained order since the dawn of creation. We must kill the demonic offspring. Wage war against the Darkness before it is too late."

Apollo, lounging in his seat with affected nonchalance, rolled his eyes. "And look where that's gotten us, old man. Powerless, irrelevant,

hiding in a backwater town." His fingers drummed an impatient rhythm on the arm of his chair, a hint of golden light flickering beneath his skin.

Athena's cool gaze swept the room. "Perhaps," she mused, her voice carrying the weight of hard-won wisdom, "it is time to forge a new path. One that bridges the divide between gods and mortals. Perhaps we can kidnap the child and raise him ourselves. He would be a powerful ally."

Micha-El shifted uneasily, torn between loyalty and reason. The conflict played across his face as he spoke. "Change is... difficult. But necessary, if we are to survive in this new world. What shall we do?"

As the debate raged on, a figure materialized at the edge of the council chamber. Hermes sauntered in, a mischievous glint in his eye. He assessed the tense atmosphere, a smirk playing at the corners of his mouth.

"Well, well," he drawled, his voice cutting through the heated discussion. "Looks like I've crashed quite the party. Tell me, is this how you lot always solve problems?"

The deities turned, startled by the intrusion. Hermes grinned, revelling in their surprise.

"What?" he asked innocently. "Did you forget to invite the god of thieves? I'm hurt, truly."

For a moment, the council chamber hung in stunned silence. Then, unexpectedly, Apollo snorted with laughter. "Trust you to sneak your way in, you silver-tongued bastard."

The tension in the room eased, if only slightly. Hermes bowed with exaggerated flourish. "At your service. Now, shall we discuss how to save our divine asses, or would you prefer to continue this riveting debate on the merits of stubbornness?"

As the other gods chuckled reluctantly, Yahweh's lips twitched in what might have been the ghost of a smile. For a brief, shining moment, the weight of their circumstances lifted, replaced by a glimmer of the camaraderie they had once shared.

The council chamber doors creaked open, releasing a torrent of divine beings into the ethereal hallway. Aodhán watched, his young face etched with concern, as the deities dispersed like wisps of smoke in a breeze. Each god's face bore the weight of unresolved conflict, their eyes distant and troubled.

Yahweh's thunderous footsteps echoed through the hall, his massive form seeming to compress the very air around him. Apollo strode past, a tempest of barely contained fury, while Athena's eyes darted about, calculating unseen variables.

Aodhán's chest tightened. "They're all so... fragmented," he whispered to himself, the words tasting bitter on his tongue.

Hermes materialized beside him, his lithe form leaning casually against a shimmering pillar. "Welcome to divine politics, kid," he quipped, though his eyes held a sadness that belied his light tone. "Come on, I know a place where we can clear our heads."

In a blink, they stood atop a verdant hill overlooking Rashford Town. The scent of pine and rain-soaked earth filled Aodhán's lungs, a stark contrast to the suffocating atmosphere of the council chamber.

"It's... beautiful," Aodhán breathed, drinking in the sight of the quaint buildings nestled among rolling hills.

Hermes chuckled. "Sure is. Hard to believe it's the epicentre of cosmic chaos, eh?"

Aodhán's brow furrowed. "How can they not see it? The potential for unity, for healing?"

"Centuries of baggage, kid. Makes it hard to see the forest for the trees." Hermes plucked a blade of grass, twirling it between his fingers. "Sometimes I wonder if we're more human than we'd like to admit."

Aodhán's gaze swept over the town, his mind racing. "There must be a way to bridge the divide. To help them remember what they once were."

Hermes raised an eyebrow. "Got any ideas, oh wise one?"

Aodhán's lips quirked in a half-smile. "Perhaps. But I'll need your help, god of thieves."

"Oh?" Hermes grinned, his eyes alight with mischief. "Now you're speaking my language."

As they plotted atop the hill, the sun dipped low, painting Rashford in hues of gold and crimson. Below, mortals went about their lives, blissfully unaware of the cosmic drama unfolding above. Aodhán felt the weight of responsibility settle on his shoulders, a stark reminder of the challenges that lay ahead.

Aodhán's fingers traced arcane patterns in the air, leaving shimmering trails of light. "Power corrupts," he murmured, "but perhaps it's not the power itself, but how we wield it."

Hermes nodded, his usual mirth subdued. "Aye, I've seen gods and mortals alike twisted by their own ambitions. It's a fine line we walk."

A chill wind rustled through the grass, carrying with it the faintest whisper of sulphur. Aodhán's

spine stiffened, his senses suddenly alert. "Did you feel that?"

Hermes' eyes narrowed, scanning the horizon. "Something's stirring. Something... dark."

Aodhán's mind raced, memories of ancient battles and fallen Eldars flashing before his eyes. "Satana," he breathed, the name a curse on his lips.

"The Deceiver," Hermes spat, his jovial demeanour evaporating. "Always lurking in the shadows, waiting to strike."

The sun dipped lower, long shadows stretching across Rashford like grasping fingers. Aodhán felt a familiar dread coiling in his gut, a premonition of trials to come.

"We can't let her win," Aodhán said, his voice barely above a whisper. "The cost would be... unthinkable."

Hermes placed a hand on Aodhán's shoulder, his touch unexpectedly warm. "We won't. Light always finds a way to pierce the darkness, kid. Always."

Aodhán turned to face Hermes, his ethereal eyes shimmering with a mixture of determination and uncertainty. "Our paths have become so intertwined," he mused, his voice carrying the

weight of cosmic understanding. "Mortal and divine, bound by fate and choice."

Hermes chuckled, a sound that seemed to dispel some of the gathering gloom. "Quite the odd couple, aren't we? A teenage-looking Eldar god and a depowered Greek trickster. The stuff of legends, or perhaps a cosmic joke."

A smile tugged at Aodhán's lips, his youthful features belying the ancient wisdom behind his words. "Perhaps both. But there's power in our union, a strength born of our differences."

The wind picked up, carrying with it the scent of pine and possibility. Aodhán closed his eyes, feeling the pulse of the world around him. When he opened them, there was a new fire burning in their depths.

"Whatever comes next," Aodhán said, his voice steady and resolute, "we face it together. The mundane and the miraculous, intertwined."

Hermes nodded, his usual smirk replaced by a look of genuine respect. "Couldn't have said it better myself, kid. Though I might have thrown in a witty quip or two."

As they stood there, silhouetted against the setting sun, the air seemed to crackle with potential. In the town below, lights began to flicker

on, each one a beacon of hope in the gathering darkness.

Aodhán's gaze swept across the horizon, his mind racing with visions of what might come. "I can feel it, Hermes. The threads of fate, shifting and realigning. Something's coming."

Hermes raised an eyebrow, his curiosity piqued. "Care to share with the class?"

Aodhán shook his head, a mysterious smile playing across his lips. "It's not clear yet. But it's big. It's... wondrous."

As night fell fully upon Rashford, the stars seemed to burn brighter than ever before. In their twinkling light, anything seemed possible. The air hummed with the promise of adventure, of battles yet to be fought and mysteries waiting to be unravelled.

Aodhán took a deep breath, feeling the weight of destiny upon his shoulders. "Ready?" he asked, turning to Hermes.

The former god of thieves grinned, his eyes glinting with mischief and anticipation. "Always, kid. Let's go make some trouble."

And with that, they descended towards Rashford, two figures united against the encroaching darkness, their hearts filled with hope and the thrill of the unknown.

A jet black raven loomed overhead, its beady eyes tracking their every move, waiting for the perfect moment to strike.

Printed in France by Amazon
Brétigny-sur-Orge, FR